Sisters in Law

NINA BELL

sphere

SPHERE

First published in Great Britain as a paperback original in 2009 by Sphere

A CIP catalogue record for this book
is available from the British Library.

ISBN 978-0-7515-3906-6

Typeset in Bembo by M Rules
Printed and bound in Great Britain by
Clays Ltd, St Ives plc

Papers used by Sphere are natural, renewable and recyclable
products sourced from well-managed forests and certified in
accordance with the rules of the Forest Stewardship Council.

Mixed Sources
Product group from well-managed
forests and other controlled sources
www.fsc.org   Cert no. SGS-COC-004081
© 1996 Forest Stewardship Council
FSC

Sphere
An imprint of
Little, Brown Book Group
100 Victoria Embankment
London EC4Y 0DY

An Hachette UK Company
www.hachette.co.uk

www.littlebrown.co.uk

To Lizzie Iron

Prologue

'I've always wondered if Sasha saw a happy family,' said Kate, 'and couldn't resist tearing it apart, or whether the cracks had been there all along, just waiting for someone destructive – or damaged – to work her fingernails into them. But when I first saw the three of you – the three Fox men – and her, I had this image of her choosing one of you to run off with. But I told myself it could never happen . . .'

'And then it did,' interrupted Olivia.

PART ONE

Two Years Earlier

Chapter 1

Kate Fox and Jonny Rafferty were late getting Sunday lunch ready. This often happened because they tried to crowd too much into their days.

'We should have done this weeks ago,' said Jonny, hefting his tool box up from the tiny cellar tucked under their narrow Victorian terraced house. 'People will be here in a minute.'

'We've got about an hour. We can get these hung in that time.' Kate unwrapped a series of family photographs, each in an identical matt black frame with a huge cream mount, transforming the image from a happy memory into a work of art. They had just finished having a modern kitchen extension built, and instead of the jumbled, friendly collage of colourful snapshots she'd crammed into frames or pinned up on the noticeboard in the old kitchen, she'd decided – no, *they'd* decided, because she and Jonny discussed everything – that it would be nice to choose one or two really beautiful photographs of each family member and frame them dramatically on the new white walls.

But they were all due round for lunch at any moment and the photographs lay on the floor, in their packaging, the 'washed and ready to eat' salad was in bags in the fridge and the rice was still in its packet, although at least there was a hunk of meat, marinated in Turkish spices, roasting in the oven.

'We couldn't do it any earlier, we had that awards ceremony, three parties, two parents' evenings at school, the Lovelace Conservation Committee meeting and we both had deadlines at

3

work.' Kate handed Jonny the first photograph, a deliciously retro black-and-white image of her mother and father, Ella and Michael Fox, as bride and groom circa 1966. Under her pillbox hat and above his kipper tie their faces looked unrecognisably young and innocent. 'Let's start with this one in the middle, shall we?'

The earliest photos were the easiest – a studio shot of Kate and her brothers Simon and Jack, aged five, seven and three, respectively, with gap-toothed smiles, and another on Jonny's side, of him and his sister squinting into the sun with buckets and spades. Kate had tried to exclude anything that resembled a traditional family photo, rejecting the garish colours and muddled composition of everyone crammed on to a sofa in their Sunday best, with unrealistically neat hair and bright smiles. She wanted simple backgrounds and casual clothes, pictures that really gave an impression of the person behind the image, like the head-and-shoulders portrait of her mother, Ella, her chin jutting out in determination, her sharp eyes seeing everything. Well, almost everything.

She'd found a good one of her father, in his late forties, with a wry smile on his face, urging them on to be the best they could be, encouraging them all every inch of the way, taking their childish worries seriously and sorting out their scraps and bickering.

Until a drunk driver on the A3 wiped him out of their lives overnight when Kate was fifteen. He had been on his way home after working late, as personnel director of an industrial components firm.

After that, the sunny childhood had become muddled and grey. They moved to a smaller house, with a back yard instead of lawns and three bedrooms instead of five, in a less 'nice' area. While Si won a scholarship to finish his A levels at the private school all three had attended, Kate and Jack had to leave, and found themselves in the school none of their friends wanted to go to. For Kate it was easier – she was starting her A levels and, higher up the school, the rebellious element had left – but, Jack, aged thirteen, had to prove that he wasn't a 'toff' and he learned to prove it with his fists. Ella, who had always been at home, checking their homework and cooking meals, had to go out to work, and the heart went out of the household. Kate cooked the boys fish fingers or sausages and beans. Simon became 'the man of the family' at seventeen. Jack, the youngest, became loud and scrappy in the school playground and was suspended three times. Kate and Si persuaded him to clean up his act, and managed to cover up a certain amount of his bad behaviour. The three of them made it work. That's what their father would have wanted. To keep the worries away from their mother. They tested each other at exam time, supported each other over boyfriends and girlfriends, and tried not to think about their father.

Si got into Oxford and became embarrassed about coming from the suburbs, then married Olivia, his long-term university girlfriend, a few years later. Kate, whose exam results were less stellar, went to London after leaving school, to become a radio journalist. Jack grew up and dropped the bad boy act, joining the army. Eventually Ella bought a tiny cottage in Thorpe Wenham, a picture-perfect Oxfordshire village. She had done her job. The family was launched. And so well. Everyone said so.

Kate took another photo out of its bubble wrap. It was a beautiful one of Si and Olivia at their wedding reception at St James's Palace – she was, according to Ella, who was impressed by these things, 'terribly well connected'. Si was the taller of the two Fox brothers, and his hair was darker than Kate and Jack's mousey blond. Kate teased Si that he should put 'dark mouse' under 'hair colour'; Jack joked that he should just write 'rat'. Olivia was tall too, and gangling, a string bean in a frothing meringue of a dress, with a generous mouth and long chestnut hair.

Then the photo of Jack and Heather: Jack was stockier than Si and tawny in colouring. Heather was strawberry blonde and tiny, like a very pretty pixie. She had a hesitant gaze, dimples and wrists so slender that they looked as if they might snap. She married in a slim silk sheath with a twist of flowers in her hair – the photo showed her peering nervously up at Jack's fellow officers as they crossed swords above the couple in a guard of honour as she and Jack left the church.

Kate and Jonny had chosen three photographs of their sons, Luke and Callum, from a serious-faced Callum with baby Luke in his arms to a pair of cheeky boys grinning at the camera to the one taken last year of them sitting back-to-back in white T-shirts and frayed jeans, with Callum's spider-long legs and arms twice the length of his brother's more rounded limbs. Luke and Callum had Jonny's blond wavy hair and penetrating blue eyes, combined with the Fox jaw. Luke was ten. Kate still ferried him to and from school, and knew all his friends, while Callum, empowered by going to secondary school, ambled off on his own, taking a bus, and the names he referred to at the end of the day were unfamiliar to her. He often begged Kate to walk on the other side of the road from him if they were anywhere near school, because she was so 'embarrassing'.

'Should we put the boys' pictures in some kind of age order?' she asked, 'or just dot them around wherever?'

Jonny, who as a television director had a strong visual sense, spent a few minutes experimenting, then tacked them up in exactly the right place. Kate kissed him.

'And now,' he shot a teasing look, 'we've actually got some representation of my family to go up. I didn't think you were going to allow them on the wall.'

'Of course I am. Don't be ridiculous. It's you who barely keeps in touch with your sister. It's none of my business if you don't.' But it had been with secret reluctance that she'd rummaged through his photographs, although she'd found a wonderfully nostalgic-looking photograph of Jonny's parents, both now dead, looking rather like the Duke and Duchess of Windsor and another she quite liked of Jonny's sister, Virginia, as one of the 'girls in pearls' in the front of *Country Life* when she got engaged to Angus. Such photos did look great in huge frames, even if she wasn't terribly fond of the people in them.

But the most difficult task had been to find the right photographs of herself and Jonny. There was an arty shot of the whole family tangled round a ladder, all with bare feet (no conventional line-ups for the Fox-Rafferty household), and a heavenly close-up of Jonny outdoors, with his lazy, beach-bum smile and creased blue eyes.

When she'd first met him – she'd interviewed him as the hot new director of a cult documentary series – the first thing she'd noticed was a pair of tanned and muscular legs emerging from shorts. In November. And she'd thought that any man who smiled like that instead of speaking and had hair down to his shoulders might well be both stupid and vain. He's got a lot of women after him, she thought – accurately, as it turned out. He needn't think I'm going to be one of them.

But she soon discovered that he used his smile to give himself time to think, and that, far from being vain, his hair was long because he could only be bothered to have it cut once a year, when he would have it virtually shaved off. And those shorts had been the first thing that came to hand when he'd opened the wardrobe that morning.

He was certainly a man who needed looking after. Kate had risen to the challenge, but had made it clear that she wasn't going to pander to his every whim like all the Jennys, Janes, Jamilas and Janelles that seemed to clog up his answering machine. The relationship would be on her terms, and if he didn't like it, he knew where the door was. If he wanted someone adoring, or even a histrionic diva, he could go and find one.

So far, he hadn't. She thought of the first time she'd 'accidentally' left her make-up at his flat. He hadn't said anything, so she left a pair of jeans, then some shoes, kicked under the bed so they could seem to be there by mistake. Over the next few weeks, her possessions crept into his place under their own volition, like guerrilla fighters sneaking over the border, and draped themselves over bits of furniture, challenging the now invisible Jenny, Jane, Jamila and Janelle, until he suggested that she have a drawer and a corner of the wardrobe.

She'd seen that drawer as an interesting sign that they might have some sort of a future together, and that, for the time being, the Js were in retreat. So she brought out the big guns, inflicting damage invisible to the naked male: two little dark smudges on the corner of a towel to signify 'mascara-wearer was here' or flowers in a vase. Men never put flowers into vases. Women knew that.

There was no answering fire: no single earrings on the floor near the bed or discarded female razors in the bathroom waste-paper basket.

Her first pregnancy had been an accident – she had been quite frightened by its suddenness, barely a year after they'd first met – but Jonny seemed unfazed, and they'd decided to buy a place together. 19 Lovelace Road.

So here they were. But she couldn't quite identify a photograph that said 'this is us'. They'd never married – they'd talked about it, but somehow there'd never been the time or the money. Throughout her twenties, Kate had come away from weddings storing away little details that she liked or making mental notes as to what had been wrong. Your wedding day was the most important day of your life, and she didn't want to do it until she was ready to do it perfectly. And not, of course, until she was down to a size ten. And Jonny agreed. Or rather, he didn't really seem to care.

Men didn't. Thinking about this, Kate suppressed a very faint worm of unease. Very few people got married these days. There was no point. It was absurd to abide by old-fashioned conventions. It just meant there were no photographs. And none of the pictures of him looking cool and her in a big, unfortunate hat at various friends' weddings would do. There were several photos of them on holidays, but Kate thought she looked like a fat, white slug next to the tanned, relaxed Jonny. In the end, she'd discarded the beach-bum shot because there was no equivalent one of her, and decided to frame a stylish photograph of him taken for a media magazine after he'd won an award for one of his series, and one of herself in the kitchen at 19 Lovelace Road taken when she'd been interviewed by a woman's magazine about one of her programmes. Both had the right kind of relaxed, cool seriousness and were well composed.

It was only when they were up that she realised that she and Jonny were not only in separate photos but they seemed to have defined themselves purely in terms of their work. She shot a look at him. Had he noticed?

'That looks great,' he said, looking at his watch. 'So who's coming?' He put away the tool box and moved over to the wine rack, recently installed in the sleek new kitchen. 'Do you think we'll need more red wine or mainly white?'

Kate whisked a bag of carrots out of the fridge and began to grate furiously, a new Middle-Eastern cookbook propped up in front of her. 'Olivia and Si. Olivia drinks white, but don't forget that she hates Chardonnay, and Si likes really good reds. Don't give him any rubbish, you know what he's like, he'll get pompous.

Heather barely drinks . . .' Kate put down the grater. 'I get the impression that her parents might have been teetotallers or something, maybe a big ban on wicked alcohol in the house when she was growing up, what do you think?'

Jonny shrugged. 'She's never mentioned any of her family to me.'

'Don't you think that's odd?'

'I think we need to get on with sorting out lunch.'

'Oh, OK.' But Kate frowned slightly as she picked up another carrot. 'Jack, of course, knocks back anything, and the children will stick to orange juice. Mumma likes sherry. Oh, and I've invited Sasha Morton. That woman I met at the drinks on Thursday. She's the daughter of the painter Roderick Morton, so she could be quite interesting. She's going through some hideous divorce and is on her own this weekend, so I felt sorry for her.' Kate flicked hair out of her eye. Her arm ached and there were still seven carrots to go. 'And she's trying to get into "the media".' She put down the carrot and wiggled her fingers to indicate quote marks. 'She said she'd love some advice. She seems really nice.'

'Just don't put me next to her.' Jonny's voice came from the fridge, where he was having difficulty finding space for a few extra bottles of white wine. 'The weekends are my time off, and I don't want to have to give the ten reasons why it is almost impossible to get into TV.'

'Me too. But to be fair,' said Kate, who was always trying to be a better person, and rather guiltily feeling that she'd failed, 'I thought she was rather interesting. And her ex-husband sounds awful.'

Jonny rolled his eyes. 'You never stop, Kate, do you?'

'What do you mean? I'm just trying to be nice. If you walked out, you wouldn't want people to leave me on my own all weekend.'

'If I walk out, it'll be because you invite people round the whole time.' He began opening the red wine, shaking his head in mock despair.

The doorbell rang twenty minutes later. Ella was always the first to arrive.

'The traffic was terrible.' She handed over the pudding that she'd made as her contribution to lunch, plus a bunch of daffodils from the garden. 'Really awful. I think I'm going to have to stop driving. I'm getting far too old. I'm seventy this year, you know.' She delivered these lines in crisp tones.

'Oh, no. Seventy is nothing nowadays. Just the right age for trekking in the Himalayas or taking up parachuting.' Kate was disconcerted by Ella's admission of frailty. She wanted Ella to go on exactly as she was, the mainstay of the Thorpe Wenham allotments, a demon bridge player and, twice a week, a volunteer at the charity shop.

Luke came racing up to kiss his grandmother, and her face softened at the sight of him.

'Come and see the new extension.' He took her hand and pulled her towards the back of the house.

Ella nodded, conveying approval. 'I love the light. And it's so big. But wasn't it very expensive?'

'Oh, not really.' Kate knew the question of how much they'd spent would be a hot topic amongst the family for weeks to come, with lines being drawn and sides being taken. She would be labelled extravagant. Quite unfairly. This was an investment. She avoided the question. Ella settled herself on one of the huge dark sofas, and accepted a sherry from Jonny. 'Tell me who's coming.'

'Everyone. Si and Olivia, and Jack and Heather with the girls, and someone I met last week called Sasha Morton. She's the daughter of the painter Roderick Morton. She's getting divorced, and doesn't have her children this weekend, so she's a bit lonely.'

Ella frowned. 'I thought we would just be family. It's not a good idea to invite divorced women round, you know.' She indicated the stairs. Jonny had disappeared with Luke, to check something on the computer. 'I mean suppose *he* fancies her? You're not married, you know.'

Why were mothers so infuriating? 'Mumma, that has absolutely *nothing* to do with *anything*, and the reason why Jonny stays with me isn't about a meaningless piece of paper, but because he knows that we're both free agents.' She picked up the carrot she was about to grate, held it as if it were a microphone, and tried to sing. 'He knows my door is always open and the sleeping bag . . .' She couldn't quite catch the tune. Or the words, for that matter. Ella looked perplexed.

'What *are* you doing?' Jonny came back into the room.

'Karaoke with the carrot.' Kate began grating again. 'Trying to remember that song that says how your sleeping bag stays rolled up behind the sofa because the door is always open. "Ever Gentle On My Mind", that's it. That's what I am, Mumma.'

'Kate, you're many things when you're on my mind,' said Jonny, 'but ever gentle is *not* one of them.'

'You never could sing.' Ella was thoroughly disapproving. 'Si and Jack both have lovely voices, but you always sounded like a frog trying to get through a grating.'

Kate giggled. 'Mumma thinks this new friend of mine might be after you, Jonny, because she's a divorcee, and therefore, by definition, must be looking for a man. I was saying "so what?"'

Ella's cheeks went pink. She firmly believed in keeping secrets from men. And any kind of female machination. Then she raised her chin towards Jonny. 'Well, she might be after Jack, he's got no sense, or Si, because anyone who works that hard is bound to have an affair at some point.'

'It sounds like fun.' Jonny laughed, leaning against the chunky black granite 'island' they'd installed in the middle of the room. 'But as Si and Jack are so busy, shouldn't we worry more about Olivia and Heather – they're obviously on their own so much?'

'Don't try to tie me in knots, you know what I mean.'

'I look forward to being fought over,' said Jonny. 'Bags I, in fact. Jack doesn't deserve it, and Si only thinks about money anyway.'

'Dream on,' said Kate, squeezing lemon over the carrots and adding caraway seeds. 'She can have you if she wants you. Which she won't unless you shave before they all arrive, you look as if you've slept on a park bench.'

Jonny saluted and went upstairs.

'Anyway,' said Kate, feeling guilty about teasing her mother, 'I don't believe that someone can just walk in and destroy a good relationship. There'd have to be something wrong to start with, so she won't get far with any of us. I mean, both Si and Olivia and Heather and Jack are really strong together. Don't you think? In their different ways?'

11

Ella regarded her steadily over the rim of the glass with a knowing expression. She was not going to be persuaded. 'Where's Callum?' she said, changing the subject. 'And isn't that the doorbell?'

'I hope we're not late,' said Heather, edging in the door nervously, kissing Kate, hugging Luke, and proffering a large flat box, slightly dented. 'Sorry, Molly sat on the apple tart. It's a bit squashed. Sorry. Sorry.'

Heather's constant churning anxiety made Kate want to shake her. She was beautiful, bright, slim and nice – why did she have to apologise for herself the whole time? 'Don't worry, Heather, it's fine. Callum . . .' she called upstairs, 'everyone's here.' An indistinct snarl from the top floor indicated that Callum had heard.

'Molly sat on the tart!' shrieked ten-year-old Daisy, as she was towed in the door by Travis, their chocolate labrador. 19 Lovelace Road's long, narrow hall had little space for enthusiastic labradors. He barrelled past Kate, almost knocking her down, dragging Daisy behind him as a motorboat tows its water-skier. 'The tart was on the seat and she just didn't look. She sat right down on top of it!' Almost everything Daisy said had exclamation marks.

'It wasn't my fault.' Twelve-year-old Molly followed, the image of her pale, slender, strawberry-blonde mother. 'It's not very sensible to put a tart on a seat, is it?'

'Well, where else you would you put it? Not on the floor,' said Jack, coming in last with his arms full of bottles of wine and a jar of Heather's home-made marmalade, which he pressed on Kate. 'Can you pump up the apples somehow?'

Kate kissed him. 'I'm sure I can do something with it. How lovely. I adore Heather's marmalade.' She expected this sort of thing from Jack. He was the family hero – he was in military intelligence, which he self-deprecatingly referred to as 'a contradiction in terms', completely at home with obscure snippets of information from tribal elders in terrorist-infiltrated villages, but vague about domestic matters. How he had managed to persuade the immensely competent Heather to agree to marry him was a mystery to them all, but it proved that he did have some sense, as Heather was, everyone agreed, the perfect wife. They had lived in a series of army quarters, which varied from depressing 1960s boxes on windy

12

estates to the current rather pleasant – even lavish – 1930s colonel's quarters in Halstead Hill, just inside the M25 in Surrey. Their various houses were usually too small – or too far away – for full family gatherings, and Kate's other sister-in-law, Simon's wife Olivia, hated cooking and was too busy 'sorting out the world' as the family legend had it. So family celebrations were usually directed by Kate and centred round 19 Lovelace Road.

'Oh, wow!' Heather stopped. 'This is amazing, Kate. What a transformation.'

'How much do you think it cost, Heather?' asked Ella. 'Kate never tells me anything.'

Heather paled. She always seemed terrified of Ella. 'Oh, I . . .'

The new extension stretched out before them, all thirty feet of it, with its width spanning the entire twenty feet of 19 Lovelace Road's plot. There were lantern-windows in the flat roof and a full wall of glass ahead of them, flooding the room with light, and, along one side, a steel double fridge, range and line of units. Daisy and Molly rushed round the chunky island unit in the middle, shrieking. Their voices bounced off the hard surfaces.

'It's amazing,' repeated Heather. 'And, oh, look the photographs. Aren't they lovely? You're so clever.'

'Are you sure we're not too grubby and stained to be allowed in?' asked Jack. 'Now I can see all sorts of things I would never have noticed before. Like your roots.' He grinned at his sister with brotherly venom.

Kate blushed. 'I haven't had time to have my roots done,' she said. 'Or the money. We went over budget.'

'So it *was* very expensive,' confirmed Ella, with triumph in her voice. 'I thought so. Now where is Callum?'

'Have a drink. We've got some elderflower cordial and there's masses of wine.'

Jonny kissed Heather and shook hands with Jack. 'What can I get you?'

'Mm. This is a smart bottle of red, Jonny,' said Jack. 'Have you won the Lottery?'

'Jonny, this is lovely,' said Heather, accepting her glass of elderflower cordial, and looking round again. 'You must have added so much space to the house.'

'Not to mention the space you must have added to your bank account,' added Jack.

'I would like to see my other grandson,' declared Ella. 'I've been here for half an hour and there's been no trace of Callum.'

'Callum!' Kate screamed up the stairs. 'Granny's here. And everyone else.'

Callum slouched down around ten minutes later.

'You look terrible, darling,' said Ella. 'Are you getting a cold?'

'No, Gran, I'm fine.' He kissed her, glared at Kate, then poured the entire contents of a carton of orange juice down his throat.

'Goodness,' said Ella. 'You must be about to start growing. It's so important for men to be tall. Now where have you been?'

'Out.'

'And what have you been doing?'

'Nothing.'

Ella smiled indulgently. 'Jack was exactly the same at his age,' she said to Heather. 'Boys will be boys.'

Chapter 2

Olivia knew they were late for the Fox lunch, and that it was her fault as usual. Si, casually dressed in cream chinos, a checked shirt and a well-cut dark blazer, was all ready to go, checking his emails on his BlackBerry with a pile of documents from work on one side of him. Si never wasted time. The Sunday papers, four different lots of them, lay unread in a heap on their long, solid dining-room table. He would work through them this evening.

At first Olivia hadn't wanted to get out of the bath. She worked hard. Very hard. As a divorce lawyer with a top London firm, she had to keep her mobile on at all times of the day and night. A client had once called her at four in the morning, drunk and weeping. They often called at weekends, lonely and angry. Olivia's clients were rich enough to expect this to be part of the service.

With only one morning a week to indulge (Saturday always seemed so full of urgent chores), she suddenly resented the necessity of rushing in order to beat the traffic, and knew that she would resent things even more if she didn't. She dreaded the idea of sitting in a car, edging forward, then stopping, over and over again, as her few precious moments of free time drained away.

She wiggled her toes and added more hot water. They had a huge limestone bathroom, with views over the city skyline, and you could lie and soak while looking at pigeons wheeling round the sky.

Olivia and Si had once owned a terraced house like Kate and Jonny's, but when it had become clear that they wouldn't be having a family, they'd decided to buy a big central flat right on the river. They'd bought it off-plan and it had gone up in value quite amazingly – with its treble-height ceilings and wall-to-wall glass open-plan existence – even when everyone else's houses were dropping. Of course, Si knew the developer before he became famous. They'd had to get rid of a great deal of their old furniture, jettisoning the reproduction mahogany dining table and friendly, moth-eaten sofas to the auction rooms, and buying large, sweeping blocks of furniture in colours that could not quite be described, but were somewhere indeterminate between grey, charcoal and beige. Olivia had felt that in doing so they'd thrown off the past, or at least the parts of the past that she'd wanted to get rid of.

But, of course, it hadn't changed the Sunday lunches, inter-mittent though they were, with the extended Fox family. Mostly Olivia enjoyed these, and she knew that they were a lifeline for Si. It was, she thought, perhaps the only time he really relaxed. He stopped pretending.

No, that wasn't entirely fair. Si didn't pretend. Si was just Si, ambitious, dynamic, hard-working and determined to be the best. The scholarship boy from the Home Counties who always wanted to be one step ahead of the rest. He was Finance Director of Rifle & Rod, what had been a sleepy old family firm selling sporting goods. He had been part of the team that had transformed the company into a major premium brand name, the intertwined RR now found on everything from sunglasses to suitcases. Now he was helping to mastermind their current expansion scheme, as RR swallowed up smaller premium companies, gobbling up almost everything that spoke of luxury and exclusivity.

Si wore bespoke suits from Savile Row. Except, of course, he didn't get them from the West End because he knew the 'little man' who worked in Shoreditch – or perhaps it was Hounslow – who actually made the Savile Row suits and he went straight to him. He had his shirts hand-stitched in Hong Kong as he flew through. Even his shoes were made-to-measure, from a cobbler in Clapham, once again the craftsman behind a great name. Si liked to be on the inside track, and he wore his status proudly.

Occasionally Olivia wondered if she, too, had been part of Si's acquisition process, the girl from the right background to go with his hand-made shoes. When she met Si she'd felt awkward with men, because she was tall and gawky, with a dowdy, outdated dress sense. Si had showed her how to turn thinness into elegance, and had enjoyed shopping with her, bringing out what she soon discovered was her own innate sense of style. But she had wondered if she was like the companies that he invested in, bound to repay a dividend in the end. Her father had certainly thought so.

'Never trust the middle classes,' he'd warned over dinner. 'They're too keen on getting on in life. I shall tell him I'm putting all your money in trust. See if he stays keen then.'

But Si's subsequent interview with her father had gone well. 'Very wise, sir, it's certainly what I shall do with our daughters.'

'And our sons,' said Olivia when Si reported this conversation to her. 'Sons and daughters are equal.'

Si kissed her. 'I narrowly avoided telling the old fart to stuff his inheritance. He obviously thinks I'm marrying you for your money.'

Olivia laughed. 'Aren't you?'

'No, I'm marrying you because you're beautiful, intelligent, kind, delicious, sexy, clever, my very best friend and I love you to bits. Will that do?' They kissed again. 'And speaking of daughters and sons,' he added, 'how many do you want?'

'Loads of each.' Olivia had snuggled into his arms, secure in his love for her and in their future together.

It had not quite turned out that way. Olivia and Si had buried the pain of childlessness in a deep involvement in their nephews and nieces, and knew that they, in turn, unfettered by the need to impose discipline of any kind, had been awarded the title of favourite aunt and uncle by Molly, Daisy, Callum and Luke. And she genuinely liked both Kate and Heather, although Kate could be a bit bossy and Heather rather too – well, they would have called it 'wet' at Olivia's boisterously expensive private girls' school. But when you heard about the sisters-in-laws some of her friends had to suffer she knew she was lucky.

But she didn't want to go to 19 Lovelace Road that Sunday. Eventually, after delaying tactics that included emptying the dishwasher and checking her emails, she gathered up the huge, soft, very expensive handbag that she'd bought on Friday – full of little treats for the children – and headed down to the underground car park. Simon had brought a chilled magnum of champagne in a cool bag, which he tucked behind the seat, so that they could celebrate.

'They'll think we're having a baby,' Olivia said, as they did up their seat belts.

'Don't be ridiculous, of course they won't.' Si's voice was sharp. 'They know we're past all that.'

She was instantly furious, but tried to suppress it. 'Why should they? People do have babies when they're forty, you know. And they don't know about . . .'

'Not many people. Face it.' Simon cut across her indignation as they pulled out into the traffic. 'Let's just enjoy the day, OK? It's a celebration. Your celebration.'

'I wish you'd let me tell them . . .'

Si's hand tightened on the steering wheel. 'Olivia, we've been over this. Again and again. I'm just not comfortable with it. And it is my secret to keep, don't you think?'

'But they think it's my fault.' Sometimes she hated Si for being so traditional.

'No, they don't,' he said, patiently. 'Nobody is talking about "fault". I think they quite like us not having children, because then we can spoil theirs, and rich, doting aunties and uncles are always appreciated.'

Olivia suspected Si was right. They all had their roles in the family, and everyone was happy with the way it was. But she wanted more time to go over this, to scratch the sore that festered between them, even though she'd seen enough scratching of sores in the divorce courts to make her understand the value of being calm and rational. As she looked out of the window, she indulged in a short fantasy of announcing Si's problem to the Foxes.

'We don't have children because Si fires blanks.' The gravy, or the garam masala, or the whipped cream – whatever was being passed down the table – would halt in its progress as everyone looked at each other, then Kate would jump in first, with cries of sympathy. Jack would try to defuse the situation with a joke, and Heather would grasp his arm in warning, while Ella would fix

Olivia with a firm gaze and ask someone to tell her what 'blanks' were – she hated slang, and always pretended not to understand it. She would then confuse male infertility with impotence, although her razor-sharp brain was quite capable of making the distinction, and refuse to believe it. 'That sort of thing doesn't happen in our family.'

Ella would then spend the rest of lunch shooting suspicious little glances at Olivia, while Heather would tentatively suggest acupuncture or fostering. Kate would start talking about a programme she'd made about women and donor sperm, offering to dish out websites and helplines, throwing herself into the problem with vigorous determination, oblivious to the fact that Olivia herself had already found every single website, helpline, leaflet and specialist available, and that Si had, after long, anguished consultations, decided that he couldn't bring up another man's child, not even one conceived with something as remote as donor sperm. 'It wouldn't be a Fox,' he said. 'It would be different.'

'Nobody would know,' Olivia had begged.

'I would know. He or she wouldn't really be a cousin of Luke and Callum or the girls.'

No, Si was right: telling the Foxes about Si's infertility would achieve nothing more than a volley of sympathetic telephone calls from Kate, possibly interspersed with requests to talk about it all on the radio, which would go on for several months, until either Jonny calmed her down or some other person in trouble came on to her radar. And the mild distrust with which Ella Fox viewed her daughter-in-law – indeed both her daughters-in-law, in turn – would deepen. Ella had been brought up in an era when nothing – particularly childlessness – could ever be a man's fault and she would regard Olivia's words as baseless, rather snide and disloyal. 'I would have thought better of Olivia,' she would have said, possibly to Si or Jack, maybe to Kate, even to Heather. Or perhaps to all of them at different times. And someone, thinking that Ella's attitude was hilarious, would have passed it back, not meaning to hurt, of course . . . Olivia sighed. And as for the strategy of just telling one of them and allowing the news to leak out discreetly – well, she and Si definitely agreed on that. There would be as much fuss and it would be strung out over a longer period, and neither of them could face the thought of Kate spreading it round the family, her friends, the school run, the PTA, the Lovelace Conservation Area Residents' Association, the ideas meetings she had with the BBC, and very possibly even the Armenian dry cleaners on the High Road. And neither of them wanted Heather's pity, either, or her firm belief that being a mother was the only true way for a woman to fulfil herself.

But still. The unfairness of it burned in her. She was sure the Foxes did blame her, deep down, for not giving Si another generation of the family. Her own relations weren't a problem: her wealthy, distant parents had both died over ten years ago and she had one elder sister, married, with children, living in Hong Kong. Apart from that there were some cousins on her father's side, with whom they exchanged Christmas cards, and, on her mother's, one cantankerous bachelor uncle, living in a decaying cottage in rural Kent, who'd made it very clear that he didn't need nieces or fuss, and that he would prefer to be left alone. So she only had the Foxes to contend with, at Christmas, Easter, Sunday lunches . . .

Olivia sighed again and the car surged forward before coming to a stop at some red lights.

A small pair of eyes peered at them through the letterbox. 'It's Auntie Olivia,' squeaked a voice. 'And Uncle Si.' They opened the door to them, shrieking in excitement and delight.

Like a pack of elves, Luke, Molly and Daisy tugged Olivia in. While Molly took after Heather, with a delicate oval face, dimples, gooseberry-green eyes and slightly flyaway strawberry blonde hair, the others were all pure Fox: mousy and tousled-haired, with tawny eyes, strong eyebrows and jaws, each cleft with the Fox dimple and a relatively stocky build. The Foxes weren't tall – Olivia herself was a centimetre taller than Si in her highest heels – but they all had presence. You noticed the Fox family, especially when they were all together.

If she had a baby by donor sperm, it might be like her, tall and chestnut-haired, or it might look completely different from all of them. She thought about Si being reminded, every time they lunched at 19 Lovelace Road, that their child was not genetically his.

She shook the thought out of her head – those battles had been fought years ago, she didn't quite know why it had suddenly all come into her mind today – then hugged Molly, Daisy and Luke, and worked her way through the grown-ups. Callum, she noticed, had made himself scarce.

'This is fabulous,' she said, walking through the narrow Victorian hall to reach the doorway to the extension. 'It transforms the house.'

'Doesn't it?' Kate sounded excited. 'Opens it up, and it's such a flexible space now.'

'What a great party room.' Olivia took a glass of white wine from Jonny. 'And has your relationship survived? I can't tell you how many of my clients come to me at the end of a house renovation.'

Kate looked slightly surprised.

'Oh, not like you,' added Olivia, keeping her tone jocular. 'The problems happen when a couple move out to the country and the husband commutes while the wife does up the house. Then, after a year or so of builders going bust, workmen being late and mess everywhere, the husband finds it easier not to come home in the evening—'

'Sounds just like Jonny,' interrupted Kate.

'I've been working late,' said Jonny, giving Si a glass of wine. 'Things are difficult in TV at the moment. Nobody's got any money.'

'You creative people just aren't businesslike, no wonder you all have such cash flow problems,' said Si. 'Some time I'll show you how to structure your business properly.'

'Sorry, go on with your story, Olivia,' said Kate, giving Si a quelling look. 'Jonny's being facetious. And Si, you're being pompous.'

'I was only suggesting . . .' Si began.

But Kate raised her voice over his: 'Olivia is talking. What happens after the husband starts coming home late?'

'Oh, the husbands I'm thinking of soon get themselves stashed in a PAT in London, so they don't come home at all . . .'

'PAT?' queried Heather.

'Pied-à-terre,' interpreted Kate.

'Well, anyway, not like you and Jonny at all . . .' Olivia was beginning to feel uncomfortable. 'Because you're not married.'

As soon as she saw the change in Kate's face she wanted to take the words back. Kate had always insisted that she and Jonny didn't have time and they didn't need a piece of paper from the government or the church to cement their lives together, but Olivia suspected that there was some underlying issue. In her opinion, Kate was not as secure as she pretended to be. And that made her sometimes more difficult to deal with.

'Not that whether anyone's married or not makes any difference, of course,' Olivia added, conscious of digging herself into a deeper hole. 'The difficulties arise from couples having different lifestyles and even different homes, you see, like ninety per cent of my clients who . . .'

'Sounds good,' muttered Jonny, with a wink to Heather. 'Can I have a PAT?'

'Shh,' said Kate. 'Olivia hasn't finished.'

'Well, one's in the PAT and the other's poring over historic paint charts, then as soon as the last brush-stroke has dried, bingo, one or other of them are in my office talking about adultery.' Olivia wished she'd never started this particular anecdote. 'But that's not relevant here, not at all. Because you were doing it together. And it all looks lovely,' she added, hastily. 'A real triumph. Hello, Ella, how are you?' She kissed her mother-in-law.

'Olivia, Si does nothing but travel and work these days,' complained Ella. 'Can't you stop him? He'll have a heart attack if he goes on like this.'

'No, réally, Ella, I'm afraid I can't. He loves what he does.'

'Do you think I should ring this Sasha person?' asked Kate. 'Find out if something's happened to her? She might have had a breakdown.'

'Nervous or mechanical?' enquired Jack.

'Either,' said Kate, punching numbers into her phone. 'Why don't you ever take anything seriously?'

One o'clock ticked by, then one-thirty, and by two, Kate, on her third glass of wine, began to look harassed. Olivia was beginning to feel slightly tipsy herself.

22

'Do you think we should feed the children now?' suggested Ella. 'This is so rude of this Sarah person. Why did you invite her, Kate?'

Heather looked anxious. 'Do you think she might have got lost?'

'Actually she lives quite near you. I should have suggested you gave her a lift. Never mind. It's fine. How's Halstead Hill?'

'Oh, we really like the house. But Halstead Hill itself isn't as friendly as our last patch. Ever since the army sold its housing off to a private company, and they then sold some of the surplus homes off to civilians, the nicest patches haven't been the same.'

'That's awful,' said Kate, dishing food out to noisy children. 'I wonder if I can make a radio programme about it.' She was given to saying this about anything.

'Oh, no, the army wouldn't like that . . .'

'And the civilians are dreadful,' interjected Jack. 'Badly behaved, sloppy, no taste . . . late night parties . . . even their dogs don't have any discipline. They crap on the pavements.'

'Jack!' reproved Heather. 'You're being a stuffy old colonel. And you're not yet forty.'

'No, I'm not. I've got standards, that's all, and the civilians haven't.'

'But the civilians don't know they're civilians, they just think they're people,' said Kate. 'While you know you're army.'

'What's that meant to mean?' Jack demanded.

'It means you can't lump us all in together.'

'That's what I think,' urged Heather. 'It's just two families who are a bit . . . well, they give large, noisy barbecues, fill the street with cars, play music late at night and have kids who hang around the streets. And rather a nasty dog who took a chunk out of Travis's ear. Jack pretends that all civilians are like that.'

'They are,' said Jack, not entirely joking.

'I just find they're not very friendly,' added Heather apologetically. 'They know we move on, and they can't be bothered. You can see their point of view.'

Olivia could see Callum polishing off another pint of juice. 'Callum looks positively hungover, don't you think?' she murmured to Heather in amusement, as Kate and Ella bent over the meat, making contradictory assessments of whether it was drying out or not.

'Surely not?' Heather's eyes widened in horror. 'He's only fourteen.'

'That's about when they start these days,' said Olivia.

'I think that's dreadful! Do you think one of us should say something to Kate?' She looked so shocked that Olivia wished she hadn't said anything.

'No, no, I'm sure it's fine.' Olivia looked at her watch. 'Ten past two. It really is getting very late for someone to arrive for lunch.'

'Perhaps something awful's happened to her,' suggested Heather.

Chapter 3

The bell rang in two sharp, staccato bursts and was followed by a demanding knock on the door.

'Whoever that is sounds as if they had the hounds of hell after them,' said Jack.

'Don't answer, children. Let a grown-up do it.' Heather got up anxiously. She always seemed terrified that something dreadful was about to happen.

'It's all right, I'll go,' said Kate.

But the girls had already opened the door.

'It's someone called Sasha,' shouted Daisy.

It had better be, thought Kate, who had eaten a whole bowl of crisps. Olivia, who must have been just as hungry, had waved them away, while Heather had nibbled two or three. She got up to welcome the newcomer.

'I'm so sorry, I can't tell you, it's just been the most terrible morning, and you've all been waiting . . .' Sasha said, in low, husky tones. 'My ex and . . . then I couldn't get a taxi . . . and it was all . . .'

Kate thought she heard a squeak of sympathy from Heather.

Sasha thrust a bottle of champagne and a rather classy bunch of flowers at her.

'Oh, how lovely,' said Kate.

Sasha was dark and petite, with surprisingly deep lines across her forehead and in a deep upside-down 'V' from her nose to her mouth. She looked like someone who baked in the sun, smoked a lot and lived on her nerves. She wasn't pretty, not exactly, but she had a certain style.

'Don't worry, we always eat late on Sundays,' added Kate. 'This is my mother, Ella Fox.'

Ella treated Sasha to a steely smile. 'How do you do?'

'This is Jonny, my er . . . or did you meet at the party last Thursday? And this is Si and Olivia – Si's my brother and Olivia is my sister-in-law, and then this is Jack, my roughy-toughy army brother. And Heather, and Daisy and Molly, of course. And these are our sons, Luke. Callum! Say hello to Mrs . . .'

'Morton,' said Sasha. 'But I'm Sasha. Not Mrs anything. Any more. Hello, Callum.'

Callum looked impressed. 'Hi,' he muttered and edged out of the room.

Olivia and Ella sat down and Heather went to sort out a query from the girls, leaving Jonny, Si and Jack standing in a row and giving Kate the brief image of a line-up, as if Sasha might make a choice between them. Would she go for blond, intense Jonny, with his rimless glasses, creased linen trousers and air of an intellectual surfer? Jonny's looks, someone had once said, were only just at the cool end of English eccentric.

Jack, whose broad shoulders and muscular stance almost amounted to a swagger, kissed Sasha. He always kissed women he'd just met, it made them blush. Might Sasha be the type who falls for an action man? Or maybe Si, a little darker and taller than his brother, and every inch the successful executive on his day off, all his clothes perfectly chosen and beautifully cut, coming smoothly forward to welcome Sasha into the room?

Kate shook the image out of her head. Ella's old-fashioned ideas were clearly getting to her. Sasha was, potentially, a new friend. Seeing her again, in bright sunlight rather than the deceptive twilight of a drinks party, she thought Sasha's body language was confident but her eyes were frightened. She needed a helping hand, badly, thought Kate.

Kate told herself to stop fantasising and set about introducing her properly.

'Sasha actually lives quite close to you and Jack, Heather,' she said, as Heather came back into the room again.

'Oh, really, where?' Heather looked alarmed at being drawn into the conversation.

'Richmond,' said Sasha. 'But I'm being thrown out of my home by my ex-husband so I'm looking at new areas. What's it like here?'

'Oh, it's going up,' said Kate, as Heather continued to seem mutely terrified of the new arrival. 'Definitely. But still affordable. Even here in the conservation area. That's Lovelace Road, Lovelace Square, Lovelace Crescent (where the grandest houses are, we can only aspire to those) and Lovelace Gardens, a massive twenties apartment block which is listed, and there are two little linking Victorian terraced streets called Love Street and Lace Street.'

'Is the shopping good?'

'Well, there's the High Road.' Kate paused, as this had failed to 'come up' with the area. It was a ribbon of sari shops, dry cleaners and betting establishments, along with the shambolic Lo-Pryce supermarket and a remarkably empty off-licence. The Lovelace Conservation area was bordered to the south and west by industrial units and graffiti-covered tower blocks, so few people even knew where it was.

'It's a wonderful friendly place,' she reiterated, casting around for another way to get the conversation going. 'Olivia's a divorce lawyer,' she said, as Olivia looked up from a conversation about compost with Ella. 'Sasha's in the middle of an awful divorce.'

For a moment, both Olivia and Sasha looked perplexed as to how they could take this topic further.

'Don't worry, I won't ask you for any tips,' murmured Sasha.

Olivia smiled politely.

'Shall we eat?' suggested Kate.

Si told everybody Olivia's news when they were all seated and the fuss of passing plates down the table was over.

'I'd like everyone to raise their glasses to Olivia,' he said, looking at her. 'Tell them, darling.'

Every face turned towards her, expectantly, and the pride in his voice almost brought a sob to Kate's throat.

'Oh, well, really, it's not *that* exciting . . .' Olivia looked down at her plate.

'She's only been made an equity partner at Campbell Carter,' interjected Si.

There was a chorus of congratulations. Opposite her, Jonny raised his glass and met her eyes. 'Well done,' he said. 'That's quite a triumph.'

'Oh, no,' she replied. 'There are lots of senior women solicitors now.'

'Will you earn more?' asked Ella, with her usual directness. She always asked the questions that no one else dared to.

'It means I get a share of the profits,' said Olivia. 'And, of course, of the losses.'

'Losses! That'll be the day. I've worked out that she'll be earning about twice as much as I do,' said Si.

'And that's saying something,' said Jack to Sasha. 'He's the original bloated capitalist, can't you see?' Si, with his city lifestyle, was less rugged-looking than Jack, and his brother never let him forget it. 'My brother went to Oxford, unlike the rest of us,' Jack added to Sasha, with a touch of malice. 'He fell in with the Brideshead crowd, and suddenly we weren't good enough any more.'

'Don't be ridiculous, Jack,' snorted Si.

There was a brief silence after that as everybody looked at each other. Kate was used to her brothers taunting each other, although sometimes she thought that the knife went in a little too deep. But it was true, Si had won a scholarship to Oxford and had either sought out or fallen in with a group consisting, apart from himself, of those whose families had estates of at least a hundred thousand acres. Ever since then he'd pretended to a grandeur that the last family home – the little three-bedroom semi in Surrey – couldn't justify. Now Olivia might be earning more than he did. Si was not only the eldest brother, the 'head' of the family and the person everybody looked up to but also acknowledged as the top earner in the family. Was earning the most money part of being Si?

She caught his eye, and he gave her a quick smile, reassuring her that nothing had changed within the family. He was genuinely delighted at his wife's success. 'I'm looking forward to being a kept man,' he chortled. And he looked at Olivia again, and Kate saw a message of love pass between them.

'What about you, Sasha? What do you do?' demanded Ella.

'Well, I've got a daughter and a son,' explained Sasha. 'Tom and Grace. So I've been at home looking after them since they were born, really. I know it's rather old-fashioned of me, but . . .'

Kate wondered if Ella would be mollified. She disapproved of Kate working.

'The children are with their father today.' She smiled bravely at them all.

'So, er, have you been divorced long?' As a freelance radio producer, Kate was always on the lookout for subjects for new programmes. She worked from the box room at the top of the house, where two computers and a bank of mixing equipment constituted a 'studio', and she survived by pitching ideas to the BBC, along with a few others, such as the Open University or the British Council. But finding genuinely new ideas and angles that they were prepared to commission was very difficult. She hadn't 'done' divorce for ages. Could Sasha offer a new angle?'

But no. 'It's all very predictable, I'm afraid,' said Sasha. 'He ran off with his younger, prettier, less harassed secretary while I was looking after the children. Grace, our daughter, was very ill for a while so I . . .' her voice trailed off and the lines deepened.

'That's awful!' Kate's vision was temporarily blurred by the terror of either Luke or Callum being very ill, before she switched into her usual mode of wondering whether there was a programme in linking childhood illness to the divorce of the parents. 'What did she have?'

'Leukaemia.'

Kate was shocked out of any thought of radio programmes. 'That's terrible. Is she . . .?'

Sasha nodded. 'All clear. Although, of course, you always worry . . . anyway, I was spending most of my nights sleeping at the hospital, and, of course, that left the coast free for my ex-husband to wine and dine his personal assistant. While the cat's away, you know.'

'How awful.' Kate was horrified. 'But what about Tom?' she remembered, with the automatic reflex of a working mother. 'Your son. Where was he?'

She saw a flicker of something in Sasha's eyes, just for a moment, and she inhaled deeply. 'Tom,' she shrugged, as if he were irrelevant. 'Oh, Tom stayed at my mother's. Anyway, I'll have to go back to work myself soon. My husband is shafting me for every penny he can get. There's no way I'll be able to buy anything for me and the children anywhere near their school. Which is what matters. That's where their friends are.'

Kate felt sorry for her and, not for the first time that lunch, looked round at the big white room with satisfaction. 19 Lovelace Road was now perfect, with its two large, light rooms on each of its four floors and now this big family room on the back. While it wasn't one of the biggest or grandest houses in the area, it had a welcoming elegance and was usually filled with the warm, fragrant smell of good cooking.

'So,' she said, 'I gather you're interested in getting into the media. What did you do before?'

'Oh, I . . . well, I used to be an accountant. I thought I'd like to do something more creative. I thought I might become a novelist, perhaps, or maybe a journalist. But for something decent, not a tabloid rag or a crappy women's magazine. Of course.'

'Well, radio is a very difficult area to make a living from.' Kate launched herself in. 'You see there's either the BBC and that's very difficult to get into as a trainee, particularly if you're, er, well, not just recently out of university. And there's—'

A family hubbub broke out around them, as everyone got on with their food and the children started teasing each other.

'—there's the independent sector,' Kate continued over the noise, 'which is competing for a tiny number of slots, because the BBC have to find work for all their internal departments first, regardless of whether the ideas coming from outside are better. I spend half my time making programmes and the other half the time fighting for commissions, and—'

'Maybe it would be better to try television, in that case,' Sasha cut in. 'Would Jonny mind giving me some advice? Or Si? Is he in the media, too?'

'No, he's an accountant, actually, like you, but he works as Finance Director for a big luxury goods company. You know – Rifle & Rod?' Kate always liked telling people what Si did. Rifle & Rod was a stunningly successful combination of old money and contemporary fashion.

Sasha looked impressed. 'How great.' She looked around, then dropped her voice. 'Haven't Si and Olivia got children? I don't see them here. Or are they with their exes or something?'

Kate smiled. 'Oh, there are no exes in their lives. Olivia and Si have been together forever,' she continued. 'They were first boyfriend and girlfriend at university. They've been together for over twenty years. And,' she dropped her voice, 'they haven't got children.'

'Is that a problem?' asked Sasha, still in an undertone.

Kate shook her head. 'We don't like to ask. I suspect Olivia is quite keen on her career. Campbell Carter are a pretty hot-shot law firm so she has to work very hard.'

'Now that is amazing,' said Sasha thoughtfully, inhaling deeply again. 'A divorce lawyer who never divorces. Over twenty years together. Well, well, well.'

Kate had a brief stab of misgiving. There was something about the way Sasha sat there, in the middle of the long dining table at 19 Lovelace Road, that suddenly reminded her of a cuckoo sizing up a nest.

But Sasha lent towards her. 'Thank you so, so much, Kate, for having me round today. You don't know what a lifesaver it's been. You are so good to think of me. Spending Sunday alone, knowing that everyone else is in a happy family . . .' Her words trailed off.

Kate immediately forgave Sasha her lateness and her slightly predatory air. It was probably all nerves. The poor woman was clearly in pieces over the way her life had fallen apart. And who could blame her?

It was six o'clock by the time everyone went home, although Olivia and Si left early, at about half past four. Kate did the washing-up while trying not to remember that, as well as leaving early, they had also arrived late. Perhaps, with her new promotion, Olivia was going to leave the family behind. Would a very rich Olivia want to bother with 19 Lovelace Road?

Heather stood beside Kate with a tea towel, drying everything up and putting it away.

'Olivia's done so well, don't you think?' This was Kate's foray into the possibilities of a bit of mild family bitching about the sister-in-law who wasn't present.

Heather's great gooseberry eyes widened. 'She's so clever.' She

31

shut the dishwasher with an unusually loud bang. 'But you do wonder, don't you, why they've never had children? Do you think Olivia is just too career-minded?'

And they were off. Kate felt a link with Olivia because they both worked, and a link with Heather because they were both mothers.

Beyond the kitchen area, Sasha sat on the sofa with a glass of wine, listening avidly to Jonny. Kate, in between theorising about Olivia's amazing work ethic, wondered what they were talking about. Why was Jonny sitting there, having a good time, while she and Heather slaved away?

'Jonny,' she said, sharply. 'Can you take the bottles out? It's recycling day tomorrow.'

Jonny looked up and for a moment she thought he was going to snap back, but he just raised his glass to her. 'I'll do it in a minute.'

She frowned. 'Sasha. Heather and Jack are going your way. Would you like a lift with them?'

'That would be so kind.' Sasha turned her attention to Heather. 'Would you really? You are an angel.'

Eventually everyone went home, and after reading a good-night story to Luke, trying to persuade Callum that he really did have to have some kind of bedtime, putting through a round of washing so that everybody had some pants in the morning, and getting everything ready for school, Kate and Jonny took the papers up to bed. It was one of their traditions – one of their best traditions – to spend most of Sunday evening in bed, flipping through the five Sunday magazine supplements Kate deemed necessary if she was to sit in her boxy studio, coming up with ideas that she could submit. The BBC had a programme commissioning round twice a year, to which she put forward ideas, and she needed to put forward about twenty ideas each time, after which she was usually asked to develop about eight of them, then she'd finish up getting commissioned for no more than three or four.

Lying in bed, contemplating another Sunday evening, Kate suddenly felt as if she might never have another idea in her life. But she had to keep her foot on the accelerator.

Wearily, she picked up another Sunday supplement. Maybe there would be something there that would set fire to her brain cells. 'So what did you think of Sasha?' asked Kate, skimming an article on the 'new anorexia'.

'Hm?' Jonny looked up. 'Rather sexy, don't you think?'

'Sexy?' asked Kate, experiencing an unexpected thud of fear, like a punch to the breastbone. She tried to think what Sasha had been wearing. Kate wasn't so naive as to imagine that 'sexy' was short skirts, cleavages and red lingerie, but Sasha had been dressed very soberly indeed, in something that might have been dark grey or blue. Or even brown. It fitted quite well, Kate remembered, and might even have been quite expensive, but nothing had been flaunted. 'I wouldn't have thought *sexy*,' she said. 'I thought she looked quite drab. And terribly tense.'

Jonny lowered the business pages for a second and treated Kate to a mischievous smile. 'She's sexy. I hope she hasn't run off with Jack on the lift home. And proved Ella right.'

Kate dropped her magazine in indignation, gripped by a perverse desire to defend Sasha against male innuendo. 'Don't be ridiculous. That's the sort of thing everybody thinks about divorcees – that they're desperate to get another man.'

'Oh, she's desperate all right,' mused Jonny, rustling the business pages, folding them into four, then bashing them into shape so he had a good grip for comfortable reading. 'Hm. It seems the travel industry's not doing well. Still, it means there might be some cheap last-minute holidays this year.'

'She's had a terrible time, that's all.' She eyed him suspiciously. 'Apparently her husband is trying to get her and the children out of the house they live in. He's insisting they sell the family home.'

'Well, perhaps he needs somewhere to live, too.'

'He doesn't have to throw his own children out. He could live in a flat,' said Kate.

'I understand the principle is that possessions are divided between husband and wife in the case of divorce,' said Jonny. 'I imagine his view is that they should sell the house and each buy two smaller houses.'

'Still, there are more single mothers living below the poverty line than any other sector of society. We did a programme on it last year, and . . .' Kate was off, her indignation in defence of single mothers mounting with every half-recalled fact.

Jonny, she thought, seemed to be shrinking away from her words, but she couldn't stop. The more she talked, the less he seemed to listen.

Eventually, feeling bruised, she ran out of steam. 'I'm just saying that we can't just rely on the courts to look after women who've been abandoned, that's all. We all need to help.'

There was a silence between them and she picked up another magazine, flicking between articles on the latest vitamin craze and how some young starlet was launching her own range of shoes. Jonny worked his way quickly and methodically through the broadsheets, even more distanced from her.

Kate couldn't bear it any longer, and threw down her magazine. 'Anyway,' she said, in as neutral a tone as she could manage. 'Did you give her any advice on getting into TV?'

'What?' Jonny's nose remained buried in the business pages.

'Sasha,' Kate reminded him. 'You were talking to her on the sofa while Heather and I were doing the washing-up.'

'Oh, yes, well, I was doing what you asked me to do. Telling her how to get into television.'

'And?' Kate's skin crawled with trepidation. He was holding something back. She could tell by the tone of his voice.

'I'm letting her do a couple of week's work experience with us so that she can find out.'

'But you're always being asked for work experience! And saying there's nothing much you can give people to do. When I asked you on behalf of that neighbour's son, Tom Whatsisface – you know that woman with the dogs – you said that someone who doesn't know the ropes can even screw up getting a parking permit for a lighting truck or alienate an interviewee by getting their hackles up with the most basic questions.'

'I'll make sure she's not given any responsibility.'

'But I thought you'd decided to say no unless there was a really good reason?'

'I thought some of her ideas were good,' said Jonny neutrally. 'If she wants to try and drum them up into something, I don't mind lending her a desk and a telephone.'

'OK,' Kate forced herself to sound calm. 'Well, that's very kind of you.'

34

He smiled, briefly. 'I am doing my bit to help single mothers. As you said we all should.' He raised his newspaper a little higher than usual, as if to create a barrier between them.

Kate knew she'd been shrill. She must change the subject. She lifted a paper up, but the words were meaningless on the page. After a few minutes, she lowered it. 'Don't you think it was odd that Olivia and Si arrived *so* late and left so early?'

Jonny folded his paper up and tossed it on to the discard pile beside the bed. 'What's up?'

'What do you mean?'

'I mean, you're upset about something, and I presume it isn't me giving that tough little nut a week's work experience.'

'*Do* you think she's a tough little nut?' Kate couldn't help being delighted. Poor Sasha.

'Hard as nails,' he agreed. 'But that's not what's worrying you, is it?'

Jonny, Kate reflected, was almost like a woman sometimes in terms of his ability to pick up light and shade.

'It's Olivia,' she admitted. 'I just felt she didn't really want to be here, and I thought perhaps now she's earning so much money, maybe she doesn't want to come to little old Lovelace Road any more. Maybe we're not grand enough, or interesting enough for her.'

Jonny made a noise that sounded like 'pah', shook the next newspaper into shape, and sighed. 'Katie, Katie. You're inventing problems. As usual.'

She raised her paper slightly higher. 'I don't invent problems. Sometimes I see things coming a bit earlier than other people, that's all. And she said that doing building work was one of the main reasons for couples splitting up and made slightly snide comments about us not being married.' She and Jonny had stopped discussing any possible wedding once they'd made the decision to go ahead with the new kitchen extension. The time and money involved in weddings and building work meant you could do one or the other. And a wedding was just one day, while a back extension was for life. Wasn't it? She peered at him over the top of the paper.

'Well,' he said evenly. 'It's none of her business, is it?'

'No, of course it isn't.' She fell into an uneasy sleep, and woke the following morning with the edge of a hangover.

Chapter 4

Sasha sat in the front seat of Jack and Heather's sensible estate car. Heather squeezed in the back with Molly and Daisy. Travis whined intermittently from the boot, while Sasha mentally reviewed the lunch. Kate, who had been so friendly at the party where they'd met, had not liked her as much this time round.

Well, stuff Kate. But, for the time being, she needed Jonny in order to get into the world of television. Whatever Kate said about it being a young person's business and impossible to get into when you were older, Sasha knew she'd be good at it. Perhaps she'd overdone the lateness bit, but she always liked to make an entrance, and then, having calculated that she would be the right amount of late, genuinely hadn't been able to find a taxi.

Well, women like Kate had no idea how hard it was to be on your own. It was interesting, though, to see from the photos on the wall, no sign of an actual wedding. If that was the case, then Kate might not be quite as secure as she seemed to think she was.

However, for the time being, that was irrelevant. Sasha needed to keep tabs on the Fox family in order to stay in touch with Jonny, who was the only TV director who had given her any encouragement at all. And his intense blue eyes and the passionate way he cared about what he did was very sexy. How had Kate, who was nothing special to look at and not even rich, landed him?

Sasha brooded over why some women seemed to get more than they deserved. Admittedly, she conceded to herself, Kate was quite pretty, in a girl-next-door way, and her boho style, all chunky necklaces, long peasant skirt and boots, was definitely a good look for her because it lifted her out of the ordinary. She had nice, brown eyes, if you liked that shaggy-puppy look, and the strong, determined chin stopped her looking too cute. But, even so, surely a man like Jonny could have chosen someone far better, like Olivia, with her top-model looks and inherited money? It was a mystery.

Sasha resolved that one day she'd be re-established in a decent house, and she'd be able to resume her social life. She would invite Si and Olivia to dinner parties. They were the sort of people she belonged with. Until then she might try to get to know Olivia a little but she didn't hold out much hope. High-flyers didn't come to little rented flats in the back of beyond. Indignation at what her husband was putting her through burned again in her breastbone.

She forced herself to plan rather than fume. Heather was the way in, she decided. Nervous, people-pleasing Heather. She'd recognised Heather as soon as she'd seen her. They were alike – two people who didn't fit in. The sister-in-law who was almost ignored by the Foxes – in the hubbub of Jack's telling funny stories, Kate's command of the room, Ella and her sharp questions, Jonny with his quiet, intense conversations and Olivia's elegant cleverness, there'd been almost nothing of Heather. She'd jumped up and down to help with the dishes, and kept an almost obsessive eye on the children. So she liked to be useful and had no confidence? Right. Good. There was an opportunity there.

'Heather.' Sasha craned her head round to the back seat. 'Grace and Tom are just the same age as Molly and Daisy, and we live quite close to each other. Would you like to come round for lunch this week with them? There's a lovely playpark just at the end of my road.'

She watched Heather conceal surprise. 'Oh, that would be so nice.'

They agreed on Wednesday.

Yes, Heather could be a very convenient friend.

But Kate was different. Sasha burned with fury at the memory of watching Kate withdraw from her, so subtly that most people would have barely noticed. Kate was one of those women who'd never had it tough. Never had to fight. Kate didn't realise it but she was soft, soft, soft. Not a survivor, thought Sasha maliciously. She obviously came from a nice middle-class household where a broken tennis racquet was an 'absolute disaster', and economising meant buying a smaller second car. Kate, secure in her position as the Queen of Fucking Everything, with her Sunday-supplement perfect home (just slightly trashed so it felt warm), smart media job (how quickly she had discouraged Sasha from trying to get one similar) *and* her mum-at-the-school-gates credentials, had no idea how hard life could be, with her cries of 'there's lots for everyone' and 'the more the merrier'.

There isn't lots for everyone, Kate Fox, thought Sasha. More isn't merrier, it just means less for each person. And it's time you learnt that.

Chapter 5

Olivia Fox click-clacked across the polished marble floors of the vast office building that housed Campbell Carter, feeding her identity tag through an automatic gate, and stepping into a glass lift which swept her up to the fifth floor. It stopped with an electronic 'ping'. Around her, lifts arriving on every floor echoed in the building's glass atrium like an ongoing symphony of experimental music.

'Good morning, Olivia,' said the Campbell Carter receptionist. 'Congratulations on being made partner.'

'Thanks, Cheryl,' replied Olivia. 'Did you have a good week-end?'

Cheryl said that she had, because she'd been able to get out into the garden for a change. 'I did seven trips to the tip,' she said, proudly.

Olivia smiled vaguely, her mind already on the week's caseload of expensive malice and misery. Her secretary, Cat, was already in and had started the coffee percolator, and her assistant, Sarah, was talking about her weekend. Olivia sank into her chair and contemplated the rows of files on her shelves. The law was not a very forest-friendly profession. Every case had generated a huge bulk of paperwork, and the shelves themselves covered two whole walls of the office. On her desk, a photo of Simon sat alongside presents from clients — a half-dead cactus, a tacky, but curiously charming 'good luck' angel holding crystals, a joky mug, a painted wooden parrot and, propped up in one corner, a teddy bear. In her desk she kept a stock of emergency equipment: a sewing kit, spare tights and a few painkillers for the occasional headache, and underneath the desk were a few extra pairs of shoes, suitable for court appearances. The office was a second home for Olivia, somewhere where she was judged for herself, not as wife, daughter-in-law or sister-in-law. Or non-mother. She belonged here.

'Olivia.' Nigel Stuart, the most senior equity partner, put his head round the door. 'Good weekend?'

'Mm,' she said. 'Nothing special. Bit of shopping. Lunch with the in-laws yesterday.'

'Rather you than me,' said Nigel. 'My wife's family make the Borgias look naive and trustworthy.'

'Oh, Simon's are nice,' she said, vaguely. 'Really. We get on very well.'

'You'd get on well with anyone,' he said. 'Which is why we think you should do this latest case that's just come into my office.'

'Me?' She was surprised. They were each responsible for getting their own cases, and while it wasn't unheard of to pass a case along – for example, if someone was a personal friend – it wasn't usual, either. 'Fine. Who is it?'

'Allison Green.'

Her heart sank. 'Not the serial divorcee?'

Nigel's smile was predictably wolfish. 'The one and only. Getting rid of her fourth husband, the one she claimed was the "love of her life" only, what was it . . . four and a half years ago?'

'Nigel, is this some kind of initiation ceremony for a new equity partner?' asked Olivia. 'I mean, it's hardly fair, is it?'

Nigel twinkled back at her. 'On the contrary, you'll do it beautifully, won't you? And you'll look so good in front of the cameras. Much better for the firm's image than fat old me.' He chortled.

'Rubbish, you look . . , er . . . fine.' Olivia was disconcerted. 'We'll never be able to get her a decent settlement, you know that. Not after last time. And she's divorcing Housewives' Choice. Everybody adores Ted Lloyd.'

'I have the greatest faith in you. Our reputation as the hottest divorce firm in London must not be allowed to be annexed by Frank & Fifield. Or Dunwoody Grant Murray. Or anyone else, for that matter.'

'What reputation?' she muttered, but Nigel had already glided out, with a satisfied look on his face. Olivia knew she was acquiring a reputation for handling difficult clients, and she suspected that, although you couldn't be a shrinking violet and be a successful divorce lawyer, the others had dumped this case on her because they simply couldn't face it. Allison Green, a woman who had made seventeen million pounds out of her first two divorces, and had been furious at the mere two million awarded her for her third, had then gone on to marry a chat-show host called Ted Lloyd, nicknamed Chat Show Ted by the tabloids, beloved of the afternoon sofa audiences. Ted, with his rough-and-ready charm and twinkling smile, was seen, publicly, as one of the world's nice guys, while Allison Green was hated and despised as a money-grabbing nobody. Then there was the shortness of the marriage – just four and a half years – although there was one baby. Ted Lloyd's only child, and Allison Green Lloyd's fourth. They had signed a pre-nup before their marriage, but this still wasn't legally binding in Britain, and would be even less so now that there was a child involved.

She sighed as she sat down. Another small forest in Finland would be cut down before this case was resolved. It would be very messy and no one would come out of it looking good, particularly not Allison's lawyer. Was getting more money for someone who already had quite enough really what she wanted out of her life?

The phone rang. 'It's a Sasha Morton for you,' said the receptionist.

Olivia couldn't think who Sasha Morton might be at first. 'Oh . . .' She was about to say she was too busy, then decided that she had better talk to her. Sasha was clearly Kate's latest project, and if she avoided her, it would go right round the family, and her reputation for being a materialistic witch who put her career before . . . no, Olivia, she told herself, they don't think that. They really don't. And even if they do, it doesn't matter what they think. Si is the one who matters, not his family, and Si knows you better than anyone. But she didn't want to get on the wrong side of Kate.

'Sasha,' she said. 'How can I help?'

'Oh, I do hope you don't mind me calling you, but I didn't know where else to go, and Heather and Kate both said you were *so* marvellous, so very clever and absolutely the best divorce lawyer in town, and that you would be kind, too . . .'

'It's very nice of them – and you, of course – to say so,' said Olivia, feeling surprisingly cheered by her sister-in-laws' faith in her. 'But I don't think they know very much about divorce lawyers, so I'm sure they've over-exaggerated my abilities.'

'Well, I don't know much about divorce lawyers either, and I really need someone to help me – because of the children, I have to put them first . . . well, to get to the point, I'd like you to represent me.'

Olivia was taken aback. Surely she already had a solicitor? She'd steered clear of talking about divorce to Sasha the day before, but had got the very strong impression that there was very little money in the pot. She didn't want to say 'but you couldn't afford me'.

'Um, I think I'm probably not the right person to do that. We, er, tend to handle quite high-profile cases and that makes us quite, um, er, expensive. I mean, I'm sorry . . .' Why, she thought, could she be firm in court but barely able to finish a sentence when it came to Sasha?

Because Sasha was vulnerable. When Olivia became a lawyer, she'd promised herself that she would stick up for people who had no one else to speak for them. It was nice, of course, to be well paid for it too, but she'd always said that she would never do a case just for the money. She'd heard the pain in Sasha's voice, and she couldn't turn her away. Not completely.

She retrieved her brisk, professional persona from the floor. 'Look, Sasha, I don't think I'm the right person to represent you, but let's meet, and we can talk about the best direction for you to go.'

'Oh, would you? That would be so kind of you. So very kind . . . let me take you out to lunch, of course.'

'No, no,' Olivia heard herself saying. 'Absolutely not. You must be my guest . . . My treat. It's the least I can do.' How had she got suckered into that? A whole lunch with someone she didn't want to represent and didn't really know? Still, when Kate or Heather came to hear of it there was no way they could accuse Olivia of failing to help a friend.

Not that Heather would ever criticise anyone. Her nice girl-next-door persona never slipped. Ever. Which made Olivia feel a bitch in her company. Olivia sighed again. She ought to try and find out a bit more about Sasha, if she could. Checking her watch, she googled the name, but got no hits.

Perhaps she should have a lunch with Kate first, to thank her for Sunday and do a little discreet digging about Sasha. Catching Kate after the school run, she arranged to have lunch with her that Thursday.

Kate and Olivia met at Koko, a new and much-praised restaurant. Kate arrived first, loaded down with carrier bags and a bulging handbag, and spread herself, her coat and her bags all over the banquette, occupying space that really belonged to the tables on either side of them, and began to send emails via her BlackBerry. She disposed of six, mostly to do with work or children before Olivia arrived.

'This is great,' she rose up to kiss Olivia. 'What a treat. I've been dying to come here.'

Olivia was relieved to see that the slight frost between her and Kate had thawed since Sunday. She knew that her story about clients splitting up after decorating houses had gone down badly, but had decided perhaps it would make it worse if she apologised. If you're in a hole, stop digging.

Ella had collared Olivia quietly at yesterday's lunch to ask her how much she thought Jonny and Kate had spent on the extension – which, luckily, Olivia hadn't been able to answer – and to ask Olivia, for the hundredth time, why Jonny and Kate didn't get married. 'Really, all they need is a church or a registry office, and a few people for lunch. How on earth could building the back extension possibly affect that? Do you think they aren't really committed? Jonny is such an attractive man, and all those TV girls are so slim and pretty – do you think he's making excuses?' And so on. Heather always tried to reassure Ella that if you had children together and joint ownership of a house, then 'it was as good as' and 'nobody cares these days', but Olivia just said 'I think Kate just wants the day to be as special as possible,' and kept her counsel, turning the conversation away to compost and the weather as soon as she could. Legally, it was not 'as good as' and Kate, even as co-owner of 19 Lovelace Road, could be left in a very precarious situation if they split.

She pushed these thoughts out of her head, and smiled at Kate. 'Well, I thought I owed you lunch and I don't know how long it'll be before I have time to do any entertaining myself. We've just taken Allison Green on as a client, did you know?' Olivia arranged her long limbs under and around the tiny table for two, managing to look both elegant and slightly ungainly at the same time. Her chestnut hair was twisted up in a chignon.

'I love your hair like that,' said Kate. 'Very French-looking. Yes, I saw about Allison Green in the papers. If she's interested in talking about it . . .'

'Kate,' said Olivia, firmly. 'Part of my job will be to keep her out of the media. As much as possible.'

'You're up against it, then,' said Kate. 'She adores publicity. When it goes in her favour.'

'Which it mostly doesn't. As I shall be pointing out to her.'

They ordered two salads, risotto, baked cod and sparkling mineral water. Kate also had a large glass of white wine, but Olivia shook her head. 'Daren't. Can't doze off this afternoon.'

'Not now you're so important, anyway. Congratulations, by the way, aren't you thrilled?' Kate buttered a piece of bread hungrily and devoured it.

'It's great. If it wasn't for Allison Green, of course. I have a sneaking suspicion that they only made me an equity partner so they could lumber me with difficult cases. Still, so far she's been perfectly sweet. If you can judge by one telephone call.'

'Speaking of perfectly sweet divorcees, I gather Heather suggested that Sasha come to see you.'

Olivia was wary. 'I'm really sorry, but I can't take her on as a client. I'm pretty sure she can't afford me, and I try to keep my pro bono work strictly for people who really do need me, like homeless victims of domestic abuse. But I thought I'd take her out to lunch to tell her nicely. What's her story, though, so I can have a think about anything that might help?'

Kate mapped out Grace's leukaemia, Sasha's husband's infidelity and Sasha's fear that she and the children would be stuck in a tiny flat. 'He sounds like a right bastard.'

Olivia had heard too many one-sided divorce stories to be drawn. 'Well, the trouble with middle-class divorce is that there's often only so much in the pot. If you've got a huge mortgage and you've been living beyond your means for a few years, when it comes to divvying up, both partners have to take a pretty big drop in living standards. It can be absolutely catastrophic for one or both of them, and, although some people are amazing and just get on with it, others crumble.'

Kate looked anxious. 'I suppose so.'

'I think she needs to consider mediation,' said Olivia. 'I'll do my best to point her in the right direction. How close a friend is she?'

'Oh, not close at all, I've only just met her. But I thought I should invite her round, as soon as possible, because so many people stick to that two-by-two Noah's ark thing where couples never invite single people round. I think that you need more support and more invitations, not fewer, when you're going through divorce, and . . . well, I think women should stick together.'

'That's all very well, and very ethical of you,' said Olivia. Kate always tried so hard to get things right, although she surprisingly often got them wrong. 'But, although I think she's obviously very stressed at the moment, I'd say she's a survivor. You don't have to take her on as one of your lame ducks.'

'I don't have lame ducks. You're confusing me with Heather.'

'Heather has worthy causes. She always seems to be getting involved in some charity or other.' Olivia smiled. 'You have lame ducks. All quacking round your kitchen table when they've got a problem.'

At last, she got a laugh out of Kate. 'And what about you, Olivia? What do you have?'

'Oh, you know me.' She spoke lightly. 'Good old Olivia. Puts her career first. I get paid for helping people. There's nothing noble about it.'

Kate smiled, but didn't contradict her. That hurt. Perhaps the Foxes did really think she was tough old Olivia, only interested in earning money.

'Let's talk about something nice. Isn't it Ella's seventieth birthday soon?'

'Oh, yes.' Kate dug happily into her baked cod. 'This is delicious. Yes, I was going to contact you about that, to see if everyone wanted me to do some sort of special party at 19 Lovelace Road. We could cover over the back garden with a marquee and invite all Mumma's old friends, and . . .'

'That sounds lovely,' said Olivia. 'Although I had been going to suggest that, as Si and I don't have any . . . er . . . responsibilities, then perhaps we could do something for a change. Like rent a villa abroad for a week. We'd pay for everything – all you would need to do is get your flights. You've done so much, it would be nice for you to have a rest.'

Kate didn't look as pleased as Olivia had expected, and she was disconcerted. What had she done wrong? Olivia pursued the seventieth birthday idea for a few minutes, and still didn't get much response.

'Are you all right, Kate?' asked Olivia.

Kate made a pattern in the breadcrumbs on the white tablecloth. 'Yes, fine.'

'Well, what do you think about my suggestion?' Olivia wondered if she'd said something tactless. 'What about Sardinia? Or Barcelona? Or even Morocco?'

'Or Cornwall?' suggested Kate. 'She might be a bit fussed by the air travel.'

Surely Kate could show a bit of enthusiasm? Irritated again, Olivia waved a waiter down and asked for the bill. 'She flew to New York last year, didn't she? Well, let's all think about it, shall we?'

Chapter 6

Heather Fox lay on her kitchen floor and used a knife to wiggle open a tiny hatch at the bottom of the washing machine. She pulled out a small bit of piping, then unstoppered it and let the dirty water that had been trapped in the machine slowly dribble out into a tray.

It occurred to her, as it did only occasionally, that it would be nice if Jack were around sometimes to unblock washing machines. But Jack, like most of her army friends' husbands, was never there when you needed him.

She sighed and stood up. The washing machine would be fine for an hour or so, but she'd have to keep an eye on it or the water would eventually flood all over the kitchen floor. She washed her hands, catching sight of herself in the mirror as she did so.

'I look like my mother,' she said, out loud to herself. Because, of course, as usual, there was no one to say it to. No, that wasn't strictly fair, because she would be picking up Molly and Daisy from school soon, and the house would be full of shrieks and laughter. But she couldn't tell them that she looked like their grandmother, because they wouldn't understand. She wasn't around. That's what Heather always used to say. 'Their grandmother isn't around.' People assumed that she was dead, and murmured their sympathy and Heather would change the subject brightly, offering another slice of cake or an additional cup of coffee.

Of course she didn't really look like Mo Spencer, although

she'd inherited her slender frame and strawberry-blonde hair from her. It was the lines that were being etched on her face, the beginnings of a set look, of disappointment – even anger – that worried her. Heather, all her life, had been determined that she was never going to be like her mother.

She would never, ever want Molly and Daisy – or even Jack, from whom she kept no other secrets – to find out about her.

Jack would never understand. Heather needed Jack to think of her as he always had – as a princess he'd rescued from dragons, a fair maiden who had been literally swept off her feet by him, as the vulnerable woman who relied on him utterly . . . that was their story, it was how they'd met, and it was how they still operated, in spite of Heather's increasing ability – which she played down – to mend washing machines and the like.

Fourteen years earlier, she'd come out of Waterloo station on a summer's evening, at about six o'clock, and was walking back to her flat in Lambeth when she was pushed roughly to the ground. She hardly had time to put a hand out to break her fall, and she lay there, unable to move, winded and confused, feeling a pain radiate up her arm, vaguely aware of feet around her.

'Are you all right?' As she struggled to sit up and get her breath back, she could hear a low, pleasant man's voice, and looked up to see broad, strong shoulders blocking out the light. There was concern in a pair of tawny eyes. 'Don't move if anything hurts,' he said, gently.

'My arm aches a bit, but I'm sure it's nothing.' Some of the feet moved away. Everyone was in a hurry.

'How many fingers?' He waggled his hand in front of hers, and she could see that his arm was muscular and dusted with faint blond hairs, as if he had been out in the sun a lot.

'Four.'

'What day is it today?'

'Wednesday.' She smiled weakly, and struggled to talk. 'I don't think I was hit on the head. I just can't breathe very well . . . oh . . . my bag!' She felt around her, panicking. She'd taken two hundred pounds out of the cash machine that day, she didn't want to lose it.

'Don't worry,' he said. 'I got it back. It's here.'

'Oh, thank you. Thank you so much.' She managed to get up, but still felt dizzy, and continued to hang on to his arm.

'I think you need to see a doctor. St Thomas's hospital is just across the road, and I'm going there to see my sister. She's just had her first baby. Come with me.' He took Heather's arm, and she walked very slowly, with cotton-wool legs, while Jack explained that he'd been behind her when two youths ran up, one grabbing her bag off her shoulder and the other pushing her to the ground.

'I didn't have to chase them far,' said Jack. 'They were only kids.'

'You could have been knifed,' said Heather.

'I don't think so. They didn't know what had hit them.'

'Or you could have been sued for assault.'

'They've gone,' he said. 'They won't be making any formal complaints.'

They reached the doors of the hospital.

'I feel much better now,' said Heather. 'And my arm's obviously not broken, because I can move it.'

Jack felt it carefully. 'I still think you should be checked over.'

'Honestly, there'll be a four-hour wait, and it's really not necessary.'

'Still, I'd like to keep an eye on you. Come up and see my sister for ten minutes, and then come out to dinner?'

Heather would normally have adamantly refused to visit a woman she'd never met – she was far too shy, and she thought it was rather a peculiar invitation, but there was something about either Jack or the mugging that had taken her breath away.

'Oh, I'll just wait outside,' she said, pulling back when they reached the door of the ward.

'Nonsense.' Jack steered her in. 'This is Heather, everyone, the girl I'm going to marry.'

He was obviously joking and Heather laughed nervously. She never believed a word men said, anyway. She muttered something about having just met him but nobody seemed to listen, shaking her hand and smiling as if Jack was always turning up with strange girls he thought he was going to marry.

He probably was. She tried to make herself invisible amongst the Foxes as they all talked at once. She was introduced to Ella,

Jack's mother, then Olivia and Si, some cousins, then tall, cool, slightly crumpled Jonny Rafferty, and, of course, Kate, tired and flushed, but smiling, with the smallest scrap of baby Heather had ever seen. 'This is Callum,' she said.

I want one of those, she'd thought, overwhelmed by the sudden tug of desire.

'Would you like to hold him?' asked Kate.

Heather realised that the family really did think she was Jack's latest girlfriend. As if Jack would ever go out with someone who didn't even know who her father was and who'd grown up with a series of 'stepfathers' and then in a children's home called the Caldecott Foundation. Well, she wasn't going to tell them. She took the tiny, light, almost boneless being in her arms and felt faint again, this time with longing. This was what she was born for. She knew it. 'Thank you,' she said to Kate, handing the baby back, and Kate smiled. Heather almost liked her for that, which was as far as she was prepared to go on her first meeting with anyone.

'How long have you known Jack?' someone asked.

'Oh, about five minutes.'

They all laughed, thinking it was a joke.

Jack romanced her. He called her every day. He sent flowers. He took her to countless restaurants and away on a country-house weekend. Heather had been wary. She always was. You never knew when someone wasn't going to turn nasty.

But Jack never turned nasty. There was something about his persistence that reminded her of the people at the Caldecott. 'You've got to get out of bed,' they had said to the frightened child. 'You must get out of bed. I'm not going until you've got out of bed. Everyone has to get out of bed. I'm still here, and I'm staying until you're out of bed.'

In the end the sullen, angry, ten-year-old Heather had uncurled herself from under the blankets and sulkily got out of bed. It was the same with breakfast. She'd never seen the point of breakfast, because there'd never been any, but at the Caldecott she was expected to eat it every day. At first she'd thrown the bowls of cereal on the floor, then eventually she'd given in. After that she worked out quite quickly that if you did what was expected of you, you could live quite a pleasant, quiet life, and that at least there were rules to rely on. She was now very afraid of breaking rules, in case the dark days came back again. She had fallen in love with Jack because he was so surrounded by people and structure. He made her feel safe.

Sometimes she wondered if she should tell Jack about the Caldecott, but decided that it had better stay a secret. She remembered the first day she'd arrived there, with a social worker holding her by the elbow, gazing up at the massive steps and giant pillars, and looking at a house that looked more as if it had been built for a King and Queen in a fairy tale rather than to house a collection of deprived, mistreated, frightened, suspicious children. 'This is the Caldecott Foundation,' the social worker had said. 'They look after children like you.' In spite of herself, she was impressed, and even stopped spitting and swearing for long enough to take it all in. There was a possibility, in its endless corridors and sweeping lawns, that life could be different.

So the army worked for her. Even being an army wife worked for her, because she could understand institutions. Everyone was friendly, but they didn't want to own your soul. People moved on before they really got to know who you were. It was safer than the unpredictable real world. Heather watched the other army wives and girlfriends and modelled herself on them, hiding the real Heather in anxious smiles and a very clean house. His family always made her nervous, though, because she'd never known anything like it. They all seemed to speak in code, and she couldn't quite understand the switch back and forward between bitching and supporting each other. But it made Jack happy, so she treated the Sunday lunches at 19 Lovelace Road as another form of institution.

It took Heather a while to discover that the Foxes, seemingly so secure and happy, also had a shadow in the background. The sudden death of Michael Fox, their father. Even after all these years, she could sense the shock and grief the accident had caused. Especially for Jack, she thought, who had been far, far too young to lose what had obviously been a steadying influence. For Jack, it was as if he'd never had a father. She thought Si, too, had been affected far more than he admitted, because he had married his first proper girlfriend, as if seeking security, and behaved like a

51

middle-aged man even when he was in his twenties. Heather sometimes wondered if Si would explode one day and ask himself where his youth had gone.

And just before she'd met Jack, there had been more recent changes. Ella had moved into the tiny two-bedroom cottage in Thorpe Wenham, away from where Jack and the others had grown up. Jonny and Kate had changed, too – they had apparently been real party-goers, often taking Jack with them when he was in London, being seen at this new restaurant or that hot club, always up-to-date with the gossip. Now Kate was tired and pale because little Callum rarely slept, and she had to divide her attention between him and keeping her career together. Jonny did the media entertaining on his own, and their lives were planned for weeks ahead, with a complex schedule of babysitters and taking turns, so they couldn't do anything on impulse. Heather thought Jack must have felt excluded from their lives.

When Heather first put it all together, she regarded it as irrelevant. Past history. Now, looking back, she wondered how threatened Jack had felt by these changes. Even his dog, Toffee, a chocolate Labrador he'd taken almost everywhere with him, had recently been put down. Suddenly it was time for Jack, the baby of the family, to grow up.

He had, she later suspected, turned into a man with a mission, looking for his own princess to sweep into his arms. And Heather had been there, lying on the pavement, waiting to be rescued.

They'd married in the regimental chapel. When she walked out, under an arch of crossed swords, clinging on to Jack's arm, she'd thought that all her dreams had come true. Mo Spencer, Heather's mother, of course, was not at the wedding. In fact, she'd had no family at all, just some friends from work. But the Foxes were so noisy and spilled over into the bride's side of the church, that, once again, nobody seemed to notice. It occasionally occurred to her that her lack of family suited Jack very well, and that it would all have been much more difficult if she, too, had had strong ties.

Heather had left her job – which she'd hated, working as a secretary – and joined Jack in a modern box on an army estate near Colchester. She'd even bought him another dog, as a birthday present, an irresistible, wriggling brown velvet bundle of enthusiasm, with huge paws and liquid eyes. They called him Travis, and, until Molly came along, he was their baby. Heather was happy, even though she knew, from the other wives, that she would be moving house approximately every two years, as Jack changed postings. She was used to a nomadic existence. It was easier to keep moving on, then no one would ever find out who you really were.

And, slowly, she was becoming Heather Fox, and leaving Heather Spencer behind. She was nervous of Olivia, but she – albeit warily – liked Kate. She was determined to be a good army wife and had tried to take an interest in Jack's work, but part of it was quite secret and other parts were quite boring, so apart from getting on with it and not complaining, there wasn't a great deal she could do. She concentrated on looking forward to any posting where she might be expected to entertain or keep an eye on the other wives' welfare. A naturally shy person, Heather knew that she would have to force herself into this role, but she was collecting china and glass in the sales so that they would be able to have a smart dinner table, and she'd even done an evening course in cookery, half of which she'd had to miss because Jack had suddenly been sent somewhere so she'd been left without anyone to look after the girls.

She was apprehensive at the thought of being a senior officer's wife, but as long the past stayed buried, it would all be fine. And there was no reason why it shouldn't. Nobody knew anything.

Chapter 7

Kate was cross with herself as she walked back after lunch with Olivia. When Olivia had suggested a week somewhere abroad for the whole family to celebrate Ella's birthday, Kate's first thought had been that even if they only paid for the flights – and it wouldn't stop there because there would be other expenses – then that would be at least a thousand pounds down the drain. She and Jonny could not afford it, and somehow, she couldn't quite admit that to Olivia, who had never had to worry about money in her life. Were Si and Olivia so wrapped up in their comfortable existence that they couldn't even see that the average family couldn't just buy four flights somewhere whenever they liked? It was infuriating.

She and Jonny lived a good life, but it was on a financial knife-edge as they never managed to save, and every so often they even had to increase their mortgage. The cost of building had been carefully calculated, but it had still come in over budget, and Kate had been so busy project-managing the build that she hadn't had quite as many programmes commissioned as usual. Of course, it had added value to the house, but that was no good unless you wanted to sell. Which Kate didn't. She had lost her beloved home at fifteen. She was determined that her children would not have to suffer in that way.

TV had been a prosperous career when they first got together. Jonny's company Future TV had had two steady serials, one based on a children's encyclopedia called *Your World*, and a gardening programme called *Outside*. Between them these had paid all the company's overheads, but in one six-month period both were axed. The occasional one-offs or short drama-documentary six-part series, which had always created the profit on top, suddenly had to pay the bills, while TV budgets were axed left, right and centre. Each programme was being done on a tighter and tighter budget. Jonny laughed less, and snapped at her more.

As for radio journalism, it was no passport to riches, although at least she could do it – mostly – round Luke and Callum's school hours.

Even so, Kate knew she had been churlish when Olivia was trying to be kind. She ought to apologise. And perhaps she should be honest about their financial worries, so that Olivia knew she wasn't just being ungracious. But she was less comfortable with Olivia than she had been. When Si had first married her, she'd been a polite, hesitant young woman, and Kate and she had been able to bond over Ella's more irritating demands, both rather nervous of her as mother and mother-in-law. Now Olivia was self-possessed and successful, and not in the least frightened of anyone.

Kate formed the words of an apology in her head, but as she pulled out her mobile to make the call, it rang. It was a new client, the Distance Learning People.

'We'd like you to go ahead with that programme on native trees as part of our ecology degree,' said Petra, the head of commissioning.

Kate's heart leapt. A rush of adrenalin filled her with energy.

'Along the lines we talked about,' continued Petra. 'But it's also very important to be inclusive. We need to hear from all the voices in the community as to what native trees mean to them, and how their loss will impoverish their lives.'

Kate listened hard, trying to follow the brief. 'You mean pensioners and their memories of the native trees of their childhood? The way the landscape – even the streetscape – has changed over a lifetime?'

'Oh.' Petra sounded surprised. 'Those, too, I suppose. If there's room. No, we need to talk to youth today, especially marginalised youth, the ones who've slipped through the system, young kids on sink estates, teenage single mothers, a good range from ethnic communities, that sort of thing. We want to hear their voices: really hear them. We must be relevant.'

'Oh, yes, of course.' Kate tried to imagine herself heading into one of the many estates that ringed the Lovelace Conservation Area, recorder in hand, asking coked-up youths what native trees meant to them. 'You what?' would be the politest response she could expect. She would rather have been dropped into a war zone.

But she had a programme. She could do it.

'That's the good news,' continued Petra. 'The bad news is that we need it as soon as you can get it to us – say, a week next Friday?'

'No problem,' said Kate, automatically. But the Easter holidays started next week and finding childcare would be a struggle. Callum was not quite old enough – or responsible enough – to look after Luke all day. She spent the rest of the journey home on the bus texting and phoning other mothers, calling in favours, and promising various slices of holiday cover in return. The final piece of the jigsaw was Heather.

'Could you have Callum and Luke on Monday? I can have Daisy and Molly on Friday if you like.'

Heather agreed immediately. 'Great . . . but don't worry about Daisy and Molly on Friday, because I've agreed to have Sasha's Tom and Grace then.'

'Oh?' Kate was surprised.

'She's awfully nice, isn't she?' said Heather. 'She's having such a terrible time with that husband of hers, so I offered to help because she's going to see Olivia. Apparently she's going to represent her. Although it's a bit annoying because I was going to have my legs waxed.'

Kate was surprised, because she was sure that Olivia had been quite firm about not representing Sasha. 'Are you sure? Anyway, I can have all the kids. Six children are easier than four in some ways.' She wrote all the arrangements down carefully on the wall planner, frowning. Then everything else – her apology to Olivia and the intriguing mystery of this sudden friendship between Heather and Sasha, and whether Olivia had changed her mind – was forgotten. She had to find at least one really articulate crackhead who cared about native trees before next Friday.

*

When the Friday came, the post dropped through the letterbox at 19 Lovelace Road, and Kate's heart gave a little matching crash of terror. She felt like tiptoeing upstairs and cowering under the duvet. Forcing herself not to be absurd, she picked the letters up and took them to her office, opening them as if they might explode. They were indeed bills. Occasionally she wondered if it would be worth doing the Lottery, but she didn't like to admit, not even to Mr Patel at the corner shop, that she didn't know how it worked.

The doorbell rang.

'Oh, shit.' Kate jumped. She had been at her desk since 6 a.m., doing emails and putting together ideas for the next commissioning round, so she was still in her nightie, wearing odd socks, with bed hair and a furred-up early morning mouth. It was twenty to ten already. She hoped it was Heather.

It was Sasha. 'Oh, my God, I am so sorry,' Sasha cried. 'Are you feeling OK? Have I come too early?'

Kate flattened herself against a wall so that she didn't have to peck Sasha on the cheek before her shower. 'Er, sorry about this, I've been working and I forgot the time.'

'Don't worry.' Sasha fluttered delicately around like an exotic, fragile bird. Her eyes were large and dark, and she carried a big, soft, squashy handbag that looked expensive. Otherwise Kate couldn't identify anything special about her that would qualify her as 'sexy' in Jonny's eyes. Maybe the shoes? They were high and pointy, and very nicely made.

'This is just so, so kind of you,' purred Sasha. 'You wouldn't believe it, you've literally saved my life . . . look, are you sure it's OK?'

Kate nodded. 'Would you like a cup of tea?'

'It's sweet of you to ask, but I'm late already. Tom, Grace, you behave nicely for Mrs . . . er . . . Fox?' Sasha's eyebrows signalled a question here.

'Kate,' said Kate hastily, not wanting to admit that she wasn't Mrs Anybody. Not that it mattered.

'Kate has been so kind,' concluded Sasha firmly. 'I'll see you this afternoon. About three-thirty, is that all right?' She propelled two shy children in jeans through the door and backed off down the steps. 'And mind you eat Mrs . . . er . . . Kate's lovely food, Grace, you must keep your strength up.'

Kate opened her mouth to ask if either child had any allergies or special dislikes.

'And Tom, don't forget to say please and thank you,' added Sasha before Kate could speak. 'And both of you, do as you're told.' She hopped into the waiting black cab and slammed its door. She was still waving from the back window as it drove off, leaving Kate on the doorstep with the two children.

Ah, yes, thought Kate, looking at Grace. The girl who nearly died of leukaemia. Grace was like her mother, with dark hair and pale skin, and a small pointed face. She had huge shadows under her eyes.

'Good morning, Mrs Fox,' Grace said, politely. 'Thank you so much for having me. What a lovely house. Have you lived here long?'

It was like talking to someone of about thirty-five, thought Kate. Perhaps that's what illness did to children, made them very at home with grown-ups and old before their time.

Maybe there was a programme in that. Kate couldn't wait to get back into her office and scribble down a few notes. She was relieved to see that Tom seemed as inarticulate as any eleven-year-old, and looked as if he hoped to be swallowed up by Kate's over-busy hall wallpaper. She'd chosen it during a fashionable revival of authentic historic wallpapers, and now wished they could afford to get rid of it.

But they couldn't. So that was that. No money for treats.

'Have you had breakfast?'

They both shook their heads.

'Well, Callum and Luke are being terribly lazy so let's get them up and have something to eat. Do you like toast and jam?'

Tom and Grace continued to look politely terrified, as Callum flounced downstairs in an outgrown pair of pyjama bottoms, and draped himself over the sofa with a bowl of cereal, switching on the television.

'Callum, you should ask Tom and Grace what they'd like to watch. They're the guests.'

Callum looked scathingly at his mother and left a thirty-second pause. 'Whatever.' He turned to Tom and Grace. 'D'you like this programme?'

They nodded enthusiastically.

'See?'

Luke wriggled on to the sofa, demanding toast and Marmite. Kate had just got all the breakfasts sorted by the time the doorbell rang again. This time it was Heather, beautifully neat and pretty as usual, in tight jeans that showed off her slender legs and a sweater that clung in all the right places.

'Sorry, sorry, I haven't properly got up yet.' Kate hung on to the door, feeling as if the day had been going on too long already.

Heather smiled nervously. 'Oh dear, we've come too early, I'm so sorry, shall I hold the fort while you have a shower?'

'Would you?'

Kate fled upstairs, knowing that Heather would wash and put away all the dirty dishes, wipe down surfaces and tidy up, and might even turn the television off and begin playing a game with the children. It was all very well for Heather to be so organised, thought Kate defensively, shampooing her hair as fast as she could. She didn't work.

She came downstairs to find the kitchen looking fresh and tidy, and all six children seated at the table drawing, Callum helping Daisy to sketch a horse.

'Thanks. You are an angel. Coffee?' Kate felt ashamed of her earlier thoughts. Heather might be fussy, but she was a genuinely nice person. 'So you've become quite friendly with Sasha, then?' she asked, as the kettle boiled.

Heather went pink as she brought four empty juice glasses back to the sink. 'Oh, not really, I'm just doing what I can because the husband, Adam, I think he's called, is trying to take the kids away from her.' Heather dropped her voice to a whisper. 'Can you imagine anything more terrifying? He's just using them as pawns to get at her, she says, because he was never interested in them when they were married. So I offered to help out, and she was so sweet, she took us all out to lunch at Pizza Pozzo the other day . . .' Heather sipped her coffee. 'What do you think about Si and Olivia offering this villa for Ella's seventieth? Jack's managed to get a week's leave.'

*

The day turned out to be one of the longest Kate could remember. Six children did not prove to be less work than four, particularly as Dan, Callum's friend from down the road, came round and they barricaded themselves in Callum's bedroom, leaving Molly and Daisy wailing on the other side of the door. Grace and Tom remained quiet and polite, appearing to eat everything and do everything suggested to them.

'But they don't talk!' hissed Callum, when Kate finally caught up with him and begged him to be 'nice to the little ones'. 'They haven't said a single word. Not one!'

'They're shy, that's all. Their parents are going through a divorce, and Grace has spent about a year in hospital. Of course things will be difficult. That's why we've got to be nice to them.'

'Be nice to them yourself,' said Callum, swishing into his room with Dan and slamming the door again.

Heather came back in the afternoon, and offered to help out while Kate went back to her desk. She had some editing to do on the trees programme.

By six o'clock, when Jonny came through the door, Sasha still hadn't returned. 'I'm a bit worried,' said Kate, rummaging through the fridge to see if there was anything in it she could turn into a meal that night. 'She said she'd be back at three-thirty. But I don't want to frighten the children by saying anything. I wonder if Grace has her mobile number? Then I could find out when she might be coming back.'

But Sasha's mobile was turned off.

'It's my bathtime now,' said Grace.

'Oh dear. This is all my fault,' fretted Heather. 'I should have realised that Sasha's not very reliable when it comes to time. I'm so sorry, so sorry, perhaps I should take Grace and Tom home with me, because Jack's away and . . .'

'It doesn't matter at all,' said Kate, trying to calm her down, 'in fact, why don't you suggest that Molly, Daisy and Grace all share a bath, give them some old T-shirts and pyjamas of the boys I've been meaning to throw away, and you can stay for supper while they all watch a video together? Then we won't have to worry about when she's back.'

Heather fluttered upstairs, obviously still upset about having got

Kate into this situation, and Jonny poured them all large glasses of wine.

'Vile day,' said Kate, chopping up vegetables for a stir-fry. 'I hardly got any work done. Where can Sasha be? I hope she hasn't had an accident.'

'I expect she'll be here in a minute. She came to see me, by the way.' His voice was casual. 'This afternoon. To talk about the work experience.'

Kate felt the thud of terror again, striking her heart like a gong. 'Oh? How odd that she didn't mention it this morning. Frankly, I think the idea of a thirty-something doing work experience is quite funny.'

'Give her a break,' said Jonny, a warning in his tone. 'Good for her that she's prepared to try something new. She's going to start next Monday, for a fortnight.' He sat down on the sofa and opened up his briefcase, pulling out what looked like some accounts, and spreading them across the coffee table. 'After all, you never know, we may all have to reinvent ourselves at some point, and we'd want people to help us.'

'Will we?' Kate wondered what she could reinvent herself as. She liked her life as it was, being a radio producer and living with her family at 19 Lovelace Road. Would reinvention threaten this, was it related to the rows of figures she could see in front of Jonny? 'I wish she'd phoned me to say that she'd be late.'

'She left us at about three-thirty,' offered Jonny.

'Exactly when she said she'd be *arriving* here. It's not that I mind these things, I'm quite prepared to be flexible . . .' She tried Sasha's mobile again. It was still switched off, so Kate pulled some more vegetables out of the fridge and carried on chopping.

'I'll get it,' said Jonny, when the doorbell rang again.

Kate could hear squeaks and kisses from the hallway. It was Sasha. She suppressed a sense of resentment, especially when Sasha glided in, in a cloud of scent and a flurry of expensive-looking carrier bags, and gave her a beautifully wrapped present.

'I cannot tell you how sorry I am,' she said. 'I've had the day from hell, but *you* must be exhausted. I tried to phone a couple of times, but it was engaged, and then I got tied up . . .'

'Don't worry.' Kate began to unwrap the present, surprising

herself by how excited she felt. She hadn't had a present for ages — these days she and Jonny 'gave' each other things they needed.

Sasha had bought her a particularly stylish scented candle.

'Thank you. Thank you so much.'

'Drink?' asked Jonny.

'Well, only if it's no trouble.' Sasha shed her coat on to the sofa and seized a glass of white wine. 'Kate, I am so grateful for all this, and I do know it's been a hideous imposition.'

'Not a bit,' said Kate, stoutly. 'I'm just doing a quick stir-fry for supper, would you like some?'

'Oh, I couldn't, I've put you to enough trouble already . . .'

They soon agreed that Sasha would stay, and she bubbled away, being amusing, as Kate chopped and stirred and fried, Heather laid the table, and Jonny leant back against the kitchen island, his face creasing into a smile from time to time.

'This is a real family house, isn't it?' said Sasha. 'And the way you all help each other. It's all down to you, Kate, isn't it? You pull everything together.'

Kate mumbled something self-deprecating into the stir-fry.

'And what about you, Jonny?' She cocked an ear up at him. 'Do your brothers and sisters all congregate here, too, enjoying Kate's delicious cooking?'

'Jonny's got one older sister, who disapproves of me,' said Kate, from inside the fridge. She pulled out a jar of hoisin sauce and shook it over the stir-fry with extra vigour.

'I'm afraid Kate has a problem with my sister,' said Jonny to Sasha. 'She really doesn't like her.'

'It's not *me* disliking *her*,' said Kate, thumping plates of food on to the table. 'It's Virginia who has a problem with me. Jonny and Virginia are Scottish,' she added, to Sasha. 'She's very grand. Married to someone who owns tens of thousands of acres, so she thinks London is a dirty, seedy, overcrowded place where children turn to prostitution and drugs at the age of twelve.'

'To be fair to her,' said Jonny, 'it is. In some places.'

'She thinks I persuaded Jonny to stay down south because I'm a London media type and that I'm keeping him away from his native Scotland . . .'

Jonny laughed. 'Ginny's a really nice person. If you got to know her, you . . .'

Kate's stir-fried chicken turned rubbery in her mouth. She always felt slightly shut out when Jonny and Virginia got together, but Jonny always just shrugged, laughed and said that she was just being a typical older sister, that was all.

'Anyway, Virginia never comes here because it's not smart enough. She goes to Sloane Square sometimes, but she'd be terrified of being mugged if she went south of the river.'

'She's genuinely frightened,' said Jonny gently. 'She lives in the middle of the countryside and whenever she reads about London in the papers, all she sees are stories about gangs, gun crime, muggings and stabbings. It's not surprising that it makes her very nervous.'

'Well, she must see that we don't get knifed or shot at,' said Kate, now tired and slightly drunk. She turned to Sasha and Heather. 'She expects us all to go up to Scotland to see her, she never comes here. It's like a royal invitation.'

'New Year in Scotland *is* the best,' said Jonny, with a warning in his voice. 'And she works really hard to make sure we have a good time.'

'So you're Scottish, are you?' Sasha turned to Jonny. 'I think that's so romantic.' Her dark eyes targeted Jonny like heat-seeking missiles.

Kate tried not to feel threatened. She slugged down another large mouthful of wine and tried to turn the tables. 'Have you got brothers and sisters, Sasha?'

Sasha hesitated. 'Yes. Four.'

'Four!'

Sasha seemed reluctant to say more.

Kate thought she remembered a profile of Roderick Morton in a recent Sunday supplement, and resolved to find it again. He'd died several years ago but there'd been a retrospective in a smart Bond Street gallery. He had had several wives and an irregular domestic set-up, so perhaps that was why Sasha was so reluctant to talk. 'I'd love to have had a painter for a father. Mine was a personnel director of a widgets company.'

Mike Fox now seemed so very far away, as if he'd never existed, but she suddenly saw an echo of him in Jonny. Her father had been the rock on which their family had been based, and it had been terrifying when that rock was no longer there. It went beyond the way they both did the household accounts and mended anything that was broken. It was a certainty that if they said they would do something they would. Mike Fox, the day before he had been killed, had promised to come to a play she'd produced at school the following Saturday. It had been the first promise he had broken. It had been incomprehensible, and because she could not understand it, she never talked about it.

She and Jonny, however, had not made each other promises. They just muddled along, trusting each other. At least, she hoped they trusted each other.

Sasha was prattling on over Kate's thoughts and suddenly turned to Heather. 'What did your father do, Heather?'

Heather jumped, and went slightly pink. 'What?'

'We were talking about what our fathers did,' said Kate.

Heather's eyes flickered from Kate to Sasha, and back. 'Oh, um, mine was in the civil service.'

'Really?' asked Sasha. 'What part of the civil service?'

'Oh, he was in several different departments . . . oh, no, it's getting so late, I think I should be getting back. Do you want a lift, Sasha?'

Sasha said that it would be very sweet of Heather, if she really meant it, and Heather went off to round up children and check the house for possessions that might be left behind.

'I gather you had lunch with Olivia today,' Kate said into the silence that followed.

Sasha looked slightly surprised. 'Oh, yes. Olivia says that what Adam is offering me is appalling and that I've got grounds for getting a lot more off him. I've really been taken for a ride.'

Kate was surprised. This wasn't the kind of thing Olivia usually said. She was always cautious and conservative, although apparently her sweet, reasonable manner in court was considered deadly. 'Oh, is Olivia going to represent you?'

'I couldn't possibly afford her,' Sasha smiled. 'But it makes me feel so much better just knowing that she agrees with me.'

Kate wondered if Sasha had misunderstood Olivia, and whether she should phone her to sort it out, but she didn't dare. Olivia would never, ever break any confidentiality, and was unlikely to say anything about Sasha at all.

'You wouldn't believe what my ex has done now,' said Sasha, fixing her eyes on Jonny again. 'That's why I was so late. I was just getting on the tube when he rang and said he had to see me. So I dashed over to his office, and then he told me.'

'Told you what?' Kate leant forward, and Sasha's gaze swivelled round to include her.

'He told me,' there was a catch in Sasha's voice, 'that his girl-friend was having a baby, and that's why we – the kids and me – have got to get out of our home. There won't be room for a baby at her flat, so he's got to get as much money as he can from me so they can buy a house. We'll be chucked out on the street.'

'But surely,' said Kate, who had done a little research on the matter, as she hadn't totally given up the idea of Sasha being useful radio material – although she certainly wasn't going to risk inter-viewing her live in case she was late, 'doesn't the law start with the presumption that the children of the marriage must have an appro-priate home, a reasonable distance from any school they attend, with enough space for them to live?'

'Now you can see what I'm up against,' replied Sasha. 'In theory that's what's supposed to happen, but in practice I'm being given a paltry sum that would barely buy a one-bedroom flat any-where near the children's school.' Her eyes filled with tears and she scrabbled around in her bag for a tissue. 'I'm so sorry, I didn't mean to bother you with all this, you've been so kind . . .'

Kate could see Jonny looking concerned, but Sasha pulled her-self together. 'Sorry,' she said, again. 'Sorry.' She smiled bravely. 'Less than two years ago I thought I was happily married. I thought my daughter was going to get better and we could go back to being a normal family again. Then, a year ago, Adam told me he'd been having an affair, but we went to counselling, therapy . . . I've done everything – *everything* – I could to make it work, for Tom and Grace's sake, and now it's clear that he was never serious. He obviously never stopped screwing her. She's seven months preg-nant. That was bang in the middle of all our counselling. When he *promised* he'd stopped seeing her. I was in a daze when he told me.

I couldn't believe it. So I sat down on one of those benches by the Thames, and I don't know how long I was there. Just staring at the water going by, and wondering what was going to become of us. So I'm so sorry I was late. I didn't realise the time. But it was unforgiveable of me, especially when you've been so amazing, Kate, just taking care of everything for me. I can't thank you enough.'

'If there's anything I can do, just call. Really.' Kate felt guilty at her earlier irritation. Poor Sasha. What did a few hours' lateness here or there matter?

In fact, what about doing a programme on punctuality and lateness, and what it showed about people's characters, and how much lateness cost the economy . . .? After Heather and Sasha and the kids had gone, Kate left the washing-up to fester and raced upstairs to her studio to make notes. On the way upstairs, she could hear music thumping out of Callum's room. She knocked on the door.

'It's quite late.'

Callum and Dan looked up, surprised.

'Music down.' She signalled.

'What?'

'It's late. And the music's too loud. And what's that smell?' She sniffed their air and thought she could detect a sweetish note amid the odours of strong deodorant and unwashed socks. 'Have you been smoking?'

The boys pointed towards the open window. 'There was a bonfire outside. Earlier on,' said Callum.

Two whole sentences. It was the nearest thing Kate had had to a conversation with her son for weeks. You were supposed to keep the channels of communication open, and she didn't want to be a 'heavy' mother, so she nodded and closed the door behind them.

Everyone said teenage boys were difficult. Everyone.

Chapter 8

On the way home Sasha kept up a trilling conversation with Heather, based on clichés, disguising her fury at the hand life had dealt her. Isn't Kate wonderful? Didn't the house look lovely? Working mothers always look exhausted. There's always a silver lining to every cloud. It'll all turn out for the best in the end.

Sasha hardly knew what she was saying, because her brain was whirring over the day, and whether she'd blown it again with Kate and the lateness. Kate had kept on looking at her watch when Sasha arrived. She hadn't even been polite enough to conceal it.

What was it about some people and punctuality? Kate worked from home so it was hardly any skin off her nose if Sasha was an hour or so late. Anyway, Sasha suspected that Kate's alleged 'work' as a 'radio producer' was more about having something interesting to talk about at dinner parties or a reason to avoid helping out at the school fête than being a serious career. Sasha knew her type of woman. They infested every private school these days, and they had four children (how had Kate allowed herself to get away with only having two?), a house that gets featured in magazines and an internet company selling frippery of some kind or a part-time role in the media.

Well, they didn't fool Sasha, none of them, especially Kate. They were all just housewives trying to seem clever and interesting, while having their children coached in French, Mandarin and tennis. They were hideously, frantically competitive while pretending to support their fellow woman. But she had better tread carefully, because she needed everyone on her side.

She needed Olivia, particularly, because she had googled her and found out that she could get blood out of a stone when it came to divorce. And Adam was definitely a stone. And she'd been nice at their lunch. She had listened carefully to everything Sasha said, leaning towards her over the restaurant table, with her large brown eyes fixed on Sasha's face. But she had refused to get involved.

'One of the things we're having increasing success with at Campbell Carter is collaborative law,' she said, 'which is a process where you search for solutions that work for the family as a whole, rather than automatically making the assumption that husband and wife must be pitched against each other. I think you should try mediation, which aims to achieve a practical, rather than a confrontational, approach to working out how much money each partner should have.'

Sasha thought she was mad. 'Adam has gone off with his secretary and wants to turn me and the children out of our home,' she said. 'The only way he is going to understand that what he's done is wrong and that he's got to pay for it is if a judge tells him. That's the only way this will be settled. He owes me.'

Olivia sighed. 'I don't know the ins and outs of your case, so I can't comment.'

'Well, what happened was . . .' Sasha saw her opportunity to get Olivia drawn in. Surely, if she had any decency, Olivia would agree to help. Didn't all lawyers do a certain amount of pro bono work for people who couldn't pay?

Olivia cut gently across her. 'Going to court costs a huge amount of money, and there's no sign that it makes people see sense. In fact, it may make them more entrenched in their own position. And, of course, Adam isn't paying you because he's done wrong – that concept has gone from our divorces. The reason why he needs to pay you is so that you can bring your shared children up. The most important thing you need to do now is to move forward so that you can create the best possible future for yourself and the children. You can't look back – it will only slow you down.'

Sasha decided that Olivia was obviously determined to spin the company line, and clearly wasn't going to come up with anything for free. So she switched the conversation to Si, and how Olivia managed when he was away so much.

Olivia smiled as she waved away the dessert menu, and ordered the bill. 'He and I are alike. We both love our work, so we understand each other.'

Lucky Olivia, thought Sasha sourly, as they tussled over who was going to pay. Olivia won, but then, she could afford to. You'd have thought she could have spared just a bit of free advice, wouldn't you? But no, Sasha wasn't important enough to be taken on as a client. Olivia could only be bothered with the Allison Greens of this world and their multi-million-pound settlements. The frustration of being nobody burned again, furiously, under Sasha's breastbone.

As Sasha kissed Olivia goodbye – a peck on either cheek – she almost felt like warning her. 'You know what they say,' she thought. 'Life is what happens to you while you're making other plans.'

But she didn't. There was something almost too stable and sterile about Olivia and Si's world, and Si was an attractive man. Watch out, Olivia, thought Sasha, as she waved her off down the street.

Chapter 9

Heather enjoyed ironing. She wondered if she was the only person who did, as she refilled the iron with water. But then, she enjoyed cooking, too. There was even a certain satisfaction to be had from making beds, washing up and tidying up because it all added up to a warm, comfortable, happy home, which was all she had ever wanted.

Her mother had had odd periods of domesticity that Heather could dimly remember – there had been a kindly, older man, Gerald, he'd been called, who had brought some stability into their life for a while. He'd had had a nice little house by the sea in Broadstairs, a regular job and, while her mother's other boyfriends had mainly seen her as a nuisance – or worse – Gerald seemed to have genuinely tried to give her some kind of childhood, although she remembered screaming at him that he was a boring old git. She remembered her mother screaming at him too.

Gerald had got sick of them – sick of her, Heather – in the end. It was Gerald who had sent her to the Caldecott, her mother had said. He'd called the social workers and they had taken her away. Well, that was what you did with rubbish children that nobody wanted, wasn't it? There'd been too much fighting in the playground, apparently, and the school said she didn't fit in. She remembered that life that she'd briefly glimpsed, though, that world of being invited to tea with other little girls whose mothers baked cakes. Or had she just read about it in a book? Had she and her mother really lived in Broadstairs or had she invented it?

From an early age, Heather had discovered that it was easier to be responsible for getting her own washing done, because her mother couldn't be relied upon to ensure that she had the right clothes for school on a Monday morning. Or that she even got to school. Mo had spent most of Heather's childhood in a haze of uppers and downers mixed with lager or cheap wine, or in catatonic sessions with weed. Heather thought she remembered a period of time as a traveller, in some kind of mobile home, with a whole lot of other unwashed children whose noses streamed permanently with cold. But the memories had become a series of barely remembered snapshots, unlinked by any coherent narrative. When she talked about her childhood, even to Jack, she only ever mentioned their time with Gerald in Broadstairs, and when Jack had once asked her what her mother died of, she'd said she didn't really know, she'd been too young and she'd rather not discuss it. It was the only time she'd ever lied to him.

For Heather, making sure that Molly and Daisy's T-shirts were neatly ironed and laid out in their drawer was a part of banishing the uneasy, lonely memories of her own childhood, just as getting Jack's wardrobe ordered, with everything dry-cleaned, mended and hung up properly, was part of letting Jack know that he had a home to come back to, where everything was warm and tidy. And safe. Life was in control when it was neat and tidy.

He was due back that evening, after three days in The Hague doing something to do with NATO. She had prepared his favourite beef stew with roasted vegetable couscous, and the girls had drawn their usual 'Welcome Home, Daddy' cards.

'But he's only been away a short time,' said Heather, laughing and hugging her daughter, feeling Daisy's deliciously soft cheek against her own.

'We always do cards.' Daisy scribbled away, the tip of her tongue poking out of her mouth with concentration, as she drew a picture of a horse, just the way Callum had shown her. Daisy was campaigning for riding lessons, but Heather and Jack had decided to wait and see if it was going to be a passing phase. At least, Jack had suggested they wait and see, but Heather was already checking out local riding schools to find the best one. It would be expensive, but they'd agreed that the girls should each learn at least one extra sport and one musical instrument.

High among the humiliations of Heather's childhood was the way she had always felt so useless. She was hopeless at sport, and always the last to be picked for a team. She'd never even stayed anywhere long enough to learn how to swim, let alone a foreign language. A few of the army wives were efficient, hearty girls who played tennis, rode, danced, swam and skied, while braying at each other about their holidays, singing in choirs, speaking foreign languages, flinging themselves into amateur dramatics and making their own clothes. Heather, shy and isolated, felt hopeless. It was why she liked Sasha. Sasha was scathing about sport, or people who could do things like that. She swept Heather into a privileged little club of two, saying things like 'of course, you and I, Heather, can see through all that . . .' Heather had never belonged to any kind of clique, and she knew she was succumbing to flattery. But she couldn't help enjoying it.

Her children, she was determined, would never have to stand around, embarrassed, on the sidelines, while other people enjoyed themselves. So, as Molly and Daisy moved from school to school, she made sure they kept up their music practice, their sports and their languages. Molly and Daisy would never have to suffer the way she did, never.

The phone rang. Heather carefully switched off the iron before answering it. It was Sasha, crying so wildly that Heather could barely understand what she was saying.

'What? Sasha, I can't hear you? Have you been hurt?'

She tried to distinguish words from the snuffling sobs.

'No,' gasped Sasha eventually. 'We're fine for the time being. Until next week. But we've got to get out of the house. He's sent a court order. To turn us out on to the street.'

'But he can't do that!' Heather was appalled.

'He has,' Sasha blubbered. 'He's made some stupid judge believe the awful things he says. We literally don't have anywhere to go.'

'Well, of course you can always come here for a few days,' said Heather instinctively. 'You can have the spare room, Tom can have the box room and Grace can go in with the girls.'

'I couldn't do that,' said Sasha, sounding clearer. 'It would be too much, you can't.'

'Jack will be home soon, and I'm sure he'll agree with me.' Heather suddenly felt slightly nervous about making the offer. She didn't really like people coming to stay because she was afraid they might pry. In fact, had she made the offer or had Sasha asked? By the time the conversation was over she no longer remembered it properly. Conversations with Sasha so often ran out of control, and Heather would find herself offering or agreeing to something she really didn't want to do. But Sasha was always so grateful. And Kate and Olivia obviously liked her, or they wouldn't have invited her to things the way they had. Heather respected their judgement much more than her own.

She heard the scratching of Jack's key in the lock, and, as if a silent alarm had gone off, both girls came tumbling down the stairs, hair flying, shrieking 'Daddy! Daddy!' Travis lolloped behind them, tongue hanging out.

As Jack stood in the doorway both girls leapt up, one on each arm, locking their legs around his waist. He held them tightly and laughed at Heather over their shoulders. Travis barked enthusiastically.

'Girls, girls,' he kissed them both, and let them gently down to the floor, and Travis hurled himself at his master. 'I need to say hello to my beautiful wife,' said Jack, as Travis slobbered all over him.

The girls' hands reached out to draw her in, and for a few precious seconds, Heather was enfolded in the heart of her family, Travis's nose pressed against her knees. He had to be in the middle of every family group, right bang in the middle, always.

She was upset at the thought of Sasha invading their cosy little home. But that was dreadful – she should be more like Kate, more welcoming. And it wouldn't be for long. To her own surprise, tears rose up in her throat.

Jack sensed rather than saw them. 'Hey, hey,' he said, softly. 'What's up?'

She shook her head, and swallowed, unable to speak.

'We've got cards, we've got cards,' shrieked Daisy.

Jack lowered them both to the floor. 'Off you go and get them for me, then.' He lifted Heather's chin. 'Something's wrong. What is it?'

The words came tumbling out. 'Sasha, she's being chucked out of her home with the children and they've got nowhere to go, she's coming here . . .' Heather herself couldn't understand why she could barely speak for tears. She turned away, so that the girls couldn't see. It was often like this when Jack came back, because she was so afraid that one day, he wouldn't. But she must be brave. Men didn't like women who fussed. Army men didn't anyway. She swallowed and blinked.

Jack put an arm round her. 'Sweetheart.'

Heather sniffed. 'Do you think it's all right that she's coming?' She half hoped he'd say no, but he just smiled.

'Of course she must come,' said Jack, softly. 'We'll do anything we can to help, of course, we must. And I've got something to tell you, too, I'm . . .'

Heather drew back and looked at him, her heart sinking. 'When . . .?'

'Sorry, darling. There's an opportunity – a very good opportunity – in Temanistan, which I've said I'll take for a couple of months. Starting in three weeks' time.'

It was like a slap in the face, and Heather felt her knees begin to shake. 'Three weeks! But I thought you had this MOD posting until the end of the year, and then you'd go into pre-command training!'

'Hm,' Jack disentangled himself from her, and picked up a few letters from the hall table. Heather always kept a neat pile for him when he returned. 'Well, they needed somebody and . . .'

'Jack! Did you actually volunteer? For Temanistan? And where is it anyway?' Heather struggled to control her feelings. Jack would come back safe, it wasn't that, it was just so infuriating that as soon as they settled down anywhere, they were all heaved up again, or that the minute they started to make friends with other families, Jack would be off and often people would withdraw, suggesting that 'when Jack's back you must both come to supper'. Well, she must just get on with it. This was the job he loved, she reminded herself.

'It's a small land-locked republic which used to be part of the

74

Soviet Union. It's had a brutal civil war for the past ten years which has just been resolved. The Temanistan government has invited the Brits to help them deal with the last of their insurgents, and because there's a lot of drug smuggling and people trafficking involved, we've agreed.'

'It sounds dangerous.' Heather would almost rather he was sent out to a war zone. People trafficking and drug smuggling sounded terrifying.

'I'll have a desk job. Nothing to worry about. I'll be helping them with assessing reports that come in from contacts and giving them advice on strategy. Maybe it'll lead to other attaché jobs: Paris, Rome, Madrid . . . You could come with me – you'd like that, wouldn't you?' He moved towards the stairs, dropping the post back on the hall table. 'I feel travel-stained. The plane was packed on the way back. I'll just pop upstairs, shall I, and then we can have a drink?'

Heather tried to smile and took his bag. 'I'll throw your washing in.' She would far rather be in Warminster or Shrivenham than Rome or Paris, which sounded very threatening.

He gave her a quick smile in return, and almost skipped up the stairs away from her. He doesn't like scenes, she thought, sadly. Kate had once said that Jack had dealt with their father's death by pretending not to care about anything. He shut down at the first sign of an emotional crisis, or dealt with it by being breezy. Heather envied him that ability. Any kind of unexpected change filled her with terror.

'So that's sorted, is it?' she called after him. 'Sasha moves in here for a week or so while she finds somewhere, and you'll be away for two months?'

'Er, it's a bit more than that,' he said, quickly going into the bathroom and turning on the shower. He put his head out again. 'It's a six-month attachment. But there's a week off in the middle.'

Heather bit back a sob and took a deep breath. Right. Cope. This is what it's all about. You have to take the rough with the smooth. Travis nudged her knee, as if to say, 'I'm here. I won't leave you,' and she bent down to bury her face in his doggy-smelling fur. Heather was used to burying anger; she buried it very deep and very quickly.

Onward and upward. Heather never allowed herself more than a few moments of grief, worry or fear on Jack's behalf. She straightened up, thinking about Sasha again, remembering that there were army rules about who could live in the house. But Sasha wouldn't be around long, and who would notice? She gave Travis a last pat, and went upstairs, followed, as usual, by the dog. If Jack was going in just a few weeks, there would be a whole list of things she needed to get done, and she needed to get the diary too, and work out what they needed to cancel and what she could go ahead with.

'Jack?' She tapped on the shower screen.

He continued showering, turned away from her as if he didn't know she was there.

'Jack, it's fine. Of course.' She raised her voice. 'I know you have to go.'

He turned back towards her, opened the shower screen and kissed her very thoroughly. 'I do love you, you know.'

She laughed, disentangling herself from his damp embrace, spluttering. 'I'm soaked, look, totally soaked.'

'You'd better get out of those wet clothes, then, hadn't you? Before you catch a cold,' he said with a wicked grin.

'Jack!' Heather couldn't help laughing. 'We can't. The girls are downstairs and . . .'

He silenced her with another, very wet, kiss.

'We haven't got much time,' she whispered, her resistance nearly gone.

'We don't need much time.' Jack pulled her towards him, reaching out to slide the lock shut on the bathroom door. She could hear Travis whining to be let in, so what with the wet, cold, hard bathroom floor and other distractions, it wasn't quite the romantic reunion she'd planned.

Chapter 10

After more discussion, Sasha and Heather agreed to do a swap: Sasha and the children would live at Heather and Jack's for just over a fortnight while Sasha did her work experience at Jonny's office and sorted out somewhere else for them to live. Heather would pick the children up from school every day, and in return, when Jack came back from Temanistan, Sasha would take Molly and Daisy for ten days so that Jack and Heather could go off for a 'second honeymoon'.

'It'll be something to look forward to,' Sasha encouraged Heather, who seemed slightly anxious about the whole arrangement. Sasha got the impression that Heather's world was very fragile, and that she feared even the slightest crack in its façade.

Sasha spent the last weeks in her house packing up, arguing furiously with Adam over everything and trying to stop him taking more than his fair share. She got the removal men to come a day early, so that she could put most things in storage before he could claim them. This was all his fault, all his and Natalie's. They didn't deserve to get anything. Then, finally, they left their beloved home, walking through the empty rooms for the last time while Sasha promised Grace and Tom that one day they would have just as a nice a house again, and making sure they knew this was all Daddy's fault.

Then on Monday morning she stepped inside the narrow Soho terrace that housed Future TV and slid into the spare desk, feeling very, very nervous. What had once been the front parlour of an eighteenth-century London merchant, its panelling and fireplace now painted a historic sludge colour, was packed with the twenty-first century banks of computers and editing equipment. There were three desks squeezed into the room, and they'd even cut the loo in half to create a tiny editing suite. The two edit assistants, almost young enough to be Sasha's daughters, looked up and smiled briefly, then went back to concentrating on their screens.

'Hi. I'm Sasha. I'm here to make the coffee.'

Two heads shot up at that, and they both smiled again. 'I'm Meera,' said the dark-haired one. 'Claire,' added the other, a pretty blonde.

Sasha made a great fuss of them, making some coffee and putting her head into the other room to ask everyone what they wanted. There was an older woman – something to do with finances and management – and Jonny, along with three very young men, working intently at their screens. She carefully filed everyone's names away in her head. She had two weeks to make herself indispensable.

'Hi,' said Jonny, leaning back in his chair and swinging his feet on to the desk with a grin. 'We've got a studio shoot today for a programme we're doing on asthma, and there's a development meeting tomorrow when we'll all bat ideas around. You'll meet the whole team. And there's a bit of background research we'd like you to do, it'll just be a question of surfing the net, and seeing what you can pick up from YouTube.'

It was exactly what Sasha had hoped for. The chance to see what worked in front of the cameras and to hear how ideas were put together behind the scenes. 'I'm on for anything,' said Sasha. 'Just treat me as chief sandwich-fetcher and telephone-answerer.' By the end of the day, she was determined that everyone should know who she was, and by tomorrow, they would all be her best friends. She'd watch and wait, then work out what worked and what didn't. Two weeks wasn't long to make an impact.

As she gave Jonny his coffee, he suggested lunch. 'I'll give you the lowdown on what happens round here,' he said.

'That's so kind of you.'

She betted he wasn't going to mention *that* to Kate when he got home that evening.

Chapter 11

Kate suggested a Sunday lunch at 19 Lovelace Road so that the family, particularly Ella, could say goodbye to Jack, especially as he was now missing her birthday.

So, on the last weekend before Jack went to Temanistan, Kate spent most of the time chopping and peeling, then decorating the table with cheap, cheerful bulbs from the market and ivy cut from the garden. She stood back, satisfied that no one would know that she and Jonny had an appointment with the bank booked for ten days' time. She was too frightened even to think about it.

Kate couldn't understand how they'd got themselves into this situation, or, indeed, how they were going to get themselves out of it. Trading down might buy them a few years before the mortgage crept up again. But, if she wasn't Kate Fox of 19 Lovelace Road, who was she? She would be nobody special. Every time she got a decent cheque, it was allocated to something before it even arrived. The native trees programme would prop up their ageing car for another few thousand miles. But would it need another expensive repair soon? She remembered the day that they had moved out of her childhood home, where they each had a bedroom, to the little semi where Si and Jack had to share a room, and how a bed, desk and wardrobe had barely fitted into her little box room. Would they have to do that again? She looked out of the window where the wisteria, in full bloom, draped romantically along the back garden wall. If they moved, she might have a terrible view – traffic or a tower block, or a factory, or all three.

Don't think about that, Kate, she told herself. If you can survive your father dying when you're fifteen, you can survive anything.

Kate squared her shoulders. 'Jonny!' she shouted up the stairs. 'Please! Can you come down and do this washing-up!'

'I'm working!'

'But we've got people coming for lunch!' This at full volume, up the stairs.

Jonny came down a few minutes later. 'If you decide to have your family round, could you at least discuss it with me beforehand?'

'We did discuss it.'

'Last Friday. When I got home from work. You told me your family were all coming. I had planned to spend the weekend going through the ideas that came up at the development meeting, and see which ones I thought would really be worth taking forward.'

'Well, *you* didn't discuss *that* with me either.' But Kate knew that work always had to come first. 'Oh, go on back upstairs. I'll do it.'

'I'm down here now.'

Just as Kate was about to tell him not to be silly, and to go back and do whatever he had to do, the phone rang. It was Olivia.

'I'm so sorry, Kate, I can't make it for lunch. Something's cropped up . . .'

Kate was disappointed. 'Don't worry, that's fine,' she said, trying not to feel hurt. 'Allison Green just called me,' said Olivia. 'Her cat, who's nineteen, is going downhill fast and has got to be put down, but it's Chat Show Ted's weekend for their daughter.'

Kate thought this story sounded very shaky.

'She's insisting that Lily has got to say goodbye to the cat because apparently she adores her,' Olivia burbled on, 'and Chat Show Ted says either the cat has to wait till tomorrow or Lily can say goodbye on the phone because Allison is always trying to bugger up his time with Lily. Allison says the cat is suffering and Lily won't understand on the phone. Ted says it can't have gone downhill that fast since Friday. I've got to sort it out, and frankly, on a Sunday it will take me all morning. I'm driving the dying cat down to Chat Show Ted's place in Sunningdale as Allison Green isn't allowed anywhere near his house.'

It was so unbelievable, Kate supposed it must be true, not just a ducking out of a family lunch. 'That's fine. Don't worry,' she repeated.

'Give lots of love to Jack, won't you? And say that we'll do Ella's seventieth birthday trip abroad next year instead, when he's around.'

Good. Next year she and Jonny might be able to afford the flights. By this time, Jonny had begun the dishes. 'I've started so I'll finish,' he said, with a wry grin.

Kate was too disconcerted by Olivia's odd excuse to smile back, and she had to drag the boys out of bed. It was getting clearer and clearer that Olivia no longer wanted to spend time with the Fox family. At least she was letting Si come, though.

Ella arrived first, as she always did. 'Did you see that television programme the other night?' she demanded, as soon as she was settled with a sherry. 'That old friend of Jack's talking about the way the army is equipped these days. Was he telling the truth? Has Jack got the right equipment? Will it be dangerous in Temanistan?'

'I'm sure he's got the right equipment, those programmes exaggerate in order to have something to say. Anyway, the Temanistan job is diplomatic, a desk job,' said Kate.

'It's a bit more than that.' Ella seemed to spend every hour that she didn't spend in the garden thinking up disasters that could befall one of her children. 'He's going to be going off on expeditions, you know. To the mountains. I think he's spying. He could get shot. And they say it's very cold in Temanistan. In the winter.'

'Well, it's only April now.' Kate got up to check the progress of the curry they were having. 'He'll be quite safe on his jaunts. And if anything did happen, we would know.' She told her mother, as she already had, over and over again, that if anything happened to Jack then the family would be informed first. The army would send someone to break the news to Heather.

'But would Heather tell us immediately?' Ella always snapped.

'She's not all that strong, I don't think she's strong at all, she'll go to pieces, and then who will tell *us*?'

And she was back on the subject again. 'I hope we don't all find out that Jack's been killed on the news. Or from reporters doorstepping us.'

There were so many issues in this diatribe that Kate hardly knew where to begin. 'Mumma,' she spoke as firmly as she could. 'Heather is Jack's *wife*. Of course she has to be named as next of kin.'

'I know she's his wife,' said Ella. 'I just don't think she has enough backbone.'

'I think the army provides backbone.' Kate sighed. 'Wives are usually next of kin. And Jack will be fine.'

It had been hard to realise that once Jack was married, of course, his wife must come first. She would hear about his death before his mother and sister did.

But that was how it had to be. At the bottom of this, Kate eventually worked out, was the knowledge that if something happened to Jonny, his sister Virginia would not be the first person she called. Virginia, as well as being irritating, was geographically and emotionally remote, and it would be terribly easy to forget to call her at all.

The doorbell rang again. Jack and Heather, followed by Molly and Daisy, were all towed by Travis through the door, followed by Sasha, carrying an enormous bunch of white lilies. 'What amazing flowers. Aren't they gorgeous? Thank you so much, Sasha. Aren't Grace and Tom coming?'

'They're with their father,' said Sasha, in her bright, brittle way. 'He's threatened to take me to court for breaking the contact agreement, just because I had to take Tom to the dentist on Wednesday evening when he's supposed to have them both. So I'm letting him have an extra weekend. I can't bear for the children to go through all that again, all the interviewing by the case workers, and the pressure their father puts them under to say what he wants them to say.'

Kate had asked Sasha to come too because she thought it would be nice for Heather. Heather seemed to get on well with everyone on the army patches she lived on, but she didn't appear to have close female friends. Or perhaps she kept them away from the family, so it was good that she was confident enough to make friends with Sasha and bring her along. 'Oh, how . . .' sympathised Kate, but the doorbell rang again. It was Si.

They settled down to talk to Jack about going off to Temanistan, and how sixty per cent of its population lived in dire poverty. 'It's called the roof of the world because its mountains are so high,' she heard Jack say. 'And it's illegal to be a Jehovah's Witness. That's about as much as I know, so far.' Travis thumped himself down on his master's feet, resting his square velvet jaw on Jack's knee.

'When I married Jack, he told me that when an army officer passes out of Staff College, he's issued with a black Labrador. He thought he ought to break the mould by having brown ones,' teased Heather.

Kate noticed that having Sasha around seemed to be improving Heather's confidence. It was rare for her to make a joke.

'Passes out?' asked Sasha.

'Graduates from,' interpreted Kate. 'Although there's quite a bit of the other sort of passing out, too.'

'It's such a pity that Olivia isn't here,' said Ella, for the third time. 'She's not really a family person, is she?'

'That isn't fair, Mumma,' said Kate, looking up to see if Si had heard. But he was lecturing Jonny on his business structure. Kate's sense of justice overcame the low-level grievance that was still festering over Olivia's non-appearance. 'Olivia usually comes. She's just really busy today. With her new job. One of her client's cats is dying, apparently.'

Jack sniggered. 'That's a good one. I must remember it.'

'Well, I think she should have had children rather than work-ing so hard all the time. But she's too thin. You can't have babies if you're as thin as that.'

'Oh,' murmured Heather nervously, who never contradicted Ella, no matter how outrageous her statements. 'She always seems to eat properly when we, er, see her. I don't think . . .'

'Ooh, I don't know. I saw this programme on how women lie. To their nearest and dearest.' Ella shook her head. 'She might be doing anything. Sticking her finger down her throat after meals.'

That was one reason for going to family reunions, thought Kate, catching Heather's eye. If you weren't there, everybody talked about you.

'Olivia is *not* bulimic.' Kate was firm. When Ella got an idea in her head, it could be hard to dissuade her.

'Oh, I know all you girls stick together. But mark my words. There's something funny going on with her. Otherwise she'd be here, wouldn't she?'

Kate checked to see if Si was listening, but he had switched his attention to Sasha and was deep in conversation with her. Her dainty hands, with large silver rings, flashed in the air, as she leant towards him. 'Si,' she called, and Sasha turned her head, her eyes narrowing slightly at the interruption.

Kate noticed Sasha curving herself towards Si, looking up at him from under her lashes, and found that somehow they'd sat down together before she'd had a chance to suggest where anyone should sit.

Oh, well. Si was a grown-up. He could look after himself.

'So,' he raised his voice, to include everyone in the conversation he'd been having with Sasha, 'I gather you're staying with Jack and Heather.'

Sasha flushed. 'They've been so kind.' She twisted her hands, pulling the rings off one by one, then replacing them, in quick, nervous actions as she looked round the table. 'My husband got a court order to get us out of the house.'

'I had no idea that a man could force his ex-wife and children out of their home,' said Kate, ears quivering for something she could turn into a radio programme.

'He said that I was preventing the house from being sold. That I was barring the estate agent from bringing potential buyers round, being obstructive and leaving the house in a terrible mess . . . the awful thing is that in an idiotic way it's all true. At least, I can't say it isn't true, which is why he's managed to get the court order, I suppose.'

'What do you mean?'

'Once I had a temperature of 104, so I told the estate agents not to bring anyone round for a couple of days. And I woke up to find an estate agent actually in the room – with a potential buyer – and opening wardrobes! While I was lying there in the bed! So, naturally, I rang up and gave them hell, and then bolted the front door so it couldn't happen again until I was better. But they didn't take any notice, and tried to get in with another three buyers, then complained to Adam – who, of course, complained to his lawyer.'

'But couldn't you explain?' asked Kate.

Sasha shook her head. 'If someone doesn't want to hear an explanation, they don't. It's all about Natalie's pregnancy – that's the woman he's moved in with,' she added to Si. 'He was desperate to get us out so he can buy a new house before she has the baby, and with the market the way it has been, the house wasn't selling. So he blamed me.'

'But couldn't you have stayed until the house was sold?' suggested Ella.

Sasha's eyes flickered towards her. 'He wanted me to accept a ridiculously low offer, out of spite, I think. Or maybe he still wants to buy me out at a bargain price. So he took me to court about that, too. I showed them loads of details of houses similar to ours that were on the market at much higher prices, but the judge forced me to accept the really silly price.'

'He's a real bastard,' said Jack. 'Treating you and the kids like that. D'you want me to go round with a few friends and sort him out?' His tone was joky, and Sasha smiled up at him.

'No, really,' she said. 'I have to keep telling myself that he's being like this because *he* feels so guilty. If he can convince himself that *I'm* behaving badly, then he can justify his own actions.' There was a slight sob in her voice. 'Maybe.'

'Well,' Jack, on the other side of her, put an arm round her and gave her a hug. 'I think you're being amazing about it all. Isn't she, Kate?'

Kate felt a stirring of concern as she cleared the plates away. Jack had always seen himself as a white knight on a horse, riding to the rescue of distressed damsels. Having one living in his house . . . well, luckily he was going to Temanistan and Sasha would be gone by the time he came back.

When Kate returned to the table with the pudding, Jack's arm was still lying protectively over the back of Sasha's chair. She was leaning forward, smiling and sparkling again. Kate paused, trying to work out what it was about the scene that made her feel so very uneasy, when Sasha suddenly looked back at Kate for a fraction of a moment.

It was a look of challenge. I will take you on.

Almost before Kate registered what she was seeing, Sasha's sweet expression returned. 'Kate, I can't tell you how delicious that was. You are such a talented cook.'

At that point the phone rang, and Kate, distracted, picked it up. 'Oh, hi, Olivia, do you want to speak to Si?'

She could hardly hear her. Jack was telling a joke about the army.

'This chap was having a brain transplant, and was told he could have a physicist's brain for £20,000 or a Nobel Prize winner's brain for £40,000, but an army brain would cost quarter of a million.'

Sasha gazed at him, rapt. 'Why?' she squealed.

'Never been used,' concluded Jack.

Sasha led the laughter. Kate stood holding the phone, trying to make Si hear. Eventually, still laughing, he came to take the call and Kate finally served out the pudding, feeling, as Sasha held court with a funny story to match Jack's, like the housekeeper rather than the hostess.

'I googled your father, Sasha,' Kate decided to take up the challenge as she sat down again. She'd noticed that Sasha was happy to drop her father's name into the conversation, but rarely wanted to take it further. 'I gather he's going through quite a renaissance at the moment, and that one of your brothers is writing his biography?'

Sasha smiled and rolled her eyes. 'You know the press. It's never quite accurate. And as for the internet . . .'

Si came back into the room, and Kate saw Sasha look at him under her eyelashes again.

He halted and straightened his tie unconsciously, and she patted the seat beside her. 'Si, I'm longing to hear about how you started up Rifle & Rod in China . . .'

'What did Olivia have to say?' Kate shouted across the table, cutting into Sasha's conversation again.

'It's extraordinary,' replied Si, settling himself next to Sasha again. 'Quite extraordinary.'

'What's extraordinary?' asked Ella.

'Si's about to tell us, Mumma,' said Kate.

'What did he say? What did Si say?' Ella turned to Heather. 'I didn't hear what Si said.'

'He hasn't *said* it yet, Mumma, just listen,' snapped Kate.

'It's no good pretending I'm a bit deaf,' said Ella. 'You don't speak up, any of you, especially Si.'

Kate rolled her eyes. 'What, Si, is extraordinary?'

'Olivia and her sister have just been left a house in Kent by her uncle. You know, Uncle Malcolm, the one who never sees . . . never saw . . . the family. Apparently he died a few weeks ago. Nobody thought to tell them. And they all thought he was gay and probably living with someone, so no one ever thought he'd leave it to two girls he hadn't seen since they were ten and twelve. It's an amazing house, apparently, absolutely classic little Georgian dolls' house, and hasn't been touched for fifty years. And it's got a bit of a garden, a paddock and even an old stable block.'

'It must be worth a fair bit,' said Jack.

'I've no idea,' said Si. 'But Uncle Malcolm had a bob or two, and they've been left that as well. Although the house is pretty much derelict. We'll have to sell it at auction, I imagine, and it probably won't fetch much.'

'Won't you want to keep it?' asked Heather, wistfully.

Si laughed. 'You know my views on the countryside. All those crops rotating make me feel dizzy.'

Everyone laughed.

'Anyway,' he added. 'One thing Olivia and I have always agreed on is that we would never want the hassle or the expense of a second home. And the estate is split between her and her sister in Hong Kong. Who she never sees, and wouldn't want to co-own with. They have nothing in common.'

'Not like us,' said Ella, sounding superior. 'Some families don't keep in touch. I think that's so sad, don't you?'

'Don't be so mean, Si, you can afford a second home if Olivia wants one.' Kate felt a stab of jealousy so powerful that she almost hated Olivia. Why couldn't someone leave her and Jonny something? Anything. All she asked was to stay in her own home, and Olivia, with her fabulous flat and well-paid job, was now being left a country estate as well. Although Si would probably make her sell it.

It confirmed her fear that Olivia was getting too grand to come to 19 Lovelace Road. That was why she had cancelled, nothing to do with that ridiculous story of the dying cat.

Chapter 12

Olivia's heart had indeed sunk when Kate phoned to say that she was giving a Sunday lunch at 19 Lovelace Road so that the family, particularly Ella, could say goodbye to Jack.

Si had been away during the week, in Moscow, Dubai, New York and Beijing, for four successive weeks. Even for Si, this was excessive. Their precious weekends together – the lifeblood of their relationship – had been spent catching up with sleep and emails, and even going back into the office on a Saturday or Sunday morning. Once or twice Olivia had wondered . . . but, no. This was Si. Si, whom she trusted completely.

No, his abstraction and long hours were more likely due to the imminent reshuffle at Rifle & Rod – the old chairman, the fourth generation of Bartlett-Joneses to own and run it, had died earlier in the year, while the current CEO, his son, was nearing retirement and would be bumped up to chairman. So the CEO slot, coveted by Si almost ever since he started working there, would soon be coming up, and the decision would be made by a collection of some twenty-seven Bartletts, Joneses and Bartlett-Joneses aged between twenty-two and ninety-seven. Si was the obvious choice, but R&R had always been managed by the family. Were they finally ready to be dragged into the twenty-first century and to appoint an outsider? Si was campaigning hard amongst shareholders and almost doubling his workload. It would be so nice to have a Sunday to themselves, while Si paced up and down, talking out loud, planning his strategy . . . taking Olivia's advice, which he surprisingly often did. He needed a lot of listening to at the moment, Olivia thought.

But instead she found herself agreeing that it would be lovely to say goodbye to Jack, although this Temanistan job hardly sounded dangerous.

They managed to enjoy a lie-in – to nine o'clock – with fresh coffee and croissants before setting off for a swim in the pool in the basement of their building. It had been part of the draw of living there, to have a gym and pool on the premises. Olivia managed twenty minutes worth of swimming, while Si ploughed up and down for his regulation one hundred lengths, as determined in his fitness as he was in every other part of his life.

She dried herself and watched him, sitting on one of the sun loungers that ringed the pool. Si was at his best in the water, slicing through it like an otter, then flipping at each end of the pool in a practised arc. She threw him a towel as he hauled himself out, gasping and dripping all over the fitness centre's mosaic tiles. 'Here, sexy.'

He laughed, and Olivia, out of the corner of her eye, saw a woman in a swimsuit look at him sideways as she went past. In spite of Jack's jokes, Si was fit – not as muscular as Jack, but longer-legged, with a surprising dark dusting of body hair all over, with the same broad Fox shoulders and a shock of thick brown hair, now fading to blond.

He met her gaze, and a sudden – unexpected – flash of desire sprang between them.

'Hi,' he said, softly, kissing her gently on the lips.

She laughed, feeling giddy and irresponsible. 'Hi.'

'Shall we go upstairs?' he suggested. 'We don't have to leave yet.'

She thought of the chores she had listed neatly on a piece of paper upstairs on the long, dark dining table, and the pile of post that had built up during the week. She hadn't even time to open the letters, let alone deal with them. But they all looked boring and they could wait. She put her hand in his, and kissed him back.

Take that, woman in a swimsuit, she thought, as they left hand in hand. You can stop looking at my husband. He's mine.

But as they entered the bedroom Olivia's phone rang. It was

90

Allison Green, who had demanded all her telephone numbers: mobile, home, work and secretary. 'Ted is the most unreasonable man,' she screamed, and it took Olivia more than fifteen minutes to get her to calm down, to understand exactly what she was saying and to make a suggestion that might break the impasse.

The result was that Si would go to Kate and Jonny's on his own, while she, Olivia, drove down to Sunningdale with a dying cat in the back of the car. She then found herself taking it to the vet for its final journey because Allison Green said that she was too sensitive to do it herself. There had been a final flurry of phone calls while Olivia established whether Allison wanted the cat's ashes or to have the body frozen for burial later.

'This really is not the job of a divorce lawyer,' fumed Olivia, to herself.

So she only started to open the post at three o'clock that afternoon, and had been overwhelmed by the solicitor's letter that informed her that her uncle had died and that he had named her and Fenella as his heirs bequeathing them Providence Cottage and really quite a nice sum of money.

After that she hadn't been able to think about anything else. She had visited Providence Cottage once when she was twelve and her sister was ten, and they'd both thought it was magical. Brampton, the house where she and Fenella had grown up, had been a big, ugly Victorian pile, with endless dusty corridors, shuttered rooms and smells of boiled cabbage. Providence Cottage was a perfect dolls' house in comparison, and the memory of the sunny fields and hedgerows tumbling with blossom, stretching out from its front door, encapsulated the image of childhood happiness in Olivia's mind. Even her parents had seemed warmer and less distant that day, and more like a picture-book mother and father.

And now Providence Cottage was hers. Fenella didn't want it, she'd be quite happy to be bought out.

Si got back that evening. Olivia left the solicitor's letter lying on the table for him. He picked it up to read it himself. 'Wow. A house.'

She uncurled herself from the sofa. 'Wow, indeed. Nice lunch?'

'Mm. That friend of Kate's, Sasha, was there again.'

'I see.' Olivia kept her tone light. 'And how was she?'

He sat down beside her, and stretched his legs out. 'Oh, really rather charming. She's staying with Heather for a few weeks, seems to be bringing her out of her shell a bit.'

'Don't tell me you fancy her?' teased Olivia.

He didn't answer at first, and she almost thought he hadn't heard her, but then he looked up and held her gaze, unflinching. 'No,' he said, finally. 'I've more sense than that.' He picked up her hand and kissed the palm. 'I've got you.'

'Good.' She turned away. 'Have you eaten?'

'But I'm not sure that Jonny has. Sense, that is.'

'What?' Olivia swung round again. 'What do you mean?'

'I saw Jonny and Sasha whispering together. Upstairs, outside the loo.'

'Are you sure she wasn't just telling him they were out of loo paper?'

Si's face cracked in a smile. 'No. I'm not sure. But I didn't like the body language between them. She's like a cat, she purrs up against you and twists herself around your body. It's strangely . . .' he hesitated '. . . charming. She seems so vulnerable, she makes you want to look after her.'

'I know. She does it to women too.' Olivia made them both a cup of tea, then sat back down on the sofa and curled her legs under her. 'Sit down and tell me all about it. Do we need to say something to Kate?'

'I don't know. And what could we say that wouldn't make it all worse?' Si sat beside her, his hand taking one of Olivia's. He turned it over and kissed her palm absent-mindedly. 'It may be nothing, of course. I don't think we should say anything against a friend of Heather's unless we've really got something to go on, it would cause such a lot of trouble in the family. Can you imagine Jack roaring at me that I'm impugning the behaviour of his wife's friend? He's quite capable of coming round to punch me in the face over it.'

Olivia grimaced. 'I can just see it. And, of course, I'm not sure that Sasha is even looking for anyone else. She's still at the stage of being obsessed with her ex-husband. When she and I had lunch I tried to explain that she needs to move forward, away from what he's done to her, and towards somewhere that she wanted to be,' said Olivia. 'And to stop spending all this money on going to court. Which, when there's only the house as an asset to pay for it all, is madness. They could *both* be left with no money at all if they're not careful.'

'Well,' said Si. 'She'll probably come to her senses eventually.' He sat back. 'I do worry about Kate and Jonny, though – it's nothing I can quite put my finger on, but recently Jonny seems to have tuned out.'

'Well, it is all rather Kate's domain,' said Olivia. 'I do wonder, when she's so busy juggling all those balls in the air, whether the ball marked "Jonny" gets dropped from time to time.'

'I think that's just what happens when people have kids,' said Si.

It hurt. Even after all these years, it still hurt, when he said things like that. He sounded as if he was almost relieved they hadn't been able to have any.

'Was she cross with me for ducking out of lunch?'

Si hesitated. 'Oh . . . no . . . well, you know Kate. She never stays cross with anyone for long.'

She had no right to be cross at all, thought Olivia furiously. Kate had everything, children, an interesting job, a nice partner, a lovely house, a big family . . . and she expected everyone to come to her all the time. 'She's being ridiculously over-sensitive.'

'What do you mean?' Si raised an eyebrow. 'Being sensitive is a good thing, don't you think?'

Olivia remembered that, even if you'd been together for twenty years, you couldn't criticise their sister. 'Being sensitive about other people is a good thing. Being sensitive about yourself is less attractive. She doesn't seem to realise that when you've got a client like Allison Green then you have to jump.'

Si raised his shoulders in a shrug. 'I don't think she's going to hold it against you. Did you sort the cat, by the way?'

'Cat sorted. Sadly. Copious tears from both Allison Green and daughter Lily. What do you mean, not hold it against me? It's absolutely none of her business. If I've got work, I've got work. She should understand that. Except, of course, I think she's pretty part-time about how she works. Did she think I was lying?'

Si sighed. 'Olivia, can we leave this topic alone? I've no idea what Kate's thinking. She didn't say anything specific. She didn't complain about your not coming. She sent you her love. What more can you ask? From something Jonny said, I think they've got money worries, and she looks a bit tense. She's put on weight again. You know how she comfort-eats.'

'So the problem with Kate might be money, not Sasha at all? And not me, either?'

'I don't see why it should be anything you've done.' Si kissed her hand again. 'Just forget about the bloody cat and the lunch, it's all a question of least said, soonest mended.'

'Right,' said Olivia. 'Well, if it's money that's at the bottom of it all, I'd better keep quiet about my lovely new house, then, hadn't I? Or she'll think I'm crowing.' She picked up a dog-eared black-and-white photograph from where it had been lying on top of a magazine. 'While I was waiting for you, I dug this out. A photo Daddy took of Providence Cottage when I was little. Isn't it magical?'

Si looked at the photograph. 'It looks rather rundown. And that photo must be thirty years old. I don't suppose anything has been done to it since. What happened to the actual farm itself?'

'Uncle Malcolm sold off the land when he retired in the 1980s. There's just a garden and a paddock now. And some ramshackle stables and a barn where he used to keep his clapped-out Morris Oxford. It's *so* exciting, oh, Si, can we keep it and do it up? Fenella can have the money, I rang Hong Kong and she's not interested in the house at all, and . . . I would love a garden again.'

'You're joking.' He touched her cheek. 'That sort of thing can be very expensive, you know. And a lot of work and responsibility. We'd feel we had to go there all the time.'

'Please. Please. I'd like to make things grow. It would be a weekend place, obviously, and maybe we'd save a bit because we wouldn't go abroad on holiday so often oh, Si, if you could see it, I know you'd fall in love with it, too.'

'Where did this sudden desire to be Marie Antoinette come from? Have you been reading glossy magazines again? No, Olivia, it's madness. Just when you're taking on new responsibilities at work,' he drew her close to him, and kissed the top of her head. 'We don't know anyone down there . . . and it's in the middle of the countryside . . . and, er . . . farming communities don't welcome outsiders.'

'They do now. It's not like the old days.' Olivia knew that he was calculating it all. Would it be grand enough to invite people to? Were the sort of the people who lived nearby worth getting to know? Might there be some kind of unexpected benefit? Si always looked at the pros and cons of everything. There had to be a point, a goal, a reason.

'Would you just come and see it? With a completely open mind?'

'OK. We'll certainly have to see it anyway, whatever we do.'

Olivia knew that Si rarely said 'no' to her about anything she wanted. Except the donor sperm, of course. That was a very big no. So he owed her. He owed for that, big time.

She was determined. This wasn't a sudden desire to be Marie Antoinette. She'd always had a faint hankering for somewhere in the English countryside, but Si so clearly didn't and she'd kept quiet. She lay awake until 2 a.m. with excitement, until she remembered her conversation with Kate about renovations and the strain they placed on a marriage.

But that wasn't her and Si. They wouldn't be living in mess. They wouldn't be living apart. No, this was going to be pure fun. For both of them. Together. They would do it together. Providence Cottage could be the child they'd never had.

Chapter 13

In Halstead Hill, three days before Jack was due to go to Temanistan, the doorbell rang. Two police officers wanted to know if Heather Spencer lived there.

'Heather Spencer?' Heather wondered if she could lie.

'Also known as Heather Fox.' They made it sound like a crime.

'Who wants to know?' Heather felt the years of respectability drop away into great chasms on either side of her.

'What is it?' Jack, a towel round his waist. 'Hello, I'm Colonel Fox.'

They were deferential at that, but still wanted to know if she was the daughter of Maureen Spencer, known as Mo. Heather avoided Jack's eye as she admitted she was, and they told her, quite gently, that they believed her mother had died in a fire in Brixton, but they'd like her to make an identification, if she didn't mind.

'Brixton!' Heather was mortified to think that her mother had been so close. Just fifteen minutes from Kate and Lovelace Road, in fact. She was so stunned that all she could think was *I could have walked past my mother any time I went to 19 Lovelace Road.*

'I thought you said . . .' Jack put an arm round her shoulders, and steered her inside. 'Let me get dressed and I'll come with you. Pity Sasha's away, but I'm sure the girls can go next door for a few hours.'

Heather couldn't think how to stop him, because the less he knew the better, but she accepted because it was easier not to make a fuss. Somewhere, deep down, she'd always hoped that her mother would come back, not drunk or stoned, and they would be able to talk, and say all the things that had never been said. That hope trickled away as she stood in her hall, rooted to the spot.

'Heather?' he peered at her, from a long way away. 'Heather, are you all right?'

She put a hand to her face. 'Fine. Of course.'

'I thought you said your mother died when you were eighteen.'

Heather shook her head, unable to reply. She let Jack find her handbag and steer her into the car. 'I thought she had,' she murmured, halfway through the car journey, trying to recover the situation.

'But surely you couldn't have gone to her funeral, could you? How did you come to think that she'd died?' Jack sounded puzzled.

Heather didn't answer. That was one of the tricks she'd always used as a child. If someone asks you a question you don't want to answer, don't. They can't make you. Don't tell anyone anything. It's much safer. Whenever she was really frightened, she thought of Broadstairs and how Gerald would have wanted her to behave. Or the social workers at the Caldecott. That was Good Heather. Bad Heather was . . . She shook her head and clenched her fists tightly, feeling her nails dig in. She would not let Bad Heather out, no matter how much she screamed and kicked inside. Bad things happened to Bad Heather. But she didn't dare say anything more to Jack, and blocked his questions out by gazing at the road ahead.

The police informed them that the fire had been accidental, apparently – she must have fallen asleep smoking.

She nodded, still unable to feel anything. 'She always smoked in bed.' She tried not to look at Jack. His expression was confused.

The police officer looked at her. 'Are you feeling all right?'

Heather nodded and sat silently in a daze, feeling sick, while forms were filled in, and people were notified, and Jack guided her up corridors and fetched her a paper cup of water. She felt safer in the police station because Jack couldn't question her there.

'Does she look . . . is she very . . .?'

'She died from smoke inhalation. She hasn't been burned.'

Heather wondered if she would remember what Mo looked

like, but recognised her immediately. But she looked about eighty, with deep grooves in her face, and harsh, bleached blonde hair. The pretty girl of Heather's memories had gone completely.

The forms stated that she was fifty-two.

'Heather, she must have been only about sixteen when she had you. Only a few years older than the girls are now.'

'They're ten and twelve.' Heather didn't want to imagine any comparisons between her and Daisy and Molly. She sorted through the scraps of clothing, still smelling faintly of patchouli and tobacco.

'Most of the contents of the flat were burnt,' said the police sergeant.

'There's nothing I recognise,' she said, but picked up a bangle, an Indian silver piece in the shape of a dragon. Gerald had given it to her. 'Except this.' The memories of the house in Broadstairs assailed her, and for a moment she thought she might cry.

But she heard Jack questioning the police officer, who told him that Mo had been an addict and a prostitute, turning tricks for fixes. She had to concentrate on getting him out of there, before he could find out any more. It would be so awful, so bad for Jack's career, if he was ever in a sensitive position and had to be positively vetted . . . A prostitute's daughter was hardly a suitable wife for an ambitious army officer. Jack would be furious when they got home . . . her panic-stricken thoughts whirled round and round, each one a silken cord of guilt and shame, tying her tighter and tighter, strangling the words in her throat.

'Sign here.' The police sergeant was matter-of-fact. She signed her name in an illegible squiggle and fled, stuffing the contents of the box into the first rubbish bin she found. The dragon bangle she put into her bag.

'Heather, why didn't you tell me?' asked Jack on the way home.

Heather shook her head, but couldn't speak.

'Don't you think I deserve to know? Trust me, Heather. Tell me about it.'

But Heather did not trust anyone. She put her hands over her ears and scrunched herself into the tightest ball that the car seat and its seatbelt would allow.

When she got home, she pulled out the contents of the kitchen cupboards and scrubbed the backs of them. 'Don't you dare tell your family,' she hissed.

'Of course, I won't, but all I want to know is . . .'

Heather shut her ears to him, and turned the radio up as high as she could. Now he knew what a truly awful person she was.

'Talk to me, Heather,' pleaded Jack, in bed that evening.

She wouldn't be so stupid. He suddenly seemed like the enemy.

They spent the weekend like that: Jack alternately cajoling then ordering her to talk. Heather made sure that she was in the same room as Sasha as much as possible, so that Jack couldn't bring it up. Sasha, obviously picking up that something was wrong, filled in the silences and kept up a constant stream of amusing chatter. Heather could feel Bad Heather struggling to get out, wanting to fight Jack or storm out, and she wouldn't. She wouldn't because she had too much to lose.

So she worked twice as hard to get everything looking nice before Jack went, and to get any paperwork in order. It was always busy before your soldier was posted away, everyone knew that. On the odd occasion Jack managed to catch her alone, she was defensive, and occasionally Bad Heather broke through, frustrated and angry.

'Yes, I am capable of paying an electricity bill by myself,' she shouted at Jack once. 'Just because I never went to university, it doesn't mean I'm completely thick, you know.'

Jack looked amazed. 'Of course, I don't think you're thick,' he explained. 'I just want to make sure that everything runs smoothly in my absence. That you don't suddenly find yourself with the electricity cut off, or anything like that.'

'Jack,' said Heather, her throat blocked with the effort of not screaming at him, '*I'm* the one who does everything round here. Your going away isn't going to make the least difference to . . .'

But Jack had gone out the front door and slammed it, and she could see him walking stiffly off down the road, hands in his pockets.

Heather buried her head in her hands. There was so much to organise: a list of chores he wanted to get done before he went, the extra bits and pieces he needed – a new torch, his favourite boiled sweets, some extra thermal underwear – getting his car off the road and claiming back the six months' road tax. It all whirled round in a tempest of misunderstandings and frayed nerves, but Heather had learned to deal with it by never losing her temper. This time her temper was too close to the surface. Travis, who hated shouting as much as she did, whimpered and pressed himself against her for reassurance. She dropped down and stroked his fur, clinging to him for unconditional love. The dog licked her face.

'Are you OK?' Sasha stood in the door of the kitchen. 'I'm sorry, I couldn't help . . .'

Heather wiped her face with her hands and stood up. 'I'm being silly. Just tired.'

'Of course, it's only natural.' Sasha touched her sleeve with sympathy. 'In the past has he always been like this? When he's posted abroad without you?'

'The past?' Heather was filled with panic. The word made her brain go blank, and reminded her of Mo. She and Jack had, until now, suited each other very well in their lack of desire to talk about the past. Jack was adamant that he could barely remember his father, and that his death had not affected him in any way because there had been Si and Kate instead. He changed the subject whenever Mike was mentioned, usually by Si, who still seemed mentally to refer everything to his father for approval 'Dad would have wanted . . .' or 'Dad always said that . . .' Kate always discussed her father's death in the context of Ella: 'My father always used to look after all that . . .' or 'ever since Dad's death, Mumma's been . . .'. It was hard to tell what Kate herself felt, but Heather detected a streak of resentment, as if Mike Fox had let his daughter down by dying. Jack almost refused to concede that he'd ever had a father at all, and as Heather literally hadn't they'd rubbed along very well. Until this business of Mo, of course.

'The past?' echoed Heather, again, numb.

'Yes, when he's been posted away before.' Sasha peered at her, worried, nurse-to-patient. 'Is he always on edge?'

Heather forced herself to respond. 'Oh, er, yes, always on edge. A bit. It's quite normal.'

'Shall I go after him and see if I can calm him down?'

Heather hesitated. She should be the one to go after him, she knew she should, and she couldn't bear to think that in three days' time he would be gone, but what if he really insisted on answers to his questions? At least this time he wasn't going into physical danger, and when he came back he'd have forgotten about her mother and it could all go back to normal. She wasn't quite sure exactly how that would happen, but she was relying on Jack being totally engaged with whatever was going on in Temanistan and herself being able to be sweet and normal-sounding down the phone, which she was having trouble being in person.

Until then, Sasha was a good barrier between them. Having Sasha, Grace and Tom in the house meant there was always clutter everywhere, but every time Sasha suggested leaving, Heather urged her to stay until she found the perfect place.

'I think we should leave,' said Sasha, softly. 'This is such a strain on you, and it's not helping, having us here.'

'Oh no. Not until you find somewhere else.' The thought of being left alone with Jack was terrifying. He would find some way of getting the truth out of her. She had even managed to book a couple of appointments at the school the morning he was leaving, so that she had an excuse not to drive him to the airport. 'Really, it's always like this just before he goes.'

'You are so good to him,' said Sasha. 'He takes you for granted.'

In the end Sasha offered to take Jack to the airport, and although Heather hesitated, she couldn't see any good reason to say no, especially as she herself had no intention of risking nearly three hours alone in a car with him and his questions. They were almost back to normal with each other now, both of them pretending that nothing was wrong, and she didn't want to risk a last argument.

Once Jack had packed, she could see that he'd mentally left them, and she relaxed. They kissed goodbye – Jack dropping down to pat Travis – and she stood on the doorstep waving and smiling as Sasha drove Jack off in her black sports car. Travis looked despondent at the sight of luggage, but Heather scratched his ear. 'He's forgotten about Mo Spencer, hasn't he, Trav?' she whispered. 'When he comes back, it'll all be like it was before.' Travis wagged his tail in agreement.

Sasha returned just as Heather switched on the ten o'clock news that evening.

'I'm surprised you can watch that,' said Sasha, whose eyes were bright. 'Don't you worry every time a bulletin starts with "two British soldiers were killed when . . ."'

'It's fine,' said Heather. 'Some army families have the news on all the time, some don't watch it. I don't think it makes much difference in the end. We would always be told first if something had happened to Jack. And I can't imagine anything about unrest in Temanistan would ever be on British TV anyway.' Weariness seeped through her. It had been exhausting keeping up the pretence of being fine in front of Jack, and she now rather wished Sasha would go away.

'How do you do it, though? Be so calm, I mean. I looked Temanistan up and there's still really quite a lot of fighting going on.' Sasha poured herself a glass of wine.

Heather forced a smile. 'I switch off. That's how you do it. You just don't feel.' This wasn't completely true – her heart flipped over at the beginning of every announcement that a serviceman had been killed – but she'd learned that it was never Jack. And they would have told her – the efficiency of the army's communications machine soothed her whenever she woke up, frightened, in the middle of the night.

She could have added that she found it harder and harder to switch back on again when Jack returned, though. You get used to being numb. Instead she just smiled at Sasha again.

'I don't know how you do it,' gushed Sasha. 'I do admire you. You're so brave.'

Heather eyed Sasha suspiciously. In her book, people who were nice to you usually wanted something of yours.

But that was Bad Heather's book. Good Heather thought the best of people. Oh, if only the memory of Mo Spencer, with all its fear and anger, would go away and Heather could go back to the person she'd been before the trip to the police station.

Chapter 14

The appointment with the bank came up almost too soon. Jonny and Kate sat down to explain their finances to someone who looked almost young enough to be their son. His name badge said he was called Gavin Small.

'You see,' said Kate, 'if I work longer hours, then I'll have to pay for childcare. I would be worse off. And our children are ten and fourteen years old. I can't leave them to let themselves in after school or trust them to do their homework without help.'

Gavin Small looked sympathetic, but she doubted he understood. He looked too young to have children himself.

'The school day,' she added, 'ends at three-thirty, whereas the working day is rarely over before six, and there are also four months of holiday a year. Leaving the boys alone for that length of time is asking for trouble.' As if Callum wasn't enough trouble already. She had found cans of lager under his bed the other day, but he'd said his friend Dan had drunk most of them.

'Hm,' said Gavin Small. 'What about expenditure? It seems very high. Particularly the food and drink bills.' He frowned at them, as if in disbelief.

'Well, of course it's been a bit difficult recently . . .' said Kate, wondering if she should ask for the financial crimes of the ten previous years to be taken into consideration before sentencing. 'We've had our kitchen redone, so we've had to . . .' She waved a hand to indicate the dangers of no kitchen, and banished the memory of her usual supermarket dash, flinging everything into

103

the trolley against the clock, but alas, without a game-show host with an open chequebook to pay her bill at the end. 'From now on, I will have a shopping list,' she stated. 'And I will stick to it. Instead of making out a list, then leaving it behind. Although I read the other day that that's an excellent way of training your brain, so . . .'

Gavin Small looked alarmed. He didn't seem much more familiar with shopping lists than he was with the complexities of childcare.

'A shopping list could halve our grocery bills, couldn't it, Jonny? Don't you think?' She was determined to prove to this fresh-faced young man that she wasn't a mad middle-aged woman with an out-of-control spending habit.

Jonny leant back in his chair as if to edge away from the meeting altogether, and caught her eye. His face clearly told her that burbling on wasn't helping. 'That's your area,' he said. 'I'm game if you are.'

But Kate, nervous, couldn't stop. 'I mean we'd be quite happy to make our own loo cleaner out of borax and live on sausages, wouldn't we, darling?'

Jonny's eyebrows shot up. 'Fine, but . . .'

'Not delicatessen chorizo,' she added, in warning. 'Plain boring old English pork sausages. Although chorizo would be cheaper than steak . . . but of course we hardly ever have steak. But we could make our own washing powder out of soda crystals and I'll start making Christmas presents in August and all that will save . . . oh . . . well, at least ten pounds a month.'

Gavin Small looked from one to the other, as if in a tennis match, and looked doubtfully down at a piece of paper that probably made it very clear that ten pounds a month was not going to help. 'Now,' he turned to Jonny. 'The business.'

A light flickered on behind Jonny's eyes.

'That doesn't seem to be turning over quite as much as . . .'

'We're actually being commissioned for as many programmes as we were before,' said Jonny smoothly. 'In fact, our business is rising year on year . . .'

Kate looked at him in surprise.

'But we do have a very short-term cash flow problem,' he

admitted. 'We had two long-running series which came to the end of their contracts . . .'

She remembered his despair when he'd told her that first one series, then the next, had been axed.

But to the 'personal banker' he was smiling and positive. 'These series were not hugely profitable, but they did give us a steady income. That income will take a short time to replace, and with any luck we'll replace them with more profitable programmes.'

Kate hoped Gavin Small didn't read the media press. 'More profitable' was not a phrase he would have found in any of the columns about independent television.

'We've got a couple of exciting projects waiting for approval,' he concluded.

Kate refrained from saying anything. Jonny, over the past weeks and months, had withdrawn into himself like a tortoise curled up inside a very hard shell. She had no idea what projects he was doing. Once they had discussed everything. When she'd met Jonny that had been part of the appeal. They came from the same worlds. They had the same media friends. They lived in the same parts of London. Every single box was ticked, perfectly.

'And the house, of course, is the security for the business . . .' the young man droned. 'As well as having its own mortgage outstanding.'

'It's worth a lot,' Kate blurted out. 'Especially with the renovations. If we remortgaged again, we could manage the higher payments because of the savings on the grocery bills, and . . .'

After another very unpleasant half hour, they agreed that this is what they would do.

As they left the bank, Kate knew they'd bought at least another year at 19 Lovelace Road. And by then, Jonny's company could be back on its feet. Both children would be at secondary school. Maybe somehow those hours between four and six would magically disappear, along with the school holidays.

Next year it would be different. They must keep the house, they must.

'What programmes are you putting forward at the moment?' she asked Jonny, as they drove away from the bank.

'Oh, you know, we've always got various things going through the system.' He frowned as a motorcyclist cut them up.

'Oh, I meant to say, I found lager under Callum's bed. Do you think we should be worried?'

'I tried a can or two myself at that age,' said Jonny. 'It's what kids do.'

'Would you try talking to him when you take him to football this weekend?'

'Oh, er, I don't think I'll be able to make that. Could you drop him off?'

This was the third weekend in a row that Jonny had ducked out of spending Saturday morning with the boys, taking them to the local park for football training, watching them, buying them burgers afterwards and discussing the game.

'Jonny! You aren't seeing the boys enough. And I'm worried that . . .'

'I have to put work first. You know that. Otherwise . . .'

Kate did not want to think about 'otherwise'.

Chapter 15

A month later, Kate was trying to put together a short resume of her possible programme on 'punctuality and personality' and had found a Professor Leith who specialised in theories about obsessively punctual people suffering from anxiety and consistently late people suffering from social phobias. At 5.33 p.m. the phone rang, presumably the professor, because he did not suffer from either anxiety or social phobias. But it was Callum. She couldn't understand what he was saying.

'I can't hear you, what is it?'

She thought he said something about the police.

'What's happened? Are the police with you? Can I talk to them?' She was anxious to get him off the phone so that it would be clear for her essential call. He had probably had his mobile stolen. Again. It never occurred to her that he could be in trouble. 'Hello?'

A Detective Constable Michael Barnes ascertained whether she was the mother of Callum Rafferty, who had been arrested and was being held at the police station under suspicion of theft and actual bodily harm.

'There must be some mistake. Callum's a very gentle boy and he would never . . .'

'Two youths answering to the description of your son and another boy pulled an elderly lady's handbag from her arm. The old lady fell over and has broken her arm, and a passerby identified your son later, a few streets away.'

'But that's not possible! Callum would never do that!' Kate was shocked beyond being able to think. 'Is he with his friend Dan?' Dan, perhaps, might . . . no, he might be a difficult boy, but he would never hurt anyone, surely? Frightened and confused, she pulled together her coat and bag and hurried to the police station, images of Callum playing through her head. The sweet smell in his room, the cans of lager, the end-of-term reports from school that said he had lost concentration . . . why hadn't she acted on her instincts earlier? She tried to get hold of Jonny, but had to leave a message.

Callum was sitting on his own in an empty detention room, his head in his hands, and she saw how his bony wrists protruded from his too-short sleeves. There was something unexpectedly masculine about those wrists. She hadn't realised how fast he was growing.

But his face was still a child's. He was pale with fright. Her phone rang.

'It's Professor Leith here.'

Kate signalled to Callum that she had to take the call, and then she saw the dejection in his expression. He was resigned to never coming first. Throughout their childhood, she had always had to stop what she was doing to take 'work calls'. Perhaps this was why they were here now.

Kate took a deep breath: 'I'm sorry, Professor Leith, I have a family emergency . . .' She paused while the professor explained that he would be studying time in the Amazon for the next six months. 'If I can contact you in six months, when you return, perhaps we can resurrect the programme then?' She snapped the phone shut and sat next to Callum, putting a hand on his.

'Callum, did you steal that old lady's purse?'

He shook her hand off, angrily. 'Mum! How can you ask that?'

She replaced her hand. 'I have to ask it, because I have to hear you say, quite clearly, what has happened. I will always love you, whatever you do, but I must know the facts.'

His eyes flickered from side to side. Was it guilt? 'Dan and I were walking home and suddenly this police car came up and arrested us. That's all. Honest. I never even saw an old lady.'

'Right,' said Kate. 'I will find out what has happened, and we will sort this out.'

They waited for an hour, Kate fidgeting with her phone and leaving messages for Jonny. *I need someone else here, someone who knows what to do in this situation,* she thought.

Olivia. Kate hadn't spoken to her since the cancelled lunch two months ago.

But Olivia took her call immediately. 'Kate, how awful. I'm not a criminal solicitor, though, but I could recommend someone.'

'How much do you think that would cost?' Kate was ashamed that she had to ask, because she would pay anything to help Callum. But they didn't have much in their bank account.

Olivia hesitated. 'Look, if you'd like me just to pop down, I could get in a taxi now. Just as long as you know I'm not an expert. But I am a solicitor, so I can represent Callum if it would help.'

'It would help a great deal,' said Kate.

The custody officer returned and led them through doors and down grey, anonymous corridors to a small, plain room. Just as they entered Jonny arrived, followed by Olivia in a grey pinstriped suit with a short nipped-in jacket and wide trousers that made her legs look endless.

'Dad!'

Jonny hugged Callum. 'Are you OK?'

'I didn't do anything, Dad, I promise.'

Jonny nodded and took Kate's hand. 'Where's Luke?'

'With friends,' she murmured. 'I didn't want to bring him here.'

'I'm acting as this young man's solicitor,' said Olivia to the custody officer. To Kate and Jonny she said, 'We'll have something called Full Disclosure now, when the police will tell me what the case is against Callum.'

Kate, Jonny and Callum spent another thirty minutes waiting, until Olivia beckoned them in.

'Apparently the old lady was walking along Forbes Road from the Post Office when two youths, one dressed from head to toe in dark clothing and another in a grey sweat hoodie, came running up behind her, the one in the grey hoodie seized her bag, she fell over and they both went running down an alleyway that leads to the road Callum and Dan were found in.'

'When did this happen?' asked Kate.

'About twenty minutes before Callum and Dan were picked

up. The old lady doesn't remember much, and didn't see her attackers, but there was a retired gentleman walking a dog on the other side of the road who saw it all and phoned the police. They drove him round the area, and he pointed Callum and Dan out.'

'On the basis of a grey sweat hoodie? But that's outrageous,' said Kate. 'And surely if he and Dan had taken the purse, they'd have run a bit further in twenty minutes than the next street?'

'I'm not, as you know, a criminal solicitor,' said Olivia. ' If you want someone more experienced in . . .'

'No! That would mean more waiting, and I'm sure they'll see sense. It's totally unfair to pick up a boy on nothing more than the basis of the clothes they're wearing.'

Detective Constable Brown and his detective sergeant were, however, very keen to maintain that the description given by the witness matched Dan and Callum. Dan, they said, would blame Callum and if Callum wanted his side of the story to be believed, then he had better speak first.

Callum looked even younger and more frightened.

'The only side of the story that Dan will be giving is that they had nothing to do with it,' said Kate. 'Unless he's being persuaded to lie.' Jonny touched her knee, discreetly. Don't antagonise them.

'Anyway,' said Kate, suddenly remembering that it was Thursday, 'if the crime happened twenty minutes before they were picked up, and they were picked up at 5.18 p.m., as we've been told, then Callum would still have been in his guitar lesson. His guitar teacher can testify to that.'

They looked at Callum.

'Uh . . . my guitar lesson was . . . uh . . . cancelled.'

Kate's eyebrows rose. 'So where were you at five o'clock?'

Callum looked down.

'Callum, this is important. Wherever you were, you've got to tell us.'

He shook his head. Kate could see his profile, mirroring Jonny's more solid one beyond, his smooth skin contrasting the roughness of Jonny's five o'clock shadow. 'Callum. Please. This is serious. You could go to jail or have a record for life. People can't automatically see that you are innocent.'

'I . . . uh . . . we . . . uh . . . were on the school computers.'

'Well, that's fine, isn't it? You'll be logged in, and we'll be able to prove where you were.'

'Callum?' asked Jonny. 'What is it?'

'Uh . . . we were hacking . . . into the school mainframe . . .'

Kate could see the expressions of the two officers. Another set of irresponsible parents who had no idea what their children were up to.

'I think it's quite clear that it's provable what they were doing and when they were doing it,' she said. 'The school will have to be involved, but it will be quite conclusive.'

Callum was released on bail, although he still had to be photographed, fingerprinted, and had a DNA swab taken. 'It will stay on record,' said Kate. 'Even if you're not charged. I hope it won't cause trouble for you later in life.' She had visions of job offers being rescinded and visas being impossible to obtain. 'But thank you, Olivia, for dropping everything and coming. It made all the difference to feel we had someone on our side.'

Olivia smiled and kissed her. 'I'm sorry I couldn't do more. How are you? Have you seen Heather? How's she managing without Jack?'

'She always seems to manage very well. She and the girls came for lunch last Sunday. I think having Sasha to stay must be helping, although she seems to go abroad a lot too. It must be more than two months now, which is a long time not to have a proper home.'

'It's an odd friendship,' mused Olivia.

Kate wondered if she could say that she thought it might be a marriage of convenience. Sasha getting a free place to live, with built-in babysitting. But she didn't want to bitch. Everyone except her seemed to like Sasha, and she didn't want to seem churlish. 'Oh, well, maybe opposites attract. Sasha having so much confidence and Heather having so little.'

Olivia smiled. 'Well, she's obviously had a very interesting life. Roderick Morton was one of the best-known painters of his day, Si says, and Si knows a lot about art.'

Kate had an idea. She could do a programme about British figurative painters of the twentieth century, featuring Roderick

Morton, and use it to find out a bit more about Sasha's family. There was something about Sasha that made Kate feel very uneasy, and she didn't want to let the others know how she felt. But first she had to sort Callum out. She looked at her son, her heart wrenched out of place at the thought that she had let him down. Somehow she had failed him, she must have done. 'I think I'll have to find out what's really going on with Callum.'

'Yes,' agreed Olivia. 'It's clearly time to keep a closer eye on what that boy's up to.'

Kate frowned as she watched Olivia hail a taxi and glide off in a flurry of kisses and expensive bags. Businesslike but stylish. Kate sighed. There went someone who never had to worry about how she would pay for her summer holiday or her council tax, or choose between taking on an interesting case and getting back in time for the children's tea. What did she know about it?

But she had been very kind to drop everything. Kate reminded herself to ring and thank her properly.

Jonny put one arm around Callum and the other around Kate. 'Headmaster next,' he said.

They had a difficult interview with the headmaster, who said that hacking into the mainframe was a matter for considering expulsion very, very seriously, particularly in the light of Callum's falling grades and failure to turn up to either sport or music.

'He needs his father,' said Kate that evening, after Callum had gone to bed. 'You're hardly spending any time with him at the moment.'

'As his mother, you should know what he's doing,' said Jonny. 'You can't let a boy of fourteen roam the streets.'

'I don't "let him roam" the streets. None of the kids in his class are picked up from school any more. They make their way home. But boys of his age need a role model. A male adult they can talk to. I think that's where it all went wrong for Jack because Dad had died when he was thirteen, and he was always getting into trouble, truanting or fighting, or . . .'

'Jack's fine now. He's an officer in the army, with a beautiful wife and two children.'

'Yes, but . . .' Kate never really believed that Jack was fine. She worried about him, almost the way she worried about Callum and

Luke. 'Anyway, you're working all hours at the moment, you're never here.'

Jonny slapped his hand down on the kitchen table and she jumped. 'He needs a home to live in,' he said. 'He needs food on the table, and clothes to wear. And where is that to come from unless I'm working all hours, as you put it?'

Kate had no answer to that. 'I'm sorry,' she whispered, as Jonny left the room.

He didn't hear. Or he pretended not to.

They had reached a turning point. Either they were together for their children or they weren't, and it looked very much as if they weren't. It's up to you, Kate, she thought. You've got to make it right for Luke and Callum. Jonny is an adult. He must make his own decisions.

If Ella had managed to bring the three of them up without a father at all, then she could certainly bring up Callum and Luke with one who was there for at least some of the time. She forgot all about ringing Olivia to thank her.

Chapter 16

A month after that Jack's leave was cancelled due to increasing unrest in Temanistan. He was snappish with Heather when she protested about it, telling her that of course he'd like to be home, but he couldn't and that was that. Heather allowed herself a short cry at not getting him back, blew her nose and got on with it. She had almost decided that she would talk to him about her mother – now that she'd had time to think about it, perhaps it would be for the best, after all, provided she edited it a bit – but not until she saw him face to face. The angry, restless person deep down inside that had been stirred up after identifying her mother's body had calmed down just enough for her to be able to function properly again. She thought she could talk now. Sort of.

And Sasha's possessions were still piled high in the dining room. Two months after that, they were still there, and Jack was due back in six weeks.

As she sewed on name tapes for the start of the new term, Heather fretted over what to do about it. Sasha wasn't exactly living with them – at weekends and during the school holidays, she seemed to have an amazing number of friends she could stay with, often in quite exotic places. She, Grace and Tom had spent the whole of August on Mykonos with an old school friend who had similar aged children, for example. Every so often she reappeared, brown and smiling, her hand full of property particulars. She and Heather would look at one depressing rental flat after another, and Heather kept finding herself suggesting that Sasha stay a bit longer, just until the right place came up. Looking back she was never quite sure how these conversations came about, because she had always resolved that, really, the time had come. Ella had asked some quite sharp questions about it. 'Is she paying you any rent?' she'd asked once, and, another time, 'I imagine she's getting a nice rate of interest on her share of her house.' She'd looked very cynical when Heather said that Sasha hadn't received any money from it yet, because there was some court case pending. And when the other wives on the patch dropped round, or asked Heather to supper because Jack was away, there was often a question mark in their voices: 'What is she doing here?'

Heather herself sometimes wondered, but how could you ask someone to leave if they were hardly ever there? It would all be different when the autumn term started and Jack was back. Heather sighed. She supposed she ought to be a bit more assertive, and not wait for Jack to sort it all out. Still, she liked Sasha's company – although she was still in awe of her – because there was a fizz about the house when she was around.

Sasha returned that evening in a flurry of presents and borrowing money for the taxi. She kissed Heather and spotted the sewing on the sofa.

'Name tapes! Heather, you are so organised. I do wish I was more like you. We've had a lovely, lovely summer, haven't we, kids? And we'll be off your hands soon. My decree absolute should be any day now, and provided Adam does actually pay me what he said he would, then we can find somewhere.'

'Oh, don't worry,' said Heather, thinking, oh, good, I won't have to ask her to leave. 'I've made a shepherd's pie for us all.'

The phone rang as Heather was taking it out of the oven.

'Shall I answer it?'

Heather nodded.

'Olivia!' shrieked Sasha. 'Have you had a good summer? Yeah, Mykonos. And before that Prague and then the South of France. There's a new R&R in Prague, I popped in and bumped into Si, did he tell you? We did a bit of Scotland, too, you know how it is. Have you been very tied up with doing up that house you inherited? It sounds divine, I'd love to see it some time. No, Heather's

115

here, she's just manhandling a huge pie of some kind. I'm sure she'd love to talk to you.' Sasha handed the phone over.

Heather fielded Olivia's enquiries. Yes, she was fine. Yes, the time had gone quite quickly and Jack would be back before they knew it.

'You know this house I've been left?' said Olivia. 'By Uncle Malcolm? We've finally got probate and it's actually mine at last. We're going down next weekend and we wondered if you'd like to bring the children down for a picnic. It's in Kent, so not far. We could meet you there. And, um, if Sasha's still living with you, do bring her.'

Heather thought she heard an emphasis on the 'still'. She agreed that it would be a lovely last outing for the summer, and Sasha said she would love to come. 'Bring your hard hats,' said Olivia. 'Apparently the house is almost uninhabitable.'

'So you saw Si in Prague?' asked Heather, over supper, wondering why Sasha hadn't mentioned this before.

'He took me out to lunch. He's such fun, don't you think?'

Heather wasn't quite sure what to think. Si was not usually considered fun. And Sasha had been flirting with him all through that last lunch party at 19 Lovelace Road. She had almost called Kate to see what she thought.

But decided not to. Better not cause any trouble. She didn't want Kate to think she was being nosy. Or critical.

Providence Cottage wasn't easy to find. Heather and Sasha wove in and out of a mesh of country lanes, passing the same pub three times. Every signpost they found was just slightly awry.

'Do you think that means that Bishop's Bottom is down the right-hand fork or the left?' Heather tried to work out, from the map, what it would mean even if they did know which road it was pointing to. Providence Cottage's address was Bishop's Forstal, but they hadn't seen any signpost at all for it yet.

'Fancy it being called Bishop's Bottom anyway.'

'I think it means a dip in a hill,' said Heather. 'And the land would have been owned by the bishop. Or maybe farmed by the bishop. Can bishops own land?'

'I expect so. But he could have signposted it better.'

'This part of the world obviously hasn't recovered from the Second World War. When they removed all the signposts to confuse the invading Germans.'

'Oh, I think it dates back longer than that,' said Sasha. 'They were probably trying to confuse William the Conqueror and his army.'

'Well, they certainly succeeded, I imagine.' Heather took out her phone and jabbed at it. 'I can't even call Olivia. There's no mobile reception, and she hasn't got a landline in there.'

They decided to try the right-hand fork, and met three women on horses coming in the opposite direction.

'Providence Cottage?' The leading rider looked surprised. 'Where old Malcolm Forbes used to live?'

'Yes. My sister–in–law was his niece, and she's going to do it up.' Heather found herself burbling. 'We're all going to look at it.'

'Nice house,' said the rider. 'It's down that lane. At the very end.' She pointed to a bumpy dirt track with her whip.

Heather's car crunched and jolted over a series of deepening potholes. 'Do you think we ought to get out? So that there's not so much weight in the car?' she asked after five minutes, frightened for the transmission, or whatever it was under the car that might get broken.

'We still don't know how far away it is.' Sasha's face was screwed up with concentration as she peered at the map again. 'I hope we don't meet anything coming the other way. I'm not sure you'd be able to reverse.'

Heather's energy was draining away, in spite of the cloudless blue sky and the fields of sheep that stretched out on either side of her. The track ended abruptly in front of a dilapidated wooden gate, flanked by a large clump of nettles. An overgrown hedge, on either side of the gate, reached towards them, its branches grasping out to her sweater. She disentangled herself carefully, craning her head to see the outline of a house through the trees. A pigeon fluttered off its roof in alarm.

'It's like Sleeping Beauty's castle,' said Molly, peering through the undergrowth. 'Are we nearly there?'

'Hiya, everyone!' Olivia came from round the back of the house, waving. 'Isn't it amazing? I couldn't get the gate open without it falling apart so we've parked round the back there, where there's a bit of a gap in the hedge. But just leave the car where it is, nobody's going to come down here.'

Daisy's hand slipped into Heather's as they got out, and she squeezed it. 'It's a bit spooky, Mummy. Did someone die here?'

'Only someone very old,' she whispered. 'And I think he would have been happy to die here. He loved it very much.'

Daisy looked unconvinced and flattened herself against her mother's legs, and, on the other side, Travis did the same. Usually so keen to explore, he picked up the family's nervousness, and Heather heard him whine.

'Oh wow,' said Sasha as they reached a clearing of nettles in front of the house. 'This is absolutely fabulous.'

The house was smaller than Heather had imagined. It was a square box with a large sash window on either side of the door and three similar windows across the first floor. Two little dormers poked out of the roof and Heather spotted several patches where tiles were missing. All the windows were either dark or boarded up, and some of the panes were cracked. To the left, in a corner of the yard, she could see some tumbledown outbuildings, probably not even safe to go near. One was a ruined barn, with a partially bare thatched roof and old beams like crooked teeth, almost falling down.

The front door had a small porch and there was a pretty fanlight over the door. Olivia put a large key into the lock and jiggled it around. 'It seems to be stuck. Oh, done it!' She pushed the reluctant door open, tearing several cobwebs apart. Heather tried to get them out of her hair.

A narrow hallway covered in old linoleum and dried-up newspapers stretched out ahead of them. They picked their way through, discovering a large room on either side, one with a single leather armchair, a television and a low table set in front of an old gas fire. In the room on the other side was a dining table covered in books and papers. Everything smelt of wet carpet and wallpaper hung off the wall in curls. At the back a lean-to kitchen housed a filthy old gas stove and a larder, along with a nice old dresser displaying a pathetic handful of mismatched plates and cracked cups.

'I thought you said he was rich,' said Tom, sounding disgusted. 'Why did he live like this?'

'That's why he was rich,' said Si, approvingly. 'He obviously never spent any money on anything. This is beyond redemption though, it'll be far too expensive to restore.'

'No, it isn't.' Olivia was defiant. 'Thank goodness I have my own money, getting any out of you is like getting blood out of a stone.'

Olivia opened up the shutters. They creaked but seemed intact. Through the gloom, the dust and the smell of damp, Heather began to see the bones of a home, and she felt a desperate pang of jealousy. Si and Olivia had so much, and now they'd been given this little jewel of a house.

As they made their way upstairs, testing each tread in case it gave way under them, they came across four doorways, two of them pasted over with wallpaper.

'It's an old tradition,' said Sasha, surprising them. 'When someone dies, you close their room for ever.'

Heather noticed Si look at her with respect. Or was it sexual interest? Heather wondered again whether Sasha was perhaps a little too perky when she was with Simon. But no, she shouldn't think like that. Sasha was their friend. Of course she would never go after Si.

They cut away wallpaper and pulled open doors to find three little square bedrooms, each with a wrought-iron bed, a chest of drawers and a wardrobe, plus one bathroom. 'When the house was built, in 1743, apparently,' explained Olivia, 'they wouldn't have had a bathroom. So someone's obviously put one in what must have been a bedroom originally. Probably in Edwardian times, by the look of it.' It had a stained, claw-footed bath with a huge pillar plug and a WC with an iron overhead tank and a chain.

'You must keep that,' said Sasha. 'They're collector's items now.'

'Great,' muttered Si. 'We inherit a house and the only thing of value is its WC.'

Olivia glared at him.

Si turned the tap on and the pipes began to clank.

'We did say we would re-plumb anyway, didn't we darling?' Olivia added.

Si cautiously tested the narrow, steep staircase that led up to the attic. It groaned and sagged, and then let out a loud cracking noise. 'Sorry, folks. It's just not safe. I'm not going up there without a surveyor's say-so.' He ignored the children's cries of disappointment and shooed them downstairs as he, Heather, Olivia and Sasha explored the bare, dingy bedrooms again.

'All the rooms are a good size, though,' said Olivia. 'The two downstairs ones are huge.' Outside they saw the four children begin to play hide-and-seek in the overgrown garden, pursued by Travis.

'They will be all right out there, won't they?' Heather felt anxious. 'They couldn't fall down any wells or anything?'

Si manhandled a reluctant sash window up. 'You lot. Be careful.' They waved at him, and Si prodded the windowsill. His finger sank into something that had the texture of damp sponge. It was wet and crumbly at the same time. He rolled his eyes and worked the window shut again. 'And we had such a perfect life.'

'It's magical. And it's going to be lovely.' Heather tried to keep the hunger out of her voice. The desire to have a little house all of her own, surrounded by blackberries and old roses, echoing to the sound of children's laughter and the cooing of pigeons, lodged like a lump in her throat. It was so unfair. So unfair.

Olivia worked the back door open to find a patch of mossy stone terrace, with self-seeded primroses in its cracks, and a wrought-iron table with four chairs. She had brought a cloth, a basin and a bottle of washing-up liquid, and she wiped them all down. They sat eating chunks of fresh bread and ripe, runny brie, turning their faces up to the autumn sunshine, and rolling up their trouser legs to catch its rays. Si opened a bottle of wine, and the children sat on a blanket, chattering and occasionally feeding bits of cheese to Travis when they thought no one was looking.

'I feel that the old man must have spent a lot of time out here in the back,' said Sasha when they'd finished the brie and the children had begun to play again. 'I can feel his spirit. There's a great sense of happiness here.' She stretched out her legs and hoicked up her skirt to catch the sun's rays. 'Must try and tan my legs. They're getting hideously white.' She closed her eyes, apparently in bliss.

Si looked at the long, honey-coloured limbs stretched out in front of him.

Sasha's mobile phone rang from her bag, and she jumped.

'I didn't think there was any reception out here?' queried Olivia.

'It's a satellite phone.' Sasha frowned. 'Yes? What? They're playing happily with some friends. You know how it always upsets them to talk to you. Oh, well, if you must. Grace! Grace!' She threw the phone at the children. 'It's your father,' she said, in tones of disdain.

Grace tentatively picked the phone up, looking nervous. 'Hello?' she whispered, turning away.

'Did you see her expression? There's no way she wants to talk to him,' declared Sasha, keeping her eyes fixed on Grace, who muttered something and handed the phone to Tom.

Tom walked towards the bushes, his back to Sasha. He returned a few minutes later and gave her back the phone.

'Well?' she asked. 'What did he want?'

'He's going to take me to a Chelsea match next Saturday. And Grace too.' He ran back to the others, joining their ball game.

'He bribes them,' said Sasha. 'Gives them amazing presents and takes them to places I couldn't possibly afford. I've tried to tell him that that's not parenting, that it's far more important for them to have the things they need first, like to go on school trips, for example, so that they can be with their friends and not miss out – they so much wanted to go on the last one, but no, he's got to be showy about it. It's always got to be his treat, not his responsibility.'

Heather thought Sasha was making a reasonable point, but wondered if she dared suggest that if she was a bit nicer to Adam, then he might be easier to deal with. And she couldn't help wondering why she had a satellite phone when she claimed to be so broke.

There was a shriek from Molly. 'The ball's gone into that shed thingy. It doesn't look safe.'

Si rose to his feet. 'OK, OK, I'm coming.'

'It's funny not having Kate here,' mused Olivia.

'Couldn't she come?' asked Heather.

Olivia, who always seemed so self-possessed, looked slightly embarrassed. 'Well, I haven't heard from her since I went to the police station for Callum. I realised, as I left, that I'd said something pretty tactless about her needing to take a bit more care of them now, and when she didn't call me, I kind of assumed she was in one of her snits with me. Which, as Si says, is probably not fair, but I did think she'd at least call and let me know how things were going.'

'Yes, wasn't it awful about Callum? So unfair. But Kate does seem a bit . . . well . . . relaxed about the boys and the way they behave,' ventured Heather, who was often shocked at the way Kate allowed Callum to just wander in and out of the house with his friends. She hardly seemed to know where he was half the time. Molly and Daisy were never going to roam the streets at fourteen, armed only with a mobile phone.

'I think she's been so busy she hasn't bothered with proper boundaries for them,' said Olivia, 'Also Si says she's worried about money so I thought I wouldn't . . . well . . . show off that I'd been left a house. I sort of thought that inviting her down would be rubbing her face in it. But she and Jonny will be able to borrow Providence Cottage any time they like when we've got it done up, and we'll be able to have great family weekends down here.'

'I'm not sure she'll like that,' said Sasha, in a wry voice.

Olivia looked surprised.

'I think Kate likes being at the centre of the family,' continued Sasha. 'Maybe the reason why you feel uneasy about inviting her down is that Providence Cottage is a potential rival to 19 Lovelace Road, and that's what Kate's going to find difficult.'

Neither Olivia nor Heather knew what to say to this.

'Of course, I'm not family, and perhaps I shouldn't have said anything. Forget it. Forget it.' Sasha fumbled for her packet of cigarettes and lit one, blowing the smoke away from them.

'If it wasn't for Kate, I don't think we'd have a family,' commented Heather. 'She holds us all together.'

'Kate's amazing,' said Olivia. 'She'll do anything to help anybody. When I broke my ankle, she came over every day to take me to wherever I needed to go or to drop off shopping. But the trouble with Kate is she's her own worst enemy. I don't think I ever really understood what that saying meant until I met her.'

'In what way?' asked Sasha.

'Oh,' Olivia looked evasive. 'I think she expects everyone to give as much as she does, and is then disappointed when they don't.'

'She likes to be in control,' said Sasha. 'It's her way of keeping people where she wants them. Not too close. I think Kate has real problems with intimacy.'

'I think you're wrong,' replied Olivia. 'Kate has a great gift for friendship.'

Heather hoped that this wasn't going to deteriorate into an open argument. She hated confrontation. 'Anyway,' she changed the subject. 'Are you going to get an architect in to see what you can do with this, or are you going to do it all yourselves?'

'Oh, Si will never let me employ an architect. It'll be a straight-forward renovation, nothing fancy.' The three women sat in silence for a while, Heather enjoying the feel of the sun on her face after what seemed like a long, dismal summer.

'How's their relationship? Kate and Jonny's, I mean.' Sasha blew cigarette smoke out of her nose.

'Kate and Jonny are very solid together,' said Olivia, in a warn-ing voice.

'Good. That's good.' Sasha sounded uncertain. 'Because . . . well, there's something I thought perhaps I ought to tell someone, but I'm not sure who. It's just that . . .'

Heather leant forward. 'Yes?'

'Got it!' There was a shout from Si and the ball came flying across, nearly knocking the wine bottle over. 'There's actually a greenhouse underneath all that vegetation,' said Si, dusting himself down, and coming back to the table to pour himself another drink. 'Completely collapsed, of course. Are you driving, darling?'

'I'd probably better, hadn't I?' Olivia raised her eyebrows. 'Sasha. You were saying . . .'

Sasha stubbed the cigarette out, grinding it against the mossy stone beneath their feet and flicking it into the brambles. She shot a warning look at Heather and Olivia. Not for Si, said her expres-sion. This is not for Kate's brother to hear.

'Si, would you mind getting another bottle of fizzy water from the car?' Olivia waved an empty plastic bottle at him.

He plumped himself down on a chair with a groan and passed her another one from under his seat. 'There's some here. Look, my hands are cut to ribbons. Getting into those brambles was like doing battle with barbed wire.'

'Si, those cuts are terrible . . .' Sasha's voice was like silk rustling, as she took his hands in one of hers and turned them tenderly over. 'We must wash them, come on in and let me help you . . . the tap in the kitchen has water.'

Olivia and Heather looked at each other. Neither of them said anything. Heather opened her mouth to ask Olivia if . . . well, what could she ask? Better not to say anything. Safer that way.

'I think we should be going soon,' said Heather. 'Sasha said she had to be back in London by six-thirty.'

Chapter 17

After they waved goodbye to Heather, Sasha and the children, Olivia and Si went back to the sunny terrace and sat down again.

Olivia had fallen in love. With Providence Cottage. From its stone front doorstep, unevenly worn down by two hundred years of footsteps to the overgrown garden, with its birdsong and brambles. She planned to keep it simple – just waxed floorboards and lime-washed walls with the bare minimum of furniture. Olivia planned to take it slowly, maybe learning how to do some of it herself. She let her eye run across the cobwebbed window panes, her euphoria barely punctured by the uneven mossy roof, which looked as if it might slide down into the guttering at any moment, and the patches of visible damp on the walls. It could all be fixed. She sighed with happiness.

'I don't know,' said Si, following her gaze 'it would be easier to just send it to auction.'

'What?'

'Just teasing.' He put his hand out and squeezed hers.

Olivia laughed. 'I think I'd rather send you to auction. If you're going to be like that.'

Si smiled back. 'I'd fetch a fortune. Don't you think? One solvent husband, clean, house-trained . . .'

'And so modest, too.' But she was joking. 'Look, those dark purple berries are elderberries. We can make our own elderberry wine.'

'Or we could buy Chateau Lafitte from a wine merchant. Which would be much cheaper if you cost out our time.'

'I don't always want to be costing out my time,' said Olivia.

He raised an eyebrow. 'But that's the way it is. You can't get away from it.'

'I could here.'

'Olivia, my darling,' he leant forward towards her. 'You've always had such a privileged life. I don't think you realise how tough things can get.'

'Your life hasn't exactly been hard,' she flashed back. 'Nice Home Counties upbringing . . . lovely family,' she added, quickly, because she remembered he never liked to talk about his parents' home. Not smart enough, he thought, not after seeing where a few of his university friends had been brought up. She rushed on: 'A top university. A top job.'

'Yes, I know. But the last two of those I did myself. By working hard. Costing out my time, if you like. And if I hadn't done that and been there, I wouldn't have got the jobs I got. I wouldn't be number three at R&R, jetting around the world and we wouldn't even be able to think about a second home or smart holidays. Or living in a huge apartment with a gym, swimming pool and underground parking.'

'I've earned some of it too, you know.'

'And inherited some more, I know,' he put a hand out. 'One of the things that's great about us is that we don't argue about money. We both earn. And you had some anyway. We don't say "this is mine" and "that is yours". But apart from your various inheritances, we do both earn it all, and that means costing out our time.'

Olivia knew that, technically speaking, he was right. But she wanted more. Not more money . . . more something else. It was like a pain under her breastbone. Something was missing. But that was a spoilt, selfish thing to say.

But she thought she might find whatever it was she was looking for here, at Providence Cottage.

She knew that confronting Si wasn't the way to win the argument, though, so she backed off. 'Let's find a local pub for a meal this evening,' she suggested.

'If there was some signal I'd download some reviews,' fretted Si. 'We don't want any old dreadful pub-grub muck, do we?'

Olivia braced herself for an evening of driving round twisty lanes, checking out menus and then deciding that what was on offer wasn't good enough before setting off into the dark again, but they were both surprised to find that the Bishop's Arms, just half a mile down the road, would have passed muster in the most demanding part of West London.

'This looks all right,' said Si, cautiously, and she saw him clocking a couple of expensive cars in the car park. 'Although I don't suppose the food will stand up to close scrutiny.'

'It's got an entry in the *Good Food Guide*,' noted Olivia from a sticker on the door.

A glass of excellent claret, followed by rack of 'local marsh-reared lamb and its sweetbreads' cheered Si up. 'I wonder if many people live round here,' he mused.

'I expect there are a few.' By people, Olivia knew he meant People. Movers and shakers. People with a capital 'P' who might be useful some day, who could give him an edge in some way or make him feel part of the club. The club that he'd discovered when a suburban scholarship boy had found himself adrift amongst the scions of the richest and most influential people in the land.

Her mobile chimed, and she rummaged about in her bag.

'Hi? Heather?'

'Oh, you're back in range again. I'm so glad. Thank you so much for today. We all loved Providence Cottage, and you'll make it lovely . . .'

Olivia knew this wasn't what Heather had phoned to say.

'Sasha has told me about Jonny and Kate,' Heather continued, 'that she . . .' the rest of Heather's words were muffled in static.

'Hang on, the reception's dodgy . . .' Olivia moved around, and found a good spot just outside, facing a garden and an orchard with hundreds of neat rows of apple trees, all dotted with pink apples. 'That's better. Tell me again.'

'Jonny's doing a pilot for a TV series called *How To Be Rich And Famous*. And Sasha's working on it.'

'Sasha's working on it? But she knows nothing about TV.'

'She says she put the idea of the series to Jonny, and he's letting her do the research and some of the interviewing, because she's using friends, and they're more comfortable talking to someone they know. Although she'll probably be cut out of the final interviews, they'll just show the people talking.'

'Well, good for her,' muttered Olivia. 'But how does this affect Kate?'

'He hasn't told her about it, and he's asked Sasha not to either.'

'Why?' asked Olivia. 'Why does it have to be such a secret? Is there something else he's hiding?'

'I don't know,' said Heather. 'Do you think we ought to tell her?'

The rest of the weekend was spent sweeping and scrubbing, deciding which pieces of furniture could only be taken to the tip, and which might live again, with a little repair.

'All this chest of drawers needs is a lick of paint,' said Si.

'Oh, not paint,' said Olivia. 'We'll just clean it up. I like things to look worn.'

'Nothing in the flat looks worn,' replied Si, puzzled. 'It all looks like a catalogue for a modern furniture showroom. That's what I like about it.'

'That's the flat. It's different.' Olivia opened the drawers, and took out a few neatly folded shirts. 'And, anyway, the flat does *not* look like a furniture showroom.' She laid a pair of tattered cord trousers on top of the pile. 'It's so sad, isn't it, just his last few clothes. I don't suppose he ever wanted me to go through them, it seems so personal and he was such a private man.' For a moment, she could sense Uncle Malcolm in the room, and for the first time she thought she could remember his smile as well as his irascible manner. It was comforting, as if he'd left her the house because he cared. Or because he knew she would care.

She made a neat pile of his clothes on the bed for the charity shop and consigned others to the black plastic bag. At the back of her mind was Heather's conversation about Jonny and Sasha. She hadn't told Si yet. She was trying to work out what they should do. If Si got all protective – and he might – he could blow it all open with a furious phone call to Jonny. She sighed.

'What's up?'

She opened her mouth to say something, then thought better of it. 'Nothing.'

'Well, as long as it's nothing I've done.'

She put her arms round him and hugged him tightly. 'No. You are being the very, very best husband in the world. Beyond the best.' She kissed him. 'I love you very much, you know.'

'Silly girl.' But he kissed her back, with increasing passion.

She wriggled out of his grasp. 'Here, let's get this place properly cleaned up and sorted out before we . . .'

It wasn't until they were driving home late on Sunday evening that the subject came up again.

'Spit it out,' said Si. 'You're worrying about something. I know you.'

'Kate.'

'What about her?'

'If I tell you, do you promise not to ring Kate – or Jonny – or breathe a word to anyone until we've all decided what the best thing to do is?'

'For God's sake. What do you think I am? Don't you trust me?'

Olivia was surprised by the sudden flash of irritation. 'Of course I trust you, it's just that . . .'

'That what?'

'Well, Kate is your sister, and you're not always logical about her. Quite naturally.'

'I can't believe this. You're filtering information about my own sister. I am a grown-up, you know, I can make these decisions for myself.'

'Yes, I know you can.' Olivia tried not to snap. 'It's just that . . . well, Jonny is making a pilot for a television series, and he's using Sasha as a researcher-cum-interviewer, and he hasn't told Kate.'

'Well? I don't suppose he tells her everything about his work.'

'Perhaps not, but this strikes me as pretty important.' The traffic slowed as they entered London, and they were now edging from roundabout to roundabout. 'If they're not talking about projects like this, then what else aren't they talking about?'

'I don't know. He must have his reasons.'

'It's his reasons I'm worried about. Suppose it's not just work?'

'If Sasha's worried about it, why doesn't she tell Kate herself?'

'I asked Heather that, and she says that Sasha feels that Kate doesn't like her. You know what Kate's like when she takes against someone. The term "death stare" doesn't even come close. Although I thought she was friendly with Sasha – she always seems to be round there, so I'm not quite sure where the problem is.'

Si grunted. 'I think Sasha's become Heather's friend, really, not Kate's. But Kate's been really welcoming to Sasha. Mainly for Heather's sake, I think, from something she said.'

'So Kate *doesn't* like her, then? She's obviously put the fear of God into her.'

'Kate can handle it. And so can Sasha, for that matter.'

'I do feel a bit sorry for Sasha, though,' mused Olivia, 'because Kate overreacts sometimes. She barely spoke to me for months because I had to drop out of lunch over Allison Green's cat. After that, there was no communication between us at all until she asked me to help with Callum. And she's never rung and thanked me.'

'Olivia,' Si took his eyes off the road for a moment to look at her. 'Has it ever occurred to you that everything you're accusing Kate of – overreacting, building things from nothing, being chilly – they're all things that you yourself are equally guilty of?'

'That's ridiculous,' said Olivia. 'You're exaggerating. As usual.'

'I do *not* exaggerate.'

'Well, Kate sulks. You all do, it's in the family. You probably don't even know you do it.'

'If something upsets us,' Si's voice dropped ominously low, 'we go quiet for a bit and think about it. We don't go rushing in accusing people of things. If you choose to call that sulking, then perhaps you should be thinking about the way you handle things that upset you. Anyway I think you're reading too much into it all. Kate wasn't in a sulk with you, and there's no reason why Jonny shouldn't keep some things a secret from her.'

'So, if you were working with Sasha, you'd keep it a secret, would you?'

'No,' he pressed his foot on the accelerator, and they jerked out in front of a white van. It hooted furiously. 'Bastard!' shouted Si.

'Si, be careful! We nearly had an accident.' They got into the right lane, and Olivia returned to the subject. 'Si, are you serious? What sort of things do you keep from me?'

'I don't keep anything from you. I'm just saying that there are circumstances when it might be reasonable if I did. And when did this become about me? *You* get a phone call from Heather, you hug it to yourself all weekend, and then you accuse *me* of keeping secrets.'

Olivia almost laughed. 'I wasn't keeping it a secret. I just wanted to think about how I should tell you, in case you got very protective about Kate, you know how you do.'

'So, as I said before, you filter information.' Si's mouth set in a tight line. 'That's keeping secrets, as far as I'm concerned. Olivia, you can't have it both ways. Either we have an open, trusting relationship, and you tell me everything immediately, or you don't trust me and you decide what information I'm to have and when. Even if it's about my own sister.'

'I don't quite see why you're getting so angry about it . . .'

'I am not getting angry.' Si stamped on the brake as they reached a red light, and Olivia jerked forward in her seat.

They sat in silence as Lewisham, then Camberwell, slowly slid past.

'Is this really about the house?' asked Olivia, eventually. 'Do you really not want Providence Cottage?'

'Now how did you get to that?' Si sounded exasperated. 'I have no objection to us having Providence Cottage. If it makes you happy, that's fine by me.'

'I think I need it to be more than "fine by you". I need to know that it's best thing for *us*. Is it the money? Because we do earn enough, and I'm sure that in the end it'll be a good investment. Or is it something else?'

'Fine by us, then.' Si's voice showed his irritation. 'Fine by *us*.'

Olivia looked out of the window and noted that a particularly good butcher had closed down.

'Only . . .'

Aha. He was finally getting to the point of telling her what he really thought. Olivia fumed. How he could accuse her of keeping things to herself she couldn't imagine, because there were layers to Si, and he rarely revealed them to anyone, not even her.

'Only that we'll obviously be out of London most weekends from now on.'

They finally arrived at the underground garage below their flat. Si parked in their space and switched the engine off. 'And that will mean a different sort of lifestyle,' he continued. 'Having what we need – clothes, toothbrushes, files from work – in the place where we aren't. Not being able to accept invitations. Not quite keeping up with the gym. Trying to find good builders and electricians when we aren't there to supervise them. Worrying about security in the place we're not at. Pipes freezing. All that. The trouble with you is you don't think things through. Even this journey' – he looked at his watch – 'has taken us just over two hours. That's four hours out of every weekend. Sixteen hours a month. That adds up to eight days a year. Spent in the car. It's not just a question of doing some decorating and having a few idyllic lunches in the sunshine.'

'Of course I think things through. Those are exactly the things I've been thinking about all weekend. And the journey down there on Saturday wasn't two hours, it was nearer an hour and a half. We'll learn to travel out of rush hours. And it won't be every weekend, if we get a good invitation we can . . .' She began to unload the boot, piling her arms high. You don't think things through indeed!

'I am pretty competent,' she said, over an armful of picnic rugs and baskets. 'I would have thought you might have noticed that, after being with me for over twenty years. I am quite capable of finding builders and making sure we have toothbrushes in the right place and that we don't leave our knickers in Kent.'

'Good,' he said, evenly. 'Just so long as you realise it's all going to be a lot of work, that's all.'

'OK.' Olivia turned the key in their lock.

Si sank down on one of the sofas with a sigh of relief. 'Home,' he said, sounding less hassled. 'There's nothing like it.'

'Si,' she said gently, sitting down beside him. 'I do see what you mean about the problems, and you're right in a way, because I hadn't absolutely *finished* thinking it all through, and hadn't quite got to the pipes freezing bit, but I do think it'll work, and that it's just what we need – as long as we're in it together.'

He smiled, and drew her to him. 'You're probably right. I just didn't want to feel we had to spend all our holidays there, and I do like to travel.' He kissed the top of her head. 'But let's give this Providence Cottage business a try, shall we?'

'Meanwhile,' she added, 'what do we do about Kate and Jonny? Do you think you should have a quiet word with Jonny about Sasha?'

'No.' He gave her a firm look. 'We do absolutely nothing. And you should not – and I mean that – *not* discuss it with anyone else. It's between Kate and Jonny and that is that.'

Olivia would like to have added that she was beginning to find this friendship between Sasha and Heather – who couldn't be more different – very odd indeed. But obviously no one else thought so and she didn't want to cause any trouble.

Chapter 18

Sasha thought it was unfair. Olivia had everything. Some people did, effortlessly. Like her so-called brothers and sisters. The other Mortons. The ones who belonged, who Roderick Morton, her famous so-called father hadn't rejected, like he rejected her.

Sasha had been born Sandra, and had spent most of her life in a ground-floor flat in Battersea with her mother Janet.

Janet had met Roderick Morton at the height of his fame as an artist, when he was married, with a young son, Richard. Janet had been his model. When she got pregnant Roderick explained that he had to stay with his wife Margaret. She was pregnant too, he told Janet – a drunken mistake after a party, he couldn't leave her now.

But he did. He ran off with Lucy, married her and had two more children by her. They had ridiculous names: Lalla and Jasper. Lalla was a month younger than Sandra was.

'He was fucking us all,' said Janet, over and over again to Sandra, who was too young to understand what she meant. 'Me and Margaret and Lucy. All at once. He told me his marriage was a loveless one, that he'd only married her because she was mad on him and she had a bit of money so he could paint. Then Lucy had a lot more money, so he went off with her. I never had a chance. I didn't have money, you see.'

It never occurred to Sandra to ask her mother why anyone would want to marry a man who was so blatantly unfaithful. Lucy had married him, after all, and Lucy was the Honourable Lucy, a dazzling society beauty. Sandra made it her business, as she grew up, to find out as much about Lucy as she could. It was Lucy who had stolen her father – if she hadn't existed he would of course have left Margaret and married her mother and they would have been a proper family, with all the privileges that Lalla and Jasper now enjoyed.

The gossip columns had loved it. Roderick Morton had three daughters born to different mothers within six months of each other: Elizabeth, Sandra and Lalla. It had been a *News of the World* scandal. But Roderick stayed with Lucy, and a year later, the ridiculously named Jasper was born.

Richard and Elizabeth, known as Ricky and Eliza, had the status of having been a family, they had a comfortable house, the reflected fame of their father and a well-off mother. Lalla and Jasper had a mother and father who lived together, loved each other and had a nice terraced house in Chelsea where Ricky and Eliza spent alternate weekends. Soon everyone forgot that there was another daughter. Whenever Roderick Morton did an interview he referred to his 'four children'.

But Sandra had nothing. While the other Morton children coalesced as an irregular, but real, family, Roderick's fathering of Sandra was restricted to paying for the flat in Battersea – on the other side of the river – and a small allowance. He never visited. It was a condition of the money, Janet had told her, with careless cruelty, that there be no contact at all between them. Sasha had grown up as the daughter without a father, the sister without brothers or sisters, the one in the middle, the one who was left out. The one who never had Christmas with her father, and was never invited to family weddings. She made carefully worded allusions to 'having grown up with an artist as a father' and 'her bohemian background' because Janet had at least insisted that Sandra carry the Morton name, which the adult Sasha worked into conversation whenever she could. What she didn't say was that she had barely met him.

He died when she was sixteen, and she had not been mentioned in any of the copious obituaries of 'one of Britain's greatest contemporary figurative painters'. The gossip columns, yellowing with age, had kept their secrets. Sandra had changed her name to Sasha and vowed to become someone who wasn't left out.

Her mother had never got over her bitterness about Lucy. 'If I'd lived in a smart house, like Lucy did, if I'd had a bit of money behind me, like Lucy had, your father would have married *me*,' she intoned, over and over again. 'I was every bit as good as she was, but people judge you on what you've got. Never forget that, Sandra. Never forget it.'

And Sasha hadn't. Standing next to Olivia, surrounded by everything Olivia had – a family, two beautiful homes, friends – she was reminded of everything she had lost, once again, because of another woman. Natalie had taken Adam from her, and with Adam her beautiful home had gone, and the lifestyle – the dinner parties and holidays with other couples. Natalie had taken everything, just as Lucy had. Women had no sense of loyalty to each other. They simply took. That was why Sasha had to fight to get it all back again. And fight she had. She smiled grimly.

So she thought about taking Si from Olivia. She had tested him when Olivia and Heather had left them alone upstairs, like someone inserting the tip of a knife under a tight lid. How easy would it be to work him free? Si was a wealthy man. And attractive – he was always so perfectly judged, almost like someone modelling the role of successful executive, with his touch of grey at the temples and handmade shoes. Sasha had tried to work out what Si must earn in a year, and Olivia, too. And Sasha's finely attuned antennae had also picked up that, although they had everything they could possibly want, something was missing. Everyone talked about how great they were together, but Sasha thought that there were tiny cracks running through the edifice of their perfect lives. She'd watched people for too long – she'd spent all her life on the outside, watching – and she could always spot the weaknesses.

'You seem to know a lot about houses,' she had murmured, looking up at him as they stood amidst the bare boards and peeling wallpaper of Providence Cottage.

'I know enough to recognise a money pit when I see it.'

'But money's not everything, is it?' She moved fractionally closer to him.

Si looked down at her. She could smell the lemon, lavender and sandalwood of his aftershave. 'I love Acqua di Parma,' she added, softly. 'Cary Grant used to wear it. He was such a sexy man, don't you think?' She saw an answering pulse in Si's neck, ticking away faster.

'Clever girl,' he said. 'To recognise it.' She thought his voice sounded hoarse. She knew he could smell her own fine, rare scent, Narcisse Noir. It was a vintage fragrance and she always wore it, because it started fresh and sparkly, then lingered on her skin, like silk pyjamas and sex.

'Oh, I always recognise the best,' she added, almost in a whisper, so that he had to bend towards her to pick up her words. She let her lips linger dangerously close to his for a fraction too long, and touched his arm in a caress. 'Like this sweater. You really deserve to be on the best-dressed list.'

And then, before his lips could touch hers, she turned to join the others. Keep him guessing. At the door, she looked over her shoulder. 'Are you coming?'

She thought she heard him exhale as she left the room.

Oh, yes, Si Fox, you are as vulnerable as any other man.

But what about love? Could you have the man you loved and all the money in the world? It was a dilemma. Sasha knew that she would have to choose. Quite soon.

Chapter 19

Kate began actively monitoring Callum. 'All I ask,' she said, 'is that we sit down together at supper in the evening and talk. We've got into the habit of picking at things whenever we're hungry, and sometimes I barely talk to you for days on end. I'm not going to ask you to break any confidences or tell me any secrets, but I do want to hear something about your day.'

Callum looked alarmed, but agreed. Luke was excited. 'I really like us eating together, Mummy.'

However the boys were always hungry by six and Jonny never got back until at least eight. Kate decided to eat with them, and leave Jonny's for him to heat up when he got in. After all, if she had to choose between her sons and Jonny – well, Luke and Callum only had her, but Jonny was at least an adult who could look after himself. He seemed happy with the arrangement.

She insisted that they had Sunday lunch all together like a proper family, Luke bubbling with enthusiasm about his football game, and even Callum conceding that he'd quite liked the film he'd seen the night before. Jonny teased them gently, and listened to what they had to say. Kate had studied all their faces with something approaching happiness. She'd been so proud of them. She loved them all so much.

But otherwise, watching television became the only thing Jonny and she did together. That Monday evening they were both watching a programme that claimed to lift the lid on the steel industry.

'It's like all these programmes,' muttered Kate. 'It goes over and over the same points, makes the odd outrageous statement without backing it up and, in the end, doesn't really tell you anything new if you were at all knowledgeable in the first place. Why *are* TV documentaries these days so useless?'

'If you know so much about it,' Jonny drained the last of the red wine into his glass, 'then perhaps you should start making proper programmes for a change, rather than fannying about with the odd commission.'

'What?' Kate sat up. Jonny had never, ever criticised her work before. He'd always listened to the programmes, and made a few comments, mostly positive. When he wasn't, it was usually soundly based, and after initially feeling indignant, she'd always seen his point. 'Everyone says my stuff is fresh. Funny. Different.'

Jonny shrugged. 'They have to say something, don't they? But you can't be a dilettante in this business.'

'Well, you can't talk. You've lost more programmes than you've won recently.' She regretted the words as soon as they were out of her mouth.

Jonny got up, put his plate and glass in the dishwasher and went upstairs.

Kate tried to concentrate on clearing up, but it was pointless. Jonny and she were on different planets now. She turned off the television and went upstairs. The light in the box room Jonny used as an office was still on, and Jonny was staring at the screen.

Kate swallowed. 'I'm sorry,' she said. 'I shouldn't have said that. Your . . . work is very good.'

'That's OK.' He continued to scroll down.

'Jonny, I know we're both worried, but it doesn't help if we get at each other.' She put a hand on his shoulder. 'Please let's tackle this together, not by sniping at each other.'

He swung round but failed to meet her eyes. 'I'm sure you're right.' He looked at his watch. 'It's getting late. I'll just read my last email and switch off this machine. I'll be with you in a minute.'

'And Callum. I've been doing some research. He needs a male role model at this point in his life. More than anything.'

'He also needs a roof over his head.' Jonny's face was still a blank. 'And please don't research our son as if he were a radio programme. Life isn't that simple.'

'I know it's not.' Kate tried to keep her voice calm and steady, suppressing the pathetic cry *I'm only trying to do my best.* Jonny, too, was trying to do his best. It was a pity their bests didn't seem to be intersecting.

She waited for him to come to bed, gazing at the meaningless pages of a book she had already read before. It was an hour and a half before Jonny came in, and she then lay awake listening to him sleep. The six inches between his slumbering body and hers felt like a chasm. Perhaps everything would get better once this pilot had been made for the BBC – whatever it was, he'd been characteristically vague about it.

The frustrating thing about Jonny was that he would never argue. If Kate tried to get him to talk about anything – anything that mattered – he'd withdraw behind an absent-minded, if kindly, smile. He'd bury his head in whatever he was reading or working at, making Kate feel as if she were pounding on a plate glass window with Jonny on the other side, not hearing anything she said.

But maybe he had a point. She turned over again in bed. Perhaps she should get on with this proposal about figurative artists in the twentieth century? It was a bit more heavyweight than 'personality and punctuality'. Although it had started as a way of finding out about Sasha, it could be quite a hot programme. Picasso had started as a figurative artist, after all – he had been superb at drawing, which was why his later paintings worked. But did today's artists have that underlying discipline? Had shock value obscured the real talent in the twentieth century? Or had people gone on buying what they liked in spite of the headlines and the critics? At two-thirty in the morning Kate got out of bed and tiptoed into her office to make some notes.

She started the week exhausted, and it went on like that. She went to a parents' evening at Callum's school on Monday, and was told that Callum could try harder, a view that Callum firmly refuted. 'They're all wankers, Mum.'

'But Callum, it's your GCSEs next year and I don't want you to fail them.'

'I won't.'

'You will if you don't do any work.'

He lifted the Game Boy, and that was that. Kate had promised to ring someone back that evening about some local planning application, so she had no more time to talk. She also managed to get hold of Jasper Morton, who agreed to be interviewed on the subject of his book about his father. On Tuesday she went to a private view of an interesting artist – could be useful for the possible programme on the figurative artists of the twentieth century – then dinner with her book group on Wednesday. There were three committee meetings for various charities or networking groups on various mornings, plus the need to get her proposals ready for the next commissioning round, in between school runs, shopping and trying to stop the house falling apart. It was dispiriting, researching and writing without knowing whether the programme would actually be made or not. On Thursday, after dropping Luke at school, she propped herself up with several slices of toast and marmalade and, feeling weighed down, lumbered upstairs to bed. Intending to make it.

Instead she clambered in and pulled the covers over her head, only to be woken an hour later by a mobile ringing somewhere. It was Jonny's ring tone, not hers. She scrabbled around, under the pillows, through a pile of clothes, under the bedside table, even under the mattress, and finally, just as it stopped, she caught sight of it right under the bed.

Jonny, Jonny, you are so untidy. Heaven knows when he'd lost it. She scrabbled around and retrieved it. It showed several missed calls. All from the same number. She had seen that number before. She had stored it in her mobile phone because sometimes, if she wanted to get hold of Heather but got no answer, she'd try Sasha instead, in case she was with her.

But maybe she was wrong. She scuffled around in her bag, eventually finding her mobile in her jeans pocket. It only took a few moments for her to compare its call history with Jonny's. It was indeed Sasha. Of course. Scrolling through the call history, he had called her four times that weekend alone, and she had called him three times. At ten-thirty on Sunday evening, and then again, half an hour after that, at eleven. Just when she was waiting for him to 'finish a few emails and come to bed'. Then a call also on

141

Monday, during the day.

Perhaps Sasha had left something behind at the office when she was doing work experience. Perhaps she needed a reference, or some advice.

But you wouldn't call someone about work at eleven o'clock at night, would you?

Kate sat down, suddenly feeling too shaken to stand. She must do something. She knew she ought to wait until Jonny came home, but she was no good at waiting. She always had to know *now*. She grabbed her coat and bag, and as she closed the door behind her, she looked back at 19 Lovelace Road.

Suppose Jonny was having an affair with Sasha? In that case, they must split. She had always said so. Kate could survive. She always had.

But Callum and Luke might not. They needed their father, particularly now, if they were to grow up into strong, happy men. She remembered what it had been like for Jack losing his father at that age. She wouldn't inflict it on her sons if she could help it.

And they needed a home. It was an important part of their security. If Jonny and Kate split, then they would have to sell up. The house of cards would come tumbling down – mortgages would have to be repaid and credit card bills paid off. It would be her father's death all over again – the new schools, the tiny house, the desperate worry about whether there would be enough money to eat or pay heating bills – all over again. She realised she was shivering with fear.

The phone rang. It was Olivia. Kate hardly heard what she was saying and put the phone down on her as soon as possible. She got on the bus into town, visualising the wreckage of her life after Jonny admitted seeing Sasha. Callum's sullen, confused face and the faces of his teachers, blaming them for his behaviour. Luke's enthusiasm and laughter disappearing into a monosyllabic adolescence. Two homes, both tiny. Children shuffling between them. Anger and recrimination, as Callum and Luke stood on the threshold of adulthood. How could she teach them how to live if she didn't know herself?

As she stood outside the narrow terraced house in Soho and

pressed the bell marked Future TV, she thought of Sasha's life the way it was now, measured out in court appearances over access, her bitterness and her furniture stacked up in Heather's dining room as her home was sold to another family. That life might soon be Kate's.

She climbed the narrow stairway with its sagging, polished treads, and dived into the cluttered cupboard of a loo on the half-landing to try to calm down. Her face, in the small, dusty mirror, looked like a potato. She leant her forehead against the cool glass as her whole being froze in terror. Should she turn back, and pretend that nothing had happened?

Ah, but you're no good at pretending either, Kate, said the face in the mirror. You never have been. You think of Jonny's bare skin against hers and you can't bear it. You can't stay silent.

Not even to save everything you hold dearest to your heart? Think, Kate Fox, think. Think of your family. It is up to you to keep it together. You can't rely on Jonny any more. You only have yourself.

She squared her shoulders and opened the door of Jonny's office.

Meera, one of the edit assistants, looked alarmed. She jumped up, which in itself was unusual. A tired glance upwards was all Kate usually got when she visited the office.

'Kate, how lovely to see you. Would you like a cup of something . . . or can I take your coat?' She tried to stand between Kate and her view of Jonny's desk. Kate brushed past her and stood over Jonny. He looked so happy, leaning back in his chair, running his hand through his hair. She hadn't seen him enjoy himself that much in so long.

'Yeah. Yeah.' Another laugh. 'That's good, that's good,' he said.

He looked up. 'Hey, I've got someone in the office. I'll call you back later.' He put the phone down and looked at her curiously. 'Hey, Katie. I didn't know you were coming up.' He seemed easier in the office, with none of the repressed anger that emanated from him at home. And older. Everyone at Future TV, except Jonny and his partner Alan, was in their early twenties. Nearly half Jonny's age.

She still had time to turn back. To pretend not to know

anything. If pretending would save your life, would you do it, Kate? Could you do it?

'I've got your mobile,' she said, handing it over. 'You left it under the bed.'

'Thanks. You didn't need to come all this way.'

She took a deep breath. 'And I wanted to know why Sasha is calling you three or four times a day.'

His eyes met hers. 'Not here,' he said, standing up and shrugging on his jacket. 'Come on. Let's go out for coffee.'

Chapter 20

Heather woke up with a prickle of fright crawling down her spine. The bedroom door was open, and she was sure she'd shut it.

She forced herself to turn on the light, and found Travis, who was never allowed upstairs, shivering beside her bed.

She got up, noting that the clock said 3 a.m. 'Travis!' She seized his collar, trying to drag him out of the room. 'Bad dog. Bed.'

Travis whined apologetically but flattened himself against the floor, and it was difficult to drag thirty kilos of dog in a direction it really didn't want to go. 'What's wrong, Travis?'

The dog let out a howl of melancholy and scuttled over to Jack's side of the bed, crouching down again, welding himself to the floor.

'Travis, come back! Bed! In your basket!'

Travis howled again. It was an unearthly sound, and Heather began to feel frightened. 'Sh, Travis.' She caressed his ears and tried to distract him. Could there be someone in the house?

But surely if that were the case Travis would bark, not howl? He made enough noise when the postman dropped the letters through the box. She looked around for a weapon, and not finding one, picked up the phone, then edged out on to the landing. If there was any noise from downstairs, Travis's keening was drowning it out.

The spare-room door opened and Sasha stood there. 'What is it?'

'I don't know. Travis has never done this before.'

'Do you think there might be someone trying to get in?' whispered Sasha.

'I'll go downstairs and check,' said Heather. 'You stay up here and dial 999 if I scream, or if I don't come back. Or if anything seems odd.'

She went downstairs slowly, one step at a time. It seemed very dark. But army patches relatively rarely suffered from burglary. You'd want easier pickings if you were a criminal, not to face men trained in combat, or the close relationships between the families.

But not all the houses were army now. That sense of their wagons being drawn up in a circle had almost gone. She felt her way to the light switch and snapped it on. The hall looked normal. So did the sitting room. And the kitchen. None of the doors and windows had been opened. Nothing outside. She squinted outside but only saw blackness, and her own reflection. Her heartbeat slowed and she exhaled more easily. By the time she had got back upstairs again, she'd convinced herself that nothing was wrong.

But Travis let out another unearthly howl. Heather jumped. 'Travis!' she hissed. 'Bad dog!'

'Fireworks, do you think?' Sasha sounded frightened.

'I haven't heard any.'

'Well, we can't hear anything with that noise going on. I'm amazed the children haven't woken up.' They went into Heather's bedroom.

'You're very brave,' said Sasha. 'I couldn't bear to go downstairs.'

'I've had to be. I'm in the army. Even just as a wife.'

'It's rather creepy, isn't it?' They both looked at Travis, the picture of dejection, apparently locked into a cycle of whimpering, whining, and then building up to an unearthly howl, before dropping away again.

'Do you think he senses something we don't?' asked Sasha.

Heather thought of Jack, and suddenly knew he was in danger. It had never occurred to her before that he might be, but she knew now, as surely as if she'd already had the visit from a Casualty Visiting Officer. The certainty lodged like a splinter of ice in her heart.

'It's Jack,' she said, jumping into bed and pulling the duvet up. 'He's . . .' The words stuck in her throat.

'Nonsense,' said Sasha, getting into bed beside her and grasping Heather's hand. 'When I said "senses something we don't" I didn't mean some kind of extrasensory perception beamed halfway across the world from Temanistan. I meant "senses something we don't" from outside in the road.'

Heather shook her head, sick with terror. She patted the duvet beside her, and although Travis was never, ever allowed on the bed, he jumped up and buried his face in her lap. The howling dropped to a low, mournful whine.

'I'll make us both a cup of tea,' declared Sasha.

'They'll come in the morning to tell me. As soon as it's light,' whispered Heather. 'They don't wake you up in the middle of the night now. They used to, apparently.' Odd facts whirled round her head as panic flooded her system.

'No, they won't,' said Sasha fiercely. 'Travis is only a stupid dog. He has no idea what's going on in Temanistan. Something must have frightened him – maybe there was someone skulking around outside or a noise in the distance – and he's come upstairs for company.'

'Travis isn't like that. He just barks.'

'Well, he hasn't got a hotline to Jack's regiment, that much I can tell you.'

Heather barely heard her.

Sasha went to the window and pulled aside the curtain, watching the road. The trees swayed slightly in the wind, and the noise of distant traffic drifted into the room.

'It's lovely here, isn't it? So peaceful,' mused Sasha. 'You do get nice houses in the army.'

'This is the best we've ever had, I can assure you. This sort of thing usually goes to a full colonel, but it wasn't modernised so Jack got lucky. Hence the tin sink and sixties Formica units in the kitchen. And the one bathroom for five bedrooms. And the pebbledash on the front.'

'I love it. It's all so retro.'

Heather made a face, but it was easier thinking about the frustrations of a bathroom and kitchen that had last been modernised

147

fifty years ago than it was to wonder what might be happening to Jack.

They sat in bed, talking in whispers, until Sasha went back to her room at about four. Heather and Travis maintained their vigil. She thought about Jack, determined to keep him alive by the sheer force of her love. And then her thoughts drifted. Perhaps she should go downstairs and do some ironing.

Keep busy, Heather, keep busy. Or you'll remember.

But she was too tired to get up, and as her eyelids dropped, her mother came into the room, the hard lines around her mouth pursed in disapproval. *You needn't think you can get rid of me like that*, she said, blowing cigarette smoke in Heather's face.

Heather could still smell the smoke as she jerked awake. It must be Sasha. Perhaps she was still awake.

Heather tried to force herself to open her eyes properly, but she must have drifted off again because Mo Spencer was back. 'You're such a stupid girl,' said Mo, angrily. 'So stupid. Thinking that anyone will ever love you.'

Heather whimpered and raised an arm to defend herself against one of Mo's casual slaps. Travis nudged his muzzle against her and she held on tight. Mo never let her have a pet, but Heather clung on to Travis, determined not to let Mo take him away.

All through Heather's childhood, as she was moved from school to school, given a key to let herself in and make her own tea, or even left to wait outside on the doorstep for hour after hour, even when she'd reached the relative safety of the Caldecott, she had promised herself that when she had children she'd be there for them. She would play games and pick them up from school, watch their matches and never be too tired to talk. And most importantly, she would tell them she loved them, every day, and mean it. Not like Mo, who had alternately suffocated Heather with drunken tears when her latest man had treated her badly ('you're all I've got now, love, never ever leave me') with pushing her away ('don't whine near me, it don't suit you, and I'll call the social services and they'll take you away').

Heather snapped awake as Travis howled again. Mo was dead now. She couldn't hurt her.

But Mo was back, in Halstead Hill, in the half-light before

dawn, raising a hand to hit Heather again, as she'd done so often. Heather struggled again to wake up, and finally, properly opened her eyes. It was only a dream.

She went downstairs to make tea, then got the children up for school, wearing her bright face. By the time Sasha came down, she was emptying the dishwasher and mopping the kitchen floor.

'Not long now,' she said. There was a knot in her stomach, one she remembered from her childhood. It was fear. 'They get messages to the family quite quickly. There'll be two of them. They send a man and a woman usually, that's all I know.'

'Nobody is coming,' declared Sasha. 'Jack is fine.'

For the next thirty-six hours, Heather went through the motions of living, pretending to be a mother on the school runs, smiling at all the other mothers, then picking the children up at the end of the day with the same false smile. She mentioned Travis's behaviour tentatively at one coffee morning, trying to make a joke of it. All the other wives instantly picked up on her anxiety and hastened to reassure her, but then the conversation turned into a series of anecdotes about dogs and cats that had apparently known when something was wrong, until Heather's pale face reminded everyone to change the subject. At one point she even rang the Unit Welfare Officer, who was kind but puzzled. No, he had heard of no problems in Temanistan.

In between the tasks Heather set herself, such as clearing out the attic, steam-cleaning the curtains and dusting the pelmets, she held a vigil over the telephone, quivering in fear.

'Hullo?' Heather seized it almost before it rang, and heard Olivia, sipping coffee, swallowing hastily.

'That was quick. It's Olivia here.'

'Oh.'

'Were you expecting someone else?'

'Er, not really . . . well, no.'

'I was just thinking about this whole business of Sasha, Jonny and Kate.'

'What?'

'Si says that the last thing we should do is talk to any of them . . . but surely, if the programme goes ahead, it will all be

149

made public anyway, and Kate will know that Jonny's been keeping things from her.'

'Mm.' Heather couldn't concentrate on whether Jonny was keeping secrets from Kate.

'Are you all right?'

'Fine. Fine.'

'I think it really lies with Sasha, don't you? Couldn't she just drop it into the conversation as if it didn't matter at all? I mean, she is very friendly with you all.'

'I don't think she wants to get involved in any arguments between Jonny and Kate. Not surprisingly. She says she doesn't want to be insensitive about things she may know nothing about.'

'I suppose that's fair enough. I wish she'd been a bit more sensitive about my not inviting Kate down to the cottage, though. She appears to have dropped it into conversation somehow and now Kate's clearly cross with me. Still, I expect it was an accident.'

'Oh, good,' said Heather vaguely, not having heard a word.

'Heather, what is going on?'

Heather told her about the night of Travis's howling, her voice trembling only slightly. 'He knows that something's happened to Jack. I know that he knows. But I should have heard by now.'

'Couldn't he have had indigestion or something? He's always swallowing the most extraordinary things. What about that time he ate the Christmas cake, complete with Father Christmas on top?'

'Do labradors get indigestion?'

'They must do. Anyway, it's much more likely than him knowing what's going on in Temanistan. And Jack's doing a desk job, isn't he? He's not technically in a war zone. What's Travis like now?'

'Happy as anything. Good breakfast. Tail wagging. Standing in my way every time I move because he wants me to take him for a walk.'

'Well, there you are then. Whatever was bothering him then obviously isn't a problem any more. And as you say, if Jack had been . . . hurt . . . at the time Travis was howling, you'd have heard by now. The army are very efficient about that sort of thing, I gather.'

150

'Yes, you're right.' Heather sounded brighter. 'I think I really would have heard by now. It's just that you know how I never worry about Jack, and now, suddenly, I am.'

'You don't consciously worry about him, but I think it must be quite a strain underneath it all,' said Olivia. 'It would be surprising if it didn't burst out somehow. But I don't think getting superstitious helps – and that's more or less what this is.'

'I hadn't thought of it like that. You are sensible.'

'So are you, most of the time. But no one can be sensible the whole time.'

When Heather put the phone down she felt so much better that she decided to go to the supermarket. The fridge was empty. Whenever she'd heard of anything like this everyone had been notified within six or seven hours. It was policy, so that wives and families always got the news officially, not through rumour or press reports. She looked at her watch. Travis had been howling at about three o'clock on Monday morning and it was now Tuesday lunchtime. No, Jack was safe.

Chapter 21

Leaving Jonny's office, Kate almost had to skip to keep up with his long stride, and she looked up to see him apparently lost in thought. They queued up behind two girls who had complicated orders for coffee and who couldn't speak much English. Kate felt like screaming at them.

'Cappuccino with skimmed milk?' asked Jonny, ordering himself an espresso.

Kate nodded.

Then they couldn't find a private table, and hovered while a group of mothers gathered up their possessions, strapped up their babies and made very slow progress out of the door, leaving their table littered with mugs, plates, crumbs, a pool of spilt milk and pieces of uneaten cake. Kate piled up the crockery and asked the staff to wipe the table. This took another three or four minutes, during which time Jonny gazed out of the window, obviously planning what he was going to say.

When they were finally settled, he swung round and took her hand. 'Katie.'

The unexpected touch weakened her. She knew the texture of his skin so very well.

'Katie,' he repeated, and she could hear tenderness in his voice. Or was it pity? 'Sasha often calls me because she's working on a programme for us.'

'But she knows nothing about making programmes.' Kate couldn't quite believe him.

'No, but she's had some good ideas, well – one good idea – and she's being tried out as one of the researchers on it.'

'What is it?'

He hesitated.

'For God's sake, Jonny, do you think I'd tell anyone?' Kate stopped. She knew she was often indiscreet. 'I wouldn't say anything, not when it comes to work.'

'She's come up with the idea of doing a programme called *How To Be Rich And Famous*, a reality TV show that combines financial advice with cheap ways of copying the celebrity lifestyle.'

'Celebrity!' exclaimed Kate. 'You said you'd never do celebrity.'

'This is different. We have to get the money in, Kate – shows that can be licensed out to lots of countries and which will run and run, would mean I could do the documentaries I want to do for the rest of the time. And it's a fun way of presenting financial advice – which is where Sasha comes in because she's a qualified accountant, so it ticks a few public service boxes.'

'I can see that,' conceded Kate. 'And you're right, it is a good idea. I wouldn't have thought she had it in her . . .' she stopped, catching sight of Jonny's expression. 'I suppose that you haven't told me about it because Sasha's involved? You wouldn't ordinarily keep projects a secret. Why is this different?'

Jonny stirred his coffee and avoided her gaze.

She didn't want to ask whether there was anything more in their relationship.

But she must. 'I admit that I wouldn't much have liked being told that she was working with you, but it's even worse to find that she was phoning you so often, and to think that . . . well, what am I expected to think? And why does she call at such weird times? Doesn't she understand that there are boundaries?'

'She's insecure,' he said.

'What about me feeling insecure?' flashed Kate. 'Doesn't that matter? How I might feel?'

'I do care about how you might feel. Which is why I hoped to get us through the early stages without involving you.'

'We shouldn't keep secrets from each other. That's more important than anything.'

'And she's working through her scripts when she can,' Jonny

153

added, 'which means when the kids are in bed. She's inexperienced and needs guidance. I thought I'd tell you once the programme was definitely commissioned. Until then, well, what would be the point? It would only have upset you.'

'No, it wouldn't. I can handle who you work with. You know I'm never jealous.'

Jonny started to smile, but caught her eye and stopped.

'It's the secrecy I can't bear,' she repeated. 'How's it going anyway?'

'We've got some co-production money – through a contact of Sasha's – and we're getting very positive feedback from the Beeb. We're making the pilot at the moment, and she's very good at interviewing. A real natural. And we've got a couple of good people to front the programme.'

'Right.' Kate knew that they had to go to the TV channels with a good business proposition, not just a great idea. If they could present with pre-production money, especially from a TV channel abroad, it made it so much easier to get the commission taken seriously.

'Jonny, the point of us is that we support each other. And I can't support you if I don't know what you're doing.'

'Kate,' he said, suddenly. 'I think you're not getting anywhere in your own work, and I think that's partly why you feel so threatened by Sasha. You're doing the same kind of programmes that you were a few years ago, but just fewer of them, and I don't think you're a natural freelancer. I think you work best in a team and . . .'

Kate was furious. 'Jonny, do not switch the attack to my work. I am desperately busy, trying to keep the family and the house together so you can work all hours, I am just about keeping my career afloat, too, and I know I'm treading water there, but I do not see any way out of this until Luke is old enough to be on his own when he comes back from school and that won't be for at least four years. This is not about me, it's about . . .'

'It's just that you could—'

'And you could tell me the truth and not involve Sasha. But you haven't. So let's not give each other career advice, shall we? Now, do you think you could possibly talk to me honestly about what's going on in the company, or do I have to worry about picking up your mobile from under a pile of dirty washing in case I see a number I don't like on it?'

'I will tell you the truth from now on,' he said. 'And just don't take it out on Sasha.'

'That's so unfair!' Kate registered the defence of Sasha with a fresh stab of pain. 'I've looked after her children, cooked her meals, had her to my house – I couldn't have been more welcoming, I always include her in any invitation . . .'

'But you don't like her,' he continued. 'I can see that, and . . .' He stopped as his phone went. He took it out and frowned at the number displayed, then switched it off. Kate wondered if it was Sasha.

It obviously was, as her own phone rang immediately from her bag, registering the now-hated name. 'Yes?' answered Kate, swallowing her rage. 'Would you like to speak to Jonny, Sasha? He says that you're really good at the interviewing, by the way. Well done. And congratulations on having a great idea.' There, that would show them. She handed the phone over to Jonny and folded her arms, blinking a tear away. Somehow she had come out of this the bad guy. Difficult Kate who everyone had to lie to.

'Right,' said Jonny in a low voice, his eyes flickering towards Kate. 'Yes, she's here with me now.'

There was a silence while Kate fumed.

He asked a few terse questions, then switched the phone off, and took both her hands in his, holding them firmly.

'I'm sorry . . .'

Her heart turned over.

Chapter 22

Heather sang along to the radio. It told her that she didn't know what she'd got till it had gone. She turned back into the tree-lined lane that led to 'the patch'. The familiar notice, 'Children Playing', that so often denoted army territory when combined with the military connotations of the names: Waterloo Drive, Sebastopol Lane, Gunnery Avenue, and, wittily, Letsbe Avenue, where the military police were stationed. Well, she did know what she had. The security that she'd lacked as a child. Halstead Hill still all felt very safe. A place where fathers cleaned their cars on Sunday, and took their children swimming. And watched out for them.

Heather had no memories of her father at all, although he was down on her birth certificate as Mark Browning. Mo had been a sixties flower child, and had been living with Mark Browning in a squat, with about ten other people. He had gone out one day and never come back. Mo's stories were unreliable and changed over the years – sometimes she said he'd been arrested for drug dealing, at others she claimed he'd run off with another woman. 'Dead now, serves him right, he was a right fucker,' said Mo, on one of her rambling diatribes against men. In another account, he had died of a drug overdose. Heather did not want to find out.

She drove past the row of small semi-detached majors' houses, bigger detached lieutenant-colonels' homes, then bigger again, a few for full colonels and one grand mansion for the brigadier, all built in red brick in the thirties and many of them pebbledashed to save on maintenance. Turning into the final cul-de-sac where their large semi awaited refurbishment, still with its original metal windows, she tutted as she saw Daisy's bicycle lying discarded across the lawn. Once this whole area had been a humming army community, but now it was peppered with civilians who had bought the houses and a smattering of empty properties. The army and civilian families didn't mix much, and the empty houses with their shaggy lawns and fallen fences stood as a no man's land between them.

She noted the unfamiliar car parked in the road with only mild interest. Jack always grumbled that the civilians just parked any-where. They had no consideration. Heather lugged as many carrier bags in each hand as she could manage, dropping them on the step to unlock the front door. 'Hi! Anyone home?' Travis bounded up, wagging his tail furiously.

Sasha, who wasn't filming that day, came to the door. 'Heather . . .'

Heather was aware of someone else behind Sasha in the hall, and began to feel her breath tighten in her chest. Now, as her eyes adjusted, she could see two people. It was like being kicked in the solar plexus. Hard. The pain was intense, and she put a hand out to steady herself. A man and a woman. Just as she'd said. They weren't in uniform, though. She felt a prickle of hope. Perhaps they were collecting for charity.

'I'll just put this shopping down in the kitchen.'

'I'll take it,' said Sasha, too quickly. 'You go and sit down in there.'

'I'm Lieutenant-Colonel Jackson and this is Major Harris.' Heather, hearing them from a long way away, shook hands for-mally. They followed her into her sitting room. She sat down just as she began to feel her knees buckle beneath her.

'I'm Melanie Harris,' said Major Harris softly, handing her a card.

Heather barely took in the grizzled, seen-it-all before face of Lieutenant-Colonel Jackson, and the neat, professional suit and bobbed hair of Major Melanie Harris, a decade older than she'd seemed on first glance. Sensible, weather-worn, attractive faces,

157

both of them. She gazed at them, willing them to be a dream, unable to believe that they were really here. She was dimly aware of a soft grunt as Travis settled himself at her feet.

'I'm afraid we've got bad news.' Lieutenant-Colonel Jackson spoke immediately. 'Your husband, Lieutenant-Colonel Fox, was on an intelligence-gathering mission in the mountains in Temanistan and it seems that his vehicle may have been separated from its back-up, and that there have been some further problems. We haven't heard from him since 0600 hours on Monday morning, so he and the three personnel with him are officially missing.'

Heather concentrated on the carpet. Specially chosen, she thought, by someone before her, not to show stains. You must never show the marks. 'So's he . . .?' she asked brightly, lifting her head, because she could see the man thought she wasn't listening.

'His personal locator beacon sent out a message to say where he and the three people with him were at 0700 hours, and we are working with the Temanistan army to get there, but the snow has come a month early and we're dealing with adverse weather conditions—'

'What's a personal locator beacon?' interrupted Heather.

'Every member of the army now has one on their person. If they are stranded anywhere without radio or telephone contact or transport, they can depress a button on their personal locator beacon which is transmitted to a satellite and we can then tell where he or she was when they depressed the button.'

'So he's probably fine? I mean, he must be alive, and you know where he is . . . where he was . . .?' She tried to take it all in. It couldn't be anything serious, surely.

'We don't know what has happened, and we can't speculate. His back-up vehicle suffered a breakdown and we are in contact with them, but it seems that he may have gone on ahead without full back-up. And there's no radio contact. Just the personal locator beacon.'

'Perhaps both vehicles broke down?' suggested Heather. 'There was that programme that said that the army didn't have enough spares to maintain things properly.' She looked at Lieutenant-Colonel Jackson hopefully.

'They were travelling in two CAVs, civilianised armoured vehicles, which were both well maintained.'

'But it might have happened that way? Both CAVs might have broken down, and perhaps the radios don't work either?' Even to herself, Heather knew she sounded desperate. 'But he's not dead, anyway. I thought he was dead. Our dog . . .' It was too difficult to explain.

'We're doing our best to find out exactly what happened,' repeated Lieutenant-Colonel Jackson. 'But we can't speculate.'

'Do you think they might have been attacked and taken prisoner?'

He shook his head, but not in denial. 'I really can't say any more. Because I don't know any more. He was on a Field Human Intelligence Team mission, and hasn't called in.'

Heather tried to understand what he was saying, but the words floated in and out of her head. She sat on the sofa, barely moving. 'Not dead,' she murmured. 'But surely, if he was on an FHT mission, he'll have had back-up, won't he? Don't they know what happened?' She knew she was going over the same ground, but she still didn't understand.

He inclined his head slightly. 'On this occasion there seems to have been some . . . ah . . . confusion about back-up, and why Lieutenant-Colonel Fox was without it.'

Jack had once explained how he gathered intelligence in the field: he'd have a team of around four, including himself, two of whom would be providing cover for him while he was talking to, say, local tribesmen, and then probably a translator. But behind them, at all times, would be another team, the Force Protection Unit, of around four soldiers, whose sole job was to make sure that Jack's team got back safely. 'There'll be someone with a satnav phone on each team,' he'd said, 'and we call in every three hours. If we don't make those calls, then headquarters knows there's a problem, and they'd also know where we were supposed to be and roughly how far we could have travelled since our last call. So it's not as easy to get lost as you might think, sitting here at home.' And now there were these personal locator beacons, too.

So Heather couldn't understand why Lieutenant-Colonel

Jackson didn't know more. 'But when did they first know he was missing?'

'His team was supposed to call in,' said Jackson. 'But the back-up vehicle called in to say that it had suffered a breakdown. That team is waiting for spares, and they're all still in contact. But we haven't had any contact from Lieutenant-Colonel Fox's vehicle, other than from the personal locator beacon.'

She looked at Travis. He had known. Temanistan was four hours ahead so if something had happened at about seven, that was 3 a.m. British time. He looked back at her, liquid golden eyes telling her that she could always trust him, and wagged his tail, apparently unconcerned. Did that mean Jack was safe somewhere now?

'Is he in an area where there is . . .' she paused, not wanting to spell it out, 'terrorist activity?'

Jackson inclined his head slightly. 'There is known to be some unrest in that area.'

'Would you like me to make you a cup of tea?' asked Melanie Harris.

Heather nodded. Her mouth felt so dry that her tongue seemed to be sticking to the roof of her mouth. She could hear the sound of the kettle boiling in the kitchen and Major Harris talking to Sasha before coming back with a cup of tea. Heather drank it thirstily, scalding her tongue on the hot liquid.

'We usually ask if you'd like us to call somebody,' said Major Harris. 'But I understand you have a friend staying anyway . . .'

'Yes. Just . . . just . . . for a short time.' Heather suddenly felt panicked about how long friends were allowed to stay in army houses. There was a regulation about it somewhere. Suddenly it seemed very important. 'She's only staying,' she added. 'Just a friend.' What was she saying? Would there be trouble? Heather could feel her heart pounding inside her head. She wished Sasha would go away.

'I can make calls and help out here,' said Sasha. 'If that's OK, Heather?'

Heather gazed at her, uncomprehending, but Major Harris seemed to think this was a good idea, and handed Sasha a card too. Oh well, it was easier to let Sasha be kind, she supposed.

Major Harris turned to Heather. 'I'll be your Casualty Visiting Officer, and you can reach me at any time on my mobile. As soon as there's any news, I'll be in touch, and I'll pop in every day to see how you're doing. If you've got any questions . . . any questions at all . . . just call me.'

'What about the press?' asked Sasha. 'Will this appear on the news?'

'Probably not,' replied Lieutenant-Colonel Jackson. 'It's just possible that the press may try to contact you, but we very strongly advise not talking to them.'

'I don't want to talk to them,' said Heather. 'Will they know where we live?'

'Well, they might be able to find out, but it's unlikely to catch their attention so I wouldn't worry about it too much. There's quite a lot going on over there, and most of it never hits the papers. Let Major Harris know if you do get approached.'

'Why don't you advise talking to journalists?' demanded Sasha.

'Because when a family is vulnerable it's very easy to twist what they say, and in the unlikely event of Lieutenant-Colonel Fox being taken prisoner, you don't want to do or say anything that could inflame the situation. And, in this case, it could be sensitive. Although we're there at the invitation of the Temanistan government, it's best if our presence isn't too widely known.'

'Of course I would never say anything,' said Heather, slowly absorbing the fact that Jack had downplayed the safety of this 'desk job' in an obscure embassy outpost. Or even lied about it. She rubbed her hands over her face. 'If he's been taken prisoner . . . we talked about this . . . it was one of the last things he said. He said . . .' she struggled to remember the conversation. 'It might have an impact on the safety of me and the children.'

Lieutenant-Colonel Jackson said something, but his words faded in and out through a buzzing in her ears.

'But,' murmured Heather, trying to think straight, 'if he's been captured by a terrorist group then they may find out where his family live, and they may try to get local associates to come here.'

'That is something we can bear in mind,' said Melanie Harris. 'And we can find you accommodation on a secure army base if you'd like. I can arrange it within a few days. But there's no evidence that he's been captured.'

Yet. Heather heard the word in her voice.

'We'll keep you informed,' said Melanie gently. 'And if we think there's any danger to you, we'll act immediately.'

Heather nodded. A glass shade seemed to have come down between her and the rest of the world, and their voices sounded tinny and faraway. She could see them: Major Harris, Lieutenant-Colonel Jackson and Sasha, all looking sympathetic and concerned, but she couldn't feel any of it.

She wanted to run away. That's what she and Mo had always done when things got difficult. A memory of Mo pulling her out of bed flashed into her mind. 'Quick,' she'd said. 'We're going now. No, you can't take that flaming teddy, it's too much to carry.' She'd dragged Heather out of the house with only half her clothes stuffed into a school satchel and none of her very few toys.

'I don't want to go, stop!' she'd cried, and had been too sleepy to evade one of Mo's hefty slaps. With her ears ringing she was bundled into a taxi.

'It's fer yer own sake, you don't want to turn out like I did,' muttered Mo. 'I'll tell you what my mam did to me, you're lucky to have me, you are . . .' And she went on: the usual, endless diatribe of horrors, the awful, humiliating detail of everything that had happened to little Maureen Spencer as a frightened child. That last journey, she remembered, the one that had ended at the Caldecott, Mo had said: 'I told you, people don't want kids around. He never wanted a kid, Gerald didn't, that's why he ain't got any of his own . . .'

Ten-year-old Heather had tried to shut out the rambling voice. And she couldn't believe that Gerald would try to send her away to a children's home. He had always been so very kind to her. She had trusted him. But she never saw him again, and Mo rarely. Although, as Mo had said on one of her rare visits, the Caldecott was OK. 'Nobody treats you bad here, do they?' She stubbed out a cigarette. 'I looked after you, I did, making sure you got in somewhere good.' Heather couldn't remember how or why she had got there, just that there had been a lot of screaming and shouting from her and Mo, and that the headmistress of the school she'd been at at the time had said she was uncontrollable, and that there had been assessments and serious faces. Ever since she'd had to identify Mo's body, she looked at Daisy, now ten – the same age she was when she'd been sent there – and the memories kept flooding back. It hurt. Everything hurt. Everything was so confused.

Wrenching herself back to the pain of the present day, she tried to remember that Jack would want her to keep calm. 'Shall I call Kate for you?' asked Sasha. 'Or rather, I'd better call Jonny, hadn't I? Then he can tell her. She's going to be very shocked. And then I can collect the children from school.'

'Yes. Thank you. Thank you so much.' The words came out in a whisper as a wave of nausea hit Heather and she clutched the back of a chair.

'Sit down,' said Melanie Harris, as she gently guided Heather back to the sofa, and handed her a glass of water.

Sasha disappeared to make a phone call to Jonny, and Heather took out her notebook, determined to get a grip. She was an army wife. She must make Jack proud of her.

'Right,' she said. 'You'd better tell me everything I need to know. If he's taken prisoner, for example, does he still get his salary?' Major Harris assured her that, of course, his salary would still be paid, and she found herself writing it down in the notebook. 'Salary paid. Prisoner.' They were meaningless squiggles on a page. She stood up. 'Thank you so much,' she said, holding out her hand, the adrenalin finally kicking in, helping her cope. 'I can manage now. You've been very kind.'

As she showed them out she tried to remember exactly what Jack had said. It was one of the talks they'd had to have before he went away. He'd told her that there could be a threat to the families of captured officers, particularly ones that had access to sensitive information, that terrorist groups had connections in Britain and might try to kidnap the family as leverage to get the prisoner to talk. Heather had said that she would be fine and that, in the very unlikely case of this actually happening, she would easily find somewhere to go. Now that it had come to it, she should begin phoning round their closest army friends. With no mother, father, sister or brother, or even grandparents or aunts and uncles, there was nowhere she could go. She'd lost touch with any non-army friends she'd had, and didn't think she could just ring up and say 'Hi, sorry it's just been a Christmas card for the last ten years, but now that we might be wanted by terrorists, could we come and stay? All of us? Indefinitely?' It was almost funny. No, she must sit tight, and not run away. She wasn't like her mother, she was stronger.

Chapter 23

Olivia spent a sneaky half hour searching out conservation architects on the web on Tuesday morning, knowing that she should be
sorting out Allison Green and three other divorces, one of which
was due in court later this week. One architect turned out not to
do that sort of work, she made an appointment to see the second
and left a message for the third company, Blake Allan.

Her head was so full of Providence Cottage that she couldn't
concentrate. And nagging at the back of her mind was concern for
Kate and Jonny. Perhaps she should have invited Kate down to see
Providence Cottage. It had just been easier not to, not to face the
niggling issues that had come between them over the last few
months. But perhaps Si had been right. Perhaps she was as much
to blame as Kate for the situation. She took a deep breath and
dialled her at home.

'Hello?' Kate's voice sounded thick, as if she had a cold.

'Are you all right?'

'Oh, Olivia. Yes, I'm fine, thank you. What can I do for you?'
She didn't sound very enthusiastic.

'Oh, I just . . . um . . . wondered if you and Jonny and the kids
would like to come down and see Providence Cottage some time?'

'Oh yes, Sasha said it was lovely. I gather you had a great time
there with her and Heather the other day.'

So that was the reason for the stuffy voice and stilted manner.
Kate was offended at being left out. Olivia suppressed a sigh. 'It's
just that Halstead Hill is almost out of London, so it was a

spur-of-the-moment thing. You know how it is . . . Did Heather mention it?'

'No, Sasha did. I wanted to know how Heather was, but I couldn't get hold of her, so I thought I'd try Sasha and you were all there, down in Kent.'

'She didn't say.'

'I didn't ask her to pass on a message. Look, I'm sorry, but I must go.'

'Oh, well.' Olivia was tempted to say that Sasha was a trouble-maker, but she didn't feel she could, not to the new chilly Kate.

'How's Callum?'

'Fine, thanks, and thanks so much for coming and . . .'

'It's nothing. I suppose you're having to put your foot down a bit, and it must be such a worry for you, having him go off the rails—'

'Olivia,' snapped Kate. 'You do not have children. You do not understand. You can't just "put your foot down". It's more complicated than that. I must go.' She put the phone down.

Well, that put her in her place, Olivia thought. 'You don't have children.' Well, no, she didn't. And she had a right not to have them, without being snapped at every time she said anything about anyone else's. She crashed the phone down.

Cat, her assistant, raised an eyebrow. 'Difficult client?'

'I can handle difficult clients. It's sisters-in-law that I can't take.' Olivia was burning inside. The Foxes did blame her for not having children, they obviously did. They obviously talked about her, saying she was selfish, that she didn't do enough for Si, that she wasn't good enough for him . . . She blinked away an unexpected tear.

'Tell me about it,' said Cat. 'My boyfriend's mother was in hospital earlier this year, and none of them could pick her up, so I thought I'd do the dutiful daughter-in-law bit and took her home. After which his sister, Karen, rang me to tell me off for not checking that the old lady's central heating was on. She went on a real rant: "What were you thinking of, leaving an old, sick woman in a freezing house?" I mean, how was I to know what temperature her house ought to be?'

'Don't marry him then,' advised Olivia. 'Because you're going to be taking on the whole family.'

'Oh no I'm not,' replied Cat. 'Once I get that ring on my finger, Karen is history. Believe me.'

'It doesn't work that way.' Olivia pulled the Allison Green files towards her and tried to decide how she was going to convince the greediest divorcee in town that she wasn't going to get the flat in New York, the beach house in the Virgin Islands, plus the Mayfair home and one million a year for the child.

Her phone rang. 'It's Blake Allan here,' said a voice. A surprisingly attractive male voice.

'I thought Blake Allan would be somebody Blake in partnership with somebody Allan,' said Olivia.

'No,' he said, 'just me. I gather you've got a Georgian wreck. My favourite.'

She laughed. It was so nice to hear enthusiasm.

When she made an appointment for him to visit Providence Cottage, she decided she wouldn't mention it to Si. Not just yet. He obviously didn't really want the house, and he definitely didn't want to spend money on an architect. But it was her money. So there.

'It's your sister-in-law on line one again,' said Cat.

Now what? Olivia sighed. She took the call.

'It's Kate,' said a wobbly voice. 'Jack's missing. Can you tell Si?'

Olivia's breath caught in her throat. Not Jack. Please not Jack. He had such a big laugh, and he never took life seriously. 'What happened?'

'He seems to have been out on some reconnaissance mission and hasn't called in since he left early on Monday morning their time. There's very bad weather over there, apparently, and quite a bit of unrest, so maybe it'll all be all right . . . But someone needs to tell Mumma.' Olivia heard a stifled sob, and Jonny came on the line.

'Olivia?'

'Jonny, what's happened?' Olivia struggled to believe it. 'I thought Jack was a military attaché. What's he been up to?'

Jonny told her that no one knew much, but that one of them needed to go down to tell Ella. 'I think Kate is too shaken to drive.'

Olivia tried to think straight, but all she could manage were mental images of Jack, captured or dead. 'Si's in Geneva,' she said, flustered. 'He's due back in a couple of hours though. But we need to get to Ella before the six o'clock news, don't we?' She looked at her watch, forcing her mind to work. It was 3 p.m., and she had a meeting with Allison Green at five. Allison Green did not expect her lawyer to change her appointments. Olivia realised that her hand, the one holding the telephone, was shaking. 'I'll go,' she said. 'Of course, don't worry about it. You look after Kate, and I'll meet Si at the airport to tell him in person, and then we'll both go to Ella. We should be there by about six. We should just about make it. Oh, this is awful, so terrible, I . . .' But she realised that the best thing she could do for the family was to stop talking and get the news to Ella as soon as possible.

Every time she stopped at the endless traffic lights out of London she tried to reach Si, leaving messages and texts to say she would be meeting him. She finally got out into the open road, only to be stuck behind two lorries overtaking each other uphill. Come on, come on.

Her mobile shrilled at her, and, taking her eyes off the road for a moment, she checked the number. Allison Green. She would have to wait.

The rest of the journey was punctuated by more calls, all from Allison Green, so Olivia eventually stopped in a lay-by and called her.

'This is outrageous,' said Allison. 'Have you any idea how busy I am? I've had to completely reschedule my afternoon because you cancelled my appointment at the last minute. I am not used to being treated like this, and I can tell you that I'm very seriously considering moving my business to a more reliable firm.'

Olivia tried to explain but Allison swept over her. 'It's such unprofessional behaviour.' Olivia finally managed to get the message across, to which Allison Green merely said. 'Very well. But I trust it won't happen again. As I said, the one thing I do require is professionalism on the part of my advisors.'

She tried Si again.

'Hi.' She heard the affectionate, amused intonation he only used with her. 'What's up?' He sounded happy to be back.

'I'm so sorry,' Olivia began to tell him, and heard his voice collapse.

'Jack is a loose cannon,' he said. 'He's got himself into something he can't talk his way out of now, mark my words.'

'I'm sure it's not his fault.'

'I'm sure it is,' said Si. 'Bloody fool. What was he thinking of?'

Olivia knew that that was how Si dealt with worry. By getting angry. But when she got to the airport and saw him coming through customs, she suddenly got a glimpse of how his face would look when he was an old man. An hour later, when Ella opened the door to them, her bright eyes and welcoming smile crumpled.

'Jack,' said Ella, turning frighteningly pale. 'You've come to tell me about Jack . . .'

'He's not dead. He's stranded somewhere,' said Si, catching her and guiding her to a chair.

Like everyone else, Ella couldn't understand why the army didn't know more.

'They know.' Her voice trembled. 'They're just not telling us.'

'I really don't think they do, and Sasha says that it's their policy not to speculate,' said Olivia, for the fifteenth time.

'Sasha?' asked Ella. 'What's she got to do with it? Why is she always around?'

'She was with Heather when the news came. She's been very helpful.'

'Heather should be more careful. I know that type of girl. She's after Jack. Mark my words. She's worming her way into your lives so she can get him.'

'I really don't think there's any danger of that.' Lovely as Jack was, Olivia suspected that Sasha, if she was looking for a man at all, might want one with a little more money and status than Jack had. The little she knew of her indicated that she was a high-maintenance individual.

'I have been around for a lot longer than either of you,' said Ella. 'And I saw how she was looking at him that Sunday.'

'She's like that with everyone,' said Olivia.

Si said nothing.

Chapter 24

Three days inched by. Heather wore her brave face and sent the children to school every day. Jack had always told Molly and Daisy that the British Army could do anything, so they accepted Heather's explanation that he would be found and brought back. Major Harris came by and was quietly reassuring but she had nothing to say. Heather asked what kind of a rescue was being mounted but she knew that no one would ever tell her. It would be with the Temanistan Army, they said, which didn't fill Heather with confidence. It would take planning.

The army grapevine worked well and she was inundated with calls, offers of help and even a rota of friends bringing round a cooked meal every evening. Only occasionally, though, did she dare disclose her greatest fear: that Jack was a prisoner and that terrorists might be coming after her and the girls. It seemed so cowardly to be thinking that way when Jack was in such danger, but she needed to plan out somewhere they could run to if the worst came to the worst. But she still couldn't quite work out where to go: some very close friends from their last posting had just had a new baby and another had a broken leg, then she couldn't get hold of a third, and the fourth was abroad . . .

There was nothing on the news about missing British servicemen in Temanistan. No one in Britain knew where it was, and most would have thought the British Army ought not to be there anyway. But Jack was doing something worthwhile, fighting drug smugglers and people traffickers. Heather, ironing, cleaning and scrubbing with a ferocity that wore her out, comforted herself with that thought. She damp-dusted picture rails, polished door-knobs and shampooed carpets in a desperate attempt to bring order back to her world, trying to tell herself that Jack was a sur-vivor, and that he was trained. Three days, though, three days. What would they eat? Or drink? What about the weather? It was vicious. She kept asking Major Harris questions. 'Suppose he's been captured and they've taken him somewhere, leaving the loca-tor beacon behind?' 'Suppose he's been injured and needs urgent medical attention?'

Major Harris discouraged speculation kindly but firmly.

Privately Heather obsessed over their last few telephone con-versations. They all seemed to have been arguments about something. Ever since they'd identified Mo's body at the police station there had been a wall between them. They'd even had a row about Sasha still being there. The last time they'd spoken on the phone, Heather had asked Jack if perhaps he could write to Sasha suggesting that she set a date for moving out, and Jack had exploded with irritation. 'Really, if you're not complaining about being lonely, you're grumbling about the house being too full. Sasha's had a really tough time, and she won't be around for much longer – offering her a spare room until the divorce comes through is the least we can do.'

Heather hadn't quite dared to point out that 'we' didn't come into it. She'd tried to change the subject. 'Is it at all dangerous?' she'd asked. 'Are you seeing any action?'

'For Christ's sake, Heather, stop fussing. Temanistan is the back of beyond and I will be very glad to see civilisation again.'

Now she struggled to remember what he'd said before he went about what she should do if he was captured. It had been one of those hurried conversations – she'd been cooking supper and keeping an eye out of the window at the girls playing on the street.

'If I get captured,' he'd said, 'they say there may be some risk to the family.' Had he said 'may' or had he said 'will'? Why hadn't she listened? What had he said about going somewhere safe? And when should she go?

The phone rang and she jumped for it. The line rustled at her, but there was no one there. Probably someone who'd accidentally pressed her number on their mobile, she told herself. But when she tried to check it was 'number withheld'.

Later she asked Major Harris about it, who promised, impassively, to look into it. During the major's visit Heather saw a car cruise by the window, with two men in it.

'They look foreign,' she called out to Major Harris, who moved towards the window to check.

'Mm . . .'

'They've stopped outside this house.' Heather was filled with panic. 'Look!' But the car moved off, quickly accelerating towards the main road.

'They're just lost,' said Melanie Harris. 'Look, the passenger's got a map.' But Heather saw her eyes narrow fractionally and knew that she'd clocked the licence plate. Checks would be made. But would they be made too late?

'I think Jack would want us to leave,' said Heather, urgently. 'The girls . . .' She wanted to run away. Away from the fear for Jack and the terror that someone might hurt the girls, before it consumed her. 'Of course! Kate! I could go to my sister-in-law, Kate. Although Jack would know we might go there, wouldn't it be putting them in danger?'

'I really don't think there is any immediate danger to your sister-in-law. And we can . . .'

'But she is a journalist,' hissed Sasha from the doorway. 'Don't you think that might be a bad idea?'

Heather straightened her shoulders. 'Kate would never, ever betray us. And the press don't seem to be interested.' She dialled Kate with shaking hands and Kate told them all to come now. 19 Lovelace Road beckoned like an oasis. Kate would take charge.

Ten years of being an army wife had taught Heather not to 'dwell' on their situation or to let the fear go on seeping through the cracks. It had taught her to make lists, then go upstairs, pack the suitcases, sit the children down when they came back from school and say that they were all going to stay at Auntie Katie's for a bit and put Travis's bed into the boot of the car, in a manic frenzy that made Daisy cry. Travis padded after her, subdued.

'Are you all right?' asked Sasha, who was staying behind. 'Don't worry about burglars, I'll look after the house.'

'That's so kind of you. And I'm fine,' replied Heather, automatically, striding back into the kitchen. 'Do eat up any of this fresh food . . .' She heaved the rubbish sack out and began emptying the bits in the fridge into it. 'I don't want to come back to find everything green and furry.' She stopped and looked at Sasha in horror. 'A prisoner,' she said. 'They do terrible things, don't they, nowadays, to prisoners?'

Chapter 25

The day after they'd heard that Jack had gone missing, Kate drove down to Thorpe Wenham and picked up Ella so that she could stay at 19 Lovelace Road, after which they barely left home for three days. Kate's ears strained for the phone call that might tell them Jack had been found. Jonny came home earlier than usual each night, and when he found Kate simply opening the fridge door, looking into it, then closing it again, he took over the cooking.

'Sorry,' she said. 'The fridge seems full, but I can't make any sense of what's in it. My brain seems to have stopped working.'

'It's fine. I can do it.' Jonny rifled through the fridge and pulled out eggs, salad and onions.

'We always used to cook together,' said Kate. 'Do you remember? You were better than me.'

He smiled briefly. 'Only at some things. Here, Callum!' he called up the stairs, 'come down and break these eggs into a bowl.'

Callum looked surprised, but obeyed.

'And Luke, you too, you're old enough to learn how to chop an onion.'

Luke came thundering down and picked up the kitchen knife with pride.

'No, don't wave it at everyone.' Jonny carefully showed him how to hold it.

When Heather called to ask if she could come and stay, Kate was pleased. It felt right to have everyone together, as if they were drawing their wagons in a circle.

'Heather's coming,' she told Ella.

'Good. Has she heard anything?' Ella was very pale. She had aged ten years in a few hours.

The doorbell rang. Ella and Kate tried not to jump.

'Maybe that's Uncle Jack?' queried Luke, anxiously.

'It's too soon to be Heather and the girls,' said Jonny.

'I hope Sasha isn't coming to stay as well, there won't be enough room.' Kate peered at a stiff female figure through the spyhole. There was no sign of children. She opened the door. 'Hello? Oh . . . Virginia?' Virginia, Jonny's sister from Scotland, stood there, trying to wipe some dog mess off her court shoes.

'I presume Jonny told you I was coming?'

'Oh, er, yes, of course . . .' lied Kate. 'We've just had a crisis.' She hated using Jack as an excuse, but she had to tell her.

'What a bore!' exclaimed Virginia after hearing the full story. 'They will get him back, though, won't they? But I can't impose on you like this. Taxi! Taxi!' She waved at a departing cab. It turned the corner and disappeared, and she looked marooned.

It suddenly became very important to prove to Virginia that she could manage. 'No, no,' cried Kate. 'You must stay. It's all arranged. There's no problem.'

She ushered them all through the house, raising her eyebrows at Jonny, signalling frantically behind Virginia's back.

He looked guilty. 'Ginny.' A kiss on both cheeks.

'Jonny darling, you naughty boy, you haven't told Kate I was coming.'

'Yes, he did,' said Kate, glaring at him over Virginia's shoulder. 'The spare room is all made up.'

'It's different in here,' said Virginia, looking round at the kitchen.

'This is our new extension. We only finished it a few months ago.' Kate couldn't help feeling proud of it, in spite of the awfulness of the day. The sun streamed in the windows across the white walls and black floor.

'Would you like me to fold up your laundry?' Virginia asked pointedly, looking at the sofa.

Kate snatched it all up, tucking the toppling pile under her chin. 'I can manage.' A pair of greying pants slipped out on to the floor. They all stared at them until Jonny picked them up and stuffed them into the mound of clothes in Kate's arms. She was mortified. They were so clearly hers, large, saggy and moth-eaten.

But what was a pair of pants when Jack was in danger? Kate blinked back a tear.

'Housework always takes a back seat in a crisis, don't you find?' suggested Virginia kindly, frowning at the crumbs that seemed to be blowing across the black tiles like tumbleweed. 'And these modern floors show all the dirt, don't they?'

The doorbell rang again.

As soon as Heather walked in, Kate could see that she was overwhelmed. Everybody seemed to be exclaiming over her. She flattened herself against the wall of the narrow hall, clutching Daisy and Molly, as Travis strained on his leash.

Jonny took Travis off her and released him into the courtyard garden where he lifted his leg on a pot of herbs. Virginia stifled a shriek of disapproval.

'I think everyone could do with a little drinkie, Jonny,' commanded Ella, steering Heather to the sofa. 'Sit here, Heather, and breathe. That's right. In. Out. Slowly now.'

'Shall I clean the floor?' asked Virginia. 'Jonny, where's your mop and bucket?'

'Under the stairs.' He bent over Heather, offering her a glass of water and she sat up slowly, and drank it.

'No, really, Virginia, don't bother. We'll do the floor tomorrow.' Kate tried to stop her.

Heather closed her eyes. 'Has my Casualty Visiting Officer called?'

'Nobody's called,' said Jonny.

Heather scrabbled through her bag and found her mobile, peering at the blank screen. 'Have you got an apron?' asked Virginia, filling the bucket with hot water, floor cleaner and determination.

Kate took the laundry upstairs and flung sheets on beds and mattresses all over the house, then came down to find everyone milling everywhere, with Virginia mopping the floor around everyone's feet.

'Has something spilt?'

'No.' Virginia looked pleased with herself. 'I just thought . . .'

You thought my floor was disgustingly dirty, thought Kate furiously. But she didn't say it. She turned to Heather. 'How are you?'

'Fine now.' Heather looked pale and strained, and had obviously slept even less than the rest of them in three days. Her body language was defeated – hunched shoulders, a tapping foot – and she seemed smaller than ever. 'How are you?' she whispered.

Kate swallowed. She had lain in bed for three nights overwhelmed by tiredness but unable to sleep, so she had a permanent headache. Every few hours she got up to scour the internet for any mention of Temanistan or Jack. It was a country the size of Wales, she now knew, governed by tribal ferocity and drug barons. There was a lawless frontier, where mines, left over from various wars, were common, and pockets of 'insurgency' were refuelled and re-armed with drug money on a regular basis. Oil discoveries were talked about, while the politicians pointed to the tiny republic as the sanctuary of some of the world's most wanted terrorists. Lawless, corrupt, poverty-stricken and desperate. That was Temanistan.

The thought of Jack bound, hooded and tortured, or starving and hunted in the famously wild mountains haunted Kate in the small hours of the night. She tried to comfort herself by remembering that he'd done six weeks of SAS training, and was well equipped to survive even the harshest conditions.

Joining the SAS had been Jack's dream, and when he passed the first six weeks of training he'd been elated, only to return just a week later to say that he'd failed the officer training. 'You know what it's like in these organisations,' he'd said bitterly at a family lunch at 19 Lovelace Road. 'Someone thought my face didn't fit. It's pure prejudice.'

'I know some of these chaps,' said Si, who always had to know more about everything than anyone. 'They don't do prejudice.'

'They did in my case,' snapped Jack. 'You know nothing about the army.' Kate was used to her brothers being highly competitive. Si was probably jealous of Jack. Defending your country versus selling expensive luxury goods to the super-rich – well, there was no comparison, really, was there? Si couldn't bear to think of naughty Jack, both the baby and the black sheep of the family, actually doing a more responsible job than he was.

Virginia fussed round Jonny, trying to take over the cooking. He insisted that he and the boys were in charge.

'You're so lucky, Kate,' said Virginia. 'Jonny is such a good cook, and now he's teaching the boys. It must be wonderful not to lift a finger in your own kitchen.'

Kate tried to say that this evening was an exception and that she usually cooked, but Virginia didn't listen, cutting across her with an 'I know, I know. I was only joking. Now then . . . let me take this rubbish out. This bag's about to burst.'

'No, you don't know where it goes,' said Kate, taking the big plastic sack out of Virginia's hands.' It's Jonny's job. He's the only one who can get everything in so it doesn't overflow. Or we get foxes,' she explained, for something to say. 'We probably have more foxes in the middle of London than you do in Scotland.'

'Do you shoot them?' asked Virginia.

Kate was startled. 'Well . . . no.'

'I can't see why not. We shoot foxes from the drawing-room window at home. Sorts them out a treat. And magpies. Dreadful vermin, don't you think?'

'I think we'd find ourselves surrounded by the armed response unit of the Metropolitan Police if we shot anything from our windows,' said Kate.

As Virginia was muttering about the loss of civil liberties and the plague of political correctness, Heather, who was looking stunned, rallied herself for conversation and offered the fact that she'd seen a pair of partridges in their garden in Halstead Hill. 'They were so sweet. I love partridges.'

'Oh, so do I,' agreed Virginia, warmly. 'They're so much juicier and more tender than pheasant. Although I wouldn't say sweet, they're really quite gamey.'

Heather blinked, and Kate suggested they all sit down. 'You must eat something, Heather.'

'Isn't it funny that we've never met before?' suggested Virginia to Heather.

Kate didn't think it was at all funny. If you stayed in the deepest countryside and never visited anyone else in the family, it was hardly surprising that you never met people. 'How are Angus and the children, Virginia?'

Virginia told them all, at length, exactly how they all were. Then she stopped. 'So tell me,' she leaned closer in to Heather, showing long, discoloured teeth. 'Exactly where do your people come from?'

Heather looked at her plate, then murmured something and rushed upstairs. Kate followed her.

'I'm OK,' said Heather, lying down on the spare bed. 'I think I just need to be alone.'

'I'm sorry. Jonny forgot to tell me she was coming. She hasn't been here for about six years, so it's most unusual.'

'S'fine. I just keep thinking about Jack. What he must be . . .' Heather put a hand over her mouth and rushed towards the bathroom.

When Kate got back downstairs, Jonny had obviously said something to Virginia because she was on the defensive.

'I don't see why I shouldn't ask,' she protested. 'I mean, one can see that she's not top drawer or anything like that, but there's no reason for her to feel embarrassed about anything. I mean, I'm hardly a snob. Where does she come from, anyway?'

Kate said she thought she remembered Heather saying something about Broadstairs. They'd never talked about it much.

Virginia nodded wisely. 'I thought as much. People don't live in Broadstairs, you know.'

'I think it's got a population of about twenty thousand,' said Jonny.

'You know what I mean, darling. People like us.'

'Ginny.' Jonny raised his eyebrows at her.

'Come on, darling, let's call a spade a spade . . . it's terribly middle class to be mealy-mouthed about this sort of thing. Much better to be good old-fashioned working class – which is what I suspect Heather is – than pretend to be something you aren't, and worrying about which forks to use and all that napkin–serviette thing.'

This reminded Kate that she hadn't put any out. She jumped up. 'Oh! Would anyone like a . . .' for a moment she couldn't remember which word was considered the right one. She remembered Jonny once telling her that it was fine to say 'fuck' or 'bugger' in front of Virginia, but not 'toilet' or 'pardon'.

'Well, would anyone like one of these?' she concluded.

The expression on Virginia's face said it all. She, Kate, clearly came into the irredeemably middle-class category.

'Well, Heather's a sweet girl,' said Ella, taking a crisp square of kitchen towel from Kate. 'Salt of the earth and all that.'

Kate spent the rest of the evening deflecting Virginia's relentless helpfulness. 'Where are your clean tea towels, Kate, this one needs a wash – shall I put some laundry through . . .?' She struggled to stay one step ahead of the demands for washing-up liquid, dishwasher tablets, soap powder . . . 'No, Virginia, please don't worry, we can do that tomorrow, no, really, I can manage that . . . no, that's not the right cupboard.' Eventually Virginia managed to get every single machine whirring, and the noise echoed against the hard floor and walls. Jonny hugged her. 'Ginny, you're a star. You should come more often.'

'Jonny looks tired, doesn't he?' Virginia said to Kate and Ella as they sat down to turn the news on, just in case. 'He works so hard, *and* he pulls his weight at home. I think that's wonderful, don't you?'

Ella pursed her lips. 'I think Kate is even more tired – she combines work and looking after the children in a way that no man ever does.' She looked Virginia square in the eye.

Although it was good to see Ella get some of her old spark back, Kate decided that she hadn't the strength to referee a game of Competitive Tiredness between her mother and her sister-in-law. She and Jonny played it themselves sometimes and it only led to arguments. 'I'd better check on Heather.'

Heather was sprawled across the top of the sofa bed in Jonny's study, fully dressed and sound asleep.

When Kate finally chased everyone into their various beds and got to her own, Jonny was lying on it staring at the ceiling.

'Jonny, why didn't you tell me Virginia was coming?'

'Sorry. Forgot.'

'She really is dreadful, isn't she? Poor Heather. A grilling about "her people" was the last thing she needed on top of everything else.'

'Ginny's just trying her best to be helpful and friendly. It isn't easy when you're outside your comfort zone.' And with that, he retreated behind his plate-glass wall again.

They lay side by side, not touching, until Kate, regretting her words, put a hand over his. Virginia was his sister, after all. And they didn't need any more gaps in their relationship. She thought of Callum and Luke, and how happy they'd been with their father that evening.

And then she thought of Jack again. 'They must know something soon,' she said, desperately. 'It's been three days. Do you think he's really . . .?' The words choked in her throat . . . 'been kidnapped by terrorists? I know that's what Heather believes.'

'I'm sure he'll be all right,' replied Jonny vaguely.

'Jonny!' Kate sat up, tired and a little bit drunk, furious with him. 'You just don't care. You don't care about anything except . . . except your work. When did you last do something with Callum and Luke, for example?'

'This evening,' he said, icy. 'I cooked supper with them.'

'Well, I know you did this evening, but didn't you see how they blossomed? They need more of that, and . . .' She stopped, knowing that her anger was due to tiredness and drink but not being able to help herself. 'Jonny. I spent most of this evening feeling that you were siding with your sister against me. Little in-jokes and memories I can't share. And she made the evening much harder work for me because I had to keep dealing with her trying to do everything the way she thought it should be done, but you just seemed to think she was wonderful.'

Jonny looked at her steadily. 'I was being nice. She needs to feel needed. You, of all people, should understand that.'

If every mattress, spare bed and sofa hadn't already been occupied, Kate would have stormed out. Instead she turned her back on him. 'I need you on my side, not Sasha's or Virginia's or anyone else's,' she muttered.

'Don't be ridiculous,' he replied. 'I am on your side. And I do appreciate the way you've made this place into a haven as well as a home. I'd just like you to welcome Ginny into it the way you welcome Olivia and Heather.'

Kate was unexpectedly touched, and her eyes filled with tears. 'Sorry. OK. I'm just tired and slightly drunk.'

'Yes,' he said. 'We all are.'

The following morning, as they saw Virginia off to stay with a distant cousin in Hampshire with cries of 'it's been great to see you' and 'come again soon', she asked them all to come for Christmas. 'You haven't been home for Christmas for so long, Jonno,' she said, clutching his shoulder. 'And the boys could learn to shoot.'

'Cool,' said Callum.

'Wow!' Luke jumped up and down.

'I don't think . . .' Kate's breath was temporarily taken away by the 'you haven't come home . . .' part of the invitation. *This* was his home. Not somewhere in Scotland. It wasn't even as if Virginia lived in the house he'd grown up in.

'We'd love to,' said Jonny, looking at Kate. 'That is, if . . .'

'Say yes, say yes, say yes.' Luke joggled her arm.

She looked at Callum.

'Dad could take me shooting clay pigeons, he's always promised.'

Kate liked to have Christmas at 19 Lovelace Road, with Ella, Heather and Jack, if they were around, and Olivia and Si dropping in for lunch. 'I have to be around for my mother . . .' she began.

'Bring her,' said Virginia. 'We have heaps of bedrooms.'

They would have. Well, maybe she could find a way of getting out of it nearer the time. But at least Jonny would be away from his office and with the boys. 'Thank you, Virginia, that would be lovely.'

There was a cheer from both boys. Right. That was more enthusiasm than they had shown for anything in a long time. Kate sighed as they waved Virginia off.

The phone rang, and she forgot everything else.

Chapter 26

Heather woke up early. She opened her eyes and whimpered, and Travis, in his basket beside her bed, pricked up his ears.

'Travis, is Jack all right?' she asked, hugging him tightly.

Travis licked her face and wagged his tail enthusiastically. Well, it would have to do as a reply. Heather had nothing else to cling to. She tiptoed downstairs and made a cup of tea, throwing the back door open and hearing the early morning sound of wood pigeons and starlings against the distant hum of traffic building up. She fingered her mobile phone. Please call. Major Melanie Harris, please call me. With anything, even the tiniest scrap of hope. This was the beginning of the fourth day. Jack had been outside, in hideously cold conditions, in territory where terrorists operated, with only enough provisions for twenty-four hours. It was all very well having personal locator beacons, but who was to say whether he was still with his? She frowned at her mobile phone. It seemed to be switched off.

Then she realised she'd left her mobile charger at home and that it had run out of battery. She scrabbled through her bags desperately for the fourth time, upturning everything on the spare bed. No charger. She crept into Luke's room, where Molly and Daisy were sleeping on the floor and touched Molly, then Luke, quietly on the shoulder. 'Have you got a charger?' They sleepily located theirs and handed them over.

They weren't the right make. Heather took a deep breath. Should she wait until everyone was up? No, she couldn't bear to.

She tapped quietly on Kate and Jonny's door and Kate was there immediately, tousled and blinking.

'Any news?' she asked, desperately, and Heather cringed at the hope in her voice.

'Sorry, no – have you got a phone charger I can borrow? Sorry. So sorry.'

'S'fine,' said Kate, hollow-eyed. 'I wasn't sleeping anyway.'

'I can't believe I was so stupid. It was the only thing I had to remember and I forgot it.'

'Not quite the only thing. Don't beat yourself up about it.'

They hunted through the house and found three chargers, none of which worked with Heather's phone.

'I'll have to go home,' said Heather. 'Now.'

Kate nodded.

Chapter 27

In Halstead Hill Sasha couldn't sleep either. She got up and switched on her laptop, and began to work out a list of questions for her next interview, feeling terrified in case Jonny didn't think she was good enough. Jonny was kind but uncompromising, and ran his metaphorical red pencil straight through anything unnecessary.

But it was hard to concentrate. She could tell she'd come to the end of the line with Heather, and that by now even she must be thinking five and a half months was long enough for a house guest to stay. Not that she'd been there all the time, of course, far from it, but still. Apart from anything else, there were army regulations and everyone on the patch was so nosy that at some point someone was bound to report her as living there without authorisation.

In fact, she'd had her half-share of the money from selling the house for some time. It had hit her bank account three months earlier, a fact that she'd kept from Heather and any other nosy parker, like Ella Fox, who asked the most personal questions, fixing Sasha with that penetrating gaze of hers. You'd have thought a woman of that age would have known it was vulgar to talk about money.

Of course, the money looked a lot on paper, but when you found out what sort of a house it would buy her and the children, it was pathetic. How dare Adam? How dare he? And how dare Natalie take away her home and her lifestyle and her friends and leave her on the scrap heap? It was like Lucy, Roderick Morton's second wife, all over again. Women were such bitches. It was take or be taken for a ride. At nights, she lay in bed consumed with rage, tossing and turning. Natalie and Adam had even taken her ability to sleep away from her.

And of course it was all worse because Jack was missing. The thought made her feel cold and tight inside, but nobody cared about that. It was all about Heather, of course. Wives always took the high ground. Nobody thought that other people might have feelings. It was so difficult. It was all so difficult.

Someone as vibrant as Jack couldn't be dead. She was sure that the explanation would be a simple one, to do with weather and broken-down equipment, that Jack would soon be picked up, tanned, thinner, but still with his big, welcoming smile. Heather had no idea how lucky she was. He was funny but so stable, so loving, so connected with his children, and then there was this masculine side to him – the strong, capable arms, the uniform, the guns, the danger, the heroics . . . Sasha sighed. She'd really got to know him over the time she'd been living in the house. When Heather had refused to take him to the airport (what had that been about, she wondered), they laughed and talked as if they would never run out of things to say, and when they'd said good-bye, he'd held her close, as if he couldn't bear to let her go. 'Sorry,' he'd said, huskily. 'There aren't any hugs where I'm going.'

'Well, in that case you deserve one more,' she'd replied, and they'd embraced again. She held the memory inside her, bringing out and turning it over like a secret diamond. She had a handful of similar jewels, sparkling memories that she shared with no one. Sasha didn't believe in those female friendships where you told each other everything. She knew you couldn't trust women.

Then she thought about her television interviews and felt frightened again. She needed to talk to Jonny.

After all, she had a special connection with Jonny. That was clear. Every time she realised that she was in over her head – that she might stutter during the interviews on camera, or that she hadn't perhaps got quite the right questions – she panicked, but Jonny would quietly calm her down.

Yes, a successful career in television would show Adam. She imagined him eating supper with that cow Natalie, switching on the TV because they'd run out of things to say to each other, then her face filling their screen. Adam would realise how much cleverer and more attractive Sasha was than the silly little fool he'd left her for. She couldn't wait. She'd be featured in magazines with a handsome, successful new husband on her arm, and they'd buy a huge, fuck-off house quite near to wherever Adam and Natalie were living, so that the children would find it easy to go from one to the other. Adam would feel as angry and hurt – and as vulnerable and useless – as she did now.

But for now she was living in someone else's house and would have to be satisfied with a credit at the end of the programme. She just hoped it wouldn't roll past too quickly. Sasha Morton. It was quite a distinctive name. Adam and Natalie might see it. And, with any luck, all her so-called brothers and sisters would see it, too, and they'd notice her for a change. She wondered if she should get in touch with the half-brother who was supposed to be writing Roderick Morton's biography. She didn't want to advertise the fact that she had been so utterly left out of the family, but she didn't want to be completely ignored either. She had so much to prove to so many people, and Jonny, in his quirky, intuitive way, understood that. Without Jonny she didn't think she could bear the life that she had now, without a proper home or knowing what her future would be, back to having to be grateful to everyone all the time. Back to being dreary little Sandra everyone felt sorry for.

The telephone rang.

'Heather?' asked a male voice, hoarse with shouting and dust.

'Jack?' asked Sasha. 'Is that really you? It's Sasha, not Heather. Are you all right?'

'Yeah. We had a bit of trouble, but I'm OK.'

'What, not wounded or anything?'

'Well,' he admitted, 'A scratch. Nothing much.'

'Jack, no! That's terrible! You're so brave, I can't believe it.'

'It really is nothing. Is Heather there?'

'No, she went to stay with Kate because she thought you'd been taken prisoner and you'd said that if that happened they

187

might need to move so that Al Qaeda couldn't find them.' She didn't say that Heather had clearly panicked. Lost it. He would find that out for himself. Sasha thought that Heather rather over-did the 'silly little me' act from time to time. Although men quite liked that sort of thing.

'Really?' He sounded stunned. 'Can't think why she did that. I rang her mobile but it's off. I'll try 19 Lovelace Road. Then I'm going to be debriefed and get a bit of medical attention, so I probably won't be able to call for a bit.'

'I'm so glad you're safe.' She heard her voice catch and struggled to control it. 'I couldn't sleep, thinking about you.'

His breath sounded ragged down the phone, and she wondered if he might be crying. 'You are sweet,' he said. 'So very sweet.'

'What happened, Jack?'

'Shit happened,' he said. 'I'll call you later. Don't go away.'

It was so perfect that she, Sasha, had been the first one to speak to him after his ordeal. It was just so right. She hugged the thought to herself.

Basing herself at Heather's had saved quite a tidy sum because it was rent-free and Heather had always been on hand for babysit-ting. Now it was time to move on.

Chapter 28

Olivia had also lain awake, her ears alert for the phone call that might tell them Jack was safe or might be bad news. She veered between thinking she should ring Kate or Heather to see how they were feeling, to deciding not to in case the sound of the phone got their hopes up. She had finally fallen into a heavy sleep at about five, but she had an appointment with Allison Green at eight in the morning. 'It's the only time Miss Green can manage,' her PA had said, her voice tinged with reproach. 'She's flying to a secret holiday destination at midday, so she can't be any later.'

At ten to eight, Olivia strode towards the Campbell Carter building. Two women approached from the opposite direction, heads down as if against a wind, while a small knot of people waited on the Campbell Carter steps. The two women were Allison Green and her PA, heading into a group of paparazzi. As they all reached the steps, a camera began to flash.

'Is it true that you're seeing Damon White? And going on holiday to his secret holiday island?' shouted one reporter.

'Is there any truth in the rumours that you're asking for a thirty-five-million-pound settlement?' called another, as Olivia caught up with them.

Allison clutched at Olivia's elbow as if for protection and held her handbag against her face, as they briefly fought their way through the knot.

'Excuse me,' said Olivia, firmly, pulling her client through.

'Please let us pass. Excuse me. Excuse me. Thank you.' She felt the press of elbows and hips against hers. The Campbell Carter security officer opened the door to pull them through, talking urgently into his walkie-talkie. There was a last shouted question.

'Is it true that Chat Show Ted never allowed you to wear knickers?'

Allison gasped and turned. 'Please,' she raised her voice above the traffic. 'Can't you report some real news? There are wars, there are people dying, there's starvation, and really critical things happening all over the world that affect all of us. Even here, there are more important stories. My lawyer's brother has been missing for three days in the mountains of Temanistan, probably captured by insurgents, but nobody cares enough to report that . . .' There was a catch in her voice. 'You should be covering people who are truly brave, like Olivia here, at work even though her brother's in terrible danger, not concentrating on what lingerie I'm wearing . . . He's trapped in dangerous territory because he's been let down by his equipment like so many of our brave boys . . .'

'No, we don't know that,' said Olivia desperately. 'Really, there's nothing to report.'

She hauled Allison and the PA through the door and the security guard slammed it behind them. A few flashes went off, then the small pack jumped on to their scooters and left.

'I'm *so* sorry about that.' Allison sounded genuinely distraught. 'I didn't know they'd be there. I'm mortified that you've been caught up in the circus that seems to surround me these days. And your poor family. They don't deserve this on top of all the worry. Although a bit of publicity might speed up the rescue efforts, don't you think?'

Olivia hardly knew where to begin. Heather said that the army advised against talking to the press, because it could perhaps endanger Jack. Was this true? Or was it time that there was some publicity, was Jack's rescue being shuffled around the paperwork of Whitehall and costed out as budgetary extravagance?

She pressed the lift button, casting a look over her shoulder. 'The army's doing everything it can. Publicity can only hurt Jack.'

Allison raised a disbelieving eyebrow. 'Lord knows that I've had my share of anguish over the press but . . . anyway, that's not the point. You should never have been subjected to all that, and I can only say sorry from the bottom of my heart.'

'How did they know you'd be there?' Olivia was upset to think that the Foxes might see this melee on their TV screens. Poor Heather. Poor, poor Heather.

The lift swished them effortlessly up to the fifth floor and disgorged them with a 'ping'. 'I really don't know,' said Allison. 'I have to tell people about arrangements, for practical reasons, and although I'm fairly careful about how I chat to friends, I don't know who to trust these days, I really don't. That's why I'm asking for money for bodyguards and round-the-clock protection. In a normal divorce people take sides – he or she is *my* friend or *my* family – but in this one the whole country is taking sides. Everyone loves Ted, so they have to hate me.'

There was some truth in this. 'But I think it would help if you could keep a very low profile,' insisted Olivia, showing Allison into the meeting room. 'There must be some way of keeping your movements under cover.'

'If I subjected myself to a sort of house arrest,' agreed Allison, seating herself. 'But that's not fair on Lily. She has a right to the normal life of a child, to friendships, to days out at theme parks, to go to birthday parties with the rest of her class at nursery . . . and of course these days, we have to deal with possibilities like kidnapping for ransom.'

'Not in Britain,' said Olivia. But suppose she was wrong? Suppose she persuaded Allison Green that she didn't need round-the-clock protection and little Lily was taken?

Allison grasped Olivia's hand, as if she was drowning and Olivia was a lifebelt. 'Before I married Ted I was a Z-list celebrity. I was rich, but I was nobody. Very occasionally I'd appear third item down in the gossip columns accompanied by a picture of me in an evening dress because I'm blonde and pretty. But I had a normal life. More to the point, I had a *private*, normal life. Nobody hated me. Since marrying Ted, that's gone out the window, and that's why I need the money to deal with it. What he's taken from me – even though he hasn't done it deliberately – is very precious to me. It's my good name and my private life.'

'There are privacy laws . . .' Olivia gently disentangled Allison's soft, manicured hand from her own harder, gym-toned grip.

Allison rolled her eyes. 'I invited the press in the early days – when I didn't know any better – and that will count against me. I only agreed to do a few pieces on the interior of our house, so that the fees could go to charity. I had no idea that I was setting myself up for a lifetime of looking over my shoulder.'

Once again, there was some truth in it all. Allison didn't seem like the mad, money-obsessed harridan portrayed in the press. Olivia looked at Allison's PA but her face was inscrutable. 'All I can say, Allison, is that you need to keep as quiet as you can about where you're going and what you're doing.'

'Would you like to live like that?' flashed Allison. 'Watching everything you say in case someone sells it to the press? Not being able to visit a friend in case the photographers are there?'

'I wouldn't like it at all,' agreed Olivia, opening her files, and trying to forget about her headache. She was no longer quite sure whether Allison had set the photocall up deliberately. She just hoped the link was too convoluted to be publishable: would anyone really be interested in the fact that Allison Green's lawyer's brother-in-law was missing? She sighed.

'Now, as you know, we've got the Financial Dispute Resolution coming up in a few weeks' time, where both sides present their financial case to the judge. It's the most important . . .'

'It certainly is,' agreed Allison warmly. 'Don't worry. I know what to do. A nice pale suit which can obviously only be worn once before it's dry-cleaned, my sapphire ring, my three rows of pearls, I've got a really good brooch which I call my Divorce Court Brooch because that's the only place I ever wear it, but it does scream money . . . I do realise that I have to make it clear that, during this marriage, I have become accustomed to a *very* high standard of living.'

Olivia paused. 'Allison, the problem is that you are wealthier than Ted Cross.'

Allison looked astonished. 'He's not having a penny off me. If he does, I shall sue you. I've never heard . . .'

Olivia raised her hand. 'What you brought to the marriage are pre-acquired assets, and it's unlikely he'll be awarded anything from them, and there is a child to consider, so you will get some money from him, but not as much as . . .'

'Ted is really rich, you know,' interrupted Allison. 'He hides his money in off-shore accounts. Look, I've got paperwork. And he's hung on to everything he's ever earned: he's so mean, he reuses his dental floss.' She brought a flurry of papers out, and Olivia took them. There would be piles of documents before this was over.

There was a tap at the door. 'Your brother-in-law's safe.' Cat, the PA, put her head round. 'We thought you'd like to know immediately.'

'Brother-in-law?' said Allison, sharply. 'I thought you said he was your brother.'

'That's wonderful news, thank you, Cat. No, Jack's my brother-in-law.' Olivia had had this response from one or two colleagues and friends. Jack was 'only' a brother-in-law, and therefore she couldn't be too worried about him. But she felt as deeply protective of him as she would of any blood relative. She was closer to all the Foxes than she was to her own sister, but it was hard to explain that. Olivia was not only relieved to hear that Jack was safe, but she was glad that Allison Green was there to hear it too. Somebody who had been missing and was now found was not, Olivia hoped, a news story. She still didn't quite trust Allison not to whip up some kind of link to Jack in her continual fascination with publicity, and Jack had enough problems on his hands.

Olivia picked up her pen. 'Shall we continue discussions? For example, what about Lily's holiday arrangements?'

As soon as Allison Green had been whisked off to a private jet in her chauffeur-driven car, Olivia called Si. He had been told by Kate, Heather and Ella already, as she knew he would.

'But I'm still glad you called,' he said. 'I love you very much.'

'I love you too,' she replied, feeling guilty. She had a squiggled entry in her diary for the following week, which she wasn't going to tell him about.

'Thank God it's over.' He put the phone down.

But it wasn't.

Si and Olivia had a state-of-the-art TV integrated into the door of their huge steel fridge. That evening, they watched the news with one eye, over salad and a glass of wine, perched on stools at their breakfast bar. They'd both worked till past nine that night. A salad, a glass of wine, the news and then bed. It was a comforting working-week routine.

There was a hurricane in Louisiana, house prices were still falling, the twentieth teenager that year had been stabbed in London and two British soldiers had been killed in Temanistan. Olivia didn't quite understand what she was hearing.

'But Jack's back.'

'It must be the men he was with,' said Si. 'It couldn't be a coincidence, could it?'

None of the news reports had much detail. Two British soldiers had been killed while on a routine mission in the mountain region of Temanistan and their families had been informed. A map flashed up behind the newsreader giving a vague indication of where Temanistan was, as nobody in Britain would have heard of it. Somewhere near Russia. A bit north of Afghanistan. Not as far west as Turkey. The dispassionate voice of the newsreader held no clues as to whether the deaths had been a result of fighting or an accident.

Olivia and Si had both agreed, several times, that there was something suspicious about Jack's presence in Temanistan. If the British Army were operating outside their sphere of influence, there could be international repercussions.

'Jack is clearly not doing a desk job,' Si had said, more than once. 'But we'd better not discuss that in front of Heather.'

Now he looked worried. 'What's my bloody fool of a brother got himself into now?' He took out his phone and began dialling Kate.

Chapter 29

Heather found out that Jack was safe after she'd struggled through an unusually heavy early-morning rush hour to get to Halstead Hill. There had been an accident on one road which, combined with roadworks on another, had created a solid bottleneck. The sun rose quickly and the car was airless and stifling. Heather could feel beads of sweat on her face. At the front door, it took two attempts before her hand was steady enough to get the key into the lock. As she walked in Sasha came out to greet her, with a pale, wild look on her face.

'What's happened?' Heather whispered. 'Have they phoned?' She stood motionless in the middle of the room, terrified of hearing what Sasha had to say.

Sasha blew her nose. 'Jack's safe. He was able to call himself. He was going to try you at Kate's, but then he said he'd have to go into debriefing. He's OK.'

Heather could hear her own heart thumping in her ears. 'I've been in traffic for hours. My mobile doesn't work.' She went on staring at Sasha.

'Heather, did you hear me? Jack's safe.' Sasha tried to enfold Heather in a theatrical embrace. 'It's all over. He's being debriefed.' But Heather stood like a stone, not responding in any way, and eventually Sasha backed off. 'You're in shock, darling. I'll get you a cup of tea.'

It took Heather another five minutes before she was able to get her shaking hands under control sufficiently to get the mobile out of her basket and reconnect it to its charger. She didn't dare believe the nightmare was truly over until she heard it from Major Harris.

Major Harris picked up immediately. 'Have you had the good news? Lieutenant-Colonel Fox is back at the Embassy. We've been trying to call you.'

'Yes,' croaked Heather, wondering why she suddenly couldn't make her voice work. 'I've just heard.' She cleared her throat and tried to steady her breathing. 'But I don't understand. What happened?'

Suddenly waves of exaltation washed over her. Jack safe. All over. Jack safe. It was like a heartbeat, the most precious heartbeat of all.

And then she remembered the other women, waiting like her. 'Is everyone back? What happened to the others? Weren't there three others with Jack? And the back-up team?' asked Heather.

There was a pause. 'I can't say anything about anyone else,' said Major Harris, and Heather detected something odd in her voice. 'But Lieutenant-Colonel Fox will be flown back to Heathrow tomorrow on a commercial flight, where you'll be able to meet him. You can even drive him down to be debriefed, if you like, but you won't have him home for a few days. We'll let you know the details when we have them.'

'Flown back? Is he hurt?' Her heart speeded up again.

Another pause. 'He needs to be checked out. And debriefed.'

'But everything's fine? Isn't it?'

'You don't need to worry,' said Major Harris.

'Good. Oh, thank you so much. So much. Really.'

'It's a pleasure,' came the calm reply, but Heather could tell she meant it.

Heather felt like she'd breathed out for the first time in nearly four days. Jack was all right.

Sasha came back with a cup of tea, still looking very upset. 'Now that Jack's been found, can you do the school pick-up this afternoon? After all this, I need a massage.'

Heather gazed at her in amazement. Sasha had been doing all the school runs, it was true. It was time for Heather to pull her weight, but . . .

'You're so calm, Heather,' said Sasha. 'I do wish I was more like you. I'm in bits – you obviously don't feel things like I do.'

'I'll do the school run,' said Heather, her voice sounding hollow and wooden even to her own ears.

'By the way, I got my decree absolute in the post just now,' said Sasha. 'It's all over. Now I can move out and find somewhere to live. It's all so upsetting.' She blew her nose again.

That evening, they almost missed the news. Heather, still too wired to sleep, watched a detective drama and was just about to switch off when the headlines came on.

'Sasha, two British soldiers have just been killed in Temanistan.'

'Well, I promise you it was Jack on the phone. And you had the call from the Casualty Visiting Officer. So it absolutely can't be him.'

'It must have been one of the others with him. I'll just have to wait for him to tell me.' Heather's voice shook as she thought of the women like her, also waiting, whose phones had rung early that morning with a very different message. 'It couldn't be a coincidence, could it?'

Sasha slowly shook her head.

'What did he say exactly, Sasha? What were his words?' Heather wished she had been the one who had got Jack's first call home. How could she have been so stupid as to go to Kate's and leave her charger behind?

'He didn't really say anything at all,' replied Sasha. 'Just that he was fine, to send his love.'

Heather, meeting Sasha's innocent gaze, suddenly did not believe her.

Chapter 30

When Kate ran inside to answer the phone after seeing Virginia off, it was indeed Jack.

'Jack, how amazing! I can't tell you how worried we've all been.' She put a hand over the phone. 'Mumma! Someone tell Mumma Jack's OK.' She went back to Jack. 'What happened?'

He hesitated. 'It wasn't my fault.'

'I'm sure it probably wasn't.' Kate couldn't help sounding doubtful. She'd often heard Jack say these words. So often. It transported her back to their school days, and the times she and Si had had to try to get Jack out of trouble.

'Kate! You have no idea what I've been through, you can't sit in judgement on me.'

'I'm not sitting in judgement at all. I'm just glad you're back. Have you spoken to Heather? Are you going to call Si or shall I?'

'Heather's not at home so I've missed her, but I spoke to Sasha who'll give her the news. And I've got to be debriefed so I won't have time to call Si. I haven't slept properly for four days, and I just need to get my head down.'

'Mumma's here, talk to her for a moment. And see you when you're back. Lots of love.'

Kate handed the phone to Ella with misgiving. 'No time to talk to Si' meant there was definitely something Jack didn't want to own up to. Si was uncompromising, and often accused her of being soft where Jack was concerned.

Ella's eyes were shining as she put down the phone. 'Thank

God for that. Thank God.' She put a hand on her chest and took great gulps of air.

'Are you a bit breathless, Mumma?'

'Just hurrying down the stairs to get to the phone. But isn't it wonderful news? So wonderful.' She put a hand out to the walls to steady herself as she went to sit down. Kate frowned. Ella was really getting very frail. Only last year she had walked ten miles for charity; now she suddenly seemed older than her years.

'Safe?' Jonny stood beside her with his arms open and Kate let him wrap them round her.

'Safe,' she agreed, letting the relief flood over her.

'If you don't want to go to Virginia's for Christmas, we won't,' he whispered into her ear.

For a moment Kate was tempted, but she remembered how excited Luke and Callum had looked, and even the anticipation in Jonny's eyes.

'No, it's fine,' she said, with a massive effort. 'It'll be a nice change. Boys,' she pulled them into Jonny's arms too. 'Uncle Jack is safe, and we're going to Scotland for Christmas.'

'Ya-ay!' said Luke.

Ella, Kate and Jonny watched the ten o'clock news together. Ella immediately took in the implications of the two soldiers who had died.

'Jack did something silly out there,' she said, her hand on her heart again. 'He is so rash. I can quite see why the SAS didn't want him in the end, he just rushes off and does things without thinking about them, and . . .'

Kate put an arm out to her mother. 'Mumma, you can't deduce that just from two soldiers being killed in the same country. They could have been in a completely different part of Temanistan.'

'Oh, I could hear it in Jack's voice when he spoke to me. It was like that time he had that punch-up with the local boys and you all pretended he'd fallen off his bike. I know that tone of his. You all keep secrets from me . . . or maybe you're too busy to see what's under your noses . . .' She took a deep lungful of air . . . 'but I'm not just a foolish old woman you know, I just don't want you to make the mistakes I made . . . but you won't listen, none of you.'

'Mumma?' You're sweating.'

Ella got up, flapping her hand in distress. 'I'll just have a little air, if that's all right . . . could you open the back door, darling?'

Kate didn't like the grey colour of her mother's skin, or the beads of sweat on her forehead. 'I think you should sit down quietly for a moment. Does anything hurt?'

'My chest feels a bit tight,' admitted Ella. 'But it's—' she gasped, '—nothing to worry about.

'Just stay as quiet as possible, Mumma,' begged Kate. 'I'm going to call a doctor.'

'Oh, I don't want to bother the doctor.' She managed the whole sentence, but it took time.

Callum drifted into the room, opening the fridge, but caught sight of his grandmother. 'Granny?' His voice went high with alarm.

'Callum . . .' She stretched out her hand. 'Dear boy.'

'You don't look very well, Granny.'

'It's so . . . airless . . . in here . . . too hot for September, I can't . . . breathe.'

Jonny opened the back door, looking worried, and caught Ella as she pitched through it.

After a terrifying wait for the ambulance – only twelve minutes, but the longest twelve minutes of her life – Kate followed it to the hospital, having told Callum that no, he couldn't come with her, because it was school in the morning, and spent the next four hours waiting by Ella's side. She either lay, looking frighteningly still, under her oxygen mask, or tried to talk about Jack.

'Mumma, please stop worrying about him. Even if he has got into trouble, he's back alive, and that's what matters.'

'Oh, I know you, Kate, you and Si used to try and keep Jack's pranks away from me – what about those girls he used to smuggle into the house at night? I could hear them giggling, you know . . . and the one that insisted on climbing down the drainpipe and broke it, remember? Jack said it was storm damage,' she wheezed, 'but the insurers didn't agree and I had to pay for a new one. Why she couldn't have used the door like the rest of them, I'll never know. Jack never obeys rules, and you can't be like that in the army. He won't get promotion, you know, and then . . .'

'Mumma! Please. Jack is now an adult and he can look after himself. Si and I no longer have that responsibility and neither do you.'

Ella managed a ghost of a smile. 'No, it's poor Heather's job now. I don't think she's up to it, she's such a funny little thing.'

'Heather is a lot tougher than you think.' It was true, reflected Kate. 'In fact, she's amazing, when you think of what she has to put up with – moving house every eighteen months, being left alone with the children for at least three months a year, having to make new friends, worrying about whether Jack's going to be killed . . .'

Ella flapped her hand weakly in denial, but she tried to smile. 'At least Heather is a nice girl,' she said, forcing every word out. 'And Katie . . . I'm worried about you too . . .'

'Don't be, I'm fine.'

'You should be nicer to Jonny,' wheezed her mother. 'You criticise him too much.'

Kate tried not to react. This was so unfair. Jonny left her to shoulder everything at home, and she was accused of criticism? But her mother's health came first. 'Jonny's fine, Mumma. We're fine.'

'19 Lovelace Road,' gasped her mother. 'When I die, I want you to do two things with the money: get married and pay off some of the mortgage, because you've made it a real home for the boys . . . all their security is there and . . . I'm not a rich woman, but . . .'

'Mumma, please, you're not going to die. You've got years and years yet.'

Kate looked at her mobile. It had three missed calls from Si. 'I'm just going out to call Si, OK? I'll be back soon.'

After finding out how Ella was, Si said he agreed with her. 'Jack's obviously cocked it up.'

'I don't see how you can say that. You don't know what happened yet.'

'Jack will have been in charge. The men killed were a corporal and a staff sergeant – they said so on the news when they named them. Jack's a colonel. And British soldiers shouldn't die somewhere where the British Army technically isn't operating, so someone – probably the most senior officer – has screwed up somewhere. It's logic, Kate. Face it.'

'But Jack could have been let down by his equipment. Or the soldiers themselves.'

'I know some of these guys,' said Si, who always had to know everybody. 'If Jack was out in Temanistan on a mission, he'll have had some of the best soldiers in the world with him. The British Army doesn't fool around, and they know what they're up to, whatever your soft, lefty friends might like to think.'

'I don't have soft, lefty friends.' Kate was furious. 'The people I know don't take everything the authorities say at face value, that's all. We don't automatically believe that the people in charge know what they're doing.'

'Oddly enough, the people in charge quite often do know what they're doing. Things have changed a bit since the First World War, you know. Even since Vietnam. Which is where the liberal left formed its opinions about the army, which it hasn't bothered to change since.'

Kate was irritated. 'Rubbish. Well, whatever it was, and I think it's ridiculous to speculate until we know the facts, we need to support Jack. And Mumma. You know how she worries. If Jack is in trouble, we mustn't let her know anything about it. She's lying there under an oxygen mask at the moment. It could kill her.'

'Kate, I've no intention of worrying her. In any way. Although sometimes I think she'd appreciate the truth.'

'Si! Don't you dare! I'm the one who talks to her every day. I know what she thinks and feels, and I promise you, she is *not* strong enough to cope with Jack being in trouble.'

'I wonder if we should talk to her about a will. And enduring power of attorney – that's a document she signs so that we can make decisions for her if she's unconscious or not in her right mind. I could pay her bills with her chequebook, for example. And we don't know if she's thought about proper inheritance tax planning . . .'

'Now is not the time, Si. She's talking about dying, you can't worry her. And you're rich enough to pay her bills anyway, without having to use her chequebook.' She and Jack always used to joke that Si was so tight his wallet had moths in it.

'Kate, when someone is dying is exactly the time to talk about wills.'

'Not if you upset them. She's been upset enough by Jack, we don't want to make it worse. Couldn't you just stop thinking about money for five minutes?'

As soon as she slammed her phone shut, she hurried back to A&E to see if there was any news on how her mother's tests were going. For the next four hours, she watched and waited, already exhausted from three sleepless nights. At one point she lay down on the floor beside her mother's trolley and closed her eyes, but a nurse, firm but sympathetic, told her that it wasn't allowed. It was half past four before she stumbled to the car park and drove home in a fog of exhaustion. But at least by then they had told her that Ella had had a very minor heart attack. 'We'll keep her in for a few days for a few more tests, and there'll be a programme of medication . . .' the doctor, looking as tired as Kate felt, looked down at Ella with a smile. 'We'll have you back in your garden no time.'

Ella smiled. 'I'm a tough old bird. You won't get rid of me easily.'

The doctor smiled again. 'I can see that.'

Chapter 31

Jack returned from Temanistan on an ordinary commercial flight. Heather took Daisy and Molly out of school to greet him at Heathrow. Eventually he emerged from customs, his face gaunt and his clothes hanging loose. The girls raced to greet him, jumping up and locking their legs round his waist. Travis wagged his tail so hard that his whole body wriggled from side to side.

'Travis knew,' said Heather, her words choking in her throat. 'He told me you were in trouble.'

Jack bent down so that Travis could slobber all over him. 'Clever dog.'

'And a kiss for my wife.' He pulled Heather towards him, as he rose to his feet. She was shocked by his thinness and the lines on his face. Stocky, well-built people like Jack looked almost distorted when they were too thin. He was brown, too, and there were two weathered sores on his forehead, as if the sun had burned holes in him.

'Are you all right?'

'Just tired.' He disentangled the girls and took Heather's hand. 'I can't come home with you, you know. I have to go straight to be debriefed.'

She nodded. 'I just wanted to see you. And I'm going to drive you there. It's all arranged. Sasha's going to take the girls home.'

'Sasha? She's here?'

'She's waiting in the car park. We came in convoy.'

'That was kind of her.'

'She's been great. But she's leaving. She's got a flat nearer London. Not too far away, though. Look, there she is.'

Sasha, dressed in black, in tight trousers and high boots, like a principal boy in a pantomime, had the sun behind her. Heather caught a flash of the deep lines around her smile and her hair swinging across her face in a dark, glossy chunk as she reached up to kiss Jack.

'Welcome home, hero.'

'Hardly, I'm afraid.'

'You're a hero to us,' said Sasha in her deep, throaty tones.

'What happened, Jack?' asked Heather as she unlocked their car. She couldn't keep the worry out of her voice.

'For God's sake, Heather, I've already had to tell everyone at the Embassy, over and over again, and now I've got to go through it all again. Just let me rest for the time being.' He threw off his backpack, levered his seat back and closed his eyes.

'I was terrified. For four days I thought you might be a prisoner.'

He opened his eyes. They were bloodshot. 'Not as terrified as I was, I can assure you. Try four days with your back to a pile of rocks, with a limited amount of food, water and ammunition, a dying man beside you and a valley full of insurgents below, all armed to the teeth, while the fucking Temanistani Army looks for its socks and cranks up its only Jeep in a pretty bloody shambolic attempt to come and find you. Oh, and I don't think I mentioned the weather, did I? The kind you can't get helicopters through? Or the communications? Or do I mean lack of them? Except the personal fucking locator beacon, of course.'

'Please tell me about it. Then I can understand better.'

'Really? Like I understood the unexpected death of your mother better after you talked about it?'

It was a slap in the face.

'OK. Here it is.' Jack filled in the silence. 'We got news of a contact who was willing to talk to us. Not just about the situation in Temanistan but also about the training camps we think they've got up there in the mountains. I mounted an FHT . . .'

Heather darted him a quick glance, which he misinterpreted.

'Field Human Intelligence Team.' He spelt it out as if she was stupid. 'We were in two CAVs, as usual . . .' he glared at her.

'Civilianised Armoured Vehicles,' she whispered. 'Really, I do remember these things.'

'Good. It's nice to know someone listens to me occasionally. Well, we got to within half an hour of the meet, and the back-up CAV, carrying four of the close protection team, broke down. I don't know why, don't ask me to explain it, but it couldn't be repaired by any of us. So we radioed for another vehicle, which they told us would take a day to get to us. But that contact we were meeting was very important.'

Out of the corner of her eye she could see a muscle working furiously in his cheek.

'We had one narrow window of opportunity to make the most of the best lead I'd had since getting to Temanistan,' continued Jack. 'We couldn't get there a day late. He wouldn't be there. There were lives resting on that intelligence.'

Heather could hardly bear to hear what was coming next.

'I decided we had no option but to go on alone. I mean, what choice did I have?'

'None, I suppose, but . . .'

'Shut up,' he said. 'Just shut up and listen. You know nothing about it. You haven't been out there with lives depending on you. You didn't have to take that decision. I did.'

'What happened then?'

'About two hours later, we hit a roadside bomb. Maybe a land-mine. We weren't sure. It pretty much took all our heads off, and when I came to, Corporal Parker . . . was dead. Very dead. He was the driver and he had the satellite phone. It was wrecked. Nothing of it left. And Staff Sergeant Mayhew's leg was across the other side of the road, still with its boot attached.'

Heather gasped in horror. 'No!'

'Yes!' he shouted. 'You ask me what went wrong, and I'm bloody well telling you. If you can't take it, I'll shut up now.'

'No, really, please . . . it's better if I know.' It began to rain, and Heather switched her windscreen wipers on, peering over the steering wheel at the spray thrown up by huge lorries. She was busy working out what to do. The risks of post-traumatic stress had been drummed into her. If your husband came back from war a completely different person, then he would need urgent help for

PTSD. It was the only explanation she could think of: what he had gone through had broken him. He would never have spoken to her so cruelly before.

'You don't exactly come out of a bang like that thinking straight, you know, but I knew that if it was a IED . . .' He shot a look at her.

'Improvised Explosive Device,' she whispered. 'Everyone knows about them here now.'

'Well . . .' He spoke slowly, as if she was very stupid. 'If it had been an IED, there would have been someone setting it off, which in turn means you get company pretty soon. People shooting at you. So I got a tourniquet on Staff's thigh, and we grabbed our bug-out sacks, and we grabbed Staff and Parky's H&K's . . .' He caught Heather's eye again. This time she really didn't know what the acronym stood for. 'Those swanky little machine guns you see toted by the police at airports. And we had a couple of rifles, too, and the ammunition in the bug-out sacks, plus an under-slung grenade launcher. So we had to get all that, plus Staff, who was practically unconscious, to a position we could defend before whoever set off the bomb came back to finish us off.'

He sank into a long silence, and Heather gripped the steering wheel as they overtook another huge truck in the rain. The windscreen wipers slapped back and forth.

'We found a rocky outcrop about half a mile from the vehicle,' he said, eventually, 'with a bit of shelter, and we got ourselves set up there, me and the interpreter, Sergeant McKenzie, plus Staff, who was in a pretty bad way. Then we set off the personal locator beacon and waited. The weather got shittier and shittier, and we knew there was no chance of any kind of helicopter rescue, so we'd have to make the rations and ammunition last.'

The dual carriageway contracted to a two-lane road and Heather slowed down to thirty miles an hour. The oncoming traffic turned into a succession of headlights emerging from the murky rain and her knuckles gleamed white with tension.

'Staff died that evening.' Jack's voice closed up. 'We used up all our morphine, and I think he floated off. Then Sergeant McKenzie and I took turns to keep watch.'

'Did you . . . get attacked . . . by separatists in the end?' Heather tried to imagine a gun battle, with Jack and Sergeant McKenzie against dozens of ragged men.

There was such a long silence that she thought Jack had fallen asleep. 'There were a couple of armed men,' he said, eventually. 'On the second day. I think they'd come to take a look at us. We pointed our guns at them and they ran away. Maybe they were farmers, or just curious. But we knew it was just a question of time after that.'

They drove on through the rain for another ten miles, and the road opened out again. 'The fog cleared up on the third day,' he continued. 'Easier for the helicopter to find us. Easier for the terrorists, too. Luckily, the Temanistani Army helicopter got there first. I think it was a close thing, though, because when we got back to the CAV, it was completely stripped out. Someone – locals, farmers, terrorists – had taken everything they could find. It was just a twisted frame and Parks's body when we got to it. At least we got that back.'

Heather didn't understand the obsession with getting bodies back. If you were gone, you were gone. 'Was he married?'

'He was. They both were.'

Heather didn't dare ask about children, but her heart contracted to think of two neat army sitting rooms, and the pale shocked faces who would now have just a smiling photograph to remind them of what their lives used to be like. And the mothers and fathers whose sunshine had been blotted out forever. The sisters and brothers, and cousins, and aunts and friends, who would struggle to understand that someone they loved really wasn't coming back. Not ever. She concentrated on driving through the rain, occasionally using the back of her hand to sweep a tear off her cheek.

'They're going to blame me,' said Jack. 'But what could I do?'

'Oh, Jack!' It was worse than she'd even dreamed. 'Why was . . .'

'*Oh, Jack*,' he repeated, cruelly. 'That's why I don't tell you things, Heather. Because it upsets you.' He closed his eyes again.

'I think I have a right to be upset. It's because I love you.' Heather kept her voice even and calm, trying not to feel hurt. But she was shocked to her core. Of course, Jack had been through a life-threatening experience. It seemed to have changed him. There was no trace of the old loving, laughing Jack left. She had always thought he was so strong, but perhaps it was the strongest that fell hardest.

She turned the radio on, softly, and tried to tell herself that maybe it was natural for him to be tired and tetchy, and that she must be understanding. After a few minutes, the tinny music terminated in the news.

'Questions are being asked about the deaths of two British soldiers in the remote mountain region of Temanistan . . .'

Jack turned the radio off without opening his eyes.

'Jack, what were you really involved in? Was it spying? It was obviously more than just a desk job, wasn't it? Surely it would be much better to talk about—'

'For Christ's sake,' he said. 'Spare me the cod psychology. Coming from you, that's rich. We talked about everything, Heather, didn't we? Except that we didn't. While I've been away, I've been wondering who you actually are. Why, why, *why* keep things a secret from *me*? A marriage is based on trust, Heather, and you obviously never trusted me. Do you know how much that hurt? Have you given it any thought at all?'

She wasn't going to turn this into a conversation about herself. 'Are you in trouble?' She could barely concentrate on the road ahead. Her hands had begun to shake, just thinking about Mo again. And Jack didn't understand. She couldn't tell him, he wouldn't understand.

She was suddenly overwhelmed by despair, and by her own stupidity. She could hear Mo's voice telling her she was useless, and had a sudden desire to drive the car straight into the face of an oncoming truck.

Two glaring headlights bore down on them through the rain and the sudden boom of the truck's horn resonated in the car.

'Christ!' said Jack, as she swerved at the last minute. 'What were you thinking of?'

'It was the rain. I didn't see that truck coming.' She drove on for a few miles. 'So will you be disciplined?'

'You're sounding like my mother,' he snapped. 'It's none of your business. So just give me a break.'

'I'm your wife,' she replied, her throat closing up. Jack hated tears. 'Anything that hurts you is my business.'

'Funny kind of wife,' he muttered. 'One who keeps her own mother a secret.'

She didn't reply and a few minutes later he was snoring.

Or was he? There was something about the tension in his body that made her think he was acting. Heather blinked away more tears, wiping them furiously away, and tightened her grip on the steering wheel. It would be difficult for Jack to adjust to being back, but provided she kept up a good front, and kept the house tidy, everything would be fine.

Later that day, after a total of almost seven hours' driving, Heather let herself into the house in Halstead Hill. The girls were with Sasha, Tom and Grace somewhere. She was bone-weary and her head ached. Jack had never been like this, never. She wondered if there was anyone she could talk to about it, but it would be disloyal – and perhaps even risky to Jack's career – to take anyone in the army into her confidence, and friends outside were even less likely to understand.

But she could call Kate. Kate knew Jack better than anyone else. Nervously, Heather called Kate, ostensibly to see how Ella was.

Kate was at the hospital with Ella again. 'She seems a lot better this morning. How's Jack?'

'In a filthy temper. Whatever I say seems to make him angry.'

'I should think that's pretty normal,' said Kate. 'Give it a couple of weeks, and with any luck you should have the old Jack back.'

Heather told Kate what Jack had been through.

'Oh, dear, it sounds as if Si was right about Jack cocking it up. I suspect he shouldn't have gone ahead once the back-up was out of action.'

'I'm sure of it,' agreed Heather. 'I think I remember Jack telling me about how rules were rules and you didn't break them unless you had to because without discipline an army can't function safely. I think it was in the middle of an argument we were having about the girls. So I can't imagine what could have got into him. It's all top secret, by the way, so don't tell him I told you.'

'Of course not.' Kate rang off.

Heather made herself a cup of tea. Almost immediately there

was a ring at the door. Maybe Major Harris? She opened it to see a clean-faced young man with clipped short, army hair, standing there with an open smile and a large bottle. Behind him was a car, its bonnet up.

'I'm so terribly sorry to disturb you,' he said. 'But my car is out of water and I wondered . . .' He waved the bottle.

'Oh!' Heather looked up and down the road to see if anyone else was around. Jack had impressed basic security precautions on her, and opening the door to strangers, however pleasant they seemed, was a silly thing to do. 'Well, all right, but . . .' She held her hand out for the water bottle.

'These houses all used to be owned by the army when I was stationed round here,' he commented, wiping his feet carefully on the door mat and coming in.

'Most of them still are. My husband's in the army.' Heather scuttled ahead of him to the sink, thoroughly unnerved by the way he'd got into the house.

'Really? What does he think about this Temanistan thing then? My name's Tim, by the way. Tim Proctor. I was in the Guards. Just for three years.'

Posh then, thought Heather, filling up the bottle and heading back towards the door. 'He hasn't said anything about it.'

'I'm not surprised,' said Tim. 'It doesn't look good for the British Army and the officers involved, does it?'

'Doesn't it?'

'Well, I gather that the British Army were on an undercover mission inside Temanistan. Which the Russians are not going to like. Considering it's their sphere of influence.'

'But they were there at the invitation of the Temanistani government,' Heather blurted out, and then felt herself go pink. 'One of them was a friend of ours,' she added, nervously.

'Really?' Tim raised his eyebrows. 'Poor bloke. I expect they'll hang him out to dry, don't you think? Save the government embarrassment by blaming an individual? That's what they do, isn't it?'

'Is it? But it wasn't Jack's fault, there was a bomb . . .' She caught herself just in time. 'Apparently.'

Tim hovered on the doorstep, barely seeming interested. 'What, not a Russian bomb, surely?'

211

'Insurgents, I think. I don't know. I don't think anyone knows.'

She waited until he drove off. By now Heather was badly frightened at the thought of what could happen to Jack. Would he be thrown out of the army? The phone was ringing and she rushed to get it, hoping it was Jack.

It was Sasha. 'How was Jack?'

Heather was always careful not to say too much to anyone. 'He was in a bit of a mood.'

'He's been through a lot,' said Sasha. 'He must have been so frightened. Although of course he'd never admit it. Personally I think he did the right thing – of course he had to go on and try to find out information that could save so many people's lives. The army are just being stuffy about it.'

Heather tried to think what she'd told Sasha. She was talking as if she knew what had happened.

Or maybe not. Maybe she'd just been making assumptions like everyone else.

'Heather, you've been through a lot too,' said Sasha, in honeyed tones. 'Perhaps you're just raw with it all. This is probably the point at which both you and he need a shoulder to lean on, and neither of you are strong enough to be that shoulder.'

'You're probably right.'

'Well, if there's anything I can do . . . I'm pretty tough, you know, and I'm more than happy to be an ear whenever you or Jack need one. You don't want to talk to anyone in the army, do you? Not if it's going the direction it seems to be going?'

Why did everyone seem to know so much more than she did? 'Thanks,' said Heather, humbly. 'That means a lot to me. And I will call you, if that's OK.'

'Anytime. I mean that. Even the middle of the night. You know how I never sleep.'

Heather frowned as she put the phone down. Sasha seemed to know an awful lot about it. Well, never mind. The whole family was speculating madly, and she'd probably just picked up on it somehow, maybe from Kate via Jonny. Kate could transmit gossip faster than the speed of light.

Chapter 32

A week later Olivia was setting off for Providence Cottage, having sneaked a much-needed day off into her crowded schedule. She pressed her foot down hard on the accelerator, enjoying the powerful surge forward and the throaty roar, leaving the roundabouts, pedestrians and traffic lights of south London behind in a cloud of fumes. She loved her car. While Si was only interested in the name on his, and whether it could be relied upon and whether the colour was suitably fashionable or tasteful, she knew what went on under the bonnet.

Olivia's father, Sir Fergus Montmorency, had been a keen amateur racing driver and it had been almost the only thing she'd done with him, sitting for hour after hour beside him from the age of four onwards, passing him spanners as he repaired and rebuilt his collection of vintage racing cars in the coach house at Brampton. They'd sold Brampton when she was twelve, she'd been sent to boarding school and her father had stopped racing. He began to look bent, and older than his age, and she began to find him fussy and crotchety. They'd never been close again. He'd never lived to see her buy a Ferrari, and he would have been proud of that. Or would he? Olivia would never know. In every other way she had been distant from her parents, brought up by the nanny, fed by a cook-housekeeper, and only allowed to eat with her parents once she and her sister reached the relatively civilised age of sixteen and fifteen, respectively. By which time, there wasn't really much to say.

Her mother had been smart, vague and preoccupied with 'good form'.

When she stopped for a coffee, Olivia thought about turning her mobile off, but decided that it would be too wicked. Allison Green wasn't likely to call from whatever private island she had been invited to, and most other clients could be fielded by Cat, but Si had been up half the night working on a proposal he was putting to the board of R&R, and then he'd been picked up at five-thirty that morning by one of R&R's company drivers and taken to Heathrow for a six-day trip to Russia, to oversee budgets on the setting up of a flagship R&R Moscow store.

The phone lines had hummed between the Fox family almost incessantly for the last week. Jack had been debriefed by his senior officers who had said that, with the back-up team out of action because of their broken-down vehicle, Jack's responsibility had been to abort the mission. The rules had been quite clear.

Because he had set off alone, and without back-up, two men had died. It was useless for Jack to protest that the bomb would have been there whether there had been one car or two. If both armoured cars had been together, they would at least have been able to get Staff Sergeant Mayhew to medical treatment in time to save his life. Jack was removed from Temanistan immediately, because the Russians were asking questions about what he was doing there. After more growling from the Russian bear, the Temanistan government had decided that it didn't want the British helping them defeat terrorists after all, and the whole mission was closed down. Quite a nasty diplomatic incident had been narrowly avoided without anything very much getting into the press, and now the British Embassy was supposed to go back to developing cultural and commercial links. 'I think they've got to concentrate on Shakespeare and fish and chips from now on,' muttered Jack.

Olivia had hardly exchanged two words with Si since Jack had been found. Every evening he either worked late or engaged in endless Fox telephone conversation: Kate would call about Jack or Ella, then Si would call Jack, then he'd call Kate again. Of course, it was very sad that two other servicemen were dead, and Olivia felt sorry for their families, but she didn't know them and that was that. But Si and Kate were chewing over it endlessly, turning it into another instalment of the Fox Family Saga, when perhaps there was nothing more to say. Olivia and her sister, Fenella, had polite telephone conversations twice a year. They never seemed to need this ongoing narrative.

Ella's illness was a worry, though. Olivia decided that she would try to get back to London early enough to visit her in hospital. But until then it was a day off, and nobody knew where she was or what she was doing.

As she turned off the motorway she passed harvested fields striped in a dozen shades of muted greens, greys and browns, studded with huge, round gold bales of straw. Or was it hay? The tangled hedgerows were full of berries. Olivia wasn't used to feeling so ignorant. Her uncle would have known. And her mother, of course, grew up in these farmlands.

Perhaps she, Olivia, was coming home. Maybe Providence Cottage and finding her roots would fill the sense of longing she occasionally felt inside her. The void she filled with work, and buying expensive things. She slid the car round the back of the house, through the gap in the hedge and inserted her key in the lock. This time it turned easily, and a spider scuttled away from her as she entered. The sunlight streamed through the pretty little fanlight and the curling lino revealed surprisingly good oak floorboards beneath.

'Hello, house. You're all mine. Nobody else's.' Her voice echoed in the silence, and the dust danced in the air. She looked at her watch. Half an hour until Blake Allan was due. Half an hour of blessed, healing silence. She opened the back door, working it gently open because it had stuck, and sat down to watch the birds fluttering in and out of the still-green blackberries.

A large, smart off-roader drew up outside Providence Cottage.

'Hi. I'm Blake Allan.' He had a surprisingly firm handshake – just the right side of painful – and Olivia took in springy dark curls above a tall, lean frame, a mischievous smile, a moth-eaten black jumper and a pair of muddy wellingtons. The four-by-four was muddy too in spite of its new number plate. 'Sorry to be so scruffy,' he said briskly. 'Thursday is my day for working at home.'

She had expected quietly cool, well-cut clothes in black or grey.

'Beautiful.' He strode round the garden, looking at Providence Cottage from all angles. 'Bloody beautiful!'

'I think so.' Olivia was pleased.

'Roof's about to slide off,' he added. 'But that doesn't matter. Doesn't matter at all. We'll pop it back on again in no time. So what do you want to do with the house?'

'As little as possible.'

'Quite right. Quite right!' He dug his finger enthusiastically into one of the window frames and it crumbled like cheese. 'Rot. Such fun.' He looked at her intensely. 'Don't you think?'

'My husband doesn't agree.'

'Divorce him then.' Blake gave her a quick sideways grin. 'Houses are more important than husbands.'

She couldn't help smiling back. 'It might come to that.'

He continued to check the house over, and eventually turned to her. 'The only two windows that are rotten are these two under where the guttering's gone. Let's start with popping up a bit of temporary guttering, eh? I've got a good company I can recommend.'

Olivia opened her mouth to talk about other architects and getting three quotes, but only managed to murmur agreement.

He whistled when he saw the cellar. 'Hm.' His torch picked out a clump of foaming mushroom growths. 'I do like a bit of drama in a cellar. Dry rot. But never mind. I reckon we've got it just in time. It probably happened when the cellar stayed closed up after Malcolm's death? I expect he kept it fairly well ventilated when he was alive. Let's get it fixed sharpish, though.'

'What do you mean by sharpish?' Olivia had visions of having to take more time off work. She was beginning to see Si's point about Providence Cottage and its responsibilities.

Blake looked at his watch. 'About five minutes ago.' The big grin again. 'I've got a company here I can call.'

As he spoke into his mobile, Olivia wondered if there was a decorating mafia in the area who fleeced weekenders and those down from London in search of a good life.

'Did you know my uncle?' she asked after he'd closed his phone, curious about his relaxed use of Malcolm Forbes's name.

'He was a total recluse but everyone knew him.' He gave her a quick grin. 'If that doesn't sound like a contradiction in terms. Pest-Out can come next week. If you like I can let them in. I'm not far away, as I said.'

Olivia knew that Si would disapprove of her engaging him to help before he'd even quoted for the work, but she gave in. She liked Blake Allan. She didn't think he was trying to con her. Si would say that she was being a typical woman, falling for a pair of dancing black eyes and a strong pair of arms. Only Si wouldn't put it like that.

'Thanks,' she said.

'And if you want to make sure the growths don't do anything between now and then, I could take a blowtorch to them.'

'Would that be safe?'

'Can't guarantee it. No indemnity insurance. At your own risk. Etcetera, etcetera and blah, blah, blah. But it's what they used before chemicals.'

'Your blowtorch. Is it nearby?'

'Not too far away. We can go home and discuss things over a civilised cup of coffee and then I can bring you back here and we can torch the cellar together.'

Olivia nodded. Si would be furious at her letting anyone do anything that wasn't covered by indemnity insurance. 'I'm game,' she agreed. 'I don't get the chance to take many risks these days.'

'Sorry, I can't offer sky-diving.' He opened the door of the Land Rover and brushed aside a collection of newspapers, old sweet wrappers, some empty plastic sandwich cartons and a dog lead. In the footwell, a ginger-and-white spaniel wagged its tail with unbridled enthusiasm.

'This is Brandy. In the back!' Brandy hopped through to the back seat, her silky ears flying upwards as she jumped over.

'She's so sweet.' Olivia tried not to gasp as the four-by-four shot out of the gate and bumped erratically over the rough track.

After a sick-making series of jolting twists and turns ('Don't worry, I'm not trying to kidnap you,' said Blake), the car followed a long yellow-brick wall and turned in between two gateposts.

'What a lovely house.' A pair of chunky yew trees, clipped to an irregular geometry, stood guard in front of a gingerbread house with three half-timbered gables and a big studded door. A jigsaw of beams and old bricks irregularly adorned with tiny-paned mullioned windows, jutted out over it. Olivia was enchanted. Her eyes were used to rows and rows of London terraces.

Blake jumped out of the four-by-four and opened the front door for her. 'After you.' Brandy scuttled in ahead of them, her paws pattering on the worn slate floor.

'Drink?' he offered.

She shook her head. 'I'm driving. But . . . oh, why not? Just one.'

As Blake poured her a glass of white wine she tried to ignore a chattering voice on her shoulder. Say no. Walk away. Don't risk your licence. There's no such thing as 'just one'.

But I want to enjoy life, she told the voice, feeling alive at the touch of his fingers against hers as she took the glass, meeting his dancing eyes and laughing herself in return. I'm sick of saying no, of putting everything else ahead of my own happiness.

Chapter 33

Ten days after Jack returned, he and Heather went to Corporal Parker's funeral. Jack was stony-faced, while Heather tried to choke back tears discreetly. Jack disappeared, and spent most of the time talking to Sergeant McKenzie. Later, in the car going home, he told Heather that he was going to meet him and three of those who'd been in the back-up vehicle in London the following day, and that he would probably stay overnight with them.

Heather was worried. There were lines in the army – social lines – that were rarely crossed back home in peacetime. Jack had been the boss on that fated mission. Bosses usually licked their wounds in private. But she didn't say anything. 'Should we make a date for going to see Ella again?' she asked, carefully. 'She'll want to see you, and you've been home for nearly two weeks now and only visited her once.'

Jack sighed. 'I'd be really grateful if you could stop all this endless organising of parties and people to see. I need to relax.'

Heather bit back a retort.

She dropped him at the train station, and he returned two days later. 'Sergeant McKenzie's going through a bit of a bad time,' he texted her, several times, and repeated it on his return. 'He doesn't get on with his family.'

'The girls were asking where you were,' said Heather. 'They need you, too.'

Jack strode up the stairs without answering and switched his computer on. He spent the rest of the evening up there, but took Molly and Daisy to the playground the following morning.

Heather gazed anxiously out of the window. Was he getting back to normal? But when he returned, she came up behind him as he was reading a paper and tried to hug him.

'For Christ's sake!' He threw her off. 'You gave me a fright. Don't creep around like that.'

'I wasn't creeping, I was trying to give you a hug.' Heather tried to keep the tears out of her voice. They had barely touched each other since his return.

That evening, she bathed in her favourite bath oil, smoothed on a perfumed moisturiser and put on the silk, lace-trimmed, champagne-coloured bra and knickers set that Jack had given her for Valentine's Day – and which she had barely worn. Her reflection in the mirror told her she looked, well, OK. She shook her hair loose and brushed it, then shrugged on her dressing gown.

'Jack,' she said, shyly, as she went back into the bedroom.

As he looked up from his book, she let the dressing gown slip softly to the floor, and stood there, begging him with her eyes. 'Look what I'm wearing. Your present.'

Jack sighed and put down his book. 'Heather, I . . .'

'Never mind.' Blushing furiously, she picked up the dressing gown and put it back on, rushing back into the bathroom to get her nightie on again.

'Jack,' she said, when she returned, summoning all the courage she had. 'I will tell you all about my childhood, I . . .'

He looked up, and his eyes were cold. 'It's a bit late now. It's not that I wanted to pry. I thought we were partners, Heather. Now I don't know what we were.' He switched the light off and turned away from her.

The following morning the first thing she saw – with a thud of alarm – was a photograph of herself on the front page of the *Sunday News*, looking – not too bad, she couldn't help thinking – in black, wiping away a tear. The picture was captioned 'Heather Fox, wife of Lt-Col Jack Fox, at the funeral of Corporal Lance Parker yesterday.'

Jack was standing over her holding the paper. 'What the fuck is this?'

She sat up. 'I don't know. Someone must have taken it at the funeral. Why did they blow it up so big? I'm not important.' Or she hoped she wasn't. Could someone start digging into her past? Might someone recognise her?

'This makes it sound, Heather, as if I have leaked the story to the papers, and am blaming the army. This really is the final death knell in my career. Have you told anyone?'

Heather scrambled up and began to dress. 'Of course not.'

'Heather, let me ask you again, because I don't believe a word you say these days. Have you told anyone, anyone at all, exactly what happened in the four days I was missing in Temanistan.'

'Nobody,' she said, her eyes filling with tears again. 'I promise, except, oh, well, I did mention it to Kate. But you've been talking to Kate yourself . . . so . . .' She picked up the paper and gasped.

'What?'

With a shaking hand, she pointed to the byline: Tim Proctor and Andrew Wakefield. 'Someone called Tim Proctor broke down outside our house, and he came inside for some water. But I didn't tell him anything he didn't know already, I promise. He must have been gathering information since then.'

'You little idiot. He was fishing. He knew fuck all, so he span you a line and you confirmed things he was only guessing at. My God, what did I do to deserve quite such a stupid wife?'

Jack stomped downstairs, and she heard him shouting down the phone at Kate as, trembling, she tried to pull on a pair of jeans. What had she done? Would Jack be court-martialled?

He came back, angrier than ever. 'Kate denies it. But I know it's her. It's just the sort of thing she'd do. Unless you're lying to me again?'

'I don't lie to you.'

'Really? What do you call the first eleven years of our marriage then, when I thought your mother was dead. One big lie, that's what I'd call it.'

'It wasn't, it was just one . . .'

'Silly me. I thought we had so much in common. Our fathers

both died when we were children. We were brought up by our mothers. We both had a fairly ordinary home counties background – I lived in Surrey and you lived in Kent . . .'

'I did live in Kent, and my father was dead,' whispered Heather.

'Really? And how can I be sure of that? Perhaps he, too, will pop up one day in some police station?'

'That's exactly why I didn't tell you,' hissed Heather. 'Because I knew you'd be like this.'

'So glad to hear you have such a high opinion of me,' retorted Jack. 'If that's really what you think, why did you marry me in the first place? Just for a bit security, perhaps? A meal ticket that you didn't have to prostitute yourself for, like your mother did?'

It was exactly what Heather had feared would happen once Jack found out. She ran upstairs, locked herself in the bathroom, and curled up in a ball.

'Heather,' he rapped on the door. 'Heather, I'm sorry, I didn't mean it.'

Of course he did.

'Heather, let me in.'

She concentrated on listening to her own breathing.

'Is there *no* way I can get through to you?' He banged angrily on the bathroom door in frustration.

She wasn't going to come out to more insults. She put her hands over her ears.

Chapter 34

Kate picked up the Sunday papers from the mat, planning to take them back upstairs to Jonny with a cup of tea, and drop a few sections off with Ella who had been released from hospital into her care.

She stopped still. It gave her a shock to see Heather's face staring up at her from the mat. She looked exquisite, and almost timeless, in a high-collared black jacket and tiny hat, wiping away a delicate tear. Kate seized the paper and skimmed it hastily.

It seemed to be a reasonably accurate account of the story Kate had heard from Heather, plus several references to the shortage of spares and equipment in the army. It said that the responsibility should lie with the government for not equipping troops properly, rather than on one individual officer who had been forced to make impossible decisions. As the days had gone by it had become clearer and clearer that Jack could say goodbye to a high-flying army career – it sounded exactly as if he had put his case to the press and was positioning himself as a whistleblower.

She raced upstairs to Jonny, throwing the paper at him. He sat up, looking sleepy, taking it all in. 'Well, well. Heather looks good.'

'It's a bit odd that they'd show her, rather than Corporal Parker's wife, isn't it?'

'You know how it works: slow news day, great pic of a gorgeous young woman, two deaths, chance to blame the government . . . Jack's been unlucky because I don't think it would normally have hit the front pages, but what with that documentary the other day, and Heather looking like that, well, it's too much for them to turn down really.'

There was a pause while he read the article. 'It seems that the press are on Jack's side.'

'It is an amazing photograph.' Kate studied it again. Heather looked hauntingly sad and fragile, almost incandescent, as if she stood for all the grieving women that war left behind. The other front page items were about a disgraced company chief executive (middle-aged, male, jowly, hence a very small photo) and the slowdown in car manufacture around the world, plus a peppering of small items about research into foodstuffs and the price of cancer drugs. Quite clearly, Heather had been the photo-opportunity of the day.

'"Questions are being asked about the presence of British military intelligence vehicles in the troubled border region of Temanistan,"' she read to Jonny, alarmed. '"In the past, US forces have been accused of planning military strikes against terrorist training camps in the region, while Russia has made a formal complaint to the British Government about the incident. Could Temanistan be the next area of global conflict?" Do you think the fact that it's all out in the open helps Jack or is it bad news for him?'

'Hard to say,' mused Jonny. 'I think his next promotion has already become very questionable. How did the papers get hold of it, by the way?'

'I expect the MOD sent out a press release about the two deaths, then someone picked up on it, and a photographer went to the funeral, and it went on from there. You know how it is. I'd better keep all the papers away from Mumma, it'll kill her. And warn the boys.'

Callum thought it was extraordinary of Kate to wake him at nine o'clock on a Sunday morning just to tell him not to talk to Granny about anything in the papers. 'I don't read the papers,' he said, sleepily. Luke looked pleased to be entrusted with a secret. 'We can hide all the papers and stand in front of the television during the news.'

The phone rang.

'Kate, who have you been talking to?' roared Jack. 'You must have told someone.'

'Me? Why should I have told anyone anything?' Kate was indignant.

'Because all your friends are journalists.'

'I haven't said a single word. I wouldn't dream of it. Anyway I don't know anyone on the *Sunday News*.' Kate heard the sound of urgent talking in the background – Heather's apologies and Jack roaring with rage.

'Well, someone must have tipped them off. My idiot of a wife did the rest. She let a journalist in to fill his water bottle the other day, or some such. And chatted to him. Sometimes I wish she'd get a brain, I really do.'

'Don't blame Heather,' retaliated Kate. 'Journos are very clever.'

'Yeah, well, I'd like to know how he found out in the first place, and then knew where to come. I expect you turned it into a funny story for one of your friends, and they passed it on, don't you think?'

'Jack, that's a terrible thing to say. I have not told a single soul. Not one.'

'That's what Mum used to say when she'd told half the neighbourhood.'

'It's true, I haven't! And speaking of Mumma, you seem to have forgotten that she's been quite ill. I can't keep the papers away from her forever, and you've only been to see her once, when she was first in hospital. She's had a minor *heart* attack, Jack, as you very well *know*, and the least she should expect is that her sons visit her. Si manages it, and he's in Moscow half the time, but why haven't you come over?'

'Oh, for God's sake.' He sounded impatient. 'OK, I'll get in the car *now* and drive over. Is that enough?'

'That's not necessary, I just want to know when . . .' But Kate could hear raised voices at the other end, and Heather came on the line. 'I'm so sorry, so sorry – I did tell him Ella was ill and that he ought to . . .'

'Never mind.' Kate was fuming. 'I really haven't told anyone anything, Heather . . .'

'I know, I know, it's all my fault, I'm so sorry. Oh, dear, Jack has

225

just stormed out and driven off . . . he hasn't taken his coat with him. Oh, no, I'm so sorry . . . is it all right if he just turns up?'

'It's fine.' Why couldn't Heather have a bit more gumption and stand up to Jack? Kate slammed the phone down. He really needed a wife who could calm him down and stop him doing silly things.

Kate put together a tray of breakfast for Ella. Luke offered to take it up for her. 'You look sad, Mummy. Everyone looks sad. Granny looks sad. So does Dad.'

She hugged him. 'We're just worried about Uncle Jack. He's getting into trouble over what he did out in Temanistan.'

'But he was very brave,' insisted Luke, wrapping his thin arms tightly round her.

She held his slight body close, wanting to protect him from adult worries. 'He was, but he disobeyed orders and that's very important. You see it can be very dangerous to disobey orders and . . .'

But Luke could spot a lecture coming up and broke away. 'Let me wake Granny.'

'And no mentioning the papers,' she warned him again as he wobbled upstairs with the tray.

She thought about Luke's words. We all look sad. Dad looks sad. Well, he was working hard and worried about money. Or maybe he was having an affair with Sasha after all. She was still the poison that infected all their exchanges. She was careful with Jonny now, polite and guarding her words. Kate was determined not to show jealousy, but she was still hurt. A secret was a secret, and Jonny had kept one from her. She just wasn't sure how big a betrayal it was. Or how much the boys had picked up. Luke certainly knew something was different.

'Kate, Kate,' Ella's voice called from the spare bedroom. 'Are there any Sunday papers?'

'They haven't delivered any.' Kate called, knowing she was a bad liar, but disguising her voice by shouting up the stairs.

Later on, Ella asked if anyone had gone to the newsagents to complain.

'No, er . . . I'm sure it would better for you to take a few days' rest from the news. It's very depressing these days, all stuff about companies going bankrupt and starvation in Africa, you know how it is.'

'But I always have the news.' Ella looked at Kate shrewdly. 'What is it you don't want me to see?'

'Oh, just the way the world is so . . . so . . . well, miserable now. I don't think it's good for your health. I don't think it's good for anyone's health for that matter. I'm going to take a break from the news myself.'

'There's something in the papers about Jack, that's what you're keeping from me . . . it's those two soldiers that died, there's something funny about it all . . .' Ella's voice rose in distress.

'Mumma, Mumma, please keep calm. Jack will be fine. He always is.'

'I'm perfectly calm. Oh, Jack is a fool. He takes risks. Stupid risks. I remember your father saying when he was little . . . oh, if only Michael was here, he would be able to talk to him.'

Kate never liked to talk about Michael Fox, their father. It hurt too much. She didn't want to think about his sunny smile and his way of making you feel that everything would work out for the best in the end. When her father died, a door had closed in her heart with a sickening thud. She'd known she'd have to look after herself – and her brothers and even her mother, up to a point – from then on, not rely on anyone else. One day, they had been a normal, happy family. The next day they'd been marked out by tragedy. When the drunken driver had got into his car and driven it into her father's, he had taken away the person they all relied on most – for no reason, and with no warning, and from then on Kate had tried to make it better for the others. She remembered girls at school who had crossed the road to avoid talking to her. She was now adult enough to realise that they had all been awkward children with no idea of what they should say to her, but it had all been very difficult to understand then, and it still was. It was easier not to think about it.

Kate tried to reassure her mother. 'Jack's grown up since then, Mumma, you must stop worrying. You must look after yourself.'

'Kate, I can tell you're keeping something from me, and I want to know what it is.'

'Jack's coming over.' She looked at her watch and frowned. Jack should have arrived by now. 'He phoned up to see how you were, and I suggested he pop round for coffee. He'll be here soon,' she went on. 'It's much better to hear everything from him, you know how stories get exaggerated and the press simply never get anything right. But it really will all be fine.'

She would make sure that Jack downplayed everything.

'You look a bit red and blotchy, darling, are you sure you're all right?' Ella raised an eyebrow.

'Yes, it's a bit hot where the sun is streaming in downstairs.' Kate hated it when her face betrayed her.

Ella looked out of the window, puzzled.

'Surprisingly hot for October,' added Kate, plumping up some cushions behind her mother. 'It just shows you, doesn't it, how important it is not to leave dogs in parked cars?'

'I suppose so.' Ella looked puzzled at the change of topic.

'Which is why they have these notices in car parks now,' Kate continued, in case Ella got too worked up about it. 'So I expect it hardly ever happens any more. Now then, would you like any more tea?'

'Darling, we don't want *another* cup of tea, do we?'

Kate was irritated. 'Well, I do, Mumma, because . . .'

'Come in and chat.' Ella indicated the little bucket chair beside her bed, and Kate tried to think of a reason why she couldn't.

'How is everyone in Thorpe Wenham?' she asked, for the third time that day. There were so many no-go subjects – so many things she couldn't talk about because Ella would worry – that it was difficult to find a topic of conversation.

Ella put down her copy of yesterday's paper, and took off her glasses. 'Kate, dear, what on earth is the matter?'

'I'm just concerned about you,' said Kate, not meeting her eye.

'The doctor isn't. And he's the one who would know.'

Her mother's 'doctor knows best' attitude infuriated Kate, and she opened her mouth to say so, but decided that she didn't want to alarm Ella.

There wasn't much to say after that, and Kate flicked through a copy of a magazine, while Ella went back to the crossword.

'Where do you think Jack's got to?' asked Ella, when her little bedside clock chimed four.

'I'm sure there's absolutely nothing to worry about,' snapped Kate, who was almost sick with fear by now. And anger. How dare Jack do this to them all?

'Well, I can't help it,' said Ella, 'when Callum and Luke are driving, you'll understand.'

'Mumma, all this worrying you do, you know, it's not good for you. Have you thought of talking to the doctor about anti-depressants? They work on anxiety, too, you know.'

'Kate, darling,' said her mother, putting the paper aside again. 'There is only one person in this room who might need anti-depressants, and it certainly isn't me. You've had a face as long as a horse's for months now. It must be very hard on Jonny, living with someone who is so gloomy all the time.' About to pick up the crossword again, she sought Kate's eye. 'Surely, darling, you can see that it's not nice for a man to come home to.'

'Don't be silly, Mumma,' said Kate, furious. 'I'm absolutely fine. There's absolutely nothing wrong with me. Well, I get a bit tired sometimes but that's being a working mother, nothing more. But you've just started getting very worked up over relatively minor worries . . .'

'Like Jack nearly getting killed in what might turn out to be a serious international incident, and him being' – she looked at her watch – 'four hours late?'

'He's not four hours late. We don't know what time he set out.'

'Kate, are you lying to me or fooling yourself? I never quite know, and I don't want to upset you. Not when you've got so much on your plate.'

'I don't lie.' Kate was indignant.

'I'm not senile, you know,' said Ella, gently. 'Although you seem determined to treat me as if I were.'

'I don't. I . . .' Kate tried to think of a way of saying that she was only trying to protect her mother, without seeming to be conde-scending.

'It's Jonny, isn't it?'

'No, Jonny's fine.' Kate wanted to throw herself on her mother's bed and sob, the way she had when she was eight and her best friend had told her she didn't like her any more. But she was no longer eight, and she had to protect Ella, the way she'd protected her in the darkest days after her father's death. She had stopped confiding in her then because her mother had had enough problems of her own. The best thing Kate could do to help her was not to burden her with any more. Don't tell Ella, she'd warn Si. Don't tell her that Jack's been smoking dope. Don't tell her that Jack's been given another detention. And she certainly wasn't going to tell her that she had any doubts about Jonny's fidelity or commitment. Ella wouldn't understand, she would worry too much about the effect on her grandsons.

'You don't feel he's really committed to you, do you?' asked Ella. 'And that means you're not happy.'

'You're harking back to what it was like in your day,' said Kate. 'That's why I don't talk to you about it. Nowadays it's perfectly normal – actually it's more common – for people *not* to be married. But you think it's all wrong, and that therefore it's the root of my problems, and it's as if it's this whole big . . . ISSUE. Which it just isn't. So everything has got to be about us not being married. When it's not important in the least.'

'Oh, you may think it's not important these days,' said Ella, 'but what worries me is that you and Jonny drifted into a relationship, then drifted into parenthood, and now you seem . . . well, adrift.' Her eyes, as sharp as Kate remembered them from her childhood, focused on her daughter. 'You never seemed to make a conscious decision about whether you were committed to each other or not.'

'That's just not true.' Kate thought of the dizzy, funny, happy times she and Jonny had had when they first discovered each other. He never really asked her out, just suggested, casually, that maybe she'd like to come with him to a party, and in the morning he'd suggest going to a market or taking a walk in the park before she could hurriedly pull her clothes on and go. She'd always been absolutely determined never to be one of those clingy girlfriends.

Maybe a bit of formality might have helped, though. She'd sometimes felt she was just tagging along. And then she'd got pregnant, accidentally, and she'd been terrified. But he'd seemed pleased, and seemed to think that buying a house together was a natural thing to do. They hadn't known each other long, and it

230

was still one big, fun adventure. But had he felt trapped? What would have happened to their relationship if she hadn't got pregnant? Well . . . she wasn't going to start being clingy now. If Jonny didn't really love her, well, she could survive. That's how she always thought of herself: as a survivor. She and the boys and 19 Lovelace Road. The house was at the heart of it – it was safer to entrust your heart to a house, it couldn't go out and get itself killed one night. Although if you didn't have enough money . . .

But she wouldn't think about that now. Kate was very good at not thinking about anything she didn't want to think about. Have another biscuit instead.

She snuck a ginger biscuit – a slightly soggy one – off the plate in front of her mother and looked up to see Ella looking at her, concerned. 'Mumma, you don't understand how things are now . . .'

'I don't think they've changed so very much. Not at the heart of it all. I think you should be married. I really do.'

'Mumma, we can't afford it. It's a big expense.'

'It doesn't have to be. You could just turn up at the registry office and have lunch at home afterwards.'

'No, if I'm going to do it, I would want to do it properly,' said Kate.

'Now tell me,' said Ella. 'I want to know. Have you got very into debt?'

'No, of course not. We have a mortgage, but doesn't every-body . . .'

'If I die . . .' Ella plucked at her bedspread, 'there'll be a bit of money, not much and . . .'

'Mumma, please don't talk about that again. You're going to get better and get back to the garden, and . . .'

'No, I want to say this. If I die, will you use some of the money to get married?'

Kate thought of saying that it wasn't entirely down to her, and hesitated.

Ella was on to it in a flash. 'Is Jonny having an affair?'

'Of course not.' Kate's heart clanged loudly. 'There's Jack's car.' She jumped up, desperate to stop her mother talking.

Soon Jack's outline filled the doorway. The spare room seemed much too small for him.

'Jack,' Kate hugged him. 'Thank God you're here. We thought you'd had an accident.'

Jack embraced Ella and sat down beside her, drawing up a small chair and squeezing himself into it, taking her hand and looking into her eyes as he talked. Kate saw her mother sparkle in return, a delicate flush on her cheeks. Kate had another biscuit as Jack talked.

'Now Jack, now that the dust has settled I want you to tell me, from the start, exactly what happened. I've heard lots about it from everyone else, and I don't know what to believe. I want to hear it properly, from you.'

Kate tried to signal 'no' over Ella's head, but Jack ignored it.

'And you've been disciplined?' asked Ella, anxious, when she'd heard his story. 'Is it serious?'

Kate wished that Jack would be a little more sensitive. He shouldn't be telling his very ill mother all this detail. She tried to nudge him, but he took no notice.

'Yes. I won't be getting my command. I probably won't be promoted again. Probably my best option is to leave the army, unless I just want to stick it out to get a good pension in thirteen years' time. But that's a long time to push a pen around in the postings equivalent of utter darkness. So I don't know what I'm going to do.'

Ella patted his hand, then squeezed it. 'Do you think it was a trap all along? Was the contact genuine?'

Jack ran his hands through his hair in despair. 'I can't believe that. I just can't believe it.' He folded his other hand over Ella's. 'But it's possible,' he whispered, his head bowed. Ella stroked his hair.

Kate was just sneaking out of the room, when he spoke again.

'There's something else I need to tell you.' He got up and paced around like a caged zoo animal.

Kate tried to catch his eye again. Protect Ella. Don't say anything that will worry her.

He sat down again suddenly, one knee juddering up and down in a nervous twitch. He leant forward. 'Mum, it's so good to see you. You look well, I was told you were at death's door.'

'I didn't say that,' said Kate, indignantly.

'What is it, Jack? I know you when you fidget.' Ella put a hand on his knee and he stopped, briefly.

'I've got some very serious news.'

Kate's heart turned over. What more could possibly happen now?

'I'm afraid my marriage to Heather is over,' said Jack. 'As you may already know, we haven't been getting along for a while, and now we simply don't have anything to say to each other. She doesn't understand the support I need, and I can't give her what she wants. I wasn't going to tell you until we'd . . . talked, which is why I haven't been down, so I hope you'll keep this strictly to yourselves . . .'

'You mean you haven't even told Heather?' gasped Kate.

'It's not a question of my "telling Heather",' he said, sharply. 'Communication has broken down between us completely. She won't talk to me about . . . well, she just doesn't talk to me full stop, and I . . . can't go on. I think she'll be glad to see me go actually, she barely addresses a word to me now.' He looked out of the window, away from Ella's sharp gaze. 'But, no, those final details haven't quite been discussed. I'm doing that tonight.'

'But the girls,' said Ella, faintly. 'What about the girls?'

'Heather's a wonderful mother, and we will both put them first. Always.'

'Is there someone else? Where were you all day?' shouted Kate.

'Katie, Katie.' He tried to smile. 'What's all this about? You know Heather's never been exactly . . .' he hesitated, 'well . . . my equal. She's a gorgeous, gorgeous girl, and terribly sweet, but I have to carry her every inch of the way. She has no confidence, she's terrified of everything and I feel that I'm propping her up, dragging her on . . . it's hard work, you know, and I'd like life to be fun.'

'There's more to life than fun,' said Ella, two spots of colour rising on her cheeks. 'Heather is an intelligent, loyal and hard-working young woman. She is a wonderful mother and a supportive wife. And you have taken leave of your senses.'

'I think you are being completely and utterly despicable,' hissed Kate. 'Get out now, and take your revolting self-justification with you.'

'No, Jack, wait,' commanded Ella. 'Sit down here with me. And Katie, off you go. For a walk, or to phone someone, or whatever.'

Jack smiled his most charming smile, although he looked shaken. 'I really haven't got time, Mumsy . . .'

Ella raised an eyebrow and he hastily sat down.

Kate backed out the door, as she heard her mother say, in an urgent, intense voice: 'Jack, this is quite, quite wrong, I beg of you . . . if your father could see you now, he'd be so . . .'

'Dad has nothing to do with it,' said Jack harshly. 'We've had to make our way without him, and that's all there is to it.'

Outside, the dusk was falling and the street lights flickered on. All Kate could see was space, shadows and menace. She paused at the window, waiting, cold with terror, trying to hold herself together until Jack strode down the stairs and out of the house, his face set. She let him drive off because she didn't know what to say to him.

If Jack could do this to Heather, to beautiful, loving Heather, then nobody was safe. She went back in to see Ella.

Her mother looked old and grey. 'That boy,' she whispered. 'He makes me so angry. So very angry. He has no sense of responsibility, none at all and . . .'

'Shh.' Kate tried to calm her down. 'Please, don't think about it. It isn't good for you.'

'And Kate, I'm worried about you, too . . . the money, and Jonny and 19 Lovelace Road.'

'You mustn't be. This house is fine, and so am I.'

Chapter 35

In Halstead Hill, Heather gave Molly and Daisy their tea, a bath, and then, looking at her watch, took them upstairs to bed. She promised them – as she had done so often – that Daddy would be back soon. He had left the house just after nine that morning, and it was now nearly eight-thirty in the evening. Should she ring Kate?

No, it would worry her. And she didn't want Kate to know how bad things had got. Jack was now often out of the house for whole days at a time, visiting the MOD, seeing Sergeant McKenzie, arranging something about his new job down in Wiltshire – he had a whole raft of excuses. Heather thought that he barely knew where he was sometimes, and had visions of him pacing the streets, lost in his memories, hardly aware of the time.

Once Molly and Daisy were sleeping, she began tidying and cleaning until the already spotless house gleamed. Pretending to read a book by the light of one table lamp, she strained her ears for the return of Jack's car.

When she heard his key in the door, she didn't dare move. He walked in, and she knew from the set, distant look in his eyes that it was over. She didn't know how she knew, just that there was a different Jack standing in front of her. Deep down, she had been waiting for this ever since he found out about her mother. But then again, all along she'd never really believed – in spite of every-thing – that he would want to stay with her.

'No, Jack, please! I don't know what I've done, but don't leave.

Don't leave me and the girls. We love you.' Heather couldn't believe the abasement in her voice. 'Please,' she whispered. 'Don't go.'

'Heather, I'm sorry.' His face was grey and he leant against the doorframe as if he could barely stand. 'Don't make this harder for me than it needs to be. I can't go on. There's nothing left.' He spoke in a hoarse whisper. 'I'm no good, Heather, you'll be better off without me.'

'No!' She almost screamed. 'Whatever it is, we can face it together.' She seized his coat. 'If we're together, we can manage.'

'You don't understand.' He prised her fingers off and backed away. 'It's over. It's finished.' He ran up the stairs two at a time as Heather sank to the floor.

He was down again, with his hastily packed backpack, and looked down at her. 'Don't, Heather,' he said. 'At least leave us both our dignity. There's nothing else left.'

She crawled over to him and tried to pull herself up. 'We love you, Jack. I love you and so do Molly and Daisy. Don't do this to us.'

Her face was very close to his, and as he looked down, she thought she saw the old Jack back in his eyes. She desperately tried to reach that Jack, the one who loved her and the girls more than life itself. 'Is there someone else?' she whispered. 'All those nights when you were supposed to be with Sergeant McKenzie. Who is she?'

His expression closed off again. 'There's nobody else. It just isn't working. You can have everything, I won't let you suffer financially.'

'No, Jack, you can't do this. You can't do this to our daughters.' He shook her off. 'I'll be in touch.'

Heather's body shook in dry, retching sobs as she heard his car accelerate away. When she finally picked herself up, she staggered into the kitchen and ran herself a glass of water, looking up at the clock as she splashed her face with cold water. She had lain there, numb and sobbing, for nearly two hours. It was now late. Who could she ask for help?

She remembered Sasha saying *Ring me, anytime. You know I don't sleep*, and with shaking hands, she managed to dial her number.

Chapter 36

In Sasha's flat, the phone rang. She was in the bathroom, showering.

Opening the bathroom door, she shouted: 'Answer that darling, could you? I'm soaking wet – I'm trying to discourage someone who's got a bit of a crush on me. Every time he has a few drinks, he calls me late at night.'

Jack picked up the phone. 'Hello?'

'*Jack?*' He could hear the timbre of Heather's voice on the other end of the line, even though it was so hesitant.

Jack put the phone down without answering.

'Heather?' Sasha stood beside him, towel wrapped round herself, still wet. She'd suspected that Heather would call her, which was why she wanted Jack to answer it. Of course she regretted that she'd had to find out the full truth like that, but Jack had originally suggested that they keep quiet until after the divorce, and then pretend to have got together afterwards. Sasha didn't think that was a good idea at all.

Jack ran his hands through his hair with a groan. 'I was hoping she didn't have to know just yet.'

'Better to have a quick, clean break,' murmured Sasha. 'Better for everyone, especially the children.' She kissed him, running her hand down his body, then drawing back as soon as she felt a response, teasing him with her tongue. She would make him wait, make him beg, make him moan . . . make him remember this night, not as the night he left his wife, but as the night he had the best, most uninhibited sex of his entire life.

'I feel guilty about . . .' he murmured.

She let the towel slip away deliberately slowly, turning away to tantalise him, just the hint of a striptease in her actions.

Sasha had won. It hadn't happened quite the way she'd planned, but love was like that. That's what had really surprised her. The hot, desperate, greedy longing she had for him, the way she was unable to catch her breath after he kissed her and the irregular, heady thumping of her heart when she heard the bang of his car door had been quite unexpected, because she'd intended to take quite a different course. Never mind, she'd fallen in love, and was nearly – not quite – out of this little rented flat and back to being someone that people took notice of again. It was just a matter of days, weeks at most.

As she slipped Jack's jacket off and unbuttoned his shirt, she thought how wonderful it would be to live in a house again, have a proper home. Not to have to worry about what things cost any more. Tom and Grace would go to a private school, she decided, as she pushed Jack slowly back on to the bed, enticing him with her tongue, allowing him almost to touch her before dancing away. You met the right sort of people in the private school system, people with villas in Spain and France, and yachts. She knew someone whose son had regularly gone on holidays with a maharajah's son, and the parents had been invited too once. She could put all the maintenance Adam was giving her towards education – as any responsible mother would – because Tom and Grace would have a family again, this time with a man who was strong and honourable. Adam had been weak. Too easily led by that tart Natalie. Too selfish.

As she lowered her mouth to his, Sasha knew that this time she would marry a man who would put his wife first. She tied one of her silk scarves gently around his eyes, after stroking it along the length of his body.

And she in turn would put him first, she thought, as she finally straddled him and lowered herself on to him, hearing his breath shorten. Give him the support he'd needed all along. When she looked at any of the three Fox women – for example – she couldn't believe it. Olivia was so selfish, always with her head in her own work and her own plans. They'd barely heard from her since she'd inherited Providence Cottage. No wonder Si was lonely – and so often alone. Kate was a lazy lump who had no appreciation of how gorgeous Jonny was, and who did nothing to make his life pleasant when he came home exhausted in the evenings, and Heather was simply a doormat. How was Jack going to become a general with that behind him? If there was one thing that getting to know the Fox family had taught her, it was that if you didn't work together, things began to fall apart.

It was a pity she'd never quite got Si to come up to scratch – at one point all that had been quite promising but somehow it had come to nothing. Sasha frowned. She hoped she wasn't slipping. And of course her relationship with Jonny had had to stay strictly professional. Much better that way. So everything had all turned out for the best.

As she bounced up and down on top of Jack, stopping when he came too close to climax, occasionally withdrawing from him and tormenting him by brushing him gently with her nipples, slipping through his hands like quicksilver, reproaching him for being a naughty boy, Sasha began planning what she was going to wear for her second wedding. It must be chic and discreet, in a very expensive hotel, with just a few people and no family.

Definitely no family. She had no intention of putting up with all that. Why should she? That very morning that cow Ella and that bitch Kate had tried to persuade Jack to stick with Heather. He'd come back from talking to them, and it had taken another two hours of intense discussion before he'd finally stood up, and told her that he was ready to talk to Heather now. Sasha couldn't believe it. Ella and Kate had nearly taken Jack away from her. It was none of their business. They had no right.

In indignation she began to move faster, and Jack shuddered under her, with a groan of ecstasy. She accompanied his cries with her own, and collapsed down beside him, soaked in sweat.

Yes, sex with Jack was quite enjoyable, which showed you. She must be truly in love. And it wasn't as if Jack loved Heather any more anyway.

Chapter 37

Jonny was non-committal about it all.

'Jack's leaving Heather.' Kate waited until Callum and Luke had gone to bed to talk to him. 'He says that she's so lacking in confidence that he has to carry her all the time, and that he doesn't feel she's his equal.'

Jonny raised his eyebrows. 'That figures.'

'What do you mean?'

'He doesn't have a lot of confidence himself, so he can't give her any. It was always the weakness in that marriage. I guess that after Temanistan his self-esteem is at rock bottom, and that makes people selfish.'

'Jack's got bags of self-confidence. Far too much in fact.'

Jonny picked up a newspaper. 'What? Hm? Oh, Jack, no, he's a frightened little boy who thinks he's got to fight his way out of the playground. That's why he's such a bully.'

'Jack is not a bully.'

Jonny looked at her over the paper. 'Jack is a bully. He always has been. He married Heather so he could have someone to bully, and now he's tired of her. Or . . .' He stopped, looking as if he'd had a sudden thought.

'Or what?'

'Nothing.'

'You can't just start a sentence and not finish it. What did you mean?'

'I don't want to make everything worse.'

240

Nothing Kate could say could persuade Jonny to explain what he had been about to say. In the end she returned to his earlier words.

'You don't sound as if you like Jack very much.'

'He's your brother. That's fine with me.'

'But you don't actually like him yourself? You wouldn't choose him as a friend if I wasn't here?' Kate had always thought they got on, had congratulated herself on the way Jonny fitted into her family so well.

'Kate, what is the point of this?' Jonny continued to skim the paper.

'Why can't you look at me when you talk to me?'

He tore his eyes away from the newsprint. 'OK.' They stared at each other for a moment.

'What else do we need to say?' he asked.

Kate felt like slapping him, hard, but restrained herself. 'Oh, OK. Nothing.' She picked up a paper as well, but she couldn't concentrate on it. She was frightened, and she didn't know why. That night she couldn't sleep until light began to creep under the curtains.

When she went into Ella's room, her mother's face was grey and seemed to have collapsed in on itself.

'Mumma. Shall I call a doctor?'

'No, no, I just couldn't sleep, thinking about Jack, and Heather and those poor girls . . . This is terrible, Kate, terrible. Those young lives. Ruined.'

Kate sighed in frustration. 'Mumma, divorce is what happens now. Nobody talks about 'broken homes'. The girls will be in classes at school with dozens of children of divorced parents. It's just life, and we have to get on with it, and do the best we can to support them both. They'll be all right.'

'No, no, they won't be. Jack wasn't all right when your father died . . .'

'We survived. We're all fine now. And that was different, that was death.' Kate flicked the curtains open. She couldn't bear to talk about her father because it hurt too much, and her mother always seemed to want to, whenever something major happened. 'Now, what about breakfast?'

'No thank you, darling. I think you and Si were all right, but Jack . . . Jack never got over it.'

Nor did I, thought Kate, but she had no intention of saying so.

'That's why he's doing what he's doing now.'

'No, he's doing what he's doing now because he's suffering from post-traumatic stress disorder. I'm sure he'll come to his senses.' Kate was trying to convince herself.

Her mother sighed, and Kate looked at her more carefully. 'I really think I should call a doctor.'

'Oh, that'll mean a long wait in a waiting room, and I don't have the energy to go out.'

Kate phoned anyway, but Ella's symptoms were too non-specific to justify a call-out, or even to warrant taking her out on a cold day and sitting her in a waiting room.

Kate took a cup of tea upstairs. 'We've got to help Jack and Heather, haven't we? What did he say last night?'

Ella sighed. 'I'm not sure you're in a position to help anyone. You've got so much on your plate.'

'Don't be silly.' Kate felt threatened. 'Helping people is important. More important than anything.'

'I think Jonny might not like it. He needs you too, you know.'

'He's got me. And Jonny's not like that. He's not selfish.' Kate was irritated. This was typical of her mother's 1950s thinking. Men had to be cosseted and treated as gods, and they had to come home to a sparkling home and a smiley wife every night. Life wasn't like that any more. If indeed it ever had been.

'No, Jonny's not selfish,' agreed Ella. 'He's a really nice man.'

This, too, was more of a reflection of Ella's man-worshipping attitude, born out of her upbringing, than a real assessment of Jonny's character, thought Kate. Jonny could be very selfish at times, but he wouldn't mind her helping Heather and Jack, say, with the children. 'You mustn't leave Jonny, Kate.'

Perversely, this gave Kate a strong desire to pack her bags and leave everyone. 'Of course not, Mumma.'

'Katie, if Jonny is having . . . an affair . . . don't leave him. It isn't the end of everything, it doesn't need to be . . .'

'If Jonny's having an affair, he's out on his ear,' joked Kate, but her mother caught her arm.

'No, no. This is important, Kate, you mustn't make the mistakes I did . . .' she took a great gulp of air.

'Shh, stop talking, and calm down.' Kate was worried.

'I have to tell you . . .' She was struggling for breath now. 'Your father. He wasn't coming home from work when he had that accident. He was leaving.'

'Leaving work?' Kate couldn't understand.

'I . . . told him he had to go. He . . . was being unfaithful, and I said . . . like you, I said . . . he couldn't stay . . . I was only thinking of myself . . . not about you three, you needed your father . . . but I thought . . .'

'Dad having an affair?' It was incomprehensible to Kate.

'He said it was over, he said he was sorry, wanted to try again, but I thought . . . I thought . . . no, I'm not having that . . . and . . . I told him to go now, and that . . .' Ella clung to Kate's arm.

Kate tried to calm her. 'I'm sure you were right. You can't stay with an unfaithful man, no one can.'

'But I sent him away, I sent him to his death, and then you three didn't have a father, and I never thought about what it would do to you all . . . when I sent him away . . . I sent him, I shouldn't have . . . I killed him . . .'

'Mumma, please, I don't blame you.' Kate hardly knew what she was saying, just that she had the urge to comfort her mother, not to hear the truth, to make it all better . . . 'No one could blame you. The person who killed him was the driver who got behind the wheel when he was drunk. And if you had tried to make it work, who's to say that Dad wouldn't have been unfaithful again?'

Ella sank back against the pillows. 'If I could have my time again, I wouldn't have cared if he did. People make mistakes. They shouldn't have to pay with their lives. Because I promise you, having an affair is nothing compared to death. Nothing. He could have had . . . oh, ten affairs, I would rather that than he was dead.'

For one second, Kate agreed with her. At least he would have been there. But then the anger flooded in. How could he do that to them? 'Don't think about that now. I'm sure you did the right thing. We've got Heather and Jack to think about. I'll ring both of them, and tell them I'm here to help whenever,' she asserted. 'It's terribly important that we don't take sides.' Her chest felt tight, as if there was a large stone lodged there. It was the weight of the pain she'd lived with since the night her father died. She had to keep moving, not to feel it sitting there, dragging her down.

Kate stomped off and tried Jack, to offer her services in looking after Molly and Daisy. She got his messaging system, then got Heather at home.

Heather – a hesitant, broken, whispering Heather – thanked Kate for offering to help, and told her about the telephone call with Sasha.

'Right. Now we know what's at the bottom of all this.' Kate, too shattered from Heather's revelation to think about protecting Ella, went back into her mother's room, and sat down heavily on the end of the bed. 'He's run off with Sasha.'

'Yes.' The colour returned briefly to Ella's face. 'I know.'

'And you didn't say anything?'

'Jack told me yesterday. But he asked me to keep it secret. So I did.'

Kate pushed her hand against her head. 'Yes, well, you've been keeping secrets pretty much all your life, haven't you? You accuse me of not telling you what's worrying me, and where did I learn that from, do you think?'

Ella looked surprised. 'Well, of course you don't tell children the whole truth. You try to protect them, and it was much better that none of you knew anything. He was a very good father and you all adored him. I didn't want to ruin that.' She sighed. 'Let's hope this Sasha thing is temporary, and partly a reaction to Temanistan, because if she and Jack are seriously going to stay together . . . well, we'll have to make the best of it, that's all.'

'She's not coming to this house. Jack will have to come on his own with the girls. I couldn't do that to Heather. And Jonny will have to realise he can't do this TV series with her.'

Ella said nothing.

'Jonny will agree with me, I'm sure,' added Kate.

'Well, maybe it'll just be a fling,' added Ella. 'I've met women like that before, and, believe you me, they're after the money. I'd have thought she'd have gone for Si, actually, except that Si has too much sense.'

'And he loves Olivia.' Kate pointed out.

Ella waved a hand wearily, as if to ask what love had to do with it.

Kate slammed the door behind her, and phoned Si. He'd already left for work, but she got Olivia.

'Oh, no! Poor Heather, how terrible,' said Olivia. 'Well, at least we now know why Sasha was so friendly with her and stayed so long. I was beginning to think there was something really odd about it all, but I didn't like to say.'

'I wish you had. I thought everyone liked her, so I didn't want to say too much against her either. Do you think we could have done anything to stop this, if we had talked?'

Olivia sighed. 'I don't think so. I'll try to get hold of Si this afternoon. He's in meetings all morning. But I think he's always been quite a fan of Sasha's.'

'Jonny seems to think the sun shines out of her proverbial, too. It's no good relying on either of them for support. Actually, I've just started putting together a programme on twentieth-century figurative painters, and I was thinking I could dig around Roderick Morton's life, and find out a bit more about her . . .'

'Dig away,' said Olivia, with enthusiasm. 'And let me know what you find.'

Chapter 38

Olivia and Blake had exchanged emails and texts almost every day. Allison Green's financial hearing was at the end of the next week, so she should really have been working, but that Sunday, with Si still in Moscow, Olivia drove down to Providence Cottage, texting Blake as she set off. 'Come for lunch,' he texted back. 'We can brainstorm.'

She drove as fast as she dared until she arrived at Blake's delightful Bailey House. She couldn't see a knocker anywhere on the thick studded oak door. Her knuckles made almost no noise against it, although her hand hurt.

But it opened, to the sound of furious yelping from Brandy, and Blake stood there, with his aquiline nose and the unruly mop of curly hair. 'Bell pull,' he said, indicating a rope to the side of the door.

'Silly me,' said Olivia, hesitating, wondering if they should peck each other on the cheek or shake hands. 'We don't have bell pulls in London.' She stuck her hand out stiffly, but Blake pulled her towards him and kissed her formally on both cheeks. He smelt of grass, cleanliness and wine.

'Hi.'

They looked at each other. 'Hi.' She was embarrassed. Perhaps she shouldn't be here after all. Perhaps it was inappropriate.

'Come on in.' He set off down the flagstoned hall to the kitchen, with its ancient range, large ceramic sink and dresser. Everything was painted white, and the beams were limewashed. Plans were strewn across a scrubbed-wood table.

'Drink?' he asked.

'I shouldn't.'

'I always seem to be tempting you to do things you shouldn't.' The challenge hung in the air between them.

Olivia swallowed. 'Perhaps one tiny glass of wine.' She seemed to be finding it difficult to breathe.

But as soon as they started talking about Providence Cottage, they couldn't stop, bouncing ideas off each other, laughing about the same things, instantly agreeing that anything too modern would be dissonant but that neither of them liked replica period fittings. They didn't eat until nearly three o'clock, by which time they had drunk nearly a bottle of wine between them.

'Don't go back till later,' he said.

She laughed. 'I don't think I want to go back at all. Maybe I should give up my job and move down here.' She tried to think, drunkenly, what was wrong with this scenario. Oh, yes. Si. Her husband. 'Si could come down at weekends,' she added, waving a hand in the air, and nearly knocked the empty bottle of wine over.

Blake caught her hand just before it swiped the bottle off the table. 'Careful.' But he was laughing.

'I'm sick of being careful. Have I told you how bloody careful I have to be? Checking every bloody little aspect of my clients' lives, checking every detail on the bank statement. Whether I'm at home or at work, I'm not allowed to make a single, tiny mistake . . .'

Blake continued to hold her hand, his eyes dancing with mischief. 'So you're overdue for at least one single, tiny mistake?'

She looked at their hands, now intertwined in mid-air. 'So.' She swallowed to bring her voice under control, 'Where's your wife?'

Blake grinned. 'Oh, she didn't like living here. Bolted back to the city.'

Olivia slid her hand out of his and folded her arms tightly into her chest, protecting herself against her own feelings. Mustn't. She loved Si. Too much to lose. The clichés seemed pathetic. No armour against the mounting desire she felt for Blake.

He got up and began cooking, tossing something into a pan. It sizzled. 'Clare didn't like Bailey House. Too isolated, she said.'

'So you really meant it when you said that when it's a choice between the husband and the house, you need to ditch the husband?'

'Well . . .' he ground pepper into the pan, and shook it about. 'I suppose it wasn't quite that simple. But almost.'

Olivia took a deep breath. 'Do you have children?'

'No,' he said to the pasta pan. 'Do you?'

'No.'

Ten minutes later he put a bowl of pasta in front of her, and she began to eat. It was delicious. She accepted another glass of wine.

'We can go for a walk after this,' he said. 'Clear our heads.'

They went for a walk with Brandy racing around them in enthusiastic spaniel circles and snuffling in the woods for rabbits. The path took them to the marshes and the sea, where the reeds swayed in a thousand shades of ochre, russet and parchment. A curlew soared through the arching skies and a herd of cows with large brown, beige and white patches ambled over the waterlogged pastures.

Olivia sighed, letting the weight of the city slip off her shoulders. 'I feel I belong here.'

'It gets into your blood. It's in mine,' replied Blake. 'I lived away for about ten years, then I had to come back. But Clare, my wife, was miserable. Where I see a beauty that's so elusive that painters can barely capture it, she only saw flat, windy emptiness. She likes countryside that rolls up hills and down dales, with picture-postcard thatched cottages and drystone walls, and I like the steel grey of skies over open water, and the endless whispering grasses.'

'So she left?'

'She started spending more and more time away on business, and then one day she didn't come home at all.'

'Si and I spend a lot of time apart. But that's just us, it's the way we've always been. He's in Moscow at the moment, and won't be back till Thursday.'

The information seemed suggestive, almost dangerous. 'I suppose you could define us both as workaholics,' she added hastily, as if to cover up a slip. 'We understand that the other always has to put work first.' She lowered her head into the wind and tramped along the coastal path, seeing the curving necks of swans reflected in the water, the ribs of a wrecked barge in the mud and distant sheep like tiny cotton wool balls. The sharp autumn air was like champagne. When her mobile phone rang, she looked at it, and switched it off.

'My sister-in-law,' she explained to Blake. 'There's a huge family crisis at the moment, because Si's brother went missing in Temanistan, and he seems to have disobeyed orders and got two soldiers killed, and now he's back, his wife seems to have accidentally talked to some newspaper man . . .'

'I saw that. I didn't connect the name Fox with you, though.'

'Si belongs to one of those families that all ring each other every time something happens. This'll be his sister, Kate, asking some kind of legal question about the whole thing.' She put the phone in her pocket.

After an hour, Blake turned left, away from the coast, and picked up an inland path, past a few houses and a wood. 'This track leads to Providence Cottage,' he said. 'It'll be your walk to the coast once you get to know it. Hey!' he suddenly exclaimed, and dived under a tree, returning with a giant puffball mushroom in his arms. 'Look, there are ceps too.' He took a carrier bag out of his pocket. 'Always carry a bag at this time of year,' he said. 'There's so much to pick up.'

'Are you sure they're safe?' asked Olivia anxiously.

'They'll be delicious this evening with garlic and herbs. Why not join me?'

'Well . . .' she was tempted. 'I could sleep at Providence Cottage.'

'Or you could sleep at Bailey House.' He let the invitation lie for a few seconds. 'I've got spare beds.'

'Well, er . . . I'd love to try the . . . er . . . puffballs anyway. If you're absolutely sure they're not poisonous.' She looked at the giant white ball in his arms. It looked like something out of a fairy tale, something that might turn her into a goblin or place her under a spell, not the kind of mushroom that Si loved to buy from the gourmet food shops and farmer's markets.

When they tramped back through the door of Bailey House she was glowing with the exercise, and after scraping off muddy boots she curled her long legs up on Blake's large, squashy, battered

249

sofa with a cup of tea. As the day slipped away they went on talking, and Blake opened another bottle of wine. She and Si were careful about the amount they drank, but today she was sick of counting. Measuring everything. She wanted to stop thinking about alcohol units and calories and hours worked and the amount she'd invested into a pension, and how much tax she had to pay and all the other numbers that dominated her life.

Blake put a match to the logs in the fireplace, and the flames sprang into life almost immediately. Occasionally Olivia and Si rented holiday cottages with open fires, but it always took them half an hour of arguments and false starts before smoke gusted into the room and set off the fire alarms. Blake was obviously good with hands. He could make things work, which neither she nor Si ever could.

She had better check her phone, though. 'I've got this high-level client,' she explained, fishing it out of her pocket. 'She expects me to be on call twenty-four seven.' Apart from the missed call from Kate, which could wait, there were three messages from Jack. She dialled him.

He sounded ragged. 'Olivia, I need your advice. I'm in the car. Just let me pull over.'

Olivia listened carefully. 'You mean you're on your way to tell Heather your marriage is over? Jack, you've been away for six months and you're under appalling strain. This is no time to make life-changing decisions. Go to counselling, spend some time together, Jack. Heather loves you.'

'I don't love her. I don't even feel I know her at the moment. And no amount of counselling is going to change that. I can't go on.'

'Is there . . . er . . . anyone else?'

'It's not about anyone else!' he shouted. 'It's about me and Heather.'

'And Daisy and Molly,' she reminded him.

'The kids come first, of course, that's why I'm talking to you. And I want to make sure that Heather doesn't suffer financially.'

'I can't act for you, Jack, you know that.'

'Could you recommend someone?'

'I'll try.' She ended the call and realised she was trembling as she dialled Si, going out into the hall so that Blake couldn't hear.

'Si, Jack's left Heather. He's claiming he and Heather don't get on any more, but it's clearly all about that . . .'

'Olivia, are you drunk? You're not making any sense.' He was clearly annoyed at being interrupted.

'Jack has left Heather.'

'The little shit. The senseless, idiotic, cretinous mound of ordure. I'm calling him now.'

'No, don't, please. I've never broken a confidence before, please don't . . .'

'This is going to destroy Jack financially, you know,' growled Si.

'It's not the money that worries me, I'm more concerned about the fact that it's going to tear Heather and the girls apart.'

'Come off it, Olivia, you see this every day. A family that has nice things – holidays abroad, shiny new toys, evenings out . . . suddenly one or both is living in virtual poverty. It tears their lives apart.'

'And the kids don't see their fathers every day, and then they don't see them every week, and before you know where you are, they haven't got fathers,' said Olivia. 'Or even, these days, mothers. That's what matters, not the shiny new toys.'

'The money's at the heart of it. The man who ends up in a tiny flat doesn't have anywhere his children can stay . . . people like Jack and Heather can't actually afford to divorce.'

But we could. The thought slipped into her mind and almost – but not quite – popped out of her mouth, before she shook it out of her head. She thought of Si as she paced up and down Blake's hallway, every inch the competent executive, his weekend blazer and chinos relaxed in the capacious leather seat of his car or in a suit, with a silk tie, leaning on the starched white tablecloth of a top restaurant. He even smelt expensive: of fine polished leather, cult aftershave and money.

'This will destroy him,' he added. 'It will do his career no good, and on top of his idiocy out in Temanistan. I suspect he'll be pencil-pushing in some dark corner of MOD for the rest of his days.'

'So he should stay married, for the sake of his career and his bank balance?' suggested Olivia.

'Of course he should! That's what anyone with any sense does. Especially when there are children involved.'

'But what about love?'

Si laughed. 'Darling Olivia. In your line of work, I'd have expected you to give up believing in fairy stories.'

She flipped the phone off, hardly aware that there was a tear trickling down her cheek as she leant against the doorway.

Blake gently stroked it off, and his eyes, no longer dancing, were full of concern. 'Olivia?' She leant her head against his shoulder as he drew her into his embrace. 'Bad news?'

When she lifted her face up to his, she wasn't sure if she was afraid he might kiss her or whether she would die if he didn't.

Chapter 39

After leaving Ella's room Kate went downstairs to find Jonny and to get the boys their breakfast. Callum, as usual, was reluctant to get up and Luke had a thousand questions he wanted to ask. Neither seemed to know where their games kit was, and there was the usual flurry of finding homework books and stuffing satchels. 'Callum, you must sort yourself out better. I don't want you to grow up like Uncle Jack.' It slipped out, almost before she realised she was thinking it.

'Why?' he demanded. 'What's wrong with Uncle Jack?'

'There's nothing *wrong* with him, of course not.' Kate backtracked. 'And the army's been the saving of him because he loves action, but he's blowing his chances in life by not thinking properly, just rushing into things. He decided to go ahead in Temanistan when the back-up broke down, which he should never have done, and two people died. He's left his sweet, lovely, gorgeous wife utterly devastated because he's got . . . got . . . lured away by, well, never mind . . . but I remember when he was at school, he was always leaving his homework till the last minute or not doing it, or getting into trouble for being late . . . he was always *so* careless. And now you're being careless, we can't find your history book anywhere.'

'It's only a history book. Perhaps you'd rather I was like Uncle Si,' suggested Callum. 'Earning lots of money and being pompous?'

'Yes! I mean . . . not the pompous bit. But can't you see that Si has a nice life? That's all I want for you, to be happy.'

'Si isn't happy,' said Callum. 'And Olivia certainly isn't. She's got sad eyes.'

Kate realised that Callum was growing up. Fast. She wasn't sure that she knew what to do.

When she had been Callum's age, she had looked up to her father, much more than Callum looked up to them. Had his affair started by then? She remembered him coming to her hockey matches and discussing them with her afterwards. He'd been good at maths and had coached her, because she found the subject difficult. It had been Mike Fox who had told her that a woman would always have to work in the future, that they wouldn't be able to rely on men for economic security. That self-reliance had become the cornerstone for everything she believed in now. Her mother had cooked and cleaned, and run the house. But Mike and Ella, like her and Jonny, now she looked back on it, never did anything together. Not that she could remember.

Was that why he'd had the affair? Was there any chance that the family story, like so many family stories, would be repeated? Of course not, because she wasn't Ella. That's why she and Jonny weren't married. That's why she had to work, not just for the money, but to stop the same old mistakes from being repeated down the generations. She would be different.

'Mum?' Callum waved his hand in front of her face. 'Earth to Planet Mum?'

'Right,' she pulled herself together. 'Now Si worked hard at school, got top marks in exams, went to Oxford, got a great job and has everything he wants.'

'No, he doesn't,' said Callum, surprising her again. 'They tried to have children, I know they did, because when I was little they used to tell me they hoped there'd be a little cousin, and now they don't.'

'That's got nothing to do with it. The main point is your GCSEs,' said Kate, looking at her watch. 'If Si hadn't got good GCSEs he wouldn't have done so well and . . .' When had Callum learned to tie her in knots like this?

'Yadda, yadda, yadda. I know. C'mon, Mum, you're like one of those "mind the gap" announcements at stations. Over and over again with the same message.' But he gave her an affectionate hug, and as he sloped off she couldn't help smiling.

19 Lovelace Road looked as if a bomb had hit it, with piles of clean and dirty clothing everywhere, shoes and unread newspapers scattered around the floor and washing-up in the sink. Mess was like a tide, it just came in repeatedly, however hard you beat it back. She scurried round, pulling everything together hastily, because Mumma needed breakfast, she had to do a telephone interview at 9.30 a.m., and an interview with Jasper Morton, Sasha's half-brother, for the radio programme, later on, and they were having people to dinner on Saturday, which needed planning.

Jonny was shrugging his coat on, with his hand on the door latch.

'Jonny.'

He looked at his watch. 'Mm?'

'Jack has run off with Sasha. That's what's behind all this.'

He was impassive. 'I'm sorry to hear it. I thought . . .'

'You thought what?'

He shook his head wearily. 'I'm late. We've got a production meeting at ten.'

'Awful, isn't it? So you see,' said Kate. 'You can't go on doing this pilot with Sasha. It would be so disloyal to Heather and the girls.'

He shook his head slowly. 'I'm not condoning what she's done, but I'm sorry, Kate, that's not how it works. You know that. We've got enough problems as it is.'

'But it's not as if she's one of the presenters or anything. She's just a researcher. She can easily be replaced. There are loads of bright young kids who would do anything to have a break.'

'Kate.' He put a hand on hers. 'Listen. We have to make our decisions on who is best. Sasha is doing a few pieces to camera. I know she's inexperienced, but if someone's got it, they've got it, and she has. One of the two presenters – Penny Marshall, you know her, don't you?'

Kate nodded.

'We knew she was pregnant when she agreed to do the pilot with us, but she's got threatened pre-eclampsia and has suddenly had to stop work completely. We've used some of the interviews that Sasha did as a researcher in place of pieces that Penny would have done, and we've been very pleased with the way the camera likes her . . .'

'And less pleased, I hope, with the way Jack likes her.'

'I think that what's happened between her and Jack is a tragedy, especially for the girls, but I can't bring it into work, or allow it to hold up a project.'

'So you're going to side with her?' Kate wanted to cry, but was determined not to let Jonny see it.

'I'm not going to side with anyone. I'm going to stay out of it altogether.'

'But you can't, you're family.'

'I can.' He opened the door 'It's work. Kate, where has your professionalism gone?'

'It hasn't gone anywhere. I just put my family first.'

Jonny got up. 'Putting work first *is* putting family first.' He turned to leave the house.

Kate followed. 'Jonny? Jack's rebelliousness? The way he's always got into trouble? I'm quite sure it's because he didn't have a strong father figure to look up to when he was a teenager. Our father was dead, Jonny, but you're alive. And the boys need you.'

Jonny raised an eyebrow. 'Did you know that the youngest child usually rebels? It's an established scientific fact. Later children have to find a niche in the family that isn't occupied by the eldest alpha one or the middle child who's usually a nurturer or a peace-maker. You should do one of your programmes on it one day.' He closed the door.

Kate sighed. Jonny had not said one word of criticism of Sasha and her behaviour. He clearly didn't think she had done anything wrong.

As she went upstairs with a tray for Ella's breakfast, a wave of sadness swept over her. The end of Jack's marriage was the end of an era for the whole family.

Ella lay with her eyes closed, snoring loudly. Or was she? Kate bent over her. 'Mumma?' She shook her arm, and got no response. 'Mumma?'

With shaking hands, Kate dialled 999.

Chapter 40

Heather clawed her way through the next three days as if through the mists of a nightmare. She was back in the dark, when she and Mo had left Broadstairs in such a hurry. 'Gerald don't want a little girl around no more,' her mother had said, pulling her into the car. 'It's all your fault, nobody wants a snotty-nosed brat, do they? He wants you put in a home, he does. So that's where you're going.'

And Heather had clutched her school satchel crammed with her few possessions, trying not to cry. It was all her fault, all hers. Her mother said so, and her mother was at the centre of her life.

Now Jack, like all the 'stepfathers' and uncles she'd briefly had, didn't want her either. Well, she was older now, she could look after herself. And the girls. She would never let the girls feel unwanted by their father. She would do anything to prevent them feeling even a fraction of what she had felt at their age. She just had to keep the old Heather Spencer under control, make sure that the one who fought and bit and 'was disruptive' was kept away, and that the 'good' Heather Fox, with her neat, tidy rooms stayed in control.

Jack arranged to come back and get his possessions while the girls were at school, and Heather tried to apply make-up to her reddened, swollen eyes. She found a belt to keep up her jeans. In the three days since he'd left she had barely been able to eat, and even her tightest trousers and skirts hung low on her hips. She looked at herself in the mirror and could only see an anxious,

257

stricken face with puffed-up eyes and greyish skin, the sharp angles of her collarbones above the T-shirt, and strips of bare bone rather than cleavage. She hastily buttoned up her shirt. She so wanted to look beautiful, but her reflection told her she had never appeared so plain, gaunt and desperate.

'Hi.' Jack wiped his feet with exaggerated care, and Heather wondered if she had been too house-proud.

'Hi.' She cleared her throat and folded her arms. 'Coffee?' She had prepared a tray beautifully, with their best coffee pot – a wedding present – and biscuits arranged in a semi-circle on a plate. It was a precarious attempt to keep control of the situation.

It failed. He shook his head. 'Best to get on with it, don't you think?' He strode upstairs and pulled down a suitcase from on top of the wardrobe. 'Do you mind if I take this one?'

Leaning in the doorway, wrapping her arms around herself for comfort, Heather shook her head. 'Take anything you like. I don't care about any of it.' Big talk, Heather. She did care, but she wasn't going to show him.

He briskly opened drawers, and laid shirts and sweaters in the case.

'I went to see the Welfare Officer.' She forced herself to keep her voice steady but she wanted to punch his lights out. Hold on, Heather, she told herself. Fighting gets you into trouble.

'So did I,' said Jack to the suitcase.

'Are you staying in the job? What . . . happened with the disciplinary proceedings?'

He stopped for a second. 'They're not complete yet. But I'm not being sent back to Temanistan if that's what you mean. I've been formally reprimanded for my role in that. They say I was disobeying orders. Going ahead without my back-up. Nothing is quite as bad as disobeying orders in the army. And you'll be glad to hear that it's pretty clear that there's no command job ahead either.'

'Why would I be glad?'

'Because you'd been looking forward to it. Hadn't you?' He made it sound like an accusation.

'I don't give a shit.' Heather Fox allowed bad Heather Spencer through for a moment. 'Sasha can do all that now.'

He flashed a look at her. 'Leave Sasha out of this. It's not her fault.'

'Really? I suppose you just went to her flat because you had nowhere else to go? Just for the night. That there's nothing in it?' This possible explanation had, indeed, been tormenting Heather ever since the phone call, but as the hours crept on and there had been no reassuring call from Sasha, she'd known that her friend had betrayed her. Well, that was what happened if you let people come too close. Heather knew that, why had she let herself forget it?

'Yes.' He straightened up and his eyes filmed over, as they always did when he lied. Heather had come to know the expression now. It had always been about protecting her from the reality of the work he did.

Now it was about protecting Sasha. 'Sasha's just a friend,' he added. 'She was a friend to me when I didn't know who my own wife was.'

'When you discovered that my mum was a prostitute, you mean? Yes, let's say it like it was. My mother was an addict, and that didn't fit with your nice little image of your nice little army wife. Don't tell me you would have seen me as wife material if you'd known all this when we met? If you'd known I'd grown up with a succession of fathers and uncles and then in a children's home.'

Jack's eyes blazed. 'Let me get one thing clear. I do not give a flying fuck what your mother did, and neither does the army. But when I discover that my wife has been lying to me ever since I met her, and still won't tell me the truth, well, I can tell you, that's when I felt pretty bloody lonely in my marriage.'

'Oh, yeah,' said Heather, not believing him. 'And that justifies finding yourself a new *friend*, does it? I should have known, when she was talking about what happened in Temanistan. I wondered how she knew every detail. You were with her all the time, never Sergeant McKenzie.'

He ignored the allegation. 'Pretending that Sasha is still just a friend might be best for the girls. And speaking of the girls, I think they should go to boarding school. It will be less disruptive for them, and the army will . . .'

'No!' shouted Heather. 'They need to be with me. I will not let you take my kids away, Jack Fox, and you'd better not try.'

'Or is it that *you* need to be with them?' asked Jack, cruelly. 'That without them, you don't have a reason for living? You should think of them, what's best for them, it's not just about you.'

Heather leaned against the doorway with her eyes closed. He was going to use her mother to prove that she wasn't fit to have the girls. She knew it. 'Fuck off, Jack. I'll be staying here, with the girls, for ninety-three days. After that you pay rent on a flat somewhere.'

He closed the last drawer, and opened the wardrobe. 'Fine. I'll pay rent. Honestly, I don't want you and the girls to suffer.'

'Oh, yeah, very touching. Well, the girls will suffer,' said Heather. 'Whatever you pay, they will suffer terribly. Don't fool yourself about that.'

Jack zipped up his case, caught sight of a framed picture of Molly and Daisy on his chest of drawers, and hesitated. 'Could I take this?'

'Take what you like.' She shrugged. 'You will, anyway.'

He put it in the case. 'So,' he said. 'You'll divorce me for adultery, I take it.'

Heather lashed out. The little girl who'd fought everyone in the playground and hadn't trusted anyone rose to the fore, and she began to beat him with her fists.

'Heather, Heather.' He was strong enough to fend her off, throwing her backwards so she fell against the bed, then he hefted the case up and marched out the door.

'And don't think you can come back!' she screamed after him.

He turned. 'Oh, I won't, don't you worry.'

Heather believed him. Why would anyone ever come back to her? She'd let herself believe she could rely on him, but he was like everyone else.

After he left, Heather curled up in a tight, terrified ball, unable to function. She stayed like that all day. Another wife on the patch had offered to bring the girls home, and even give them tea, so there was no need for her to move until bedtime. In fact, she thought, perhaps it would be better if she never moved again. Nobody wanted her, she was no good. It would be better if she didn't exist.

Chapter 41

Ella was admitted to hospital. Kate drove after the ambulance, racing down the hospital corridors after parking her car, phone clamped to her ear as she tried to alert the family. Nobody was answering, they were all in meetings. Except Heather, who was presumably out.

Ella opened her eyes for a few moments and smiled at Kate.

'Mumma, I'm here.'

'Jack,' Ella whispered from under her oxygen mask. 'Must see Jack.'

'He's on his way,' lied Kate. 'Just stuck in traffic.'

As Ella closed her eyes again, Kate raced outside and tried to call everyone again. She got hold of Si, who promised to be on the next plane back, but had no luck with anyone else. She also had a raft of phone calls connected with work to make, cancelling meetings and responding to queries. The next round of submissions was going through to the BBC and Kate had put forward ten ideas. She was waiting to hear if she should develop any of them further. And she had to cancel the dinner party, and a drink she was having with another radio producer in town, then find someone who could pick up Luke – Callum could get home on his own. She'd have to call him, though . . . remembering everything when she was so short of sleep was difficult. She thought she could still make the Jasper Morton interview at least, because they were meeting at three, not far from the hospital.

*

She did manage to make the appointment. They ordered coffees. Kate asked him about his father and the art scene of the seventies and eighties, where headline-grabbing installations and abstract art seemed to dominate the market. 'What happened to figurative artists like Roderick Morton?'

Jasper leant forward over his coffee cup. 'There's always been a place for people like my father . . .'

Kate took notes and recorded the session. 'And growing up with him, what was that like? He painted at home, I understand, so did you see more of him as a father or did you just feel that you always came second to his work?' The question had echoes in her own life. She wanted to hear the answer.

'A bit of both. His studio door was always closed when he was working and it would have been more than our lives were worth to go in there. But he was with us for lunch and supper, and I guess that means we knew him a bit better than most of our friends knew their fathers.'

Kate switched the tape off. 'Thanks. That's so helpful. By the way, wasn't there another daughter? The cuttings I have said that . . .'

Jasper looked at his watch, his face a blank. 'I'm afraid we're out of time.'

Kate took a risk. 'Please. I . . . we . . . our family – your half-sister, Sasha, she's just married my brother, and . . .'

'I'm sorry to hear that.' Jasper looked at her with disdain, getting up and shrugging his coat on. 'Do I take it, by the way, that this was all a ruse to see me and get me to talk about my family, and that there won't be a programme on figurative painters of the twentieth century after all?'

'No! No.' She tried to call him back, but had to run after him down the road. 'Truly. The priority is your father's work, but so many creative people have . . . er . . . irregular private lives that it is relevant. I need to understand him as a man as well as a painter. If I'm to get the programme commissioned.'

He stopped. 'You mean you want a bit of scandal to get the programme talked about?'

'I would be sensitive,' she said. 'I do understand how damaging it can be. My brother is Jack Fox, the military intelligence colonel who was involved in the incident in Temanistan last month, in which two British soldiers died. It got into the papers, somehow, and that really didn't help. The army thought he was trying to manipulate his case through the press.'

'That will have been Sasha,' said Jasper, with an unexpected grin. 'She sells leads to the papers. It was quite a big story, wasn't it? Well, she'll have been paid hundreds of pounds. Maybe a thousand or more. It's one of her sources of income. But you can't say I said that. I've no desire to end up being accused of slander. I was told about it by a friend on one of the tabloids, who knew about our links to her. And that really is all I've got to say about it all. But if you're genuinely interested in my father's work, we're holding a retrospective exhibition at the Red Gallery.' He opened his briefcase and took out an invitation. 'Do come. But no Sasha, is that an agreement?'

Kate nodded, charmed by the smile and the invitation. 'I'll see you there.'

And he raised a hand, hailed a taxi and jumped into it. Kate returned to the hospital.

The doctors would not be drawn on Ella's condition. 'She's very seriously ill. She's had a second heart attack. This one is more severe.'

'Will she recover?'

They wouldn't commit themselves.

'Is she dying?'

This even less.

It was five o'clock before she managed to contact Jonny, but he immediately agreed to pick up Luke and Callum and bring them to the hospital. 'It might be goodbye.' Kate could barely bear to say the words.

Jonny appeared shortly afterwards and wrapped her in a bear hug, as the two boys hovered anxiously.

Kate wiped her eyes. 'There's a chair on either side of Granny, just sit and hold her hand.'

'She saw us,' reported Luke half an hour later. 'She thought I was Jack, but she knew who Callum was.'

Callum's face was set, and he refused to answer any questions. His body was stiff with grief, and he threw off Kate's attempt to comfort him. Jonny took them both home, and she tried both Jack and Heather again. Neither were answering their phones.

In desperation, Kate tried Sasha. No answer. She left a frantic message. 'Sasha, can you tell Jack that Mumma's had another heart attack? A really bad one. She's asking for him, she wants to see him.'

At ten o'clock that evening, Si strode through the low-lit corridors of the hospital and dropped down in a chair beside Ella's bed opposite Kate. They spoke in whispers. Visiting hours were over, but nobody seemed to object.

Ella opened her eyes. Si and Kate took a hand each. 'Mumma?'

'Jack?' she asked.

'He'll be here soon. Very soon.'

She shook her head, clearly disbelieving. 'Si, Si, darling, I need to tell you . . .'

'You don't need to tell me anything,' said Si gently, his voice cracking up. 'Just get better.'

'In my bag . . . copy of my will . . . for you. The original is with Browne & Son in Lovelace Avenue . . .'

That was odd, thought Kate. She'd have expected solicitors in Thorpe Wenham.

'Kate . . .'

'Yes, Mumma . . .' she leaned closer towards her mother to hear her better.

'Talk to Virginia . . . she's a good girl . . .'

Mumma had obviously been impressed by the hundreds of thousands of acres in Scotland. But Kate wasn't going to argue. 'Yes, Mumma, now try to get some sleep.'

'Virginia can help.'

Virginia would just love that, wouldn't she? Helping was something she was far too fond of. And what was she going to help with? Keeping 19 Lovelace Road tidy at long distance? If Kate hadn't had tears in the back of her throat, she would have been angry with her mother, but no one could be angry with the limp bundle of bones struggling to survive amongst a spaghetti mess of tubes. A nurse bustled in and checked various pieces of equipment, but didn't tell them to go.

'Si . . . fidelity isn't important. Well, it is, but it's not worth throwing everything away for. Not always.'

'I know, Ma, I know. Don't worry.'

Why was Ella telling Si that? She must be muddling him up with Jack. Or had Si been up to something too?

'When you were born we had so many dreams for you,' said Ella to Si, 'we thought you could do anything. By the time Jack came along, we'd relaxed a bit. I've always thought maybe we were too relaxed, we should have looked after him better.'

'What about me?' asked Kate, before she could stop herself.

Ella smiled. 'You were our precious little girl. Mike had dreams for you, too, that you'd be a great journalist or a politician. He always said you'd be somebody special, but that it was harder for a woman.'

Kate was warmed by the faith her father had had in her. This was what they had missed since he'd died – the chance to re-tell the family story, to remind each other how they'd all come together. It was what she was doing at 19 Lovelace Road, creating an environment full of memories for the four of them. Except, now, one of them was hardly ever there.

'But Jack . . .' Ella plucked anxiously at her sheets. 'Jack . . .'

'Tell us. We can tell him,' said Si, stroking Ella's hand.

'I'll write. Is there a pen and paper? I must write to Jack.'

Kate handed Ella something to write with, gently propping her up in bed and watching the spidery hand, now beginning to distort with arthritis, falter across the page. She signalled to Si that they should leave the room. As she and Si bought bottled water from a machine, Kate leant against the wall in exhaustion. 'I think Ella wants to tell Jack about Dad having an affair.'

Si nodded. 'Yeah, I reckon that's what's on her mind, too. She's never got over the fact that she was the one who chucked him out, and that he drove right into an oncoming car. She knows it wasn't deliberate, but she thinks he wasn't concentrating because of the row they'd had, so she feels guilty.'

'Si! You knew?' Kate was shocked. 'All along?'

Si nodded wearily. 'I knew about the affair. I saw Dad with the woman once, and tackled him about it. He admitted it. It was almost as if he was relieved to have someone to confide in.'

'What did you think?' asked Kate, cautiously.

'I was angry at first. For Mum. But when he died . . . I thought what a bloody, bloody waste. I was determined never to let anything so messy happen to me. It was just a waste, Kate, he could have done so much more in life, and we would have been so much happier ... maybe that's why I like my life nice and organised, with plenty of money in the bank. Still, there's nothing wrong with that.'

'Do you blame Mumma? Or Dad?'

He hesitated. 'Not now. But maybe ... you know, when I went to Oxford, and met people who were more sophisticated than we were, and read up on that whole Edwardian aristocratic thing where you have affairs but they don't touch your marriage, I thought, why weren't we like that? Why were we so bloody provincial and small-minded?'

'Yes, I remember. It was as if you despised everything we came from. I thought it was just that you hated the new house we moved into after Dad died.'

'I did, it was miserable there. It never felt like home ... Let's try Jack one more time, then go back to Mum.'

Jack still wasn't answering.

'Si, did you ever talk to Mumma about it?'

He shook his head.

'I think if you did, and you told her that you didn't blame her, that none of us blame her, that we'd all have done the same, would probably still do the same, then it might give her some peace.'

He nodded. 'I'll do that. I think she feels that she's failed, especially with Jack.'

They rounded the corner and saw two nurses and a doctor bending over Ella's bed, too busy to notice Si and Kate.

The doctor straightened up, and looked at his watch. 'Death pronounced at 10.42 p.m. on Monday October twenty-second.' He looked at Kate and Si with the dropped shoulders of apology and the bleakness of failure in his eyes. 'I'm sorry,' he said.

'Jack's killed her,' said Kate, as an utterly incomprehensible world swirled around her. 'He and Sasha.' She clung to Si. 'Si, they killed her. Just as much as if they'd given her poison, or shot her or something like that. She should have lived for another ten years at least, to see her grandchildren grow up.'

'I never got to tell her.' Si's voice was bleak. 'I never got to tell her that we loved her, that we didn't blame her, that it wasn't her fault. We should have told her earlier.'

But Kate couldn't bear it any longer. She ran out of the hospital, away from the pain, through the gloomy linoleum corridors, pounding over the pavements, half running, half walking, with the Thames glittering to her right, ignoring the ringing of her mobile and hardly feeling the tears on her face. Her feet took her automatically along the river, down through the main arterial road, up to the junction, then into the side roads until she stopped, out of breath with her feet almost hurting more than her heart, at her own front door.

Jonny must have been waiting for her, because it opened the minute she tried to get her key in the lock, and he opened his arms to her. Behind him she could see Callum's anxious face.

'We heard,' he murmured. 'Si rang. We were worried about you.'

Kate buried her head in his chest and let the wings of her home settle protectively around her. 'Jack killed her,' she sobbed. 'Jack and Sasha, they killed her.'

Chapter 42

Sasha's flat in Richmond was crowded with the furniture from her marriage to Adam. She didn't want to throw anything away, or sell it, because one day she would be in a house again and she would need a huge cream sofa and two matching armchairs, a giant coffee table and swags of cream silk curtains puddling over the floor. She would have a house with big, tall windows that needed those curtains.

Jack came back late that afternoon. He'd been in meetings with the MOD all day. After his session with Heather, Sasha had been slightly anxious, and she had been unable to contact him. But he was back. Nobody had persuaded him that his duty lay with Heather. The tension seeped out of her.

He had several boxes and another suitcase. 'I don't know where we're going to put these.'

'We won't be here long,' said Sasha. 'You might fit those under Tom and Grace's beds.'

He flung his jacket over the sofa, and lugged the boxes into the room that Tom and Grace shared. The door swung shut behind him just as his mobile rang from the jacket pocket. Sasha slid her hand inside the pocket and checked the number it registered. Bloody Kate. Probably trying to persuade Jack to go back to Heather. She would be on the phone for hours. Sasha quietly turned the phone off – she didn't want Jack checking for any missed calls – and slipped it down the back of the sofa. He would never find it there.

Her own phone rang too, almost immediately, and once again it was Kate. She was so fucking persistent. Didn't she ever think of anyone else apart from herself? Well, she could wait. Sasha ignored the call. She was tempted to turn it off too, but Kate would be suspicious.

Jack, sneezing with the dust, came back in. 'Isn't that your phone?'

'Don't worry, it's my mother. I'll call her later. Once she's on the phone, she never gets off.' Sasha slipped the phone into her bag, and turned it off once it stopped ringing. She and Jack deserved some time to themselves without his family pestering them all the time. Thank God it was a rented flat, and there was no landline.

'How was Heather, darling?' Sasha went into the tiny, boxy kitchen and pulled a bottle of champagne out of the fridge. She always welcomed Jack with champagne, it was part of their ritual.

He sat down with a sigh, taking the glass from her. 'I feel such a shit.'

Sasha moved closer to him. 'She's playing the victim card. She means you to feel that way. It's not fair, darling, she's not thinking about what's best for you at all.'

He looked at the glass in his hands. 'I must stop drinking. I'm due back at work next Monday. In Wiltshire.'

'In that case . . .' Sasha began to nibble his ear. 'We ought to make the most of this week. Have a little holiday somewhere. Adam can have the children, he's always asking for them.'

'I'm not sure I can afford it, I . . .' Jack's words died away as Sasha's hand trailed across his crotch. 'Well, maybe . . .'

Sasha slid her hand up his front, unbuttoning his shirt, and then the waistband of his trousers. 'Oh, dear, I think I've spilt some champagne,' she whispered, as she scattered a few drops over his torso. 'I've been a very naughty girl, I'll have to lick it up.'

What was the saying? A standing cock has no conscience? Well, it certainly doesn't remember to return phone calls. She smiled as she bent over it. He wouldn't be thinking about his family for some time, she resolved, and by the time they finished, he wouldn't be worrying about silly little things like money either. 'Sweetie pie,' she murmured as she briefly lifted her head, 'You deserve a bit of proper time off after everything you've been through.' She was rewarded by the urgent pressure of his hands pushing her head down again.

Sasha treated him to a particularly athletic and inventive pre-dinner session, involving the champagne and some olive oil, after which Jack fell asleep. He was still sleeping badly, and often woke in the night, shouting. Sasha hoped that a new life with her would take his mind off what he had suffered in Temanistan.

Later she checked the messages on her phone and got Kate's desperate plea for Jack to come to Ella's hospital bed.

And have a deathbed scene where Jack promises his mother he'll go back to Heather for the sake of her granddaughters? No way. Kate must think she was a complete fool if she thought Sasha was going to fall for that one. Sasha deleted it, and went on to the internet to find a selection of top country-house hotels. She needed to book Jack and herself in for a mid-week break. Get him away from his family – families only cause trouble.

It was Kate who, ten days later, via Jack, forbade Sasha to attend Ella's funeral. And Jack didn't stand up to her.

'Heather's going to be there, with the girls. Kate thinks it will be too hard on them.'

'Heather needs to move on,' said Sasha. 'She has to accept that it's over between you. And Kate has no business to forbid me to support you. How would she feel if someone told her that Jonny couldn't be there?'

She dealt with Jack's incessant guilt over not getting to Ella in time by blaming Kate for not trying hard enough to contact them ('Darling, I really think she was trying to keep you from saying goodbye to Ella'), having quietly switched the phone on again the following morning. He thought it had slipped out of his jacket somehow. 'I should have checked my messages when I left the MOD,' he kept saying, until Sasha felt like slapping him.

In the end, Sasha dealt with the whole business of the funeral by being slightly frosty to Jack the day beforehand. And he certainly wasn't getting any sex, especially as he'd cancelled their mid-week break at Cliveden.

On the day of the funeral itself, she drove all the way down to the crematorium near Thorpe Wenham in dark glasses and a scarf, and parked in the corner of the car park. She watched them all walk in, Jonny and Kate hand in hand with their boys, Heather hurrying after them with Daisy and Molly, then Si, looking handsome, with his arm around Olivia, and finally Jack, his face like granite. Kate was the colour of putty, but Olivia looked elegant in black, and her face seemed lit up from within. She hung back to answer her mobile phone. Sasha watched her stalking up and down outside the dreary modern building like a model on a catwalk, a smile on her lips, talking urgently into the mouthpiece and casting quick looks up and down the street. That wasn't a business call, Olivia Fox, thought Sasha, as Olivia closed her phone and hurried back in, still smiling to herself.

The service ticked by inside. Sasha was angry about not being allowed to go to the funeral, but she was also frightened. Very frightened. She got back into the car and stared at herself in the rear-view mirror and saw the huge dark shadowy eyes of a rejected child. Here she was, on the edge of another family that didn't want her. A family where the women would not respect her, would not like her, would try to exclude her. Kate, most particularly. She didn't want her brother to be happy, that was quite clear. She didn't want to lose control, that was what it was – a control issue.

But Sasha was with Jack now, and the family should accept that. And Heather, too. Deal with it, Heather. Your marriage was a sham, you've barely seen your so-called husband over the past year, you can't pretend you have, so why ban me from the funeral? Jack needs me there, at his side. Because we're a unit.

She'd found the letter, though, the last letter that Ella had written to Jack. Si had given it to Jack, who, numb, had scrunched it up and thrust it in his pocket. Sasha always checked his pockets late at night and she'd lifted it out. 'Oh no you don't, madam,' she whispered.

It was easy to lift the flimsy flap, and she was right. Ella's letter to Jack was all about some affair Jack's father had had, and how she shouldn't have thrown him out, and how not having a father had ruined Jack's life, and that him leaving now would ruin the girls' lives. That he mustn't let his girls down, that, above all, they needed their father while they were growing up, and she apologised for depriving Jack of his. 'You were the one who suffered most amongst the three of you,' she wrote. 'Because you could barely remember him, and had nothing to cling to. Si was almost grown up, and Kate is so sensible, but you were too young to make any sense of it, and you fought it all. In the playground. By not doing your homework. By staying out late and drinking. Thank goodness you found the army, or you could have gone badly wrong. You must be there for your girls, they need a father.'

Well. That meant, presumably, that Jack ought to stay married, although she was interested to see that Heather hadn't been mentioned. She wasn't going to risk it though. Jack was going to find that he'd lost the letter. Everyone knew how careless he was.

And she didn't think Ella was right about Kate. So-called sensible Kate, thought Sasha, was trying to recreate her happy family home, as it was before her father's death, for her boys at 19 Lovelace Road. But it's not the seventies any longer, Kate, wakey-wakey. Keep your head too buried in the past trying to recreate something that was probably never there in the first place, and you could find yourself overtaken by the future, which won't be playing to the same rules.

The doors of the crematorium opened and the Fox family tottered out ahead of the crowd, as if battered by a great wind. Olivia and Si were arm in arm, Olivia crying now. The trouble with those two, thought Sasha, is that they'd been together so long they were more like brother and sister. There was tenderness there, but no passion. Unless she was very much mistaken.

Kate hugged the sobbing Luke, who seemed nearer to six years old than ten. Heather, Molly and Daisy trailed out one after another, each weeping into handkerchiefs. Heather gathered them to her, and they clustered in a tight little trio. Jonny stood to one side with Callum, both stiff and brave, accepting condolences from Ella's friends, extending invitations to the reception afterwards. He moved over to stand by Kate, and occasionally she saw their hands touch briefly. A sign of closeness or a connection that kept breaking? She studied them carefully. It was a strange relationship: tall, blonde Jonny and plain Kate. Well, not plain exactly, but she was hardly film star material, was she? Kate was Mrs Average, and Jonny was not Mr Average. Not in Sasha's book. But there you go.

Then Jack came out, raw, red-eyed and uncertain, and Heather looked at him over the heads of her daughters.

Don't you dare go to her, Jack Fox, thought Sasha, watching the scene.

She saw Jack walk hesitantly towards them, and then Heather turned away, drawing the girls with her. Sasha exhaled, not realising she'd been holding her breath.

You can't split us apart. Jack is going to put me first in the future, not his awful family or his cringing, pathetic ex-wife. You had your chance to welcome me in, Foxes, and you blew it. From now on, you'll be seeing a lot less of Jack. She drove away, quickly, so that she could get back to Richmond before Jack did.

Her hands were shaking as she poured herself a drink, and she couldn't get rid of the tight, terrified knot in her stomach. She would be nice about it this time – she would be very, very nice to him when he got back – but she must make sure nothing like this ever happened again. Jack belonged to her. Not to the past. He should not have a relationship of any kind with another woman, not even his sister. It was a betrayal.

That was what it was. A betrayal. Finally, the rage overwhelmed the fear in a hot rush, and Sasha lifted the glass to her lips.

She tried to comfort herself with the thought that there was bound to be a bit of money from Ella's will. She and Jack could have a decent holiday.

Chapter 43

Kate drove down to Thorpe Wenham a week later to meet Si and Jack there. They had to clear the house, talk to the neighbours, engage an estate agent, inform the council . . . the list of tasks was endless. Kate had had to spend half an hour rejigging her diary to create enough space in it to spend a few days at Thorpe Wenham, and she wished she had done the same when Ella was alive. She had always been too busy to come and stay with Ella, although Ella had asked her several times. Guilt and grief settled on her shoulders like a heavy blanket.

Si had rung her to ask her to arrive before Jack. 'I need to talk to you,' he'd said.

She wondered if Si was just being self-important or whether there was any real reason to exclude Jack. She sometimes felt guilty about that, too – the way she and Si had secretly conferred over everything after their father died. Mostly that was because Jack was 'the problem', of course.

But Si produced Ella's will, which he had taken from her hand-bag in hospital. 'She made a new will, and left me a letter,' he said.

'Did she leave me a letter?'

Si raised an eyebrow. 'Not as far as I know. Why?'

'It's just that she wrote a letter to Jack on her deathbed and then she left you a letter. I just wondered if there was one for me.'

'She didn't need to write you a letter,' replied Si. 'You were there. Jack wasn't. And my letter was practical, because I'm her executor.'

It still hurt. Kate would have liked a letter. 'Can I see it?'

'She's cut Jack out,' said Si abruptly, ignoring her request. 'That's why the original is with solicitors in London. She wasn't in Thorpe Wenham, she was at 19 Lovelace Road when she wrote it. I remember her "just popping out" that morning, even though she looked so ill.'

'Well, we'll just have to write him in again,' said Kate. 'I know people can do that. The heirs can rewrite the will, if they all agree.'

'Well, I don't agree,' said Si. 'She didn't want Jack to have the money. She obviously didn't want it to go on his divorce.'

'She obviously didn't want Sasha getting her hands on it,' retorted Kate. 'But Jack has a right to it. We can't just take it between us.'

Si cleared his throat, avoiding the reference to Sasha. 'Actually, she left Jack's share to me. You get a third, I get two-thirds.'

'But that's outrageous! You've got so much money already, and you don't have a family, Si – you can't take this, even you couldn't be so mean?'

'Even me? Is that what you think of me? Oh, I know the family legend is "Si's so mean. Si's wallet has mothballs in it". All the old jokes about Si being as tight as a duck's arse. Well, I've had to be tight, especially in the early years. Has it ever occurred to any of you to ask who's been supporting Mum since I graduated from university? She's had something from every single salary cheque I've ever had. She couldn't have survived without it, especially since she retired to Thorpe Wenham. I've paid all the running costs on the house.'

'But . . .' Kate couldn't take it in. 'She helped us buy 19 Lovelace Road, she gave me some of the deposit when Jonny's family gave him some.'

'Yes,' said Si. 'And where do you think that came from? And it's not as if I have an unlimited salary, you know. I have to earn every penny.'

Kate was shaken. 'Si, I'm so sorry. It was . . . very generous of you. I wish . . . I'd known.'

'I didn't want you to know. It would have been awkward. But when you were being extravagant . . .'

'If the family legend has you as mean, it has me as extravagant,' said Kate defiantly. 'And I don't think either are fair. I'll show you my bank statements if you like.'

'That won't be necessary,' said Si, his voice stiff.

'And maybe the family legend about Jack being irresponsible and rebellious isn't entirely fair, either,' added Kate. 'And Mumma's will certainly isn't. You must see that. And he will never speak to you – to us – again, if we let it stand. Do you want that?'

'Of course not. But it's my job, as executor, to carry out her wishes. Not my own.'

Kate bit back the retort that Si was being pompous. She heard Jack's car drive up outside. 'Please, Si. This will tear the family apart. Forever.'

As Jack walked up the path to the front door, she added: 'Mumma made that will in a hurry, when she was furious with Jack about him leaving Heather. It's like Dad and the car accident all over again. Don't let the family be damaged permanently by something that was a knee-jerk reaction, please don't, Si.'

'We won't talk about it,' said Si. 'Not until I've decided what to do. I'll tell Jack we haven't seen the will yet.'

As Jack stood outside the cottage, knocking on the door and tapping on the window, trying to catch the attention of her and Si inside, in the warmth, Kate had a glimpse of what his childhood must have been like. Always trying to catch up.

It went wrong from the moment he stepped in the door. 'I can't be too long,' he said. 'I've promised Sasha I'll take her away for a break in a good hotel near here, so I'm picking her up from the station at lunchtime.' He looked at his watch. 'But this shouldn't take much more than an hour, should it?'

'Really?' asked Kate. 'And who is going to clear the house? Get it ready for sale? Sort out the paperwork?'

Jack smiled his charming little-boy smile. 'You and Si are so good at all that, I don't want to interfere. Anyway, I haven't got time.'

'*I* haven't got time,' retorted Si.

'It's all right,' said Kate. 'We can make a start and I'm sure Jack won't mind coming back and helping out another day, would you, Jack? He could take all the rubbish to the tip if we sort it all out.'

'That's right,' said Jack, easily. 'Give me the nasty jobs, I'm used to it. Anyway, Sasha and I won't want much of the furniture – army houses are so small. In fact, there's really only one thing –

that little diamond brooch Mum used to wear all the time, which Sasha would like. As we won't be having much else in the way of goods and chattels, that's fair enough, don't you think? Have you got the will yet, by the way – what did it say?'

'Jack!' Kate couldn't believe his breezy tone.

He winked at her, and sat down. The little peach and pale green sitting room seemed very small with the three of them in there. 'But that's what we're here for, isn't it? To find out what it's all worth and divvy it all up?'

'Well, that needn't concern you, Jack.' Si's colour had risen.

'Si, no!' shouted Kate.

'Kate, please be quiet. You needn't worry about helping us clear the house out if you can't be bothered, Jack,' said Si. 'After all, you're not in the will, so perhaps it wouldn't be fair to ask you to pull your weight.'

The colour drained from Jack's face. 'Mum would never have cut me out, never. She loved me every bit as much as she loved either of you.'

'No one's questioning that. But she rewrote her will when she heard you were leaving Heather.'

Jack looked bewildered. 'To keep the money away from the divorce? So that it wouldn't go to Heather in a settlement? Presumably you're going to give it to me later?'

'I haven't decided what to do,' said Si, at his coldest. 'My main concern is to carry out her wishes, and she said nothing about redistributing the money later.'

'Did she say anything in the letter she wrote you, Jack?' asked Kate, with a fresh pinprick of hurt that she had no letter.

Jack looked ashamed for a moment. 'I lost it. But I'm sure that's what she would have said. Or wanted.'

'You lost it?' Kate couldn't believe her ears. 'Lost the words she nearly killed herself trying to write? Well, I'm not surprised she cut you out of the will. She knew you'd lose the money she'd worked so hard for.'

'This is about Sasha, isn't it? You can't bloody stand it that I've got her and you haven't. I know you wanted her, Si, and Jonny did, too, Kate, but she loves me. Me! And I love her. And none of you can handle that. You're bastards, all of you.'

'Jack, it was Sasha who sold your story to the papers,' said Kate. 'She's a stringer for the tabloids. That's where it came from, not from me or anything poor Heather ever said by accident.'

'Even for you, Kate, that is a pretty low blow.' Jack stared at her with venom. 'You are totally indiscreet, and you know perfectly well that you either intentionally or unintentionally told someone in the media – and I'm not accusing you of actually selling the story, by the way, I wouldn't stoop so low – and now you're trying to cover it up by blaming Sasha. I think it is disgraceful. I hope you are ashamed of yourself, if you're capable of such an emotion.' He stormed out of the house and drove away.

'It's true,' said Kate to Si. 'Jasper Morton, Sasha's half-brother, told me.'

Si shook his head. 'What a mess. What a bloody mess.'

'And Jonny didn't fancy her or have an affair with her,' she said, hastily. 'It's always been work. That's why they've spent time together.'

'Of course, of course.' Si cleared his throat, but looked disbelieving. 'Quite. And I've no idea why Jack would say . . . well, you know, my marriage to Olivia is . . . I would never . . .'

'Of course not.' An expanse of unsaid, unsayable things stretched between them.

She taints everything, thought Kate. We all trusted each other once.

PART TWO

Chapter 44

Jack didn't speak to anyone in the Fox family for over six months. Kate trudged through the landscape of grief, missing him, and angry at what he had done with Sasha and how casually he expected her to clear up Ella's affairs. And she was angry with Si for not re-dividing the money. If Jack had still been with Heather, Kate knew that Heather would have helped clear out Ella's house, with Jack or without, and Jack wouldn't have been so greedy and arrogant about the will. Anyway, the money would have been left to him, or, if for some extraordinary reason it had not, Si would have re-divided it. She was sure he would have done, if he hadn't been so furious at Jack's callous attitude. Kate thought that if Sasha hadn't existed, they would all have worked together on the slow, painful process of dismantling their mother's life, maybe even just sometimes the three sisters-in-law together, dividing up the odd pretty thing they liked. Kate never found the diamond brooch – her mother's favourite – and suspected that Jack, who like the rest of them had a key to the cottage, had simply come in and claimed it.

But Heather was so shattered she was only just functioning – Kate didn't like to ask her – and Olivia seemed to be busy all the time. When Kate asked Si if Olivia would like any of Ella's jewellery, he just said that it was only costume stuff and Olivia had plenty of real jewellery she'd inherited from her own mother.

Milestones that would have been marked with lunches at 19

Lovelace Road – when one of Kate's radio programmes won an award, Si's birthday – went unacknowledged.

At first, Kate was too angry with Ella to feel sad, as she slowly absorbed the effect of her mother's confession that she had thrown Mike Fox out for infidelity. And too angry with the father whose memory she had revered for so long.

In April Si rang her. 'Do you mind doing the final clearance of the cottage before completion on Wednesday, sis? We've got an Extraordinary General Meeting of R&R. Although it won't be the final voting, it's the ideal opportunity to get the whole family together and convince them that I'm the ideal choice for the next Chief Executive. I would send Olivia in my place, but she's frantic too, with work and this renovation project of hers . . . I never see her these days.'

'But I've got a couple of programmes to produce and Callum and Luke . . .'

Si bowled on regardless. 'Thanks, sis. You know how it is with these family firms. I'm up against a chinless Bartlett who thinks he knows it all. So no time to lose!'

Jonny said he would come instead. On the car journey down they talked about Callum and Luke. Callum, she thought, had turned the corner. 'He's a different boy.'

'Mm,' said Jonny.

On the way back, she forced herself to talk about Ella, Mike and the affair. It was burning a hole in her brain, but she'd been too proud to confide in Jonny. A whole day of working together in Ella's cottage, though, had lifted some of the shadows between them.

'She probably lost her temper,' said Jonny, about the night her father died. 'If he hadn't had the accident, she would have had time to think about it more carefully.'

'So you think she was wrong, that if she'd thought about it, she'd have had him back? That it's OK to be unfaithful?'

'I didn't say that.'

'What *do* you think?' It seemed very important to know.

He was silent for a while. 'I think that your father was obviously a good father, who loved you all and got very involved with you, but if he'd lived you'd have had the chance firstly to rebel against him like all teenagers do, and then, later, to know him as a person, not just as an omnipotent figurehead who could do no wrong. People who die early sometimes get frozen into a sort of sainthood, but he was a flesh-and-blood person, like you or me, and he made a mistake. Which had tragic consequences for you all.'

'Is this because you're defending Sasha and Jack?' Kate did not want to concede that he was probably right. They had hero-worshipped their father, but he was only another parent, just like they were now. The anger and pain shifted, just a little.

'No, I'm not defending Sasha and Jack,' said Jonny evenly.

'Because I get the feeling that you're on her side.' Kate still wanted Jonny to declare that he was for her and the Foxes. To reject Sasha completely.

'It's not a question of sides.'

'She's got Jack completely in her clutches. He won't believe it was her who sold his story to the papers.'

'Maybe it wasn't. And Jack must take some responsibility for all this, Kate. He chose to leave his wife. He chose to be unfaithful to Heather, to spend his leave from Temanistan in Paris with Sasha rather than at home with his wife . . .' Jonny broke off.

'What?' shrieked Kate. 'What are you talking about?'

Jonny ran a hand through his hair. 'Sorry. I didn't mean to say anything. That week's leave that was allegedly cancelled about halfway through his tour in Temanistan – I'm now pretty sure he spent it with Sasha in Paris. That's why they got together so quickly after he came back.'

'And you knew about this and didn't tell me?'

'I didn't know. Not at the time. I knew she was going to Paris, then someone in the office said something about a married boyfriend in the army a bit later, and then, well, I pieced it together quite recently from the odd things she's said.'

'Without telling me?' Kate repeated.

'Of course I didn't tell you,' he said quietly. 'You would have told everyone, and then you'd have tackled Jack about it.'

'Perhaps that would have been a good thing. He might have thought more about what he was doing,' she hissed. 'I can't believe you knew all this was happening and did nothing to stop it.'

'I didn't know "all this" was happening at the time. I didn't have the power to "stop it", and nor did you.' Jonny sighed. 'Be realistic, Kate, you have got to accept this. He has made his choice, and if we continue to condemn it, you'll never get to see your brother. It's none of our business.'

'I think it is our business,' said Kate. 'At least it was our business. I think if someone's family can't at least try to stop them from making a terrible mistake, then it's . . . it's . . .' She was too angry to find the words to complete the sentence.

'Kate, let it go. Make the best of it. Stop being so angry with everyone.'

'I'm not angry at everyone. I'm only angry at Jack because his and Sasha's behaviour killed Mumma, you know it did, and maybe a bit at—'

'You're angry at your father. For being unfaithful. And your mother for kicking him out that night he had the accident.'

'She had to kick him out,' interrupted Kate, hastily. 'She had every right. You don't know what it's like, your parents stayed alive, stayed together . . . or maybe there were hidden secrets there too?'

Jonny shook his head. 'I don't think so. But if there are, they'll stay hidden, as only they knew about them. No, I admit I was lucky. Ginny and I had a really happy childhood . . .'

Christmas would be in eight months, thought Kate, irrelevantly. They'd cancelled going to Virginia after Ella's death, but this year they really did have to go. Occasionally, Kate fretted over Ella's last words to her: *Talk to Virginia . . . she can help.* Ella had obviously been going a bit gaga.

She returned to the argument. 'If you came from such a happy home, I'm even more amazed that you're prepared to defend infidelity.'

'I'm not defending infidelity.' Exasperation crept into his voice.

'Well, you're backing Sasha and Jack against me.'

They were passing a garage and Jonny turned into it, parked the car and turned the engine off. 'I am not backing Sasha and Jack against you,' he said, in low tones. 'And I resent the implication that I am.' It was very rare for Jonny to get angry.

Kate realised she'd been unfair. 'No. I know. Sorry.' She looked at her hands. 'Really. I mean it.'

He nodded and started the car again. 'I know. It's like this when someone dies. I was angry at my parents when they died, even though I knew they couldn't help it and they hadn't done anything wrong. Ginny and I argued about the stupidest things.' He touched her cheek. 'It will pass, Kate, it will. Just try not to tear everything apart in the meantime.'

'Is that what you think I'm doing?'

Jonny, wisely, did not answer and ten miles further on, he changed the subject with a quick, sideways smile. 'Do you want the good news or the bad news first?'

Kate always felt this was a test of personality. If you said 'bad news' you were probably a negative person. 'I'll have the good news,' she said stoutly.

'The *How To Be Rich And Famous* programme is being recommissioned. And it's being sold to Germany, France, Belgium and Japan.'

'And you get a slice of that?' She thought about not having to worry about money so much, about being able to afford the repayments on their enormous mortgage.

He nodded. 'We should. We're not completely out of the wood, financially, but we should be able to afford to pay the mortgage and save a bit, if things go on like this. And your mother's money has helped, of course. We should be fine for a few years, and that's all you can really ask, isn't it?'

Kate's heart leapt at the thought that 19 Lovelace Road was safe for the foreseeable future. 'What's the bad news?'

'It's not really bad news. But you might not like it. They want us to use Sasha as one of the two lead presenters. They think she's got a warm, sparky personality and delivers what could be quite dry, financial advice in a way that makes it seem sexy. The camera loves her, basically.'

'That's absolutely fine by me,' said Kate, stiffly. 'I really don't have a problem with it at all. Incidentally, I've had the go-ahead for that programme on twentieth-century figurative painters, and I wondered if we could ask Jasper Morton, Sasha's half-brother, to dinner some time. Since going to that retrospective exhibition of Roderick Morton's work, I've kept in touch with him. His wife's an art dealer too, so I'd like to talk to her. Informally.'

'Sure. Ask them any time. Maybe I should be thinking about doing some programmes on the arts myself.'

'Thank you for coming with me today,' she said, forcing the words out of her mouth. 'I thought we worked very well together.'

Jonny smiled, and for a moment she thought he was going to say something. But he didn't.

Chapter 45

On the first of June, Sasha fixed a tiny pearl stud earring into each ear, looped and fixed a seed-pearl choker around her neck, and looked at her appearance with approval. She had found a pearl-grey sheath dress which clung to her contours and flattered her tan, and her hair looked good twisted up, and wound through with tiny jewels. She might wear it like that more often. She slipped on a pair of killer heels and checked her lipstick. Perfect.

'Grace, let's see you.' She turned her daughter round. 'You look very nice. And you too, Tom.' She drew her children close to her. 'The taxi's downstairs.'

She sometimes wondered what her daughter was really thinking, but not for long. Tom, grumpy about being crammed into dark trousers and a shirt and tie, kicked the taxi seats repeatedly, but Sasha was too excited to reprove him.

It had taken seven months for Jack to get divorced, and Sasha had been shocked at the amount of money he'd agreed to pay to Heather, far more than she really needed. 'Don't forget that Heather needs to work,' Sasha had reminded him. 'Her confidence is at rock bottom – sadly – and the only way to pull herself up is to get stuck into a job. If you give her too much, then you take away her only chance of making a new life for herself.' She had watched Jack's reaction. 'But I love the fact that you're so generous and caring,' she'd added. Adam was still a pain, making unreasonable demands over the children, but Sasha couldn't wait to tell him that she was going to be married again before he was. So there. Natalie hadn't won after all.

Jack was standing outside Chelsea Registry Office, looking handsome and nervous, with someone called Dan. Or was it Don? Major Donald what was it? Goring? Boring? Nobody he really knew. Jack had originally wanted Si to be best man, but that would have meant inviting Olivia along too, and if they asked Olivia they'd have to ask Jonny and Kate. And Sasha loved Jonny but she wasn't having Kate at her wedding. Not after the way Kate had forbidden her to attend Ella's funeral. When Sasha thought of Kate, she felt very angry, the way she felt about her half-sisters. They were all alike, they wanted to lock Sasha out of their smug, beautiful, safe world and keep it for themselves.

But at least it had made Jack realise that his relationship with his family was ridiculous, especially in view of this appalling behaviour over the will. Sasha couldn't believe her ears when she heard Jack had been cut out. 'Take them to court!' she screamed when he told her. 'Take them to court! You can't let them walk all over you like that. They've stolen your money, they've used undue influence . . .'

'I have no intention of ever taking any member of my own family to court,' said Jack, and that was all she could get out of him on the subject. Well, that was that. No more cosy lunches at 19 Lovelace Road. No way. She and Jack would be a new family now – her and Jack, Tom and Grace – with new family rules about Christmas, birthdays and celebrations.

One of which was that if she didn't have Grace and Tom over the festive period, then she and Jack could go skiing on their own. As Sasha had pointed out to Jack, Heather had nowhere to go at Christmas and it would be cruel to stop her from being with Molly and Daisy at the Foxes. 'I know Heather hates me,' said Sasha earnestly, 'but I still want to support her whenever I can. We've got each other, she has nobody. So we must let her go to Kate's, especially as Kate will love that. Kate is one of those people who needs to be needed, and Heather needs her. So that all works beautifully.'

Jack had suggested that Molly and Daisy, like Tom and Grace, should be at the wedding, but Sasha had pointed out how much that would hurt Heather. 'I'd love them to be there too,' she'd said. 'But it would crucify Heather, and I can't bear the thought of making her any unhappier than she is already.'

So there they were, on a Thursday morning in the sunshine of a perfect June day, with blossom on the trees and shoppers in the Kings Road looking at them both curiously, probably recognising her, thought Sasha.

Well, perhaps not quite yet. But *How To Be Rich And Famous* had proved very popular, and now that they were shooting the second series, with Sasha as one of two lead presenters, well, she was really on her way. She still didn't have anything like as much screen time as the main presenter, a well-known psychiatrist, but her face was out there, and her agent was talking about other opportunities.

So everything was falling into place at last, she thought as she took Jack's arm and stepped on to the red carpet, approaching the registrar with a slow, measured tread, even though there was no one to watch except Major Boring and his mousy wife. Just her and Jack, and Grace and Tom. As it should be. Adam could go fuck himself.

After the honeymoon – an eco-lodge on the beach in the Maldives, with a spa attached – Sasha couldn't wait to get back to London and flash her wedding ring around. She and Jack had agreed that they should marry quietly, for Heather's sake, and let the news drip out slowly, rather than make a big announcement. So the Foxes knew nothing about it, and she'd really enjoyed dropping Grace and Tom off at Adam and Natalie's between the wedding and the honeymoon, and dropping 'we've just got married, actually' into the conversation. Adam had been really surprised. She saw it in his eyes. So there, Adam Taylor. I don't need you after all. She'd clutched Jack's arm, sparkling and happy. 'We're living in the country,' she said. 'Wiltshire, of course. So much better for the children.'

So as soon as she got back from holiday, she took a train straight to London to show her ring off to the girls at Future TV. Jack had talked about 'finding the right moment to tell the family' and 'sparing Heather's feelings' but she had a right to tell the people she worked with, didn't she? Sasha suspected that he was frightened of Kate's reaction. Well, Kate could stuff it. So she didn't think Sasha was good enough for her brother? Fine. In that case, she wouldn't be included in anything that Sasha and Jack were doing. See how she'd like that when Sasha became famous.

She pressed the intercom. 'Is Jonny there? It's Sasha.' An electronic buzz beckoned her in.

'Jonny, hi.' She waggled her fingers at him, and he looked up from the screen he was studying intently with Andrea, who came in two days a week to do the accounts.

'Guess what?' She held her hand up so he could see the ring. 'I'm your sister-in-law now. Oh, of course you're not married to Kate? Maybe the term is "partner-in-law"?' She twinkled at him. He was so attractive. In that thoughtful way of his . . .

Jonny straightened up and murmured something to Andrea before coming over to kiss Sasha's cheek. 'Let's keep it simple. Sister-in-law will do. Congratulations. We must have a glass of champagne.'

Sasha enjoyed that. The whole office crowded round at lunchtime and raised a glass to her, sharing the sushi and sandwiches that Jonny had treated them to in celebration. They went over the schedule – filming was to begin in two weeks' time, and she felt so much more confident than she had before. She left the office with a smile on her face.

On the train back to Wiltshire, she decided that the only thing that wasn't working out was the house that she and Jack had been allocated. She had thought army quarters, if you were as senior as a colonel, would be like the houses in Halstead Hill – old-fashioned, but impressive and spacious. In fact the house was dreadful, a tiny, boxy modern semi, with low ceilings and square windows. Sasha had been horrified when they were shown round.

'I can't live here Jack, we'll have to look at some other army properties.'

'Sorry,' said the horrid little man who showed her round. 'If you don't take this, you go straight back to the bottom of the housing queue. You might have to take captain's quarters.' She'd been so disappointed she'd found it hard to speak to Jack for the rest of the evening, and he'd promised to look into renting something decent. 'An old vicarage would be nice,' she'd said. 'Something with some character.'

Until then it was Boxville, though. She was almost glad she had plenty of excuses to go back to London – what with taking Tom and Grace up for their nights with Adam, and filming, so she'd better look up some London friends she could stay with, and try to work something out vis-à-vis the children. Boarding school. That was the only option, she thought, talking to some of the other wives on the patch at a coffee morning. Many nine- and ten-year-olds in the army went to boarding school, in order to minimise the effect of endless moving. She thought Grace in particular might benefit from being more with other children.

Sasha planned happily as the train rattled towards Warminster. Once they got a decent house and the kids into boarding school, everything would be fine. And she'd love to be a fly on the wall at 19 Lovelace Road when Jonny told Kate about Sasha and Jack's wedding. Assuming that he did of course, but if he didn't, in some ways that might be even better. Kate would eventually discover that he'd kept it secret from her. Either way there would be an unholy row, and it would serve Kate right.

Yes, life was turning out very nicely. Except for not getting Ella's money, of course.

Chapter 46

Heather heard about the wedding by email, from an old friend of hers.

After the ninety-three days in Halstead Hill were up, Kate had offered Heather the spare room at 19 Lovelace Road as a temporary home. Heather was wary. Another person pretending to be kind. What did Kate want? But she was in too much pain to do anything more than accept. Most of the furniture went into storage, and a stunned Heather, along with Daisy, Molly and Travis, who were bewildered but used to moving, found themselves on Kate's doorstep with a pile of suitcases.

It hadn't been quite as bad as Heather had thought it would be. She was in awe of Kate's muddly lifestyle and the way she sandwiched radio interviews between supermarket shopping and school runs, and hoped there weren't going to be too many frighteningly successful people round the table every night.

But it worked well, because there were so many people around all the time. Nobody asked too much of her. She didn't have to have intense relationships with anyone, she could just say 'hi,' and then go back to her cleaning, polishing and straightening. Kate loathed housework and was remarkably unfazed by having Heather do hers. Heather couldn't understand it. She'd never have let anyone touch her house, never. The frighteningly successful people – usually from the media – did turn up, all too often, but were surprisingly kind, questioning her in such detail about her divorce that she always feared they were about to do a programme or write an article on it. 'No, really, he's giving me as much as he can afford,' she said, not wanting to talk about Jack. No wonder he had left her, she thought, she was no good as a wife, or a mother. 'No, I'll have to rent somewhere, perhaps a little flat . . .'

Kate invited Olivia round. 'You'd better check that Heather's lawyer is up to scratch,' she joked.

'What, against your own brother?' Olivia shed her coat – dark, soft cashmere and beautifully tailored – and dropped her smart handbag on the floor, accepting a large glass of wine. There was something much more relaxed about Olivia these days, thought Heather, or perhaps it was seeing her away from the big Fox family lunches. Olivia smiled at Heather. 'Tell me, can your family help at all?'

Heather felt her face go stony. 'No, no.'

Kate poured her another glass of wine. 'Not at all?'

'My parents are dead,' said Heather, staring into the glass of wine. 'A long time ago.'

'What, when you were still a child? Who brought you up?' Kate went into questioning mode, and Heather froze in the head-lights of her interest.

'They're dead.' Surely Jack had told the Foxes the whole humil-iating tale of Mo?

'That's awfully early,' said Kate. 'Was it a car accident like Dad's?'

'Sisters and brothers?' asked Olivia.

Heather shook her head to both questions, hoping that the world might swallow her up, thinking that any minute she might jump up and sweep Kate's bottle of Chateau Pretentious right off the table, with all the glasses, so that they would smash on Kate's fashionable granite floor. She glared at them both.

'Lucky you,' said Kate, apparently not noticing. 'When I look at Jack, I could . . . How's Si, Olivia? We haven't seen him either recently.'

At that moment the phone rang.

'Oh, Si,' said Kate, 'we were just talking about you. When do you hear about the job?'

She paused. 'Oh, I . . . yes, I see . . . oh, well . . . do you want to talk to Olivia?' Kate handed over the phone to Olivia.

'He didn't get the CEO job at R&R,' she whispered to Heather, as Olivia took the phone out of the room. 'It's gone to a thirty-something Jones, seventh generation of Joneses at R&R, who knows diddly squat and thinks he understands the luxury market because he goes to smart parties.' Kate put her head in her hands. 'Si has never, ever failed at anything before. He's trying to sound as if he doesn't care, but I've always felt that all our parents' aspirations were focused on him, and even with them both dead he's still deep down looking to them for approval. At least that's my pet theory. I cannot imagine how he's going to react. Really, really badly, I suspect.'

But Olivia was vague when she got back. 'Oh dear, poor Si, but you can't have everything in life. He sounds furious, but is pretending not to be. Thank goodness I'm very busy with the renovation of Providence Cottage and this Allison Green case. Now let's have a look at all this correspondence between the solicitors, Heather.' She read the letters several times, carefully. 'Heather, you should be getting much more than this. It's not enough to bring the girls up on. What's Jack thinking of? He seems to have Sasha's Rottweiler divorce lawyer.'

'I won't go to court,' said Heather, who did not trust the authorities and knew that a court would find some way of blaming and punishing her. And finding out who she really was. And digging up Mo's crimes. She was terrified at the thought and she didn't want Olivia poking her nose into it all. Jack was divorcing her, that was enough to make Heather feel she had no rights, no good qualities, almost no reason to live. Except for Molly and Daisy, although even they would be better off without a mother like her.

'Sometimes you have to.' Olivia frowned over the letter. 'Heather, you needn't be frightened of going to court. You won't be on trial.'

'Heather, you have the girls almost all the time,' urged Kate. 'Jack takes them out for the odd excursion. You're shouldering all the costs and all the work. You must get the finances sorted properly.'

'I'm going to get a job. Part-time.' Heather knew there was no point in fighting the system. Gerald had said he would look after her, and hadn't. Jack had said he'd look after her and hadn't. People gave up on her, they always did. Kate would soon, and with any luck so would Olivia, who was looking very suspicious. Might Olivia use her legal contacts to find out about Mo? Heather was afraid she could. She smiled at her. 'I'm going to be OK. Jack's giving me what he can, and I shall earn the rest.'

By June Heather had managed to rally herself enough to find a small, rented flat and a mornings-only job at a small legal firm as a general dogsbody, which was supposed to finish at 2 p.m. so she could pick the children up. She never did finish on time, and always had to go home to pick up Travis and the car, then struggle through the London traffic, so Molly and Daisy were often the last to be collected, along with the two children they shared a school run with. Heather felt as if she was swimming in a very choppy sea – get the kids off to school, get to work, get out of work, back to school, walk Travis, homework, bedtime, and, finally, a few hours to catch up on household chores before she collapsed into bed herself, with Travis apologetically slithering up and on to her feet. Molly worried her, because she kept losing things, had failed to turn in her homework several times, and had also become rather accident-prone, falling and bruising her face once, and spraining her wrist on another occasion. The school nurse reported it all, and said there was nothing to worry about, but Heather couldn't help it. Daisy, too, was waking up at night and crawling in with Heather, which made the bed very hot and crowded. 'I miss Daddy,' she whispered. 'Me too,' said Molly, slipping in quietly too. Heather couldn't bear to reject them, but it all meant she was more tired than she'd ever been. Perhaps Jack was right, perhaps they would be happier at boarding school, with their father only a few miles away and all the facilities, and the other children to play with . . .

It was too painful to think about. Jack's rejection burned into her soul every waking moment.

But she forced herself to keep going – to open her emails and email people back with bright, cheery words. She avoided the phone because that was more difficult.

'Hi,' read an email from wilcoxes@home.net. 'How's things?

Met the new Mrs Fox yesterday when she and Jack moved into our patch . . .' After chirruping on for another few paragraphs it signed off as Ann Wilcox, a friend from a previous posting.

The new Mrs Fox. Heather's heart stopped. Surely he hadn't? Not without telling Molly and Daisy. With trembling hands she texted him. 'Have you got married? When were you going to tell us?'

Then she regretted the tone of the text. Nobody likes whining, Heather, nobody loves you. She crawled into her bed and Travis bounded up beside her, settling down with a grunt, his reassuring, furry weight a bulwark against the cold outside. She was beyond tears, and lay awake all night, dry-eyed, staring at the ceiling and clutching Travis.

Chapter 47

Kate had been so bound up in her own feelings about Ella's death along with missing Jack, getting infuriated by Si who was being difficult about everything and still flatly refusing to re-divide the will up, and her lingering worries about Jonny, that she forgot about Callum and Luke. She didn't forget about them physically – she produced meals, picked them up from sports grounds, did their laundry, tested them on their homework, albeit with half her mind on work, Ella's will, her book group, the latest planning application they were fighting in the Lovelace area or the charity committee she sat on to help deprived teenagers – but she didn't realise how much Ella's death had affected them, especially Callum, until one evening in July.

They were eating together as Jonny had got home early.

'Why don't we see Uncle Jack any more?' demanded Callum.

'Er . . . well, he wasn't very happy about . . .' Kate took a deep breath. 'Granny was very sad about Uncle Jack leaving Auntie Heather, and Daisy and Molly, so she cut him out of her will and Jack blames Si and me. And he hardly ever sees Molly and Daisy, which is awful and . . .'

'Cut him out of her will? That's terrible,' said Callum. 'Are you going to do that to me?'

'There won't be a lot to inherit,' said Jonny, joking. 'Don't worry, it won't be a problem.'

'But you never criticise Luke and you always criticise me, so how do I know you wouldn't . . .'

'We wouldn't,' said Kate firmly. 'And anyway we don't criticise you, we . . .'

'What if I do something you don't like?' he asked. 'Would you cut me out of the family, like you've cut Uncle Jack out? It's so unfair, I think you're all being really uncool, just because he fell in love with Sasha.'

Uh oh. Jack and Sasha as the star-crossed lovers. Just what they needed in the family dynamic. 'It's very complicated, Callum . . .'

'So? Explain it to me then.'

'I can't, it's . . .'

'It's just something you can't handle, so you pretend it's all his fault. And people say teenagers are immature.' He looked disgusted.

'Callum, your mother's doing her best to convince Uncle Si that Jack should have his share, so don't speak to her like that,' said Jonny.

'Well, her best obviously isn't good enough, is it?' said Callum. 'And it's time to stop talking to me as if I was about six.'

'If you stopped behaving as if you were about six, we might,' snapped Kate, exhausted.

Callum walked out, slamming the front door. And didn't come back.

By midnight, Kate was terrified. She and Jonny had walked round the area and checked all the pubs, they rang his friends and were wondering when they should call the police. 'He might have been stabbed or mugged,' she said. 'The blocks of flats on the Lovelace Estate have on average three knife incidents a week . . . we should have seen this coming. He was close to Ella, and to Jack and suddenly neither of them are there any more.'

'And neither are we,' said Jonny.

'I can't help it!' shouted Kate. 'I have to keep things going. And I don't want to become the sort of woman my mother was, who had nothing but her home and family, and then she suddenly loses everything. We lost our *home*, Jonny – we had to move away and go to a different school so we lost our friends, I know I didn't do as well as I could in my A levels and didn't get into university as a result, we lost *everything* when we lost our father, and my mother couldn't do a single thing about it. I am not going to be that vulnerable. Ever.'

Jonny stared at her. 'So, finally, I get to hear the truth about what's been driving you all these years. You could have told me before, you know.'

'Told you what? You knew about my father dying and us moving and changing schools. I didn't keep it secret. And stop talking about us, we must find Callum. Shall we try the hospitals?'

'I'll go out again and look,' said Jonny. 'And you stay here in case he calls or comes back.'

Every minute seemed like an hour. She would never see Callum again. It became impossible to imagine ever knowing what had happened to him. She rang all the hospitals and the police, twice, then realised Jonny might have been trying to get through to her.

She called him. 'Did you ring? Have you found him?'

'No,' said Jonny, sounding broken. 'I thought you were ringing to tell me he'd come home.'

Kate was distraught. In desperation she called Jack.

'Jack, I'm sorry . . .' she explained that Callum had left after a family argument. 'I thought he might have come to you. You and he were very close.'

The sleep left Jack's voice immediately. 'He's not here. But I'll get dressed and go and drive around the area generally. There's no public transport down here at night, he'd have to hitch-hike to get here. I'll try the petrol stations, that's where hitch-hikers would be dropped off.'

She thanked him and called Si.

'I'm in Bahrain,' he said. 'But call Olivia, in case he's gone to the flat.'

'It's the middle of the night, and anyway I already did.'

'What, you called the flat? And Olivia wasn't there?' He sounded anxious. 'What time is it in England?'

'Quarter to two in the morning. Maybe she just didn't hear the phone.'

'Yes, of course. Well, try her mobile. Or shall I?'

Kate got the feeling that Si was planning to check up on Olivia. 'No, don't worry, I'll do it.'

Olivia sounded sleepy too, and said that she was down at Providence Cottage. 'Maybe he's gone to our flat. There's no one there, though.'

'Olivia, he's done this because he thinks the will is unfair. Please, please convince Si that it needs to be changed.'

'I'm trying. I promise.'

Kate called Jonny. 'Olivia wonders if he might have gone to their flat. There's no one there, they're both away, but maybe he's waiting for them.'

'I'm there,' said Jonny. 'I had the same thought. I'm just going up the steps.'

Kate clung to the phone, praying.

'Callum!' shouted Jonny. 'He's here.' He clicked off, as Kate collapsed in tears. She had to live a different way, she had to. But she would think about that tomorrow. As she waited for Jonny and Callum, she wondered if she ought to have warned Olivia that Si knew she hadn't been sleeping at home.

Chapter 48

Si had become impossible to live with. When Olivia got back from her evening with Heather and Kate the night he'd been beaten to the job, he was opening a bottle of whisky, sloshing it angrily into a large glass.

'Si, I'm sorry.' She put her arms round him, but he shook her off.

'Olivia, just let me deal with this in my own way. I don't need pity.'

'Drinking won't help.'

He whirled round. 'What do you know about it? You've never had to try, you get what you want automatically . . .'

'That's not fair, Si, you know how hard I work.'

'I know. You do. But you get rewarded, you get the partnerships and the top cases, because you were born Olivia Montmorency, of the Montmorencies of Brampton. Do you know what this Hunter Jones said to the older shareholders? He said: "I strongly advise that you think very, very carefully before you vote in someone who had to buy his own furniture." He had the cheek to repeat that snobby old Alan Clark chestnut that I, for one, hoped we'd never have to hear again in this century. That fucking Jones persuaded them that they couldn't have someone who grew up in suburbia running one of Britain's longest-established quality companies, because, quote, the instinctive taste levels would be questionable, unquote.'

'Si, how awful – but that's just not true these days, and it's certainly not true that I get the top cases because of who I was born. That's not how it works in . . .'

'It is how it works, even today, Olivia, and you're a fool if you can't see it. Being Olivia Montmorency opens doors that stay closed to Simon Fox.'

'Well, it's easier to blame Britain's class system than it is to blame yourself, I suppose,' flashed Olivia, regretting the words as soon as she spoke them.

Si stared at her as if he had never seen her before. 'Thank you, wife,' he said, eventually. 'Thank you for that vote of confidence.'

They barely spoke for a week, although admittedly Si had spent four days of it in Bahrain.

Olivia tried again at supper the night after Callum ran away, when Si had returned. 'Si, I think this rift with Jack isn't helping anyone, least of all you. You haven't spoken to him for over six months.'

Si's eyes bulged. 'Isn't helping what?'

'Isn't helping anything. I do understand but don't you think you'd feel better if you made it up with Jack? Perhaps we should have him and Sasha round?'

'In case you'd forgotten, Jack thinks he's entitled to money from Mum's will, and she most specifically didn't leave him any. And he's blaming me for that.'

'Well, I can't imagine that you feel you have a right to keep it, you're not like that,' said Olivia, talking very fast before he could interrupt. 'Why not put Jack's share into a trust for the girls? That might help Heather, too, who has been left almost in poverty by this divorce.'

Si glared at her. 'You've always got an answer for everything, haven't you, Pollyanna?'

It was almost an improvement on Marie Antoinette, which was his latest nickname for her now that the work on Providence Cottage was taking up so much of her time. 'You'll get sick of it once it's finished,' he said. 'I know you, you're a city girl at heart.'

'I spent the first eighteen years of my life living in the country,' Olivia corrected him.

He set up the trust, informing her in an aside a few weeks later, casually. 'The trust for Jack's girls is all sorted now.'

'Have you told Jack?'

Si glared at her. 'Just about to.' He dialled. 'Mm? . . . Uh-uh, uh-uh, mm. Mm? Uh-uh. Uh-uh. Sure. Great.' He flicked the phone off. 'Well, that went OK. Jack is pleased. Says that's fair enough. He doesn't hold grudges, I'll give him that. And he's married Sasha.'

'What? And you didn't even say "congratulations"?'

'Didn't I?' Si looked surprised. He sneezed.

Olivia jumped at the sudden noise. 'No, you said "mm" and "uh-uh" about twenty-two times.'

'Oh, well I meant congratulations. Jack knows that.' Si sneezed again, and brought out a huge white handkerchief, blowing his nose forcefully.

Olivia was repelled. Did he have to blow his nose while they were eating? She looked at Si, his eyes red-rimmed and watery. Was it flu? Or allergies? Or even emotion? Surely not. 'We ought to invite them round.'

'I thought you didn't like her.' Si trumpeted another sneeze into the handkerchief. 'I hope I'm not getting a cold.'

'It doesn't matter whether I like her or not.' Olivia decided that if Si was going down with something, she'd be sleeping in the spare room. 'We should make the effort. Get him together with Kate again, and the boys. They miss him. And he and Kate have at least talked again, because Jack offered to drive round Wiltshire the night Callum disappeared. He may not be speaking to us, but he dropped everything to help when she needed it.'

Si wiped his eyes and returned the handkerchief to his pocket. 'Oh, OK, well, isn't Providence Cottage almost finished? Let's invite them down for the weekend.'

Olivia felt like snapping that Providence Cottage was hers, and not to be invaded by his noisy, nosy family. 'Blake and I are going through the snagging next Friday,' she said. 'I've no idea how much work it'll throw up.'

Si's eyes darkened. 'I don't mind going down before the snagging's completed. Anyway I ought to check over the final finish, and make sure this Blake hasn't left too many loose ends.'

Olivia felt like screaming, but kept her voice even. 'Blake is far too professional for that.'

They faced each other down for a few moments, and then Si sneezed again.

'I'd better spend the night in the spare room,' said Olivia. 'You've had an awful lot of colds this year. Do you think you ought to have a check-up?'

'Too busy,' snapped Si. 'I'm perfectly all right.'

But he wasn't, and Olivia knew she ought to be more sympathetic. But she just couldn't be. He was being self-pitying about Ella's death and not getting the top job at R&R. She couldn't bear to see it.

He poured himself another glass of wine, and Olivia pushed her own glass forward. They were both drinking more – not a lot, but enough for her to feel tired and cross when she woke up in the mornings.

'You could always apply for another job,' she ventured. 'With your record, you'd be snapped up.'

'I've got a cold,' he growled. 'Not a career crisis. And I don't need life coach advice, thank you.'

'We'll have to have a dinner party on Saturday night if we have Jack and Sasha down,' she said, changing the subject. 'To distract Sasha and Kate from each other. Then they'll have to behave.'

Si treated her to a smile of pure malice. 'I agree. Why not ask Blake? To thank him for all his hard work? Has he got a girl-friend?'

'I expect so,' said Olivia carefully. 'I'll ask him to bring her if he likes.' Si was increasingly suspicious about the time she spent with Blake, and could never resist a sardonic remark about him.

Si rolled his eyes, and sneezed again. Olivia couldn't face finishing her meal, and tipped it into the bin. 'I'm not really hungry. I'll get on with inviting everyone.' She reached for her phone and dialled Jack, asking to speak to Sasha. 'Hi, Sasha, congratulations.'

She thought Sasha sounded wary. 'Oh. Thank you.'

'We wondered if you'd like to come down to Providence Cottage and we'll all raise a glass of champagne to the happy couple. We've finished the renovations and could do any of the next three weekends. With the children, of course.'

'Oh, that's so kind.'

'She sounded pleased to be invited,' said Olivia, clicking the phone off, then calling Kate and Jonny and getting a yes from them too. 'Do you think we should put Kate and Jonny in the best bedroom, or Jack and Sasha? What do you think?'

Si raised an eyebrow. 'Dearest heart, the bedrooms are the least of your problems. Preventing Kate from actually murdering Sasha is going to be your major challenge. She believes that Sasha and Jack's behaviour killed our mother, and it's going to require a bit more than tactful bedroom planning to overcome that.'

'Well, believe it or not, it is extraordinarily important where people sit or, presumably, sleep if you want to avoid conflict. That's why our meeting room at Campbell Carter has round tables, and we put a lot of effort into making sure that the divorcing couple aren't placed directly opposite each other. They need to feel that they aren't eyeballing up to each other, and that they're being protected by their own side. And it's a more collaborative shape.'

'Perhaps you should have got a round table for the dining room at Providence, then.'

'Oh dear, perhaps I should. Do you think we should go out and buy . . .'

'No, I do not. It would be madness. I am not going to waste money on buying two tables. This is one weekend, and everyone has got to learn to behave. Otherwise they're not coming again.'

'Si, you will be nice, won't you? Because if you're too bossy, it . . .' Olivia suppressed the desire to point out to Si that it was her money, not his, that would buy a new table. 'Anyway, Kate thought it was a good idea, as she'll have to make peace with Sasha some time,' she added. 'Although she's furious about them getting married, says they've done it far too soon.'

'Army regulations,' said Si, with another sneeze. 'You can't get married quarters without being married. At least now that Sasha's career's getting off the ground it should help Jack with the money side. As long as they don't have any more children. But I can't imagine that they will, can you?'

'Why not?' Olivia was finding it almost impossible to hide her irritation with Si, his sneezing and his general approach to life. The words 'miserable git' came to mind, she thought. 'Sasha's still in her thirties, she could easily have another baby.'

Si got up and put his plate in the dishwasher. 'I just can't imagine why they would want to, that's all. It seems a retrograde step.'

Olivia wondered if Si had ever really wanted children at all. No wonder he'd stalled when she suggested donor sperm.

Well, at least she had Providence Cottage to love, even though the renovations were almost finished. There was still the garden to do. She dialled Blake, deliberately doing it in Si's earshot, and asked him to dinner. 'And Si says have you got a girlfriend you'd like to bring?'

Blake laughed. She wished she was with him.

Behind her, Si sneezed again. Olivia couldn't bear it any longer and took a pile of papers to the spare room. It was the final hearing in the Allison Green case on Thursday, generating mountains of papers and documents. It would be a fully contested fight between Allison and Chat Show Ted, and his lawyers were wily adversaries that she had come up against before. She needed to think about that, not about Blake's golden laugh.

Chapter 49

Kate, Jonny, Callum and Luke drove up the potholed track to Providence Cottage and parked in the newly cleared drive. Kate took in the exquisitely sympathetic lime pointing between the old bricks, the careful shade of historic white paintwork around the windows, the renovated Kent peg-tile roof and the front door, exactly the right greyish, slubby shade of dusty blue. The door furniture was polished and the worn front steps scrubbed. Everything had been renovated, but it looked as if it had been there for ever. The sunset spread its rosy fingers over the landscape, and the air was cool and fresh. A perfect summer's evening.

Olivia opened the door with a cry of welcome.

The following day, after waiting too long for lunch, they ate without Sasha, Jack and the children, Olivia jumping up every time she heard a rustle at the door.

'Sasha's always late,' said Kate. 'I think she does it deliberately. To show how important she is.'

'They might have had an accident,' quavered Luke.

'Was that them?' Olivia began to get up again, but Si pulled her down.

'If it was, they'll knock properly. If Jack's being so rude that he can't even ring to let us know when he'll arrive, then he can wait outside.'

They arrived at six that evening, pouring through the door with all four children – Molly, Daisy, Grace and Tom, and Travis bounding ahead of them – with shrieks of apology and a huge bunch of flowers. 'I am so, so, sorry,' cried Sasha, kissing Olivia, 'we got stuck in terrible traffic and Molly dropped my mobile down the loo, so it doesn't work. Si, darling, you look the perfect country squire.' She flung her arms around him, and hung on just fractionally too long.

While they were taking their things upstairs, Kate muttered that surely someone else in the car had had a mobile phone.

'Put a sock in it, Kate,' said Si, sharply. 'This is the weekend where we bury all hatchets.'

Kate studied him. He was always suspiciously quick to defend Sasha.

Sasha and Jack came downstairs, hand in hand. 'Oh, you've made the cottage look absolutely gorgeous, Olivia, hasn't she, Jack?'

Kate fled as she heard them kissing. She was sure Sasha was deliberately making as much noise as she could over it.

She walked briskly down the track to find a spot with a mobile signal. She started with a call to a woman called Marina Elliott. She had recently met her and discussed the tentative idea of forming a larger production company. They chatted about other people who might join them.

'I met an absolutely charming woman at dinner the other day,' said Marina. 'She's just started TV presenting, and says she loves radio. She's called Sasha Morton – in fact, you probably know her. Doesn't Jonny direct the *How To Be Rich And Famous* series? I thought she was rather good.'

'Know her? She's married to my brother, and I'd really rather not get involved with her on a work basis.'

'If your brother's Adam Taylor, I'm not surprised,' agreed Marina. 'It was obviously a filthy divorce – although of course you always have to hear the other side of the story too.'

'No, my brother's Jack Fox, the one she's just married.'

'Are you sure? I understood that she was on her own still.'

'No, she's sitting on my brother's knee playing tonsil tennis with him at this moment. Waving a wedding ring in our faces at every possible opportunity.'

'Perhaps we're not thinking of the same person? Quite petite, thin and dark, stylish in an understated way?'

'That's her,' said Kate, grimly. 'Do you mean she's pretending to be single?'

'Well, I suppose . . . I'm trying to remember. She talked about her ex-husband, Adam Taylor, I'm sure she said he was called. Well, she talked about him and how vile he'd been quite a lot. How she had to live in rented accommodation while he has a five-bedroom palace. And someone asked her how long she'd been on her own, and she said three years. But I must have got the wrong end of the stick somehow.'

'Must have,' said Kate. 'And this was only last week?'

'Two days ago. I was up the other end of the room from her for the rest of the evening, so I really don't know if she then went on to say that she'd married again, etcetera. But she was all over the spare man she'd been invited for.'

'She'd been *invited for a spare man*?' echoed Kate.

'Yes, I started to ask the hostess about her, and she said that she did admire her, she'd had such a tough time and was turning her life around so brilliantly, and that she was inviting this American guy to meet her because he's in TV and stationed in London for a bit, and she thought they'd have lots in common. I just assumed she was . . .'

'Well, perhaps it was all about TV and wanting to seem independent for her career,' suggested Kate. 'But it is all very odd.'

'Well, maybe I got it wrong, and I only heard half the conversation . . . perhaps it's just the Chinese whispers effect . . .'

Kate struggled to make sense of it all. 'Must go.' She snapped her phone shut as Jonny came down the lane, apparently deep in thought. 'Hiya. You OK?'

'Mm? Yeah, fine, just tired. We're submitting the proposals for a third, longer run of *How To Be Rich And Famous* first thing on Monday morning. Is Sasha around? Would you mind if we did some work this weekend?'

'Not at all.' Kate was tired of being seen as the problem. 'The only thing is . . .' she hesitated. Would Jonny believe her? 'Well, a friend's just told me that she was at a dinner party with Sasha a few days ago, and she was pretending to still be single.'

Jonny turned back towards the house and Kate followed him. 'Kate, I have to concentrate on work. Please don't expect me to be distracted by every snippet of gossip you can dredge up about Sasha.'

'But what about Jack – what if she's . . .'

'You have no evidence that she's two-timing Jack. This could mean anything.'

And they were back again. Kate being indignant because of Ella, Heather and the girls, and Jonny retreating. Kate remembered the day he'd delivered the news, flatly, that Sasha and Jack were married. He would not be drawn in any way about it, would not concede that to marry secretly, without telling your family, was a betrayal. She was left, as always, with Jonny on one side of a fast-moving river and herself on the other. But what if Sasha was cheating on Jack?

'It's none of our business, Kate,' said Jonny, in a warning voice.

Sometimes Kate felt that she and Jonny were close, and that they wanted the same things, like the day they'd spent together clearing out Ella's or the time Callum had run away. But at other times, like now, he was back behind the glass wall of his work, locked away, uncommunicative and remote.

She was beginning to feel that it was not good enough. She never knew where she was.

Chapter 50

Sasha had felt quite grumpy about going down to Providence Cottage ever since she'd heard Kate was going to be there. She'd been looking forward to a relaxing weekend, reinforcing her friendship with Si and Olivia, who really were the suitable end of the Fox family. Olivia had just been in all the papers following the conclusion of the Allison Green case. Both sides had declared victory: Allison had been awarded one and a half million pounds, which was less than she'd asked for but more than Ted had wanted to give. It would have been exciting to get Olivia on her own, to talk about how she'd achieved it, because everyone had betted that this time round Allison Green would finish up paying off Chat Show Ted, not the other way round.

Now they were taking both sets of children, and Kate, Jonny and Luke would be there too. It would be mayhem, just the sort of family event she'd managed to steer clear of so far. And Jack's obvious excitement at being with his family again was irritating, considering how disgracefully they'd all behaved over the money. Putting it in trust for Daisy and Molly indeed! That money was Jack's. The only redeeming side of it was that it wasn't a lunch at 19 Lovelace Road, and provided she could get through this one weekend, she could probably avoid anything similar for at least another year. Or two. Even so it was annoying, because her time was precious, and being a mother, a stepmother, a wife and a TV presenter was a lot for one person to handle, without taking on someone's extended family as well.

She threw Grace and Tom's clothes into their bags angrily, and spent ages sorting out her own things.

It was all so exasperating. She made sure that Jack knew her views, and there was almost a complete silence between them in the car going down, except when they stopped off in a service station and Molly dropped the phone down the loo.

That evening, Kate ushered the children up to bed, while Sasha had a bath and got ready for dinner. She was first down, and the sitting room was deserted. It looked like a house that had recently been finished: there were just two large sofas in charcoal linen facing each other in front of the fire, and an over-sized coffee table on which stood a bottle of champagne on ice and ten glasses, plus a cherrywood desk at the other end of the room. Nothing else, not even on the walls. Sasha quietly slid the drawers of the desk open, and gently fingered through the contents. Some receipts and guarantees. A couple of credit card bills in Olivia's name, mostly for restaurant meals. Quite a lot of eating out, and not just for one, unless prices round here were very steep, she thought. There was a sheaf of photographs of the cottage before renovation, obviously taken as a record. Sasha leafed through them quickly. The last one was a picture of Olivia, laughing with her hair blowing about in the wind and the sea in the background. She looked carefree. On the back were scribbled words. 'Be this happy always.'

Bit of a strange one, thought Sasha, as she slid everything back into place. She heard footsteps on the wooden stairs, turning to greet Si with a smile, moving close to him. He looked down at her, and she wondered if he wanted to kiss her. She knew men when they looked like that.

'So you haven't both been down here every weekend, making sure that the builders are doing their job?' She laid a hand on his arm.

Si cleared his throat, darted a hasty look at the door and stepped backwards as if he was afraid someone might come in. 'I must open some champagne. No, we decided that it would be better for our marriage if I left it to Olivia. I didn't come down at all until yesterday.'

312

Sasha thought that was interesting. She and Jack had agreed, several times, that Si's initial lack of involvement in Providence Cottage was dangerous, and it seemed as if it had continued.

'I know Si,' Jack had once said. 'If Olivia leaves him on his own too much he'll have an affair.'

'Why? Has he had one before?'

'No.' Jack had laughed. 'But it would be expected of him, and Si always does what's expected.'

'Well, she's done it beautifully.' Sasha accepted the glass of champagne. 'In fact, I'd love to take some photographs of it, if that's all right, but I haven't brought my camera. Is there any chance I could borrow yours?'

Si laughed. 'The last time I went near a camera I broke it. In 1976, I think that was. No, I'm afraid I'm one of those people who's all fingers and thumbs when it comes to photography. I don't think Olivia has one either, it's just not our thing.'

Sasha smiled and nodded. When the doorbell rang she heard Olivia's footsteps, light and eager, click-clack to open it, and murmurs from the hallway. A tall man with dark curly hair strode in, and shook Si's hand vigorously.

'Sasha wants to borrow a camera, darling,' said Si, introducing her to Blake. 'But we don't have one, do we?'

'A camera?' asked Olivia. 'We don't, but Blake does. It's always in the car. He likes to keep a record of the houses he works on, and always takes photographs before and after.'

Bingo, thought Sasha, seeing the colour in Olivia's face and the sparkle in her eyes. Bing-*go*. No wonder Si's been looking so constipated recently. There might yet be an opportunity of some kind there.

Chapter 51

Olivia was almost exhilarated by the roller-coaster sense of risk in having Si and Blake in the same room, especially as she suspected Si had set this up to test her.

When she opened the door to Blake, out of the sight line of the sitting room, he kissed her on the lips, his tongue touching hers so briefly that she could have dreamed it. She ushered him inside, white-hot with desire for him, hating herself for doing what she was doing to Si.

She'd tried so hard not to give in. She had stumbled back to Providence Cottage when Ella had died, spending the night there alone, feverishly unable to sleep. The following day he had texted her, and every day after that, all innocent messages, shared jokes, nothing, at first, that could even remotely be called suggestive. He phoned her too, and they exchanged details of their day; she surprised herself by how much she laughed, and how much she could make him laugh, but she could not, would not betray the man she'd been married to for nearly twenty years.

It became a joke between them. 'Would you like modern taps, traditional taps or to make mad passionate love?' asked Blake.

'Simple classic taps,' she insisted, firmly.

'Old White, New White, James White, House White, Off White, Lime White, Stone White, Hardwick White or the best fuck you've ever had?'

'Either New White or House White. The others are too cold.'

'Oh no they're not,' he said. 'I'm sure I could change your mind.'

'I'm sure you couldn't.'

'Do you love your husband?' he asked once, suddenly, as they were checking the quality of the tiling in the bathroom. 'Because if you do, if you really do, tell me and I'll go away.'

'I . . . I . . . please don't ask me that. I don't want to hurt him. If that's love, then . . .'

'It's not,' said Blake softly. She could feel his breath across her face.

I must break away, she thought. I must stop this.

But I can't. The moment was frozen between them, the air dangerously still.

'Please . . .' she begged, not sure what she was asking for. She tried to breathe, to get the words out, but they wouldn't form.

'I've got to go.' She grabbed her bag and ran, driving blindly back to London. When she got there, she texted Blake. 'Sorry.'

And he texted back, and it started again.

With Si drunk or angry most of the time, Olivia was lonely: 'He was my oldest friend. Now he's like a stranger,' she said to Blake.

'In that case you'd better spend more time with your newest friend,' said Blake with a wicked grin that was very hard to resist.

It came to a head one evening, when she drove down to Providence Cottage on the spur of the moment. She'd had a bad week at work and then Si shouted at her when she asked him whether he thought she should varnish the floors at Providence Cottage or wax them.

'I don't have time to think about details like that,' he snapped, cutting into her question before she'd finished. 'You may not have work to do, but I do.'

'In fact I was going to work from home tomorrow so I might take my laptop down to the cottage tonight.' She had only been asking his opinion to make him feel included.

'I don't care what you do,' said Si, 'and I haven't got time to discuss it now.'

Olivia picked up the car keys and her laptop. 'I'll be back on Friday.'

She texted Blake, knowing it was dangerous. 'Came down for a break. Fancy a drink?'

315

When he walked in, she was so lonely and miserable, she burst into tears.

'Come here, darling.' He wrapped her up in a big bear hug, and when his lips touched hers, the fire was lit, and her life with Si was engulfed. Everything that had gone before was incinerated, gone forever. She kissed him back with a desperation borne of the time they'd spent together without touching.

'It will all be all right,' he whispered, tenderly removing her clothes, each layer drawing her away from what was right, from where she should be, drawing her down. This would destroy everything she knew and loved. She couldn't help it. The emptiness inside her suddenly seemed too huge.

That very morning, with Kate, Jonny and the boys in the house, when she'd set out on her run Blake had been parked at the coast ready to pick her up in the car and take her back to his house. He had asked her, not for the first time, to leave Si and come to live with him.

Olivia swung her legs out of bed. 'I need to get back.' Her shorts and underwear were puddles of fabric on the floor. She leant over to pick them up.

Blake put out a hand to stop her. 'Don't go. Stay here.'

'They'll be wondering where I am.'

'Leave him. Go back and get your toothbrush, and anything you care about and come here to me. Now. For ever.'

'Toothbrush? We're not teenagers, you know, there's a whole life to be unravelled. Anyway, you know I can't.'

'Why not?'

'Because his family are there. It's the reconciliation weekend between Jack and his sister. If the hostess runs off with her lover in the middle of it all, it would all fall apart.' She couldn't help smiling, though. She didn't think she would ever stop. 'It's an absolute nightmare weekend, so exhausting. Kate is manically punctual for everything and Sasha is terribly late, and I don't know which is worse. Everything takes twice as long as it needs to, and the tension is awful.'

'Well, you brought it on yourself inviting them. But I'm glad you didn't say you couldn't leave because you love him.'

She wondered if Si would miss her if she went, or whether she was just habit. Or an investment, like a really good winter coat or a pair of beautifully cut leather boots. 'I sometimes think I'm just an accessory to him. Olivia Montmorency, with lots of the right connections. All that sort of thing is important to him.'

Now they were standing in a circle: Si, Blake, Sasha and Jack, and Olivia, along with Kate and Jonny. Olivia had never seen Blake in an ordinary social situation. She was used to his ancient jeans and the confident way he drove his four-by-four across the muddy land, as if he farmed it himself. She was almost afraid of seeing him differently.

'How formal should I be?' he'd asked, and she'd said, not at all, be relaxed, just anything. She couldn't imagine him in a collar and tie, looking less than himself.

He turned up in a leather jacket that was just the right side of battered. She could see Si eyeing him up, checking out his shoes and his watch, pricing everything up, the way he always did. From the way their shoulders moved, she could see that Si was slightly intimidated. Blake belonged. His shoes were beautiful, but well worn and polished. His clothes seemed to be part of him, and part of the countryside around him. In contrast, Si looked like an advertisement for R&R's country range, which was rarely worn outside Chelsea.

Si offered him a glass of champagne. 'We're toasting the newly weds.'

Sasha shimmered at him. 'You must be the architect who's done a wonderful job on this house. You are clearly so talented.'

Blake smiled down at her. 'Olivia's got a great eye. She really understands the nature of the building. Clients so often try to turn their houses into something they're not.'

'That's my girl,' said Si, possessively patting Olivia on the bottom.

She took a step away from him and watched them, for a moment, to see Sasha work her magic but after a few more exchanges Sasha turned back to Jack, placing a be-ringed hand on his arm. He enclosed it in his and squeezed it. They quickly exchanged glances before paying full attention to Si.

'Is there much decent work for you around here?' asked Si. 'Or is it all small stuff?'

317

'I get along,' replied Blake evenly.

'No girlfriend?' Olivia murmured to Blake, as they moved aside from the buzz of conversation around them.

He looked down at her with a glimmer of amusement in his eyes. 'Should I have one?'

'Of course not. I'd better see about the food.'

'Would you like some help?' Blake followed her into the kitchen, and stopped the potatoes boiling over. 'Were you planning to make mash?' He took over, rescuing the farm shop's best ready-made chicken casserole from the oven before it burnt and mashing the potatoes.

'I'm so sorry, I'm not a domestic goddess.'

Blake ignored her words. 'Leave him, Olivia. He's an arsehole.' He mirrored her body language, folding his own arms in front of him, but standing very close. She still wasn't used to men being so much taller than she was.

'He's not. He's just rather unhappy at the moment because he didn't get the top job he'd been after and it's still not long since his mother died.'

He touched her cheek. 'You are sweet. But I mean it. Leave him and come to me. I asked you to the first time we met, remember?'

'You said "if he doesn't like the house, divorce him", or words to that effect. You didn't post yourself as an alternative.'

'No, but that's what I meant.'

'I can't do anything in a hurry. It would be splitting up a family.'

'You don't have children.'

The words twisted in her like the handle of a knife blade turning. 'Blake.' She turned back again. 'Why didn't you and your wife have them? Would it have kept you together if you had?'

He looked surprised. 'She didn't want them. But I think that was a sign that she didn't want me. Secretly. But we were younger then, it seemed less important. And would we have stayed together if we had had children? Hindsight's always so accurate, isn't it? Maybe we would have tried harder – you always would, wouldn't you – but we never talked about it much. Which is, perhaps, a sign that it would never . . . look, I can't answer that.'

It was a fair response. Olivia respected him for that.

'And you?' he asked. 'What about you and Si?'

318

She nearly told him. But betraying Si with her body was one thing, betraying his innermost secrets – especially to his rival – was quite another. She would not hurt Si's pride any more than she had to. Because it was his pride that mattered to him. She reluctantly tried to withdraw her hand, but he held it tighter. 'Oh, well, you know. There never seemed time. Babies not a priority, I suppose. I must go.' She turned back one more time.

'He's still an arsehole. You belong with me, you know you do.'

She shook her head. 'Not yet. I can't think about that yet. Not while he's so down.'

Blake kissed her full on the lips, but then Olivia moved away, sensing a movement at the door.

'Can I help with anything, Olivia?' It was Kate. Sharp-eyed Kate.

'We're just about ready to eat.' Olivia ushered them all in. She'd worked out a table plan that would keep Si and Blake apart, Sasha and Kate apart, and which would give Kate some time with Jack because she knew how much Kate missed him.

But Jack seized Sasha's hand and they sat down next to each other without waiting to be told where to sit. 'We don't get enough time together. One or other of us is away so much.'

Sasha placed a hand on his thigh and simpered. 'Sweetheart.' They exchanged a noisy kiss.

Si looked furious.

'It's no good looking disapproving, Si,' taunted Jack, 'all the old etiquette books say that husbands and wives should sit next to each other in the first year of marriage.'

'That dates back to the time when couples married very young and hardly knew each other,' said Si, who was sensitive about correctness. 'And the bride should be wearing her wedding dress, if you want to be absolutely correct about it.'

'Don't worry, it's fine, this is hardly a grand dinner party.' Olivia hastily tried to rejig the table plan round this, but ended up having Blake and Si facing each other across the table, with her in between. And although she managed to keep Kate next to Jack, Sasha was in full-on sparkly mode, and Olivia could see Kate trying to talk to Jack's shoulder.

'Are you getting up to London much now you're down in Wiltshire?' Kate suddenly launched this at Sasha in a brief silence.

Sasha looked startled. 'Well, I have to go up to work, and Adam still wants his Wednesday evenings.'

'That's a bit unreasonable, isn't it? To expect the kids to travel for two hours each way before and after school once a week?'

Sasha raised an eyebrow. 'Welcome to Adam's world. Unreasonable is the name of the planet he lives on. And I'm not going back to court unless he forces me to. It's incredibly expensive, stressful and not necessarily in the best interests of the children. He only does it to twitch the rope he's still got me on, and if I get one thing sorted out, he'll only find another way.'

'Right. So where do you stay when you're up?'

Olivia noted that Kate had her interrogation voice on.

'Oh, here and there,' said Sasha casually. 'With old friends mainly. People have been so kind.'

'Well, if you ever need a bed, do stay with us. I mean that.'

Sasha looked surprised. And pleased. 'Oh, thanks. Well, I very well might.'

'It might be quite convenient, if you're working with Jonny, that is.'

'Yes, of course.'

'That's very sweet of you, Katie.' Jack looked pleased.

'And of course that includes supper too,' added Kate. 'Or do you find that you're living the life of a spare woman when you're up in London?'

'A spare woman?' Sasha sounded bewildered.

'You know, so-and-so's just got divorced, let's have him round for supper, who do we know who might even up the numbers?' Kate was definitely up to something, thought Olivia.

'I think that's spare men, isn't it?' countered Sasha. 'No, the life of divorced women is much less sociable. There's nothing quite as protective of its territory as a woman with a man when she sees a friend hasn't got one. Although one old friend was very kind the other night. She invited me to this quite grand dinner party and paired me off with someone. It was so embarrassing, and of course I didn't want to say "actually, I'm married" because I thought that would put her in a difficult position. So I didn't say anything.' She looked round at everyone. 'What could I do?'

'Perhaps you ought to give a wedding party of some kind,' suggested Kate, 'make it all very public.'

'I think that could hurt Heather if she came to hear about it,' replied Sasha. 'Which she definitely would as we'd want the girls there. I'm trying not to rub her nose in it, so we're just letting people hear about it all as and when they need to. Gradually. Aren't we, darling?'

'Sweetheart.' Jack picked up one of Sasha's hands and kissed it. 'You're so considerate.'

'Jacksy.' Sasha gave a throaty gurgle, and they kissed.

Olivia caught Blake's eye, and her stomach lurched as if she was in a plane that had dropped twenty thousand feet. Si looked as if he was going to explode at any moment.

Sasha fixed her eyes on everyone round the table in turn. 'I am ashamed – *we* are terribly, terribly ashamed, aren't we, Jacksy, darling – of the way we've hurt Heather. It was the very last thing I ever wanted to do, but . . .' She looked at Jack again.

'We couldn't help it,' explained Jack. 'Sasha is just the best thing that ever happened to me. Losing her would have been like losing a leg.'

'That is so sweet.' They kissed – briefly – on the lips again.

Si's eyes bulged. 'You know the rules. No PDAs. No Public Displays of Affection,' he barked.

They all laughed, each for different reasons.

'Do you know what "Jacksy" is slang for?' hissed Kate furiously to Olivia a few minutes later. 'It means "bottom".'

Running away with Blake was beginning to look quite appealing.

Chapter 52

Heather was having trouble with Travis. He didn't like being left at home while she was at the office, so after a few episodes of chewed furniture and neighbours complaining about the incessant barking, she managed to persuade her very reluctant boss to let him come to work. She got off the bus two stops early to fit in an extra walk, and went out with him to the park during coffee breaks and lunchtimes. The rest of the time he was happy to curl up under her desk, nearly invisible.

Only nearly, though. Every time anyone came to the office he greeted them with a volley of barking, and on two occasions tried to shove his nose in the crotch of female clients.

'Will you get that damned dog out of here,' shouted John Lake, the senior partner, and Heather took Travis for another walk round the small, litter-strewn park. On her return, she found that another partner had been asking for her, and that some documents had been needed urgently.

'We can't have staff leaving suddenly in the middle of the morning,' said Cheryl, the office manager. 'I'm sorry, but we can't. And that dog smells.' She waved her hand in front of her nose.

For the next few days Heather shampooed Travis before work. It was a difficult task, because every time she paused, even for a second, he shook himself and droplets of water and shampoo flew all over her. She usually finished up wetter than he was, trembling with exhaustion, with her hair hanging limply over her shoulders as she put together Daisy's lunchbox and found Molly's games kit.

But Travis was the only one who offered her unconditional love. Molly was withdrawn and silent, although Daisy still seemed her usual bubbly, childish self. But she couldn't confide in a child. Travis was a warm shape on the bed in the evening, and he listened to her worries, comforting her with a lick on the nose. He never criticised her. With Travis there she never had to hear the voice inside her head that told her she was a nuisance, and that no one would ever want her.

'Now that I'm down in Wiltshire, I'd like to have Travis back,' said Jack on the phone one evening. 'It makes more sense – I'm in the middle of the countryside, and I can take him to work in this job. It's about the only good thing about it.'

She still found it impossible to say 'no' to Jack, but she couldn't bear to lose Travis as well. 'I think . . .' She took a deep breath. 'Well, he means too much to the girls. They've had to lose so much and I don't think Molly's all that happy at her school . . .'

'And that's another thing. We do need to send them to boarding school. The army would pay, and it would make it much easier for you to work, and would give them some stability. It would mean, technically, of course, that I'd have to be the parent who they officially resided with, but you could have them for as much of the holidays as you wanted . . .'

This wasn't a new demand, and had been the one sticking point in their divorce settlement. Heather had caved in to everything else, but she had been adamant that she was not going to give up on the girls. Jack never let up, though. He proposed it every few weeks and it terrified Heather. He broke off as Heather began to sob. 'Oh, for God's sake,' he said impatiently. 'I am getting really tired of all this self-pity.'

She put the phone down on him, flooded with despair. Surely he didn't think she was an unfit mother as well as an unfit wife. She couldn't bear it – surely the girls were better off with their mother than in a boarding school? But perhaps not, when their mother was as awful as she was.

Travis finally blew it when he tried to make a friend of Mrs Hussain, a pleasant woman who was visiting Barclay, Berne &

Sons about a company trust. He shot out from under Heather's desk as Mrs Hussain passed, nudging her so that her full cup of coffee spilt over her keyboard.

Mrs Hussain gasped and tried to hurry away. Heather grabbed Travis's collar. 'I'm so sorry. But he would never hurt anyone, I promise.' She saw fear in the woman's eyes, and was mortified. 'Travis. No. Bad boy. Down.'

John Lake whisked Mrs Hussain into his office and slammed the door on the scene. Heather began to clean up the keyboard as well as she could. Cheryl stood over her. 'You'll have to have a new keyboard. The contacts will get sticky, and . . .'

Heather turned the keyboard upside down and furiously shook the remaining drops from it. 'No, it'll be fine. I promise. I'm always spilling coffee on my keyboard at home.'

After Mrs Hussain had left, John appeared over her desk. 'Mrs Hussain is a very nice woman who has no intention of imposing her views on anyone. But she has been brought up to regard dogs as unclean and she is afraid of them. That incident caused her real distress and I will not have my clients upset in that way.'

Cheryl sniggered. '*That* dog is definitely unclean. Have you smelt him?'

'I wash him every morning,' flashed Heather, standing up to Cheryl for the first time. 'But I'm so sorry. So very sorry. It won't happen again.'

'No, it won't. Because you have a choice. Find another option for your dog or find another job. And take that as an official verbal warning. Meanwhile I want him out of here now.' He slammed the door of his office.

There were very few jobs that she could do from 9 a.m. to 2 p.m., and certainly none that would accept a dog. Heather looked at Cheryl, who rolled her eyes. 'OK, take him home. Have an early lunch hour or whatever. I won't deduct it from your pay.'

'Thanks.' Heather grabbed her coat and Travis's lead before Cheryl could think again, and got home at ten to twelve. Molly was at home, huddled up in her bed.

'Molly! What are you doing here?'

Molly jumped. 'I wasn't feeling very well, so they let me come home.'

'Without notifying me? That's very irresponsible of them.'

'Mummy, don't complain. Please. About anything,' Molly pleaded.

'What's wrong with you, anyway?' She sat down on Molly's bed, and Molly burst into tears.

'Nobody likes me. They say horrible things to me.'

'Well, you must ignore them. Pretend you haven't heard.'

'I do. But it doesn't help.' Molly sniffed. 'They still go on.'

'What sort of things do they say?'

'Oh, that we're posh, things like that.'

'We're not posh, of course we're not,' said Heather, bewildered, thinking of Mo and the grubby, stained bedding of the squats they had lived in. And the small, modern army houses with already outdated plumbing that she had spent most of her married life in. 'We live in a tiny flat and I'm a dogsbody for a law firm. We wear second-hand clothes from charity shops, and can't afford to go on holiday. How can that be posh?'

'I don't know, but it is.' Molly's shoulders heaved. 'I think it's because Daddy's in the army and he's an officer, and they don't like the army, they think that war's wrong and . . .' Her words disappeared into choking sobs. She gulped. 'They steal my stuff and push me over, and laugh at me, and no one talks to me. When we were at school at Warminster or Surrey or even in Germany, at least there were other army children.'

'What about Daisy? Is she having problems too?'

Molly sniffed. 'Daisy hits anyone who's nasty to her.'

Heather's eyebrows shot up. 'Does she? Right. We're going to talk to the headmistress. Today.'

'No, Mummy, please. Please don't make me go back there.'

Heather usually found headmistresses intimidating but rage propelled her into an almost immediate appointment, and just two hours later she was steaming through Mrs Burgh's door. 'Good afternoon. I'm Mrs Fox, Molly's mother.'

'Hello. I'm Mrs Burgh. Anita Burgh. How can I help you?'

Heather settled herself on one of the chairs facing Mrs Burgh's desk. 'My daughters are being bullied because their father is in the army.'

Mrs Burgh raised an eyebrow. 'Yes, we are aware that your

elder daughter is having a few problems settling in. She hasn't made things any easier for herself, you know. The other children think she's haughty. Arrogant. Apparently she won't talk to them. Just sticks her nose in the air when they say something to her.'

'I think that's because what they're saying to her is highly offensive. And she says they're stealing her stuff, pushing her over and teasing her.'

'We don't tolerate bullying in this school, I can assure you,' replied Mrs Burgh. 'But I think you should be aware that we have thirty-seven first languages here, and that a number of the children are refugees from war-torn countries such as Afghanistan and Iraq. We have to be sensitive to their feelings.'

'My daughter's father has risked – and will risk – his life for his country. I think it is also important to be sensitive to her feelings.'

'Mrs Fox, I do not approve of the British waging war on other countries for outdated imperialist reasons, and neither does anybody else here. There are children whose families and friends in their home countries have been under attack from British forces. Molly must expect a little rough and tumble in the playground, and she will have to learn to respect other people's beliefs and cultures now that she is in an inner-city school.'

'She does respect other people's beliefs. She doesn't have a problem with celebrating Diwali or Chinese New Year. Or anything else that is genuinely cultural. Mrs Burgh, she is a nice girl, and she is not trying to upset anyone.'

Mrs Burgh fixed Heather with a stare. 'She may not be trying, Mrs Fox, but she makes it quite clear that she's proud of her father and what he does. And that is unacceptable here. And I know I'm speaking for all of the staff when I say that.'

Heather got up. 'Of course she is proud of her father. They both are. They will not be returning.' She walked out.

As she drew breath, her blood flowing furiously through her veins like fire, her mobile bleeped at her. 'Where are you? JL furious. Written warning on its way. Cheryl.'

'Fuck off,' she texted back, the old feisty Heather who had survived Mo's slaps coming to the fore.

Cheryl, to her surprise, texted back: 'Will do.'

Kate phoned that evening. 'Just ringing to see how you're getting on.'

Heather didn't know how much to say. 'I think I'm going to have to find another school for the girls. They're being bullied a bit.'

'Well, the boarding school idea might be quite a good one. I read a piece recently on stability in schools and apparently . . .' And Kate was off, with statistics and advice, finishing off with, 'actually I might do a programme on it some time.'

Heather was silent.

'It would give you time to work properly, and they can usually come out most weekends, you know.'

'Yes, I know,' said Heather, trying to keep her voice steady. 'Perhaps I will discuss it with them.'

Molly and Daisy thought it was a very exciting idea ('please, Mum, please, please, I don't want to go back to that horrid school again'), and Heather, with the sensation that her heart was being ripped out of her chest, phoned Jack and in a trembling voice suggested that perhaps it might be better if he was officially the parent caring for Molly and Daisy so that they could go to boarding school. And that he could also have custody of Travis after all.

'I think that's very wise,' said Jack. 'And you are entitled to fifty-six days a year with the girls, after all, which is pretty much all the school holidays. Well, most of them, anyway, and no one wil be checking too closely.'

Just fifty-six days a year with her children. She would only be able to tuck them up in bed fifty-six times a year. Ask them how their day had been fifty-six times. Heather was in such pain that she could barely breathe. She had thought Jack leaving her had hurt, but it was nothing compared to this. She would have to find a job that would give her fifty-six days' holiday. Because she was not going to miss one moment of the time they could spend with her.

Perhaps it was just as well Travis was going with them. He would look after them.

She pasted her good-Mummy smile on her face and went in to tell Daisy and Molly that new arrangements for school would be made as soon as possible. And she herself would have to get a different job, one that followed school terms.

*

So when Daisy, Molly and Travis went to stay the weekend with Jack and Sasha at Providence Cottage, Heather opened her eyes to emptiness. The small south London flat was silent, except for the muffled roar of planes passing overhead.

She'd given in her notice, and both girls would be joining St Peter's together in a few weeks, and this was what it would be like from now on. An empty flat. An empty life.

After an uncomfortable few weeks of touring schools with Jack, with them both sitting awkwardly in headmistresses' offices while Jack did the talking and she miserably agreed with most – although not all – of what he said, she looked for a job that would give her the school holidays off. She telephoned every school in the area to see whether there were any term-time only jobs, eventually finding work in the kitchens, at the minimum wage. But it was a job, and it would leave her free for Molly and Daisy during the holidays and most half-terms. She knew that Sasha wouldn't make her stick to exactly fifty-six days. She visited the Citizens' Advice Bureau to find out what tax credits she might be due, and called her lawyer to find out how much less Jack would be paying her when she no longer had Molly and Daisy living with her. It was like being in the army, having to turn your life completely upside down at the drop of a hat, and all the organisational skills she'd learned – making lists, telephoning strangers, the determination to make it all work and make it work *now* – it all came in useful. Only this time the warmth of the patch was missing – the cheery knock on the door, the invitation to a coffee morning, the offers of help from other women, the casual, cosy suppers with friends on a weekday night – were all replaced by the occasional visit from someone trying to sell tea towels, or beg money for a lift home, or get her to join their religion. Heather was so lonely she nearly did.

It was fine when Molly, Daisy and Travis were there, sprawled on the sofa or curled up on her bed. Now they weren't. They were gone, excited about seeing their father for the weekend. 'Travis will love Providence Cottage, won't he, Mummy?' Daisy had said. 'He'll love being able to run around in a garden again.'

Heather realised that Daisy was talking about herself. The army houses might be small, but they always had a garden big enough for a swing and a trampoline and there was always a playpark on the corner, with other children, and it was safe enough to play in the street. Here, there was only a courtyard behind and a busy road in front.

How would they manage in the holidays?

She turned her face to the wall, closed her eyes and tried to get to sleep again. Think of all those mornings when getting out of bed was torture. Think how lovely it is to have a lie-in.

It wasn't lovely. It was despair.

She got up and made herself a cup of tea, picking up a kitchen knife and wondering if it would hurt if she sliced it across her wrists. She'd done that when she first went to the Caldecott, just to make herself feel. She traced it lightly across a vein and saw some red blood spurt out.

Then it came to her. She should get the girls established, and then she should kill herself. Nobody wants you, Heather. Nobody will care if you're gone. It would be easier for the girls, even, not to have to be shuttled from one house to another. They were fine with Sasha, they really quite liked her, and they adored Jack. And once boarding school was sorted, it would be like the Caldecott. They would be looked after, and would be better off without a mother as useless as she was.

It was almost a relief to realise that there would be an end to this, that she didn't have to be trapped in this nightmare forever. But it was yet another thing she would have to plan carefully, and it wouldn't be easy. As she put a plaster on her wrist, she thought about the sleeping pills that everyone always suggested she take.

A few weeks later Heather started her new job, dishing out food at lunchtime and cleaning up afterwards. The other staff treated her with reserve, but she liked the children. It was only temporary anyway, she thought, visiting her doctor every few weeks to beg a few more sleeping pills, making sure she saw someone different each time.

'I feel there's an issue with depression here,' said one locum, a young woman in a Muslim headscarf, her eyes surprisingly wise for her years. 'Looking at your notes, I don't think we should necessarily be giving you more sleeping pills. I'd like to start you on . . .'

Heather had to force herself not to lash out. 'It's only sleep I need, truly. Please give me one more prescription and if I need anything more, I promise I'll come back about something for depression.'

The young woman looked concerned, but eventually agreed. 'Just five sleeping pills this time. I don't want you getting addicted.'

'No, of course not, I promise.' Heather pocketed the prescription. For a moment she thought that the young woman had seen right through her, she'd been afraid she'd been rumbled. She didn't have enough pills yet, and she couldn't risk going too soon again for more. And she would make sure she saw someone different. It was all going to take longer, that was all.

Chapter 53

Surprisingly, Sasha took Kate up on her offer of a bed in London. Kate wondered if perhaps she was running out of places to stay. It was agreed, mainly via Jack, that Sasha would spend Wednesday nights at 19 Lovelace Road.

'I'm very grateful to you, Kate,' he said on the phone. 'It's been so hard for Sasha, having to drag the children up and down to Adam and Natalie all the time, and as she works in London quite a bit, it makes sense for her to have something of a base with you. But could I ask you to make sure she doesn't have to do too much around the house? She's exhausted at the moment with everything she's doing. She really does keep that programme going, because everyone else has such a huge ego. And she only likes cotton sheets, by the way, I thought you ought to know. She's allergic to anything synthetic.'

Kate was irritated. 'All my sheets are cotton and my guests never do anything around the house, except Heather, who was amazing and turned 19 Lovelace Road into a show home while she was here.'

'And that's another thing. I wonder if you could be a little more sensitive about the way you constantly hold Heather up as the perfect army wife . . .'

'She was,' interrupted Kate.

'It's actually none of your business,' warned Jack. 'Heather didn't have to work, and Sasha has a particularly demanding career, so obviously Sasha feels she's being criticised by you when you make remarks about how good Heather is at cleaning and clearing up.'

'But I've never even been to your new house,' said Kate. 'So how I could I be criticising Sasha?'

'I didn't say you *had* criticised, I just asked you to be sensitive.'

Kate longed to tell Jack to piss off, but she was determined to stay focused until she worked out what Sasha was up to.

Jonny seemed relieved at the cessation of hostilities, too. Kate tested him out on her observations of Olivia and Si.

'I think Olivia's having an affair with that architect,' she said, one evening as they were finishing off some pasta.

She waited for him to tell her that she was imagining things and that she had to keep her nose out of her sister-in-laws' business.

He was silent for a moment. 'Yes,' he said, eventually. 'I'm inclined to agree with you. There was a glow about her, something very . . . I can't put my finger on it. And she was out such a lot. I did think myself . . . that possibly . . .'

'Do you think Si knows?'

Jonny shrugged. 'I have no idea. He doesn't seem to think about anything except R&R.'

'He's always been like that. And he was at his very worst last weekend – pompous, aggressive, unsympathetic, snobby . . . to be honest, I'm not surprised. If that's what he's like all the time, he must be driving her away. But it will kill him if he loses Olivia as well, really it will.'

'No, it won't,' asserted Jonny. 'He'll survive. Like Heather has.'

Kate wondered if he thought the same about their relationship.

For three months, Sasha was the perfect, invisible guest. She arrived late every Wednesday evening, sometimes very late, even two in the morning, crept quietly upstairs, and left the following day with gushing thank-yous while Kate was still grappling with two lots of packed lunches, backpacks, homework, missing shoes and sports kits. Kate tried to find out what she'd done the night before, but got vague answers about meetings, friends and parties. Sasha left presents – flowers, chocolates and fragrant bars of soap – and always left the room immaculate, dancing in and out with cries of 'Kate, you're so marvellous, I don't know how you do it. This is so kind of you. You are an angel.'

Jonny and Kate made sure that they invited Jasper Morton and his wife round on a night they weren't expecting Sasha, adding a few other friends in media and the arts. Jasper's wife, India, was friendly and confiding. Kate edged the conversation round to Sasha at the end of the evening, when India had consumed almost a whole bottle of wine.

India shot a glance at Jasper, now deep in conversation with Jonny. 'Don't let Jas know I'm saying this, he absolutely cannot bear to talk about Sasha. You know that after his father's death, she tried to take them to court, egged on by her frightful mother, because she said she deserved to inherit from her father's estate? They didn't have all that much money – Jas's mother was quite rich at one point, but I think they'd pretty much spent it all. So they had to sell their family home to pay Sasha off – they weren't sure they'd win, and there'd be costs, so they couldn't really afford to contest it. Jas was fourteen. It's not the right time to lose your father and your home.'

'I know,' said Kate. 'I really do.'

India had relatively little else to say about Sasha, except that Jasper and Lalla had starting seeing her at one point when they were around ten and twelve. 'She used to hang around their house after school, watching them, apparently, and they discovered their father had a daughter, and that he paid her mother something on condition that there was never any contact between the families. They thought it was really exciting to have a secret sister at first and made friends with her. Until she began to steal their stuff and stalk them, and it all got quite . . . scary. I'm not sure how they got rid of her – is your brother rich, by the way?'

'No, not at all.'

India looked surprised. 'I always thought she was after the money.'

'I suspect, deep down, she's after love,' said Kate. 'But when she gets it, it's never enough. What must it have done to her, knowing that her father refused ever to see her?'

'Pretty shitty thing to do,' agreed India. 'I think Roderick Morton must have been a very selfish man.'

Not a good time to lose your father and your home. India's words rang in Kate's ears for weeks. There seemed to be a trail of missing fathers in all this unhappiness: Sasha's permanently absent one, the death of Mike Fox, and it was obvious, even though she never talked about it, that Heather's had not been around for most of her life.

Jonny was a good father. She and he were like members of the same relay team, passing the baton of family life on to each other as they entered and left the house. And the house itself, 19 Lovelace Road, was at the heart of it all. Still. Less so now than it had been, perhaps, but . . . Over and over again, Kate tried to persuade herself that everything was fine.

Then, one evening in early September, Sasha and Jonny came home together, at 6 p.m., with two bottles of champagne.

'We're celebrating,' said Sasha, smugly.

'How nice,' replied Kate.

'After fannying around forever, Channel Six have finally commissioned *How To Be Rich And Famous* for a third series,' explained Jonny.

Kate flung her arms around him. 'That's amazing. Quick, let's open the . . .'

'Typically, of course, they want it yesterday. All leave cancelled for two months, and you won't be seeing much of me.'

'I'm used to that.' Kate got three glasses out of the cupboard. 'I make a good single parent. Oh no, that means cancelling half-term in Cornwall though, doesn't it?'

'You can go on your own with the boys, if you like.'

'None of that matters,' said Kate, 'we'll work it out in the morning. For now, let's toast you all. We can pay the mortgage for the next year.'

Jonny raised his glass to hers. 'As long as we don't have to get a new car.'

'Ours will sputter on for a bit longer,' said Kate, touching the rim of her glass to his.

'Channel Six insisted that I be one of the main presenters.' Sasha broke into their conversation. 'Apparently they did some focus groups which showed that the audience warmed to me. I hope you don't mind, Kate.'

'Mind? Of course not, why should I? I'm delighted.' Sasha really was the most irritating woman, thought Kate. One day, perhaps, someone would shoot her when she said things like that.

A few minutes later Kate went upstairs to tell the boys the good news, and when she came down again, she overheard Sasha whispering down her phone in the corridor, telling someone else the same thing about audiences warming to her. 'Bye, darling, yes, that's fine, one o'clock tomorrow at Como Pietro's, I'll see you there. Can't wait,' she gurgled. Her eyes flicked upwards and she clicked the phone shut on seeing Kate. 'I was just telling Jack.'

'He must be pleased.'

'Oh, he is.'

On instinct, Kate doubled back upstairs and phoned Jack immediately. 'It's good news, isn't it?'

'What is?'

'Jonny getting a third series of *How To Be Rich And Famous*, and Channel Six actually asking for Sasha. We can all pay our mortgages.'

'Oh, that's great,' he said. 'I know she's been worried about it.'

'If she hasn't had a chance to tell you herself, maybe you'd better not say I've told you. It would spoil the surprise. What I'm really ringing about is Daisy's birthday present . . .'

Right. Como Pietro's at 1 p.m. tomorrow. Kate was going to be there. She made a booking for one, and asked to be put in a corner table.

Kate got to her table early, opened a large newspaper and kept an eye on the door, feeling remarkably foolish. This was ridiculous. This was none of her business, and so what if Sasha was lunching with someone? It could be her agent, or a woman, or someone from another TV company, or an old friend.

By twenty past one, there was still no sign of Sasha and her mysterious date, and Kate had finished her plate of pasta. She got up and got her coat.

Then she stepped back behind a pillar. Sasha was just coming in, followed by a tall, heavy-set man with a goatee beard. Sasha was looking up at him as if he was a god. But then she looked at all men that way.

'Koski,' said the man loudly, bending over the reservations book. 'No, K-O-S-K-I – look there it is, Chris Koski, for two. Well, I know we're late, but you must have a table. We have booked.'

Sasha stretched up to whisper something in Chris Koski's ear, and he responded by looking down at her. Their mouths seemed very close. Right. That was intimacy all right. Kate managed to sneak out while they were being shown to their table. She wrote the name 'Chris Koski' on an envelope so that she could google him later.

Kate called Olivia as soon as she got out of the restaurant.

Olivia sounded distant. 'Well, you know how flirtatious Sasha always is. There's probably nothing in it.'

'And she forced Roderick Morton's family to sell their house when he died so that she could get a share of the money. Even though it was still their family home and they were still quite young.'

'That's not unusual,' said Olivia. 'Illegitimate children often make claims when the blood relative dies. Presumably she knew she could never have claimed from the stepmother when she died.'

'Olivia, is something wrong?'

'No,' said Olivia. 'Why? I'm just rather busy at the moment.'

Olivia had a way of making Kate feel very unimportant sometimes. She decided to call Si instead.

Si was in a filthy mood, which he usually was these days, and dismissed her discoveries about Sasha completely.

'Kate, I don't know why you're doing this. You've got enough to sort out in your own life, with Callum, Luke and Jonny. You were lucky that night Callum ran away to our flat. You might not be so lucky again. Your priority should be your own relationships rather than putting all this effort into trying to derail someone else's.'

'Jonny and I are fine,' she said, defensively.

'You know it was Mum's dying wish to see you married . . .'

'How do you know? Was it in that letter she left you?' Kate was still hurt not to have had a letter, and furious that Jack had lost his.

'That letter is my business,' snapped Si.

'You can talk. About needing to pay attention to your relationship, that is.' Kate remembered seeing Olivia and Blake in the

336

kitchen at Providence Cottage. 'If you're like this with Olivia, I should think . . .' She trailed off. She shouldn't say any more.

'You'd think what?'

'Oh, just that you're probably being very difficult to live with.'

'Mind your own business, sis.' And he slammed down the phone.

Si was probably right. Crushed, Kate thought of the money she'd inherited from Ella. Ella had asked her to use some of it to pay for her wedding. Perhaps that was what she and Jonny needed. To get married. Perhaps Ella had been right. She missed her so much. So very, very much.

And now she knew about Sasha, well, what? Nobody wanted to know. Nobody wanted to hear.

Chapter 54

It was mid-October before Olivia made her decision. The wind gusted against the car and rain drummed down on her windscreen as she drove through the crowded streets of south London. The radio broadcast a series of severe weather warnings for the south-east of England. 'Police are advising drivers not to make unnecessary journeys.'

This was not an unnecessary journey. She couldn't wait. She had to see Blake. She turned the radio up and flicked the windscreen wipers on to maximum, finally pulling out on to the motorway and the open countryside. The rain was so heavy that she could barely see ahead for more than a few seconds at a time before everything was swamped in a heart-stopping blur. A moment later the wipers would whack across the screen again, rhythmically clearing waterfall after waterfall. She was exhausted because she'd been up since five. She hadn't been able to sleep.

But she knew the journey well and drove slowly, turning carefully off into the winding lanes, edging nervously through puddles that were large enough to be considered floods, hoping that the avalanche of spray being thrown up wasn't going to drench the engine. Did engines drench? Could she be stranded? There were few other cars on the road, just occasional lights behind her and one or two cars inching their way towards her, dipping their headlights when they saw her coming. She tightened her grip on the steering wheel, and was relieved when she saw the long wall of

Bailey House. The wind was so strong she had to struggle to stay upright between the car and the door.

Blake kissed her. 'This is a surprise.'

'I've come to say that I've decided to leave Si.'

Blake's smile didn't waver, but he was very still. 'This is a bit sudden, isn't it?'

'Not exactly. We've been talking about it for nearly a year.'

'And you've always said no.'

'Well, I'm saying yes now. Unless you don't want me?'

'Of course I want you.' He handed her a towel, and she followed him into the kitchen. 'Drink?'

Olivia's heart beat in double time. 'Could I have water? I don't mind tap.' She rubbed her hair dry and hung the towel on the range, then sat down, feeling sick. She always felt sick these days.

He fetched a glass out of a cupboard and filled it from the sink. 'So what's happened?'

Olivia took a deep breath. 'I haven't quite told him yet. I wanted to talk to you first. Properly.'

'Properly?' Blake laughed. 'Or improperly?'

'Please sit down. You're making me feel giddy standing up there.'

He sat down. 'All you need to do is pack a case, leave him and move in here. Everything else will follow.'

'I can't commute from here.' Olivia was used to dealing with Si, who planned everything carefully before making a move.

He shrugged. 'So? We don't need much, and you'd find some local work soon enough.'

'I don't want "some local work". How would you feel if I forced you to move up to London on the grounds that you'd find another job easily enough? Because you would, much more easily than I would down here.'

'The whole point,' he said, 'is that you would be coming down here. Where you belong. Away from the London thing.'

'Well, the London thing is where I earn my money, and it's what I love doing. And whether we sell Bailey House or Providence Cottage, or even both and buy somewhere completely new that's ours, we . . .'

'We would never sell Bailey House. Of course not. I was brought up here . . . it makes sense. Nothing else does.'

Olivia hesitated.

He read her mind. 'If you're worried that I'll never let you make it ours, then forget it. If you want this kitchen ripped out, consider it gone.' He waved a hand at the old-fashioned tongue-and-groove doors and ancient scrubbed worktop.

'No, no, I love it like this. It's just that . . . well, it's all so you and very little me.'

He leant forward and took her hand. 'We can change that. Together.'

She looked down. 'I'm not sure that you're very into change. You don't even want to move five miles down the road to Providence Cottage. Which would be just as suitable, and easier to run.'

He ran his hand through his hair in exasperation.

'No, really,' Olivia lost her nerve. 'It's all right. I'll come and live here. I do love it, and then I'll get a place in London for the week.'

'What?' He stared at her. 'Live in London during the week? Are you mad? That's not being together and you know it.'

'I need to be in London for work,' she repeated.

'Give up your fucking job.'

'So I give up my home and my job, and you give up nothing?' she asked, suddenly overwhelmed by doubt. He wasn't meeting her anywhere near halfway. She and Si would have worked it all out between them with military precision, careful to measure the feelings of each. But that was why Si was so stuffy.

'Don't twist what I say. I believe that being together is being together, not spending most of the time apart. It's what went wrong with my first marriage, and I'm not repeating that mistake again. It's probably what went wrong with you and Si, too – you were apart so much. How can you expect a relationship to work like that?'

'We need the money,' said Olivia. 'You don't earn very much as an architect.'

'We won't *need* very much,' Blake repeated, leaning back casually. 'You've got money, I've got a job, we've got god knows how many homes between us, there'll be a payoff from your marriage . . . it's not as if we've got dependants, after all.'

Olivia let the silence hang between them as she tried to get the words out of her dry, frightened, exhilarated mouth.

'That's what I had to tell you. I'm pregnant, Blake. We have got dependants. Or one dependant. We will have. You and me.'

Blake's face had drained of colour. 'For fuck's sake,' he whispered. 'How the fucking, bleeding, *hell on Christ's earth* did that happen?'

'The usual way.' Olivia was shocked at his response. All the love had gone from his voice. Perhaps it had never really been there in the first place. She felt like she'd jumped into someone's arms only to have them step backwards and allow her to fall, down, down to the bottom of a deep crevasse.

'I assumed that you would be taking the appropriate precautions.'

'Of course I wasn't. I thought I was too old, it hasn't been . . .' She paused, stunned at his response. But even now she didn't want to reveal Si's secret. 'Well, I thought it was all too late. We wanted one, I never got pregnant so . . .'

'I take it it is mine? I mean, what are the chances it could be his?'

She shook her head in amazement. He had changed, become ugly and selfish. 'Would it be such a bad thing? You said your marriage split up because your ex-wife didn't want children . . .'

'I never said that. You asked me why I didn't have children and I said we hadn't wanted them.'

'No, you said your ex-wife hadn't wanted them.'

He shrugged. 'Me, her, what does it matter? You must have known that if I was after children, I'd have found a younger woman.'

'I thought you wanted me. Not someone defined by age.' She still hoped.

'You weren't exactly going for full and frank disclosure yourself. You said you hadn't had time for babies. That it was low on your list of priorities. Not that you were desperate for one.'

She hesitated. 'I couldn't . . .' She stopped. Any further and she would be forced to say too much. Si did not want anyone to know he was infertile, and she owed him that, at least. 'I'm sorry, I just couldn't tell you . . .'

'Not a whole lot of honesty between us from the off then, was there?'

Olivia forced herself to get up and put her coat on again. 'No. Like we never really talked about where we would live or whether I would work? Tell me, did you ever really want me to leave Si, or was it just all one huge joke for you?'

'Married women don't usually leave their rich husbands.'

'Do you specialise in such affairs?'

The laughing eyes were back again. 'I have been known to.'

'Well, that's it, then, isn't it?' It was the ultimate betrayal. She suddenly saw herself as the locals must have – as Blake Allan's latest fancy woman. The dupe who bought the meals in smart restaurants. The spoilt wife escaping from her wealthy, overworked husband to do up a house. It was a classic. And she hadn't seen it coming. She'd thought she was immune to the potent cocktail of married boredom and dancing eyes.

He put out a hand to her. He was going to stop her leaving for a moment. Maybe it would be all right. Maybe he'd just been shocked. Perhaps she should trust him, give up her work and he would be there for her.

But he dropped his hand. 'Olivia . . . I'm sorry. For what it's worth.'

'I take it you don't want the baby.' Her baby deserved a father, at least.

'Sorry,' he said, again. 'Not really my scene. I'll do anything I legally have to, but . . .'

'I won't want you to do anything legal, don't worry.'

'Will you leave him?' asked Blake, as she left the kitchen.

'Well, I'm hardly going to pretend it's his, am I?' Si did not deserve that. He didn't deserve any of it, in fact.

He shrugged. 'I don't know. You've done a pretty good job of lying to him so far.'

She closed the front door of Bailey House behind her, and went out into the dark, humiliated and angry. The wind drove the rain into her face. A pretty good job of lying. Yes, that was her. Guilty as charged. Very, very guilty. She had to concentrate not to slip over in the mud. 'Hang on in there, baby,' she murmured, as she edged the car into the road, avoiding a fallen branch and switching the wipers on to maximum again. 'It's just you and me now.' She stilled the frightened beat of her heart that asked, 'And how will we manage?' She would. She always had. But she knew she had been a fool, and that made the heartache much worse.

Ten minutes later, she rounded a familiar corner to find that the very large puddle was now several hundred feet of flooded lane. She drove slowly through it, trying to minimise the spray, but she could see the nose of the car getting lower and lower in the water.

Terrified, she almost held her breath as the car inched towards the safety of the road rising up out of the water ahead.

Her shoulders dropped as they made it. They were nearly there. Just a few more miles to the shelter of Providence Cottage.

But as she turned into the lane, the car sputtered and died. She searched desperately through the glove compartment for the name of the roadside rescue package that had come with the car, but they told her she was no longer a member. 'It was a one-year deal, which expired eighteen months ago. You didn't renew.'

Hadn't she? She and Si were usually so careful about all that. But in all the excitement of doing up Providence Cottage, maybe . . . 'Can I renew now?' she asked. 'Over the phone, with my card.'

'You can only renew in office hours. It's a different department. Nine to five Monday to Friday.'

Sighing, Olivia grabbed her bag and set out to walk the mile to the cottage, in the dark and the rain. The mud clawed at her city shoes and shifted beneath her weight. Without a torch, she slipped and fell twice. She was shivering, wet through and freezing. Not much further to go, she told herself. Nearly there. You can see the lights of the cottage through the hedge.

Lights. There shouldn't be any lights. She gripped her mobile phone tightly in her hand, trying to keep it dry. A tug of pain in her belly made her gasp. Then it was gone.

She had imagined it. Don't think about that. Just get home. Perhaps she had left the lights on when she was last down. But she didn't do things like that. She had never left a light on in her life. There were lights in an empty cottage and that meant someone was there.

There's no mobile signal here. If Providence Cottage was being burgled, she couldn't call the police. She would have to walk to the nearest farmhouse, in her pumps and thin coat.

She stopped, her heart thumping. Could anyone in the cottage see her approach? If there were burglars, would they keep a watch? Her coat was dark, and the blinding rain made it unlikely. Go forward, Olivia, at least find out who it is. Go forward.

Of course she would go forward. But she was frightened. Very frightened. She had to force herself on, putting the mobile back in her pocket. On a sunny day Providence Cottage was peaceful and quiet. Now it just seemed lonely and isolated, and so very, very cold. Her teeth chattered and her body shook as she carefully placed one foot in front of another in the heavy, slippery mud, feeling it squelch up around her ankles and slither beneath her.

Chapter 55

Heather's heart broke when she took Daisy and Molly to their new school. She was keeping an eye on how they settled, giving herself until after half-term before she advanced her plans. The school was in Wiltshire, near several army bases, 'So Daddy will often be living nice and close', she told them. They were excited by it all, by being back in the countryside again, by their dormitories, and by the promise that they wouldn't have to change schools ever again.

Heather visited them after a few days and they raced round, proud of themselves and their new environment, showing off the pet shed and the games room, and breathlessly recounting their days to her. She had thought they might be homesick, or would want to be with her, but that hope died when she heard them chatter about being picked for the rounders team and what the art teacher was like. It reminded her of the Caldecott – a grand house, sprawling gardens, kind, interested staff, rules, notices – she could feel a sense of security emanate from the school's walls. When she hugged them goodbye, Daisy wriggled out of her arms after a few seconds, eager to return to her new friends.

Driving back, she remembered that she had been ten when she'd gone to the Caldecott, which was very like a boarding school, and it had saved her life. Maybe Mo, in her muddled way, had seen that she was better off there. The thought both soothed her, in an unexpected way, and deepened her despair. Jack was right. She was being selfish wanting Molly and Daisy to live with her. They were better off where they were.

Well, it certainly made her decision easier. She had enough sleeping pills now. So there was nothing else left to do. She would do it that night. She would lie down in bed, take her pills helped along by the whisky, and, if she could manage it just as she was losing consciousness, put a plastic bag over her head.

When she got home, the wind was rattling the ill-fitting windows of the tiny flat and she could hear it gusting through the plane trees. Every so often a siren wailed past or a car alarm was set off. She arranged everything very neatly as usual. The flat was immaculate, with everything gleaming and put away. She lined the sleeping pills up on the kitchen table, with a glass, a bottle of whisky and a large black plastic bag, which she would put over her head, if she could manage it, once she began to drift off.

Everybody would be happy. The girls wouldn't have to shuttle from parent to parent any more. Beside her, the phone began to ring, and she automatically reached out to answer it. Then she dropped her hand. She must not be distracted or diverted. She would clean the flat one last time so it was easy for whoever found her, and put the girls' remaining clothes and toys into boxes and suitcases. This was the only way out, and she didn't want to think about anything else until it was over.

When the pain would be over once and for all. She remembered one of the teachers at the Caldecott telling her once that it was harder for the bright ones. 'You're a clever girl, Heather, and life will always be harder on you. You'll want to work it out, to find the answers, to understand why all this has happened to you.'

But there weren't any answers. She knew that now.

Chapter 56

The shooting schedule for the next series of *How To Be Rich And Famous* was punishing, and Jonny also had several other programmes which he had to keep an eye on. As he pointed out, Future TV couldn't take their foot off the accelerator, either – they had to keep going with developing potential new programmes, plus maintaining their usual level of entertaining existing clients and potential clients in the evenings. Sasha was filming around three days a week, so spent two nights at 19 Lovelace Road, but even she seemed to be working too hard to get up to much. Kate was also too busy with work to keep an eye on her, but she listened in on any phone conversation she could. She never struck lucky again. She had googled Chris Koski and discovered that he was part-owner and director of a big TV indie – far bigger than Future TV – called KAT. It stood for Koski Anderson Tiverti, the surnames of the three partners.

There was rarely any time to talk to Jonny, until just after October half-term, when he was back by six one evening and was able to spend a few hours with Callum and Luke.

'Dad?' queried Callum.

'Mm?' Jonny was forking up risotto, studying a pile of papers in one hand, frowning over reams of statistics showing how much various programmes had gained or lost in viewers and what their share of the market was.

'Can I do work experience at Future TV?'

Jonny put the papers down, took his reading glasses off and frowned at his son. 'What?'

'Work experience, Dad. Can I do some?'

'Oh, that. Yes, of course.' He went back to the papers again.

'Jonny, I think you need to say a bit more than that,' intercepted Kate.

'It's cool, Mum.' Callum got up and put his plate in the dishwasher. 'Night.'

Jonny put down the papers again, looking at her over the top of his glasses this time. 'What more do I need to say? "Yes" seems quite sufficient to me. Luke can do some too, if he likes.'

'Oh well, I suppose so.' She decided to change the subject. 'Do you know Chris Koski?'

'Yeah, everyone knows him. He's a bit of a chancer, but he always manages to pull it off. KAT's a big, big independent operation, getting a lot of commissions at the moment, because he's got a good track record. Teflon-coated man: nothing seems to stick to him, and he knows how to schmooze. Anything else?'

'I saw Sasha having lunch with him at Como Pietro's a few weeks ago.'

Jonny shrugged. 'Like I said, he schmoozes. She's building her career.'

'It looked a bit more intimate than that.'

He put his fork down. 'Katie. Not that again, please. Not in the middle of shooting.'

She was irritated. 'I'm not saying she's having an affair with him. Just that it looked . . .' Suddenly she could bear it no longer. 'Jonny, are we OK?'

He looked wary. 'In what sense?'

'You and me. Here. At 19 Lovelace Road? With the boys? Are we OK?'

Jonny frowned again. 'Of course. Why do you ask?'

Kate took a deep breath. 'You know the money Mumma left me?' Jonny nodded.

'Well, we used a chunk to pay off some of the mortgage, but I've got some left, and she wanted us to get married with it, so why don't we? Next summer, I was thinking.' She deliberately kept it light, so as not to put him under pressure.

His face went blank.

Mistake, thought Kate. 'It's just that seeing Heather and Jack split, I thought . . .' She knew it was one of her faults, babbling when she should stay silent. 'Well, it just seems . . . oh, everything seems to be falling apart. Si and Olivia are at each other's throats, I wanted . . .' Kate couldn't think straight. 'Maybe some sort of public . . . well, maybe not . . .' Why had she done this? They were all right as they were, weren't they?

Neither of them spoke.

They both started together. 'It was just a thought . . .'

'If that's what you want,' said Jonny.

'Well, only if it's what you want.' It was absurd, thought Kate, suddenly feeling very cold. It was as if they were strangers talking politely about a possible trip to the cinema, not a major life decision.

'OK,' said Jonny. 'It's just that . . .'

'What?'

'Well, the garage phoned today. The car failed its MOT. It'll cost more to put right than it's worth.' He drummed his fingers on the table.

'Well, we'll use the money to buy a new car then, won't we?' Kate didn't want him to see that she minded. She'd always been so careful to make sure he knew she didn't. 'No question. First things first.'

'Sure?' He picked up his fork again. 'Because . . .'

'I'm quite sure. Absolutely.'

'Because, you know, if you want to . . . it's just that it would cost a bit but maybe we could borrow a bit more . . .'

'No, really, it's absolutely fine. The important thing is to keep paying back our debts, not making them bigger, isn't it?'

'Kate, have you thought about going back to work in an office, because . . .'

'I don't want to talk about it just now, if that's all right.' Kate thought she might burst into tears if the conversation went on any longer, and she certainly didn't want it to turn into a careers session.

Jonny looked at her over the glasses, and she thought he was going to add something, but he just smiled, a small, sad smile, she thought, and went back to the pile of viewing statistics again.

It was clear that Jonny didn't want to make that final commitment. They would have to do that old-fashioned thing of 'staying together for the sake of the children', then split, maybe, when Luke was eighteen. Seven years.

It was a very long time to spend with someone who didn't really love you. But she thought again of all the missing fathers: hers and Sasha's, and Jasper Morton, and Molly and Daisy, and all the pain stretching down the generations. Ella had not wanted Kate to make the mistake she'd made.

And she and Jonny were good together. Not great together, perhaps, but good. They could bring up their children, then she, Kate, would get out. Go travelling, perhaps. She looked at the beloved white walls of her home, and hardened herself to losing it. One day, she would have to close the front door forever. It was almost an unbearable thought, because the best part of her life – the boys and Jonny – had happened here. But she knew that if she and Jonny had to part, she wouldn't be able to bear to stay either.

She almost didn't hear the phone.

'Shall I get it?' asked Jonny.

But Kate picked it up. Molly was crying so hard that she could hardly make out what she was saying.

'Sweetie?' Her heart quickened.

'It's Travis.' Molly's voice wobbled, and she gulped.

'Take a deep breath,' advised Kate. 'Just breathe. Then tell me what the problem is.'

'Grace says that when Sasha goes away she ties Travis up in the garage, on a long chain, and leaves a couple of days' food and water, and the door open so he can pee and poo outside, and then just leaves him. She's away now, in London at a party, Grace says. In a nightclub. And Grace says she won't go home till tomorrow morning, or later. She sometimes stays away for days at a time.'

'That's awful! Are you sure? I think Grace does sometimes make things up a bit . . .' Kate trailed off, as she didn't want to criticise either Sasha or her children to Molly and Daisy. It would only unsettle them.

'Oh Grace is the most dreadful, dreadful liar, everyone knows that. But she isn't lying now.'

'How do you know?'

'Well, I've seen a very long chain in the garage, and two dog bowls, and when I asked Sasha what they were, she was a bit vague. Auntie Kate, it's an awful night, there's thunder everywhere, and Travis really hates thunder. He's so frightened of it, you know that. And he's quite old now. He'll be so cold and wet and frightened. Please go and get him, please. Please, please, please. He's always looked after us, we can't let him down.'

'Go and get him? But . . .' Kate hesitated. 'I'll get hold of your mother, and we'll talk about what's best to do. Don't worry, I promise we'll make sure that Travis is all right.'

'Mummy's not answering her phone.'

'Well, perhaps she's out.'

'She never goes out at night. Ever. I'm worried about her too – suppose she's hurt herself and is lying unconscious or there's been a burglary and she's being held up . . .'

Kate decided that Molly's anxiety levels were far, far too high for a thirteen-year-old. The settling down at boarding school, trumpeted as such a success by all, might not be everything it seemed. 'Molly,' she spoke clearly. 'I promise you I will drive over to your mum's house right now and make sure she is all right. And we will both discuss what's best for Travis.'

It was only when she put down the phone that she realised she didn't have a car.

'Take a taxi,' suggested Jonny. 'It's not far.'

'Heather's probably just out on a date. It's about time. Or gone to the cinema with a friend.'

'Does she have friends?'

Kate shook her head. 'I'm not sure. I got the impression that she always got on with people on the army patches, but that she wasn't particularly close to any of them. And no one ever called for her when she was living here.'

'You know, I don't have a good feeling about this,' said Jonny. 'Do you want me to come with you?'

But Kate wanted to get away from him. To give herself time to paste 'good old Kate' back on to her face. 'No, I'm fine. And we can't leave the kids alone.'

When she arrived at Heather's, she could see chinks of light through the curtains. That meant Heather must be there, because she was obsessive about turning lights off. Kate had often joked that when Heather and the girls had been staying, she'd had to walk round her own house in the dark.

But there was no answer. Kate rat-tatted the house's door knocker over and over, and pressed the bell repeatedly.

'What is it?' The front door was opened by the man who lived in the flat above. Kate brushed past him and began drumming on Heather's flat door, shouting her name.

It opened after several minutes. 'You never give up Kate, do you?' said Heather, leaning wearily against the door, obviously in the middle of cleaning because she had a cloth in her hand, sounding resigned.

The first things Kate saw, on the table, conspicuous in the tidy, empty flat, were the sleeping pills, the whisky and the black plastic bag. 'Heather, no.' She picked up the pills and stuffed them into her own bag. 'The girls need you.'

'No, they don't.' Heather tried to snatch them back.

'And so does Travis.'

'Nobody needs me,' said Heather, with finality, folding her arms and looking sullen.

'Heather, you are wrong. Completely wrong. Your daughters' stepmother is a liar and cheat, you cannot desert them now.'

'What do you mean?' The colour came back to Heather's face.

'I'm sorry, I hadn't wanted to involve you in this because I thought it would be too painful, but I've come across some very disturbing things about Sasha.' She told Heather about Sasha's behaviour to her half-brother and -sister, the lunch with Chris Koski, the little odd lies that she'd told, and finally, Molly's phone call about Travis. 'Every single incident can be explained away in some way, and no one really seems to think it adds up to anything serious, but . . . Heather, you've seen Sasha with children, and actually she's fine. She doesn't neglect them or anything, but you cannot – you must not – trust your daughters to her care, and Jack is too blinded by his obsession with her . . . I feel so, so guilty that I haven't done more, but please, please do not ever try anything like this.'

Heather's eyes grew large and dark. 'The girls,' she said. 'Do you think she would harm the girls?'

Kate hesitated. 'No . . . I don't think so . . . but she will never put their interests first.'

Heather picked up her bag and put on her coat. 'Let's get Travis. He's always looked after me. He should be curled up with his family, not chained up, scared and shivering outside.'

'I'll drive,' said Kate, hastily.

But when they got out on to the open road, she braced herself. 'Heather, will you talk to me? I promise never to tell anyone, I really do.'

Heather was silent for a few miles. 'You know what? You remind of some of the staff in the children's home I grew up in. They never gave up, either. Come on, Heather, you must get dressed. Heather, why not start with that nice top, Heather, I'm staying here until you get dressed . . . on and on. My mum never got me up, you see, either I did it myself or I slept in until the middle of the day.'

Kate didn't know how to reply.

'I'm not saying it's bad to be persistent,' added Heather. 'Of sorts. I had good uncles and bad uncles, and uncles who hit me and uncles who burned me with cigarettes, but nobody ever hung in there for me until I was sent away to somewhere called the Caldecott. My mum dumped me there, when I was about the age that Daisy is now.'

'Heather, I'm sorry. Why didn't you ever say?'

'It's not exactly the right background for the wife of an ambitious army officer, is it?'

'I don't think Jack would have cared about that. He would only have cared about you.'

'Oh, yeah,' said Heather. 'He's being very caring at the moment, you should see it. Anyway, it was kind of a good thing, because it was safe, and I learned a bit about how to survive.' She managed a shaky smile. 'Maybe not quite enough, though.'

'But it's all falling apart now, isn't it?' ventured Kate. 'Because of Jack and Sasha, and the girls going and . . .'

'Yeah, well, it started before Jack and Sasha. They found my mum just before Jack went to Temanistan. She died a drug addict, turning tricks for fixes. Jack was very caring about that, I can tell you. We didn't speak for two days.' Heather's voice was strained, and hoarse.

'He's got a lot of faults, but I can't imagine Jack would think the worse of you because of your mother.' Kate was amazed. 'And he doesn't have any pretensions. He's not like Si. Although we are all only a few years apart, we had completely different experiences in our teens, because of our father dying. Si was in his last year of A levels, so the private school we went to kept him on – he went from private school to Oxford and then into the luxury business. I was just starting A levels so I went to the local comprehensive – which, unfortunately, wasn't one of the best – when the money ran out. But that was fine, because of course most of the people doing A levels with me wanted to stay on at school, so I never had to deal with any disruptive elements. In fact, I enjoyed it a lot more than the stuffy private school where there seemed to be endless rules about which shoes you wore for chapel. But Jack went in much younger, when he was thirteen, and the bully boys from the local estates really liked to pick on "posh boy", as they called him. He really, really had to fight his way out of that, and I think that's where he got this reputation for being rebellious. But although he can seem callous and thoughtless, he isn't, and one thing he really does not care about is what anyone's mother did.'

Heather didn't reply for a few more miles. 'Well, maybe. Maybe I wasn't quite fair on him. I hadn't told him, you see. He was angry about that.'

'I should think he minded the secrecy more than anything else.'

Heather shrugged. 'Maybe. It doesn't matter now.'

The rain had stopped and the windscreen wipers scraped across in front of them. Neither of them noticed. 'Anyway,' she added. 'That's why I've got to get Travis. I know what it's like to be left alone and chained up.'

'No!' Kate was horrified. 'Really?'

Heather nodded.

'What about Broadstairs?'

'What about it?' Heather sounded defensive.

'You liked it there.'

She shrugged. 'He was all right, Gerald was, but he got rid of me because I was difficult. That's what happened at all the schools. He called in the social services, and got me sent to the Caldecott. That's what my mum said, that he wanted to get rid of me. People do if you're difficult. That's why I've learned to be so careful.'

'Have you thought that he might have called the social services because he didn't think you were being looked after properly?'

Heather shook her head. 'They didn't want me. She told me that. Lots of times. It's not like your family, everyone all happy and loving each other, and ringing each other up all the time. That's why I don't belong. I'm not a part of you all.'

'Heather, that is ridiculous. Of course you're a part of us. Even now. You're a part forever and ever. Nothing can change that.'

'Not even Sasha and the divorce?'

'Especially not Sasha,' said Kate.

Heather didn't respond.

'Do you know where their house is, by the way?'

Heather nodded. 'I've taken the girls there several times since Jack and Sasha moved out of army quarters. But haven't you been yourself?'

'Oddly, no.' Kate had been waiting to be invited down to Wiltshire, but the phone lines had been silent.

'But she stays with you all the time.'

'Invitations don't come back the other way,' said Kate.

By this time they had turned off the motorway, and were peering for signposts. 'Look,' said Heather. 'There's the Black Piper, the pub, we turn left. They're right at the bottom, past all the other houses.'

They bumped down the lane and ended up on a sweep of gravel in front of a pretty house, small and square, with three gables.

'I can see why Sasha might prefer this to army quarters,' said Kate.

'Looks lonely to me, miles from the patch. Travis!' Heather called. 'Travis!'

They listened, but could only hear the wind. The garage, to the right of the house, seemed empty and was locked. 'I wonder if she's left him inside after all because it's such a dreadful night.' Heather walked round it, listening hard.

'I think we might have been very silly,' said Kate, peering in the letterbox. 'Travis! She's obviously put him in kennels or left him with a neighbour after all.'

'Sasha doesn't really do neighbours.' Heather wiped some rain out of her eyes. 'She told me once that she hates the nosiness of it all, and never accepts invitations from them on principle.'

'Well, she's told me over and over again how nice the people are in that big house we passed on the way in. She's certainly accepted their invitations. She accepts invitations from rich neighbours.' Kate unlatched the gate to the back garden. 'Let's just try round here, and then agree that we are both completely mad, and drive all the way back to London.'

'Travis! Travis! What was that?'

They listened. 'The wind, I think.' A soft whining came from the darkest area, towards the end of the garden. 'Travis?'

'There's a torch in the car.'

Travis was lying inside a shed at the bottom of the garden, on a piece of old blanket. He tried to get up when he saw them, wagging his tail weakly and staggering on collapsing back legs. 'He's ill,' cried Heather, crouching over him with cries of anguish. 'She should be prosecuted for animal cruelty. Travis! I'm so sorry. I should never have let you go.' Travis licked her hand obligingly. 'You'd think he'd be suspicious of people after this. Look, he's got mange. And he's so thin. Oh, Travis, I'm so sorry. I'm so sorry.'

Kate, watching Heather wrap herself round Travis with cries of anguish, thought that perhaps she'd found a level of trust with the dog that she'd been unable to accept from a human being.

'I think we should find an all-night vet,' she said, unclipping the chain from his collar. 'And let's take a photo of him with my mobile phone. And I'll take the chain. As proof. They can't say I'm imagining this.'

But it was too dark for them to get any detail with the phone, just the glitter of Travis's eyes and the dark.

Later, they held him while the vet fixed up a drip. 'I think your dog should be fine, but he's dehydrated, malnourished, and suffering from mange. And because of his breed, there's a weakness in the back legs, which is probably more to do with age than neglect.

356

We'd like to keep in him for forty-eight hours, if that's OK, and there'll need to be follow-up. '

'Follow-up?' asked Heather. 'Will we be in trouble?'

'Don't worry,' said Kate. 'We'll come back in two days and get him.'

'He's not going back to Sasha. I wouldn't leave that bitch in charge of a packet of peanuts, let alone a dog,' declared Heather.

When she rifled for the car keys, Kate saw the sleeping pills in her bag. 'Do you have any more of these anywhere?'

'No, and I won't be wanting them again,' said Heather, starting the car. 'You can keep them if you like.'

'Good. And I think you should see someone, get some help. Some answers.'

'There aren't any answers. No one can help.'

'Well, you'll never find out until you try. Why not start with looking for that man in Broadstairs? He's probably still alive. And he was kind once. He could tell you what your mother was really like.'

'I don't think I want to know,' said Heather.

'It might be better than you think.'

'Kate! Shut up.'

'There's anxious Heather, who makes everything look perfect, but is terrified it's all going to fall apart, and then there's angry Heather just underneath, waiting to ambush you if anything goes wrong. I think it's time the two Heathers got together and tried to find happy Heather. She must be in there somewhere.'

'There's nothing unusual about that. There seem to be at least two Sashas,' said Heather. 'And how many Kates are there, do you think? Let's start hearing from them, shall we?'

'Oh, I'm just boring old me,' said Kate. 'What you see is what you get.'

'Kate,' said Heather. 'I've seen a lot of you in the last few months, and you're not happy. I think . . . perhaps . . . you should talk about it. Maybe to me?'

Kate was going to brush her off, but she suddenly realised how hard it must have been for Heather to suggest it. She didn't want to drive her back into her shell.

'Well,' she said, taking a deep breath. 'Jonny and I are like friends, not lovers, at the moment. He's only interested in his work and doesn't want to marry me. And I don't want to leave the boys and 19 Lovelace Road, so I was going to stick it out. But I don't think I can do it any longer. It's the loneliest thing in the world to live with someone who doesn't love you.'

'I'm sorry,' said Heather, in a small voice. 'So terribly sorry.'

'I didn't mean to say all that,' Kate struggled to control her voice. 'It just came out.'

Heather passed her a tissue, and Kate realised she was crying. 'Sorry.' She blew her nose. 'Anyway, I'm going to give myself till after Christmas and talk properly to Jonny then.'

'You always seem to get on so well,' whispered Heather.

'Oh yes, we get on fine. Absolutely fine. He just loves his work more than he loves me, and suddenly that's not good enough.'

Chapter 57

That evening, in Soho, Sasha faced a dilemma. Chris Koski. He was not going to be satisfied with flirtatious lunches forever. And he was very, very much more powerful than Jonny had ever been – or ever would be – and he had now suggested that she come back to his flat.

She had never mentioned that she was married, because it had all been such a hole-and-corner affair, and Jack's family didn't really accept her. And she and Jack barely even lived together. He was on a course somewhere, for three days, yet again, just leaving her at the bottom of a muddy lane. What did he expect? That she should sit there looking at her hands and making everything nice for his return? Unless she worked – and worked hard – they couldn't have a lot of what he took for granted. He had paid so much money to Heather. Sasha hadn't realised quite how much, until Jack took her through the finances. That money should be Jack's. Why didn't Heather get off her bum and get a proper job? And Jack should think about his future, too. He wasn't really going to get any further in the army, which was quite ridiculous, because you needed people who could act on their own initiative in war. He had narrowly avoided court martial for the incident in Temanistan. Well, it was ridiculous. Sasha had done everything she could for him. She'd even made sure that the story in the newspaper was sympathetic to him. Although the fee had been very useful, too. She smiled. You had to look after yourself in this world, you really did.

If he was going to be in dangerous places, he should be getting a lot more money, working for security companies maybe. She must look it all up, get him set up properly. It was all so different to what she'd expected. She'd thought Jack was strong, that he would look after her, but she had really just acquired another dependent, someone else who relied on her. Yet again.

She looked up at Chris, who was standing expectantly over her at the door of the nightclub.

'Or I could give you a lift?' he suggested. 'Back to yours?'

She smiled up at him. 'I think a taxi to Wiltshire might dent even Grand TV's expenses budget.'

'Ah, so you're a country girl?'

'I'm a bit betwixt and between at the moment . . . my divorce, you see.'

'A woman of mystery. I find you fascinating. My place,' he leaned a little closer, 'is very convenient. And we could talk about that six-part series on life after divorce.'

Sasha moved towards him, lifting her face for a kiss.

Chapter 58

When Olivia eventually stumbled up to the front of the cottage, wet and muddy to the knees, with her suit trousers wicking the mud and rain, she saw Si's car. She could hardly believe it, but the licence plate was unmistakeable. For a moment she wondered whether their London place had been robbed and the burglars had come down here, but then she saw Si walk across the small window in the kitchen.

She pushed open the door. 'Si?'

'Olivia?' He didn't seem surprised to see her. 'I didn't hear the car.'

'No, it broke down at the bottom of the lane.'

'I see.' He didn't ask her what she was doing there, and she didn't dare ask him. 'Drink?'

'No, thanks, I'm going to bed. I had a case at Maidstone and, with the weather, it was easier to come down here . . .'

He smiled cynically. 'Quite. I had business quite close, too. Wasn't that a coincidence?'

Olivia gave him an uncertain smile, and slipped her soaking shoes off, edging upstairs to try to get warm and dry, but the bed seemed icy cold.

Olivia was woken by a pulsating pain deep inside her, and the knowledge that Si had not come to bed. It was two o'clock in the morning and the space beside her was empty. Perhaps he had left. She gasped and clutched herself as another slash of pain sliced through her.

It stopped. Just cramp. Nothing more. Just cramp. She was filled with fear as she pulled on a dressing gown, her teeth still chattering. Surely she couldn't be losing the baby so soon after she'd found out she was having it?

She lay very still, terrified of moving in case it dislodged the little being inside her. Please stay, she begged it. Hang on in there somehow. I will lie quite still and it will be all right.

But she didn't seem to have warmed up much. Maybe she should turn the heating up. She edged nervously downstairs to the boiler trying not to jolt herself at all, creeping as smoothly along as she could, and turned the thermostat up high.

Si appeared behind her in the doorway.

'What are you doing?' Si's voice was harsh.

'I'm cold. I was turning the heating up.'

Both their eyes were drawn to the floor. There was a trail of blood across it. Olivia closed her eyes in despair. She could feel her thighs were wet.

'Shall I call a doctor?' Si spoke kindly. 'I think you should go back to bed. I'll clear up here.' He handed her a towel.

She let him help her up the stairs, but insisted on talking to the doctor herself. 'With the door closed, if you don't mind,' she added, politely. Si needn't know. Maybe he needn't ever know about the affair with Blake. She could explain the blood away somehow. She couldn't meet his eyes.

After an endless wait for a return phone call, Olivia established that there was no point in going to a hospital, especially not in this weather.

'There's nothing we can really do,' explained a nurse. 'How far along is your pregnancy?'

'I don't know,' said Olivia, her teeth clattering. 'I only found out yesterday, but I haven't had a period for . . . well, ages. I might be about ten weeks. Maybe a bit less. Or a bit more.' A cramp seized her belly, like a giant hand, gripping and squeezing in a series of waves. 'Please help me,' she pleaded. 'I want this baby so much.'

'If you are having a miscarriage,' said the nurse gently, 'there's very little we can do. Call us in the morning, or earlier if you feel you need help.'

Olivia put down the phone and lay in the dark, waiting as the waves of pain grew closer and closer together. She heard a soft knock on the door, and Si came in, sat down on the bed, and held her hand.

'Sorry,' she said, gripping it. 'I'm so sorry, I . . .'

'Sh,' he soothed. 'Sh.'

She drifted in and out of sleep, awoken by spasms of pain and comforted by Si's silent presence, until she felt an overwhelming urge and bolted to the bathroom. With a groan, she felt something leave her. It was no larger than a clot of blood, but it left her empty and bleak.

'I'll be all right now,' she said to Si, returning to the bed and crawling in.

He didn't ask any questions.

'Si.' She turned on her side, curling up in a self-protective ball. 'We do need to talk.'

'We do,' he agreed. 'But not now. Not until you're warm again.'

Warm again. It was a nice thought. A distant wonderful feeling that happened to other people. People who didn't lie and betray. Holding Si's hand had been so right. But it would never be right again. He knew what had happened, and even though they hadn't said a word about it, she knew, now, that he knew about Blake.

Si always used to say he could read her like a book. She had lost everything she cared about. Si and the baby. Nothing else mattered.

'I don't think I'll ever be warm again,' she said sadly, before finally dropping off to sleep. As if it were a dream, she heard the faint click of the door as Si left the room.

Olivia woke up in Providence Cottage to hear the rain still thundering down. Si came in with a cup of coffee.

'How are you feeling?' But the gentleness of the night before had gone. He had his hard face on again. Olivia would have given everything – Providence Cottage, even – to be able to turn back the clock and find her best friend beside her. But she'd blown it. And she knew Si well enough to know that his pride, his dreadful, annoying, stiff, outdated pride, which was the reason why he was always Si – always beautifully groomed, always so hard-working, always meticulously polite – meant that he would never forgive her, even if he wanted to.

Which he didn't, judging by the set of his body in the chair opposite her. He contemplated his fingernails as she sipped the coffee.

'Thank you.'

He inclined his head, but made no reply.

'Where shall we start?'

'Well,' Si leant forward. 'Let me see. I get home from work, and go into the bathroom to get some paracetamol, where I find the remains of a pregnancy test in the bin. A positive pregnancy test. And as the only other person who uses that bathroom is my wife, and as my wife has been extremely friendly with her architect for some time, I draw some conclusions. So I phone my wife's office, where she isn't. I phone my wife's mobile which isn't on. It is very rarely on these days, by the way, in spite of her high-profile client list who may need her at any time of night or day. And then I go down to the garage and find my wife's car gone. She does not use this car often in London, because she prefers public transport, so I . . .'

'Stop talking about me in the third person,' Olivia whispered. 'I know it hurts, but it's us. Not someone else. You and me. Use those words. We can't pretend it's not happening.'

He looked thrown by that. 'Oh. Well.' He recovered himself. 'Your car wasn't in the garage, and . . .' he forced the words out, 'I . . . knew where you'd gone.'

'So you followed me? You drove for two hours in appalling weather on a hunch? Supposing I'd been visiting someone in . . . well . . . another part of London? I could have been . . .' she tried to think of their friends, but most lived within taxi or tube distance. She and Si rarely did use their cars in town. 'I could have been visiting Kate, for example, we always drive there.'

'I called Kate. I called anyone I could think of.'

This was astonishing. She couldn't imagine Si letting his guard down enough to ring around, asking where she was. 'I'm sorry,' she said. 'That you had to do that. I thought you were working late. I was going to ring you when I . . .'

'When you knew what you were doing? Well, I got to Bailey

364

House. And your car was there. So I knew you'd gone to lover boy. The weather was so terrible, I thought I'd spend the night at the cottage. And maybe talk to you in the morning. That's my story. Now it's your turn.'

She shook her head, ashamed. 'I'm sorry. That's all I can say. I'm sorry.'

'Sorry isn't good enough,' he said, harshly. 'Is it?'

Olivia pulled her knees up to her chest. 'No. But it's over between me and . . .'

Si raised an eyebrow. 'Not happy about fatherhood? No, well, I always saw him for a selfish git. A bit too pleased with himself.' He stood up. 'But I'm sorry you lost the baby. Perhaps I . . .' He turned away and looked out over the windswept, muddy fields. 'Perhaps I never understood how much you wanted one,' he barked.

Olivia clenched her fists in an effort not to cry. She had never felt so bleak and empty in her life.

'You need to go to a hospital, don't you?'

'I don't know. I think I'm all right. The pain's stopped. The bleeding's stopped. I just feel rather weird.' Olivia couldn't bear the idea of spending hours in waiting rooms and having intrusive and pointless tests. She knew what had happened. She fixed her eyes on the bedspread. It was cashmere. Only the best for Providence Cottage.

'Si, I wanted a family. If I couldn't have a baby, I wanted to belong somewhere. Grow something. Feel the seasons change, not just look at them from behind a triple-glazed window all year. That's why here was so important to me. It felt real and old, and as if it had always been there.'

He looked at her with real dislike. 'You are a spoilt little brat, aren't you? You're a Montmorency, one of the richest and oldest families in the land. You've always had everything handed to you on a plate. But no, the plate – the silver plate – isn't big enough. You were born with everything I had to work my guts out for, and still you want more. And you don't care who or what you destroy in order to get it.'

'No! It wasn't like that. I promise, I didn't . . .'

Si got up. 'I'll tell you what it's like not to feel you belong. You go to university and find that all the other boys can shoot and fish, that they come from houses with wings and drives and stable blocks . . . most of our friends at university would have despised me if they'd seen the house we lived in.'

'No, they wouldn't,' flashed Olivia. 'They were my friends, too, and I don't believe they were that shallow.'

'Easy for you to say,' retorted Si. 'You were brought up in a grand country house. You were part of it all. And you've no idea what it was like to lose everything. Your home, your friends, your father . . . I never wanted anything to hurt that much again. That's why I've worked my guts out to get to the top, and now it's been taken by somebody who was born to it, somebody who was born privileged, like you.'

'Si, it wasn't fair what happened to you at R&R, but it's not right to take it out on me either. Stop feeling sorry for yourself, and get on with finding another job.'

'That'll sort it, will it? Easy for you to say. Everything's easy for people like you.'

'Easy, easy, easy . . . is that why you married me? For an easy life?'

Si was silent.

'Si, you had a family. A mother, a sister, a brother. Who cared about you . . . oh, I can't be bothered with this. If you can't see the value of where you've come from, then you're a fool. It's not what you're given in life, it's what you do with it. Think of the rich people we knew who've done nothing with what they've been given, then compare it to what you've achieved.' Olivia turned over, and pulled the duvet over her ears. She felt utterly defeated. 'But I'm sorry. I'm sorry about it all.' So. Si had married her because she was a Montmorency, and he was obsessed with belonging to the crowd they'd met at Oxford. That seemed pretty clear now. Snobbery was what drove him.

'You needn't worry about money, I'll see that the divorce is fair,' said Si. 'I promise. Just let me know what you need. And you can have the flat, if you want it. I'll move out now.'

She hugged her knees, trying to comfort herself. 'I'm sorry. Sorry,' she whispered, an incantation repeated over and over again that failed to comfort her.

'I'll see you in court, as they say.' He closed the door quietly behind him.

She lay watching the rain trickle down the window, numb with the pain of it, until she forced herself to go downstairs. She found a note on the table. 'Took your car. Got it started, and you'll find the four-by-four easier in the mud. I'll leave your keys on the table at the flat. S.'

She put her head on her hands and howled like an animal.

Chapter 59

Jack blamed Kate for the kidnapping of Travis. He phoned her the following afternoon.

'Kate?' asked Jack. 'Kate, what were you thinking about, driving down to Wiltshire in the middle of a stormy night to steal my dog?'

'I didn't steal your dog. Molly told me that . . .'

'I don't care what Molly told you. You've no business to get involved.'

'Heather wanted me to come, she . . .' Kate stopped. But Heather was far too fragile to cope with a furious Jack, so she'd better not blame her. 'Heather loves Travis very much, and I thought she needed company on the way down. She's . . . still very upset about . . .' It was hard to explain without betraying Heather's secrets.

'Heather would never have done anything like this without your encouragement. That's why I'm being very careful not to be angry with her. But you're different, you should have known better. Sasha put Travis in the shed before she went out that night because he'd been sick a few times, she left him with food and water, and quite safe, with the door shut, and she came back at about two in the morning and was absolutely frantic to find him missing. How could you do it?'

'It couldn't have been two in the morning, we were still there, and the shed door wasn't shut, and she wasn't—'

'You must have missed her by seconds, which makes it all the more ridiculous. At the very least you could have rung one of us about it if Molly was worried.'

'The vet said Travis was undernourished, suffering from dehydration and mange.'

'Well, that's not what the vet that Sasha took him to earlier in the day said. He's been off his food and losing weight, and has a skin problem. Sasha is actually working very hard at the moment, unlike you, yet she's still found the time to take him to the vet three times this week to find out what's wrong with him. You can't just kidnap someone's animal and take it to any old vet to get the diagnosis you want . . .'

'Jack, that is so unfair. Travis was in a terrible state, his back legs were going, we simply went to the vet who was on call, and he told us what he thought.'

'After you, no doubt, had told him that Travis was being left alone for days on end, chained up in a barn? Yes?'

'Well . . .'

'No wonder he gave you a diagnosis of neglect.'

'Jack, you're being slippery. I could show you the chain. I've got a photo, too, although it's very dark . . . Jack, you must know that Sasha lies. Look, it's not her fault, she was completely rejected by her father and she's spent the rest of her life trying to make up for it, but she's damaged. And dangerous. I talked to her brother and . . .'

'Kate, this is disgraceful. You have been spying on my wife, and inventing stories about her, and it must stop. If I hear you've been repeating any of this, and especially if you dare sell or tell as far as the press are concerned, I shall take you to court, is that clear? Sasha is becoming quite famous, and she's very vulnerable to this sort of tabloid nonsense.'

'It isn't nonsense. That chain is proof, at least as far as Travis is concerned. And if you look carefully at the picture . . .'

'No, Kate, you're twisting everything. And no amount of chains or almost blacked-out pictures can possibly prove anything. You simply cannot stand that Sasha is my wife, she is now my priority in life, and you and the rest of the Fox family have got to realise that. You have never accepted her and—'

'I've had her to stay two nights a week, I cook her meals and—'

'Well, she will *not* be interested in taking up that invitation again, I can assure you.'

'I've looked after her children. I've invited you both to family events you haven't come to. She's never invited us to your house, she screens my calls and never picks up, she always leaves it to you to call me back . . .'

'Which is exactly what you do to Jonny's sister. Don't try to deny it, I've heard the way you talk *about* her, and you practically never say two words *to* her if you can help it.'

'That's different, she doesn't approve of me, and anyway she only wants to talk to Jonny and—'

'How do you know? You've never given her a chance. Well, equally, you've made it pretty clear you don't approve of Sasha, and personally I think Sasha has been a lot friendlier to you than you've ever been to Virginia. You want to be careful, Kate, when you condemn people. You may find that what you're busy accusing everyone else of is something you're most guilty of yourself.'

'Jack. What you and Sasha did killed Mumma. It almost killed Heather. Molly is an anxious wreck. It's extremely difficult not to condemn that sort of behaviour, but I've done my best because—'

'What you can't seem to grasp is that you're not at the heart of my family any more. Sasha is. Heather fitted in, because you could dominate her, and she toed the line, but Sasha is her own person, and she's not going to fall in with the whole Fox family thing exactly the way you want her to. You can't control her the way you control everyone else, and that's why you don't like her.'

'I'm not trying to control anyone, I'm only trying my best to keep the family going because it's always mattered to us. Sasha doesn't really care about families because she's never had one.'

'Nonsense, she's got four sisters and brothers.'

'Who she never sees. They were brought up with different mothers. Have you ever even met them? Have you even met her mother? Did any of them come to your wedding?'

'Kate, families do not have to live on top of each other. The way we were, with us coming over all the time, even sometimes going on holidays together – well, it was claustrophobic. Unnatural. No wonder Sasha isn't going to put up with it. Think about Virginia again, Kate – do you go to lunch with her? Or go on holiday with her?'

'In fact, we're spending Christmas there.'

'And I bet you've done everything you can to get out of that.'

He was right, of course. Kate was taken aback. 'I thought everyone enjoyed getting together. I'm sorry if you didn't, but if you wanted it to be different, you could have done something about it.'

'As I have. This time I'm putting my wife first, and you should learn from that. You really should. You're on very thin ice in your relationship, and, as your brother, it's my duty to tell you.'

'What do you mean?' Kate was frantic. 'Has Sasha told you something about Jonny?'

'Only that you nag him all the time about domestic things when he's working all hours trying to pull the company out of the shit, and that he gets a nicer time at work than he ever does at home. Oh, and that every single female at Future TV – all of whom are a lot younger and more attractive than you are – have got their eye on him.'

'And has anything . . . well, you know, happened?' Kate's heart stopped. Even if Jonny didn't love her any more, she couldn't bear that.

'Sasha is far too discreet to say anything if it had. She's not a gossip, like some people. Your relationship is between you and Jonny. You have to deal with it directly.'

Kate crumbled. Jack sounded as if he hated her, really hated her. And he was right, her relationship with Jonny was vulnerable. And maybe Sasha hadn't neglected Travis. She wouldn't lie about taking him to the vet, would she? Not something that could be so easily disproven?

She forced herself to apologise. 'Well, I'm sorry if we made a mistake, but we thought Travis was in danger.'

'If you want to apologise, you should apologise to Sasha. She's the one who's been hurt in all this. But may I add that until you do, then I think it's probably better that we don't meet. Is that clear?'

'I've absolutely no desire to see you. But please don't shout at

Heather like this. She's incredibly fragile. She is . . . even suicidal, and she couldn't take being harangued.'

'I'm not shouting,' said Jack, 'and I wouldn't dream of haranguing Heather, as you put it. I don't blame her for any of this, because I know how much she loves Travis and how hard she's found everything. She's not a strong person, and very easily led. Which is why you should have had more sense.'

'There's more to Heather than you think.' But Kate put down the phone, shaking. Had taking Travis been too intrusive? Surely they couldn't have left an animal to suffer?

And he was certainly right about Virginia. And probably Jonny, Callum and Luke. They were her first priorities. Even if Jonny didn't really love her, they were responsible for Callum and Luke together.

And what about the girls at Future TV and Jack's hints there? Maybe Jonny wanted to end their relationship, and was just waiting for the right time.

The only thing that Kate was becoming increasingly sure of was that there were no rules to help her make her decision. No certainties. No one else's past experience.

Chapter 60

After two weeks of the anti-depressants Heather decided to risk a trip to Broadstairs. She had also been referred to a therapist. As she talked about how far she'd come, a knot inside her was slowly beginning to unravel. Maybe there was sunshine ahead. Hearing about Sasha had helped too – she wasn't the wonderful, confident woman that Jack thought she was, just another damaged, hurting person.

The therapist thought a trip to the place where she'd been happy was a good idea. There were plenty of empty weekends when the girls were at school. The flat was clean enough, and she was going to dare to do something apart from polishing, scrubbing and dusting everything yet again.

She remembered the street name and the number of the house. Twenty-seven. She knocked on the door. It was painted the same smoky blue – now peeling and battered – and a neat pile of wood sat in the porch, the way it always had. Heather sniffed the sea air, with its tang of salt and smoky fire.

The man who opened the door was exactly as she remembered him, but much, much smaller. He was almost bird-like, with thinning white hair combed across his scalp. She would have walked past him if she had bumped into him in the street.

'I'm sorry,' he said. 'I'm not interested. Whatever it is you're selling.' He began to close the door.

'Gerald?'

He stopped, the door half-closed. 'Excuse me?'

'It's Heather,' she said. 'Don't you remember me?'

He looked puzzled. 'I'm not sure that I do, to be honest.'

She lost her nerve, and began to back down the path, getting briefly tangled in the gate. 'I'm sorry. Sorry to disturb you.'

The door closed on her, and she hurried across the road to her car. He didn't remember her. Of course he didn't. Why should he? She had been nothing to him.

She heard a shout as she was getting into the car. 'Heaven!'

Hesitating, she wondered if he was drunk, or perhaps a religious nut. 'Sorry. I must go.'

'No, no, it's Heaven.' He was almost running towards her.

She wished she hadn't come.

He seized the car door. 'Heaven. You're Heaven. Mo's daughter. You look just like her.'

'My name's Heather.' Then it came flooding back. She had been Heaven until she went to the Caldecott, where they had called her by the name on her birth certificate. Mo had always called her Heaven. The memory of being Heaven, with its sweet, musty scent of joss sticks and joints, the meals she'd scavenged from discarded takeaway bags, the blows, the fear of almost everything, took her breath away. Heather was frozen to the ground.

'Come in,' he said, 'I always hoped you would come back.'

Heather followed him inside on trembling legs, Travis at her side. The little house was dark, slightly cluttered and musty with the smell of books and cooked bacon. It had always been the smell of safety to her. And of shouting. She followed him into the back room, where the same two sofas, now sagging and covered with books, lined both walls. She had the impression of a life that had closed in on itself. There were photographs on the mantelpiece. One was of her, in her school uniform.

'Would you like a cup of tea?'

'Oh, er, if it's not too much trouble.'

He gestured to her to sit down, picking up some books and magazines to clear a space on the sofa. Around her, the memories crowded in. The old clock on the mantelpiece: Gerald had been keen on doing things on time, and Mo had not. 'It's six o'clock,' he'd shout, 'we always have our tea at six o'clock!' and there would be the smell of herrings, or mince or stew calling her from her homework. Gerald had been keen on homework too, whereas Mo could never see the point of it.

He brought the tea in, on a tin tray, with a plate of biscuits. 'Would you like a shortbread?'

She shook her head, her mouth dry with fear. 'I came because . . . well, I wondered if you could tell me about my mother. Why we were here, and why . . .' She swallowed. 'Why you sent me away.'

He stirred the sugar into his tea and settled himself down. 'It's wonderful to see you. I hoped you'd come back.'

Heather laid a hand on Travis, for reassurance. 'I never knew.'

'Well, I didn't dare come after you. But I can tell you what I know. Or think I know. Your mother – she was lovely, but she wasn't always . . . truthful, you see.

'I've been a teacher all my life, and in my spare time I used to volunteer at a centre for homeless people. Your mother came in with a scruffy, frightened little eight-year-old in tow. She'd been living in one commune after the other – these weren't places based on peace and love, but communities usually heavily dominated by one strong man, who used the women, made the rules and often dealt in drugs. They were dangerous places, and your mother had pretty much been handed from man to man since she'd run away from her foster home at fourteen. She was fifteen when she had you, and only twenty-three when she arrived at our centre. She was very frightened, but determined to make a better life for her little girl.'

'Me.' Heather took in the room, which seemed darker and smaller than it had in her memory, but there were the same Victorian paintings of the sea on the walls.

'As you can see . . .' He spread his arms wide, 'I'm not exactly a dreamboat, I never was. Other men got the girls, I always got their shoulders to cry on. So when Mo told me she'd fallen in love with me, I fell for her. I wanted to rescue her. And you. For us to be a family.

'But the drugs and the drink got in the way. She'd manage a few months clean, and then she'd sneak out of the house with some money she'd taken from me and score. Or she'd go shopping and just buy cheap cider instead of food. I started to do all the shopping myself, so that she didn't have access to money, but sometimes she took things and sold them. She stole my cheque-book and forged my cheques, then she'd apologise and promise never, ever to do it again.

'And there was you. I watched you go to school in a nice, new uniform and lose that hungry look. I loved it when you asked me to help with your homework, or when we went along the beach for an ice cream. I could pretend you were mine.

'But you weren't. And your mother wasn't much more than a child herself, a very, very damaged one. She used to hit you. I tried to persuade her that it wasn't the way to behave, but she honestly seemed to believe that it was normal. It was all that she knew.

'And one day we had yet another terrible argument about it all, and I said that I would call the Social Services if I had to, to protect you, and she said that if I did, she'd tell them I was a nonce. That I was sexually abusing you.'

Heather paled.

'I was a teacher, I taught English at a boy's school. And I've always done voluntary work. Just one allegation, even made by someone like her, could have wrecked my career. And my life. So we staggered on for a few more weeks, while I tried to work out what to do.

'Then I contacted a friend of mine who was a social worker, and he knew about the Caldecott Foundation, and even Mo thought it had to be safer for you than a string of stepdads. The teachers at your school agreed, because you swung from being quiet and introverted, like a little mouse, to wildly disruptive.

'Your mum went with you to the Caldecott house at Mersham-le-Hatch, then came back and cleaned me out. She was gone when I got back from school. And so was anything of any value: the silver candlesticks I'd been left by my grandmother, my chequebook, my passport even, a few other things.'

'I'm so sorry,' gasped Heather.

'It doesn't matter,' he said. 'They're only possessions. Mo had always said that she had had a terrible, terrible childhood, and she wanted something better for you, and I think she thought she'd finally found it. The men she left, before me, she left them because she thought they might be turning their attention towards you.'

'I don't remember that.' But she did, an unbuckled belt and a giant belly hanging over it, and her mother screaming abuse from the door. She remembered, more dimly, the man leaving her room, walking towards Mo, and the sounds of shouts and blows from the next room. Mo had taken those blows for her.

Had that been one of the nights they'd run away, fleeing to the shelter and eventually this little house by the sea? It was so difficult to remember what had really happened.

'She told me that she'd managed to keep them away from you, and she also told me that she'd been raped at the age of eight. So, as I say, a very damaged child, but determined that you weren't going to turn out the same way.

'But I'm ashamed to say that I didn't dare go to the Caldecott and visit you. I was worried about the accusations that I thought she might have made to make sure you got in. I would never have hurt a hair on your head, but who would believe me? An eccentric single man in his thirties, taking a woman and child in? It looks suspicious, doesn't it?' His face was filled with regret. 'I had asked her to marry me, so that I could adopt you legally.'

'Why didn't she?'

He shrugged. 'She didn't trust men. She didn't want any man to have legal power over you.'

'Do you know anything about who my father could have been?'

He shook his head. 'She didn't know herself. But the only thing you need to know was that she really did try to be the best mother she could be. And she did love you very much. She was just a lost soul.'

He got up stiffly and went to the mantelpiece. 'Look. Do you remember this day?' He handed her a photograph.

It depicted a beach. Mo was laughing and glamorous in sunglasses and a bikini, a ten-year-old Heather had an ice cream and Gerald, in a striped deckchair, squinted into the sun with a panama hat on his head.

'That was us,' he said. 'When we were happy.'

She studied the picture before handing it back, feeling something tight unravel inside her. She did belong. She was wanted.

'When Mo wasn't drinking or using,' Gerald said, 'she was

lovely. She gave me the most fun and the most love I've ever had from a woman. Even though I knew she was only doing it for you.' He took out a handkerchief and wiped his eyes.

Heather waited.

'Don't mind me,' he said, eventually. 'I'm just a silly old man. Tell me about you, what you have been doing?'

And Heather told him. Everything. About Jack and Molly and Daisy. About Sasha and Travis. About her sisters-in-law whose marriages were also breaking up, 'and they've been the closest I've had to a family since you.' Three hours later she was still there, talking.

'Well,' he said. 'There's one thing I could help with. If you want me to. I could take the dog whenever you're too busy.'

Travis settled his head on his paws with a grunt of satisfaction as Gerald scratched his ear.

'We could be two old men together.'

Chapter 61

October drizzled into November, followed by the tinsel of Christmas. In her office, Olivia was offered a mid-morning mince pie by her assistant, Cat, and realised that it had become something of a habit. The one good thing that had come out of the miscarriage was that the nausea had disappeared a few days later, leaving her hungrier than she'd ever been in her life. She'd got thinner while she'd been pregnant, but ever since then she couldn't stop eating. As she crumbled the mince pie over her papers, revelling in the sugar hit, she couldn't help another long, deep sigh of regret for what had been wrenched out of her. Perhaps she was getting like Kate, comfort eating when things went wrong. Life seemed very flat without Si. She often lifted her head from the newspaper to speak to him, and the fresh realisation that he wasn't there was like a punch to the heart. They had always planned everything together, sometimes months ahead, with their diaries or organisers side by side. Now there didn't seem to be any point.

'Are you OK?' asked Cat.

'I'm fine. Perfectly fine.' Olivia's eyes filled with tears, but she finished every last crumb, and looked around for something else to nibble. Her clothes were even beginning to feel tight. She was now, for the first time in her life, beginning to have to worry about her weight. But she had always gone to the gym with Si. Or swum with him. It was part of the pattern of their life together and without him she was too tired for exercise at the end of the day.

379

There was a box of chocolates in her top drawer, given to her by a grateful client. Olivia quietly snuck one into her mouth when Cat wasn't looking.

'It's Si on line one.'

Olivia's hand hovered over the phone. She didn't really want to talk to him. But she could tell from the expression on Cat's face that she ought to. 'Si, hello.'

He wanted to meet to discuss getting some of his pictures back.

'Just go along to the flat any time,' she said. 'You've still got the keys.'

'Aren't you worried that I might take something you wanted to keep?'

'Not in the slightest. You're scarcely likely to be interested in my collection of handbags, are you? Or should I be concerned about whether you'll be slashing one of my twelve black jackets or if my thirty-seven pairs of black trousers will all be in ribbons when I get back?'

Si laughed. He actually laughed. He was clearly enjoying life as a bachelor. They agreed on a date for him to take his art collection from the flat.

She almost hoped he would take something he wasn't entitled to, just so she could hate him, but when she got home, the squares on the wall exactly corresponded to the pictures he'd asked for. Perhaps it would all hurt less if she saw him and reminded herself how pompous he could be.

Their lives continued to unravel slowly. She would keep Providence Cottage and the flat, but he would get a payoff. She wasn't going to make any claim on his pension or he on hers. There was, of course, no child maintenance or alimony to bicker about. It was all hideously easy, just like tearing an envelope in half before you threw it away.

'Let's have dinner together,' he suggested. 'To celebrate our financial agreement in a civilised way.'

She shuddered. 'I don't think so, Si. I think that's rather a grisly suggestion.'

Once he came to the office, to give her his set of keys for the flat, and rang from reception to ask if she'd like to come down for a coffee. She was almost tempted, but couldn't face it. 'Cat, tell him thanks, but I'm just going into a meeting – could he leave the keys downstairs?'

Cat's eyebrows rose at this. 'Are you ever going to set eyes on your ex-husband again?'

'Not if I can help it,' grimaced Olivia. It hurt too much.

But eventually, with great reluctance, she agreed to have a Christmas drink with him. It was the last thing she wanted to do, she was so busy at work, and she knew she was looking terrible: fat for the first time in her life, pallid and moon-faced, and her hair needed cutting. She was tired, too, and would rather have gone home to bed. She arrived late at a bar she'd chosen for its subdued lighting and sat down hastily.

Not before he'd given her the quick once-over. He stood up to kiss her on the cheek, and poured her a glass of champagne. She sipped it, but asked for a sparkling mineral water too.

'So where are you spending Christmas?' she asked, although she knew, from Kate.

'I'm going skiing. With a group of people I've met. Most of us are single. Newly single.'

'What fun.' The thought of it repelled Olivia, but she could see that she would have to start doing something similar.

'I gather you're going up to Scotland with Kate and Jonny?'

She nodded. 'It's rather an odd thing to do, I suppose, to spend Christmas with one's ex-sister-in-law's sister-in-law.'

'Are Kate and Jack talking to each other yet, do you think? I had him on the phone after the Travis episode, furious with her.'

'What did you say?'

'I'm staying out of it. Kate and Jack used to have terrible scraps when they were kids, and it was usually just best to leave them to it. Apparently Kate was accusing Sasha of mistreating Travis, lying and not answering her calls.'

'With some justification, as far as I could gather.'

Si shrugged. 'Jack feels that Sasha's been cast as the Evil Other Woman, and that Kate has taken sides with Heather. I think he's quite hurt about it.'

'Well, she isn't taking sides over us. She invites me to dinner, and I say yes. And I know you go there, too.' Olivia paused. 'I do say that I don't think we're quite ready yet to be in the same room at the same time, publicly.'

'That's fine by me,' said Si, sharply. 'And Christmas is OK, too.'

'I think it's been a bit of a tussle between Virginia and Kate,' said Olivia, with her first smile of the evening, 'with Kate saying she had to be in London because of all the family split-ups and Virginia saying "bring everyone, the more the merrier". Heather's coming too, because she's got the girls and Kate doesn't think she should be on her own. Apparently Virginia's got ten bedrooms.'

'She sounds a bit like Kate, only on a larger scale.'

Olivia shuddered. 'Don't ever say that to Kate, she doesn't seem to like her much. I think she's only going because Jack accused her of being unfriendly in the argument over the Travis incident, and now Kate's going around with a hair shirt on wailing that she's never been nice enough to Virginia and she ought to give her a chance.'

Si laughed. 'They always say that men marry their mothers, but I suspect that in Jonny's case, it's the sister. I look forward to hearing who wins over Christmas.'

'What about you and me,' she asked, before she could stop herself. 'I'm not a bit like Kate or Ella, am I? Perhaps that's why we didn't work out.'

'No, you weren't like anyone,' he said. 'You were just my soulmate.'

'Until I screwed it up,' she said to her glass.

'It wasn't just you.' He put a hand on hers.

'Why? Were you unfaithful too?' She slid her hand away. 'And what's the point in going over it?'

'The point, Olivia, is that I gather from Kate that you are blaming yourself entirely for the collapse of our marriage.'

'Well, I am to blame.'

'Not entirely. I think we'd grown apart. I spent too much time on my laptop and not enough on you. And I know I reacted to not getting the top job at R&R like a spoiled toddler.'

'I don't blame you.' Olivia was suddenly exhausted. She wanted to go to sleep. This was all about Si's pride again. He couldn't bear to think that his wife had been unfaithful. He had to persuade them all that he was the one at fault. 'So,' she said. 'Carry on.'

'I lent Sasha some money. Ten thousand pounds. She needed smart clothes . . .' He raised his hands, 'and things. She said that Jack was giving every penny he had to Heather, and that she needed to look smart for TV.'

Olivia frowned. 'He's given Heather barely enough to live on, while he and Sasha have jetted around the world on expensive holidays. So when did this happen? And in what circumstances?'

'When we were all down at Providence Cottage.'

Olivia remembered that weekend, and the way she had sneaked off to be with Blake. 'And?' she added, coldly, although she knew she had no right to be angry.

Si looked uneasy. 'She was following me round, pressing herself to me, and I kept thinking Jack was going to find us . . .'

'You mean she was chasing you?' Olivia was incredulous.

'Well, yes, that's what it felt like. I have to admit, I'd flirted with her a bit, but I never thought she'd take it seriously. It was like being chased by candyfloss, all rather sweet and sticky and very difficult to beat off. I kept thinking Jack was going to come in. It was terrifying. '

Olivia laughed.

'Olivia,' he snapped. 'I was actually in quite a difficult situation. My own wife was nowhere to be seen, and my relationship with my brother was already very dodgy. As soon as she hinted at a loan, I jumped at it. Wrote her out a cheque there and then, and then tried to keep myself locked in my room.' He paused. 'And she was making innuendos about you and Blake, too, and I remembered how she'd sold Jack's story to the press. You'd just had this amazing success with Allison Green, and I thought she was quite capable of selling that to the gossip columns too. So I 'lent' her the money on the promise that I'd never see anything about my wife in the papers.'

'That must have been a tricky conversation.' Olivia looked at him with respect. 'So you knew about Blake from then on?'

He nodded.

'I'm sorry,' she said. 'From the bottom of my heart.'

There was an uneasy silence between them. 'Ten thousand pounds buys an awful lot of things,' she added. 'Did she pay you back?'

He grinned ruefully. ''Fraid not. And not likely to either, as far as I can see. But I don't think we should tell the rest of the family.'

Olivia was nonplussed. 'I've never known you give anyone ten thousand pounds before.'

'No.' He drained his drink and stood up. 'I think we've finished here. By the way, did you ever go and see a doctor after your miscarriage?'

She shook her head. She did not want to discuss it. It was too raw. 'No point. I feel fine. Just tired.' She got up herself, and pulled her coat on.

'Well, I think you should go now.'

'I don't see why I should, I . . .'

'Olivia.' His eyes were dark with regret. 'Have you seen yourself in a mirror recently?'

She was surprised. 'I'm a bit fat,' she said, her heart thudding furiously. 'I eat too many mince pies.'

He put a hand gently on her stomach. 'That is rather too large and tight a bulge to be a mince pie.'

She involuntarily held his hand there for a second, and suddenly felt a stirring as her eyes met his. 'No,' she whispered. 'I'm not going to hope again. I daren't.'

She felt another movement under Si's hand, just before he pulled away. 'I don't think we're talking about hope, are we? We're talking about being absolutely bloody certain.' His smile was crooked, full of tenderness and regret. 'Sometimes a miscarriage leaves a baby behind.' He kissed her on the cheek and left. 'Just check it out.'

But as soon as he'd spoken Olivia had known he was right. She put a hand on her tight waistband again and felt the hard, round dome. And, once again, she could feel something stirring.

Chapter 62

Angus and Virginia lived near Inverness in a house called Glenwallace. It was not beautiful – it had been built in the days when Georgian meant 'very plain indeed' and was known in the family as The Bunker. But its industrial-strength furnace was easily equal to the cutting north winds, and Virginia was an excellent cook, having cooked city lunches for high-powered businessmen before she'd married Angus.

Glenwallace took almost all day to reach, with a flight to Edinburgh, and then a terrifyingly fragile small plane further north. The plane vibrated furiously for all forty minutes of the journey and Kate expected them all – she and Jonny, the boys, Heather and the girls and Olivia – to drop out of the sky at any moment. She could see the news reports now. 'A family of eight were among the dead when a small passenger plane crashed into the sea . . .'

But they arrived, and Angus was there to greet them, his big open face smiling, and his reddish-grey curls almost ripped off his head by the wind. 'It's so great to see you,' he said, wrapping Kate, then Olivia and Heather in bear hugs, and shaking hands with Luke and Callum. He and Jonny banged each other hard on the back and shook hands, and he ruffled the girls' hair.

The Land Rover bounced over mile after mile of heather and gently rolling hills. After half an hour Kate felt slightly sick. Land Rovers always got her that way. But they were almost there, turning in past the pretty Gothic gatehouse – now a holiday let – and down the long twisty, rhododendron-lined drive that led to Glenwallace.

'The rhodies were fabulous this year,' said Angus. 'You should come up in spring because the drive is just ablaze with pink and red.'

At the house, Virginia was waiting with Archie, Donal and eleven-year-old Caitlin, whose red curls streamed out behind her as she raced down the drive alongside the car. Archie, just a few months older than Callum, was now tall and also ginger-haired, like his father. Bertie, two years older, had something of Jonny's blond good looks. Callum brightened.

'We've built a tree house overlooking the burn,' announced Archie.

'A tree house?' echoed Callum, looking disdainful.

'It's more like a tree palace,' said Virginia. 'No mothers allowed.'

'Definitely no mothers allowed. Come and see.'

'I think they drink beer in there,' said Virginia, as Luke and Callum followed their cousins towards the river that ran at the bottom of the Glenwallace gardens. 'I hope that's all right. But it was quite good that they built it themselves, don't you think?' Virginia had always been the most strictly controlling of mothers. She seemed to have let go a bit.

One of Angus's businesses was selling Christmas trees to West End stores, so there was a twenty-foot Christmas tree at the foot of the big staircase battling it out with gigantic portraits of Angus's ancestors, one of whom had been an ancient Scottish warlord of almost mythical reputation.

'Reminds me of the Caldecott,' whispered Heather, looking up at the high, ornate ceilings. Kate giggled. Heather was slowly opening up. Still apologetic, and still, she admitted, cleaning things that didn't need it, but she now had glimmers of confidence.

They were all dispatched to bedrooms with names like 'Rose', 'Yellow' and 'Bluebell', decorated appropriately to their names by Angus's mother thirty years earlier. 'But we've had a round of new mattresses on the beds,' said Virginia smugly, thereby depriving Kate of anything to grumble about. 'We've got the neighbours coming for supper, Jonny, do you remember Rory and Lorna Macdougall? Old man Macdougall died in February so Rory's come back to run things, and they've got Lorna's sister and her new husband with her. They're all frightfully nice. Rory will be so pleased to see you again.'

Virginia was in the habit of referring to people who lived five miles away as 'the neighbours' because their land bordered on to Angus's. The real neighbours, a string of stone cottages, a pub and a post office a few hundred yards along the road past the gatehouse, didn't seem to count. People were always 'frightfully nice' or 'a bit of a bore'. Kate dreaded to think which category she fitted into.

'So,' trilled Virginia. 'Drinks in the drawing room in half an hour.'

As Kate threw herself on the bed, and found it firm but comfortable, fingering the 400-thread-count cotton sheets and lambswool tartan throw, she had to admit defeat. She looked up and met Jonny's eye. He grinned.

'Fucking perfect, isn't it?'

She giggled back. 'What do you think about Olivia, though?'

'I'm glad for her,' said Jonny. 'She's wanted this for a long time. But it'll be tough on her own.'

'Luckily she can afford it. It can't be Si's, though, can it? Or they'd be back together?'

Jonny hesitated. 'Probably not.'

'Did you like Blake?'

'No, I didn't. I thought he was a chancer. And I don't understand why Olivia fell for him.'

'She was lonely. Si was so tied up with work, and she got involved in Providence Cottage. It was exactly as she said, remember, at that lunch party. They were living separate lives.'

She thought Jonny was about to say something, but he didn't.

'Let's go and be frightfully nice to Rory and Lorna,' said Kate, getting up. It was all getting a bit close to home.

Jonny was waylaid by Angus, who wanted to show off a new project, so Kate entered the drawing room alone. It was of generous proportions, with full-length windows on two sides, big squashy sofas covered in floral fabric, and a huge piano covered in photographs in silver frames. The big stone baronial fireplace jutted out into the room and was blazing with logs. Two dark-haired women, unmistakeably sisters, one pregnant, were perched on the sofas.

'Lorna, this is Kate, my . . . er . . . Jonny's . . . er . . .'

'Partner,' said Kate firmly, extending her hand towards Lorna. She didn't see why Virginia always had to make such a meal of it. 'These are my sisters-in-law, Olivia and Heather.'

'Kate's brothers' marriages have both broken up,' added Virginia helpfully.

Nobody knew quite what to say to that.

'This is my sister, Natalie,' said Lorna.

Natalie and Olivia bonded over the size of their bumps, and Olivia, excited, explained that she had only really found out a few days ago: 'I'm terrified. Overwhelmed. It's amazing. I thought I'd had my last chance, and then I found out I was five months pregnant. It's the most wonderful Christmas present I could ever have.'

Seeing Heather smile too, Kate finally relaxed. They all settled down on the sofas, and Virginia passed a dish of olives round. 'I don't know where the men are, I think Angus might be showing off the new billiard room.' She turned to Kate. 'We turned the old housekeeper's sitting room into a billiard room, we thought it might be more fun.'

'Oh, yes, definitely.' Kate usually loved talking about decorating but didn't feel qualified to discuss the conversion of housekeepers' sitting rooms into billiard rooms. She tried to think of another topic of conversation and settled on the failsafe one of pregnancy. 'So is this your first?' she asked Natalie.

'My second,' smiled Natalie. 'And my husband has two from his first marriage, who are with us this Christmas because their mother's working in Thailand.'

'Oh? Is she an aid worker or something?' Kate wondered if she could make a radio programme on women who were charitable in other countries while leaving their children at home.

'No, she's in TV.'

Lorna spluttered. 'Aid worker, that's a good one. I can't see Sasha on a mission of mercy. The only person she's keen on helping is herself.'

Kate nearly dropped her glass. 'You're not Natalie? Of Natalie and Adam Taylor?'

As Natalie nodded, Kate added. 'I'm Kate. Jack's sister.'

'I'm Heather,' whispered Heather. 'Jack's ex-wife.'

Natalie paled. 'Jack as in Sasha and Jack?'

Olivia looked alert.

Kate nodded. 'But Sasha isn't *working* in Thailand. Not as far as I know, and she works for Jonny, so I think he would know. She's on holiday with Jack. Because, apparently, Adam insisted on having the children, even though it's not his turn?'

Natalie looked confused. 'No he didn't, of course not.' Her face closed down.

Lorna put a hand on her sister's shoulder. 'I'm sorry, Kate, but Sasha has caused Natalie so much grief she nearly lost her first baby. I don't want her upset. . .'

'Grief?' repeated Kate.

'I'll give her fucking grief,' said Heather, then caught Kate's eye.

Lorna clasped Natalie's hand. 'Nat, darling, you mustn't get upset . . .'

'Upset?' Natalie's eyes looked up, eyes shining. 'I want to hear every word. Tell me about Jack. Sasha says he's fantastically demanding, she's always changing our times for having the children because of something he insists on.'

Kate shook her head. 'She's got Jack wrapped around her little finger. She tells *us* that it's Adam who keeps threatening to take her back to court if she doesn't stick to the access agreement to the letter.'

'Adam couldn't possibly afford to take her to court again. She was the one who asked for a divorce you know, because she was having an affair with Grace's consultant at the hospital, and it seems that he'd agreed to leave his wife. But at the last minute they reconciled, leaving Sasha up in the air because Adam had already moved out and met me. She demanded that he come back, then when he said he wouldn't, she point-blank refused to move out of the house. It was their only asset, he couldn't afford to walk away from it, and he just wanted what was fair. He paid her two-thirds of what was left when the mortgage was paid off, then he paid the legal fees and there was hardly anything left after that . . .'

'Nat, darling . . .' urged Lorna. 'Please don't go over all this, it really isn't good for your blood pressure.'

'It's very good for *my* blood pressure,' said Kate. 'I've been thinking I was mad all this time, everyone seems to think Sasha's so bloody wonderful . . .'

'And mine,' added Heather.

'I'm just fascinated,' said Olivia. 'Keep going.'

Natalie squeezed her sister's hand. 'I'm OK to carry on. Sasha said that Adam was having an affair with me all along because we worked for the same company, but we hadn't, I promise. We were friends, but I never thought of him like that until she chucked him out.'

'Doesn't she work for Jonny now?' asked Virginia. 'What does he think of her?'

Kate shrugged. 'As far as I know, he thinks she's great. He won't discuss it.'

'Typical bloody Jonny,' said Virginia. 'Never interested in anything except his work. He's always been like that. On another planet.'

Kate told them how she had met Jasper Morton, and about the way that Sasha had been rejected by her father – and how she had taken her revenge.

Heather added the story of Travis's rescue. 'And now Jack isn't speaking to Kate.'

'And I probably shouldn't say this,' ventured Olivia, 'but she chased Si all round Providence Cottage the weekend we were all down there, and he lent her ten thousand pounds to make her go away.'

Everybody laughed.

Virginia looked at her watch. 'The potatoes must be boiling dry. Never mind, I don't want to miss a bit of this.'

'She's a desperately damaged person,' said Heather. 'And believe me, it takes one to know one.'

Kate could see the others looking interested, but not daring to ask any more. 'Jack's now completely cut off from his family,' she said. 'We never see him. And yet I saw Sasha having what can only be described as an intimate lunch with yet another man. Should I try to find out more and warn him?'

'No,' said Virginia, Lorna and Natalie simultaneously.

'Absolutely not,' added Olivia.

'I mean,' said Heather, 'I think we were right to rescue Travis,

390

although I can see that some people might think it was a bit over the top. But Jack's an adult, he has to make his own mistakes. He's not vulnerable in the way a child or an animal is.' She raised her head. 'And, anyway, it would serve him right.'

They all looked at her. 'I don't hate him any more, for going off with her like that,' she added. 'But I still feel very angry.'

'I simply must get those potatoes,' said Virginia. 'Don't say anything interesting until I get back.'

'Here's my telephone number,' said Heather, scribbling on a piece of paper she'd taken out of her bag, and handing it to Natalie. 'If she gives you any trouble over children and access, call me. I won't be taking any more nonsense from Jack or Sasha in future, but if there's a genuine clash, I'll always help out. I think Sasha will find it a lot harder to do her smoke and mirrors thing with us both talking to each other.'

Natalie took it, and left the room with her sister, to look for Adam so that she could warn him.

'Right,' said Olivia. 'Has everyone got my mobile number too? I think we should stick together from now on.'

They all checked their phones. 'We can be the Sisters-in-law Club,' joked Kate.

'Can I join?' asked Virginia, sounding surprisingly nervous.

'Of course,' replied Kate. 'You are definitely a sister-in-law.'

Virginia gave everyone her number. 'What fun. I can keep an eye out if she starts to operate in Scotland.'

'It's a deal.' Kate raised her glass. 'To the Sisters-in-law Club.' They touched their glasses together, and Heather's eyes filled with tears.

After dinner they pushed back the sofas, turned on the music and finished the evening with Scottish reels. Kate found she remembered them better than usual, and Jonny relaxed for the first time in months, laughing, his eyes alight and his strong arms propelling her in the right direction whenever she got confused.

Kate wished he looked as happy at 19 Lovelace Road.

The following morning Kate woke up early and went downstairs to get a cup of tea, to find Virginia in the kitchen up to her elbows in a gigantic turkey.

'What can I do to help?'

391

'Don't you worry. Have a cup of tea.'

One of the irritating things about Virginia was her determination to help in other people's houses without letting others help in her own. Kate decided to do what Virginia did to her, and picked up a potato peeler. 'Small potatoes or big?'

'Really, don't worry.'

'Medium-sized, in that case.'

Kate worked her way through a mound of potatoes.

'Thanks,' said Virginia after she'd manhandled stuffing into the turkey. 'Peeling potatoes is really my least favourite job. Along with whipping cream, for some reason. It's not difficult because I've got an electric beater, but it just irritates me.'

'I don't mind it, so line it up for me.'

Virginia placed three pots of cream and a bowl on the table. 'Jonny seems quiet.'

'He's working hard.' Kate felt defensive. Virginia always had to criticise. 'Just while we get this next series off the ground.'

'Until last night's reeling, when he warmed up a bit, I thought he'd rather gone back to what he was like when he was little.' Virginia sewed up the turkey, to Kate's amazement. She'd never sewed up anything she'd cooked in her life. 'Jonny always saw everything through the lens of a camera. He used to make little films with our father's Super 8. He locked himself away for hours. Never did anything that our father thought he should do, like fishing or stalking or playing ball games. It was such a relief when he met you. He lightened up a bit for the first time, stopped being so introverted.'

'Did he?' Kate was astonished. She had never thought of Jonny being introverted, because they'd always had so much to say to each other. And his great big smile – the one he hid behind – wasn't introverted. Or was it?

Virginia looked at her vaguely. 'Oh, you've been frightfully good for him. Dragged him into the real world.'

Kate hoped that was a compliment.

'All that brooding Heathcliff thing is obviously very attractive in a young man,' continued Virginia, 'but it must be frightfully difficult to live with. All the girls round here were throwing themselves at him, but he never noticed them. We were beginning to think he was gay.'

'Well, he isn't,' said Kate, hastily.

'Not that it would matter if he was. If you don't mind me asking, why have you never married?'

Kate did mind. 'We can't afford it,' she said, deciding that being honest was probably the best way of shutting the conversation down.

Virginia laughed. 'God, that's so like Jonny. If he does something he always wants to do it properly. He wouldn't dream of getting married unless he's researched it thoroughly and worked out exactly what it would look like through the lens of a camera.'

Kate was surprised. She thought she was the one who was like that, and that Jonny simply didn't care. She decided to risk a question. 'Virginia, my mother, just before she died, said "talk to Virginia". What do you think she meant? Did she tell you something I ought to know?'

Virginia looked pleased. 'How sweet. Your mother was lovely. But I'm not sure I know what she was referring to. We chatted about Jonny generally, and she said she thought it was so important to know where someone had come from.'

'She was a bit of a snob,' admitted Kate.

'Not like that. I think she just meant that if you know someone's family and background, you understand them a bit better.'

Did she now? Thanks, Mumma.

'I told her that Jonny won't talk about anything that really matters to him. I think the only way you'd ever get him up the aisle is to propose to him. Then organise everything else yourself.'

Kate was sick of organising everything herself. 'I have proposed to him, and we decided to buy a new car instead.' She turned the electric whisk on loudly.

The door opened and Luke came in. 'Can we open our stockings on yours and Dad's bed? Please? Please, please? Now?'

Kate smiled. 'Of course.' She turned to Virginia. 'Do you mind? I'll be down in about half an hour if there's anything else that needs doing.'

Virginia looked at her immaculately organised kitchen, with its piles of peeled vegetables and pots of cream and brandy butter on standby in the larder. 'Really,' she said. 'There's nothing left to do.'

Chapter 63

While Olivia was lying on her four-poster bed at Glenwallace, looking at the faded yellow rose wallpaper and finally daring to believe that she might, one day, be a mother, she texted Si to say that he had been right about the baby, and got a single line, sent from his BlackBerry, probably at the top of a ski slope or in some smart mountain bar. 'Congratulations. S.'

She also sent one to Blake, saying that if he wished to exercise his rights as a father, then she would, of course, do everything necessary.

She got one back saying that fatherhood had never been his bag. This is a baby, she felt like screaming. A child who needs a father. She thought of Sasha, and her desperate need to prove herself.

The next few months slipped by in a scurry of hospital appointments – she was worryingly old for a first baby – rearranging her life, planning and letting her divorce inch slowly forward. From time to time Si suggested meeting up again, but she put him off. She didn't have the energy for it, and she didn't want to cry.

She received the decree nisi in the post in March, and Kate called. 'Heather and I thought we'd have a sisters-in-law reunion. Before you stop being one, that is.'

'Well, yes, but . . .'

'Well, I can do lunch any time, Monday, Tuesday, Wednesday,' said Kate.

'Oh, well . . . um . . . Tuesday, I suppose, although I'll have to be . . .'

'Tuesday,' said Kate.

Olivia wasn't sure she could face either of them. It would remind her of Si. It hurt, being without him, much, much more than she had ever expected. She avoided talking about the break-up, and never mentioned her affair. So far, she and Si had been model divorcees. No bitter texts or disastrous late-night emails. No bursts of frantic greed. No clawing at the possessions. So there wasn't even any need for any of those destructive disputes that so often derailed a divorce at the last minute, a hysterical claim for a pop-up toaster or a bicycle roof rack. She had been in this business a long time, and she still couldn't understand why people fought over things that could be quite easily bought again new. But they did, and she was determined not to. But she did it by not seeing him or talking to him unless it was absolutely necessary. They were both fragile, and she couldn't risk it. Kate had stayed in touch, with invitations to this and that, mostly refused because Olivia was busy and tired, and she didn't want to risk bumping into Si.

But if Kate wanted lunch, Olivia felt she owed her.

She was surprised to arrive at the table first. Kate was usually so punctual. She ordered a glass of water and studied the menu, before closing it with a snap. She was too busy for lunch, perhaps she should just leave some money and go. She could take Kate out to lunch another time, after the divorce. After all, she wasn't going to stop knowing Kate, just because of a decree absolute.

A shadow fell over her. 'Hi,' said Si. He cleared his voice. 'Is this a set-up?'

'Sort of. Do you mind if I sit down? Kate will be here soon.'

'OK. But you could have just asked to have lunch with me.'

'Which you would have refused. Again.'

Olivia shrugged. 'I've been busy. So how are you? And why have you grown a beard? You look . . . raffish.'

'It's not a beard as such, it's the kind of face you'd have if you'd been at sea for five days without shaving. It's my new image. I'm leaving R&R – did you hear? I've been approached by some venture capitalists to set up a luxury brand based on the sea rather than the country. It's a bit of a risk after my well-paid years at

R&R but at least I'll be MD for a few years before the whole thing collapses.'

'It won't collapse. You'll make a stunning success of it. Let me know when I can buy some shares. And the pirate look suits you.'

Si looked pleased. 'Thanks. So have you missed me?'

Olivia was startled, but she raised her chin. 'I have, actually, but I'm absolutely fine about it all.'

Si's eyes gleamed in pleasure. 'Good. There's something I have to tell you. Which you might not like.'

Olivia's heart stopped. This was it. The moment she'd been dreading. The day that Si found a serious girlfriend. She could just about stand not being married to him. She couldn't bear the thought of him being with someone else. She braced herself for it every time Kate phoned. Si would never allow himself to be on his own for long. 'Have you been seeing someone?'

He looked surprised. He obviously hadn't expected her to guess. 'Well, yes . . . I . . .'

Olivia arranged her face in a painful smile. 'So what's her name?'

'Er . . . Anna, but . . .'

'And she's nice, I take it?'

'Oh, very. But listen. I talked to Blake,' he said, suddenly.

'Oh.' Olivia hadn't contacted him again. If he wanted to be a father, he knew where she was.

'He said he wants a DNA test before he accepts that it's his.'

She felt her face flood with colour. 'That's ridiculous! And why did you—'

'I told him we'd already done a DNA test and that it was mine,' Si spoke in a rush. 'I couldn't help it, it was a spur-of-the-moment thing when I realised you hadn't told him about my not being able . . . well . . . he should be . . . well, anyway, I'm sorry. I wanted to give him something to think about. But I shouldn't have done it, and I thought I ought to own up.'

'Oh. Right.' She looked at him in amazement, and couldn't help laughing. 'Good. Well done you. What did he say?'

'Well, he looked pretty poleaxed. In fact, I'd really gone round to punch him in the face, but then I saw that socking great four-by-four of his and said, "Olivia always said the smarter the car the smaller the willy."'

Olivia, taking a sip of water, choked. 'You made that up! I like smart cars.'

He tried not to look too pleased with himself. 'And then I added that I'd only dropped by to let him know in case he was worrying about having to pay maintenance.' He looked at her out of the corner of his eye. 'And it was only on the way home that I thought perhaps you might want some money from him, after all, and I might have blown it for you.'

'I don't.' She smiled, feeling her face stretch in a way that had become totally unfamiliar, using muscles she'd forgotten she had. It was odd, laughing with Si again. It hurt. She stopped smiling.

'I thought so.' He fiddled with the knife and fork on the table. 'Does this baby need a father, by the way, or have you got someone? Because I thought, perhaps . . .'

'Perhaps . . .?'

'Sorry, I know it's ridiculous, but . . . maybe you and I . . . do you think . . .?'

'You and I? But what about the very nice Anna?'

'Olivia, I've met an awful lot of very, very nice women in the last few months. You have no idea how many. Anna is one of them. But I've told her.'

'Told her what?' Olivia didn't like the idea of quite so many nice women.

'That she isn't you, so it's no good.'

'But you've always said that you wouldn't want a baby that wasn't yours.'

'That was before I realised it meant losing you. Now you could have an entire villageful of babies if it would bring you back.'

'I don't want a villageful. Just one.'

He looked at her. Really looked at her. The old Si, the one who cared, who would put her before everything, was back. Olivia hardly dared look him straight in the eye. She was so ashamed. And not quite sure whether she could trust him. Would he descend into resentment once the baby was born? Would he look at her daughter every day and only see that she wasn't a Fox?

But that had never been Si's way. To give him his due. Onwards and upwards was his motto.

'If anyone could make this work,' she said. 'It would be you.'

He smiled. 'OK. So is it a deal?'

'A deal, Si? That is hardly romantic.' But she couldn't help laughing again.

'I know I'm not romantic enough. I know that was part of it. But that's just me. I do care. I do . . . love you very much. And all that sail in you.'

She placed a hand on her bump and was reassured to feel a stirring. 'I've missed you too. More than I thought I ever would.'

'Good.' He leant forward to kiss her, but as their lips touched Kate appeared, waving furiously, followed by Heather. 'So is it all all right? Was that a kiss I saw?'

'Well it *was* a kiss until you turned up. Push off, sis.'

But Kate plumped herself down, followed by a waiter with a bottle of champagne. 'I do love champagne and I hardly ever get any so it would be unfair not to share it. Sorry about the subterfuge, Olivia, but Si said you always either refused to meet or cancelled at the last minute, and we didn't think you'd cancel me and Heather. And if it had all gone horribly wrong we could have comforted whoever was left.' She knocked back a slug of champagne.

'As it is, we don't need comforting.' Si stood up and put a hand on the back of her chair. 'Off.'

'I think we should go,' said Heather, laughing. 'Can I just go to the loo? Then I'll prise Kate away and we'll have lunch somewhere else.'

'Just one glass, then.' Si poured one out for Kate, who sighed. 'What's up, sis?'

'I wish I was going to have a romantic lunch.'

'Why don't you?' suggested Olivia.

Kate looked at her hands. 'No point. It would be a waste of money. Jonny and I are good friends, but the sparkle has gone . . . you know. It happens.'

Olivia looked at Si, who took her hand. 'What makes you say that?'

'We function,' said Kate. 'But we don't live. He looks after the boys while I work. Then when he works I chase round picking the boys up and sorting out the house. We're like those couples on Swiss clocks. He goes out, I come in.' She straightened her shoulders. 'There's nothing wrong with it. Lots of people do that.'

Si and Olivia both frowned.

'Look at you two,' said Kate. 'You've both got identical expressions on your faces. But you needn't worry that we're going to split up, because I would never do that to the boys and nor would Jonny.'

'I didn't think for a moment you were going to split up,' said Si. 'I've always thought you two were right together.'

Kate got up as she saw Heather come back. 'That's what we all thought about Heather and Jack. Remember? And you and Olivia . . . oh well, who cares?'

She left Si and Olivia holding hands.

'This is what's been missing from my life since we split.' Olivia attempted a joke. 'Family drama.'

Si smiled and kissed her. 'Thank God you're back,' he murmured. 'I feel as if I've been carrying a stone around inside me ever since you went. But I don't like Kate's state of mind. She seems to have given up, and that's not like her.'

'I think she wants to leave him,' said Olivia. 'But she thinks she can't. So she's trapped.'

'Should we try to do something about it? Or could we?'

'Can we just spend some time together first? On our own?'

Chapter 64

Walking back home from lunch, Kate felt doubly lonely. Would she and Jonny – could she and Jonny – ever achieve that level of loyalty, forgiveness and love? He had been trying to talk to her about something, but the finality of his tone frightened her and she kept him away. She wasn't ready to be Heather, struggling on her own, or suffering.

He had tried to talk to her in Scotland, his face grave and his voice hesitant. It was the voice he usually used for bank statements. Bad bank statements. Virginia's determination not to allow anyone to help in the kitchen was often an impenetrable barrier, and the boys were happy with their cousins. Olivia spent most of the time asleep, and Heather was with the girls, doing sewing or craft projects.

Kate and Jonny talked about work as they tramped through the heather or along the side of the burn that ran through Angus's land.

'I thought there might be something in the twentieth-century figurative artists idea,' he said. 'Would you mind if I did a programme on it too?'

Kate thought it was a good idea, and sketched out the areas she thought needed looking into. When they stopped talking, it was dark. It was only four o'clock in the afternoon.

'Kate, there was something I wanted to discuss . . .'

Kate's heart shrivelled with fear. She wasn't ready for the Big Conversation yet. She would have it when she was ready to deal with all, or any, of its consequences. 'We're not lost, are we?' She shivered. She didn't know which way it was going to go.

Jonny looked up at the clear, starlit sky. 'No, the house is east of us.'

'You can navigate by the stars?' This was a side of Jonny she didn't know.

'Of course. We all could. There are no A–Zs up here.'

It took them three-quarters of an hour to find the house, but there it was, solid and forbidding against the stars. Inside there was whisky and the fires were blazing. Kate had a hot bath and a sense of wellbeing enfolded her.

It all seemed much easier up here, but like all holidays it was away from real life. She still, ultimately, had a decision to make, and she didn't want to talk to Jonny until she had decided.

The following day Jonny took his long walk with Callum, and then the next Luke.

'Dad's teaching us to navigate by the stars,' Luke reported back. 'Because it gets dark so early here. You should learn, Mum, then you won't get lost.'

And Kate felt very lost as she walked away from Si and Olivia, through Soho. Out of the corner of her eye she caught sight of two heads, close together, intent on conversation, through the glass of a restaurant window. It was Jonny. He was lunching with a woman, and he was intent on what she was saying. Kate couldn't see who she was, because Jonny and the woman were seated three tables back from the window.

Kate stopped. Then she turned on her heel and flung open the restaurant door. Jonny and the woman laughed. She could see, from his body language, that he was relaxed and engaged, listening to every word she said.

'A table, madam?' A waiter in a white shirt approached.

'No, no. I just thought I saw someone I knew.'

But she didn't know him, did she? When had Jonny last leant back, with the wide, lazy grin and told her, Kate, that he loved her? When had he ever told her?

She walked round and round, past the delicatessens, fabric shops, restaurants roaring with diners, and the last few remnants of the famous Soho sex trade, thinking. Now that she knew what real love was – she'd seen it in the faces of Olivia and Si – she couldn't just carry on, even if it cost her her home.

She passed the restaurant again. It had emptied out, but Jonny was still there, with the unknown woman.

She walked in again and batted off another query from the waiter. 'Jonny?'

He turned. 'Kate.'

The woman got up. 'I must go.' She kissed Jonny effusively on both cheeks.

'Work,' he said in brief explanation. 'Do you want a coffee?'

'Yes. I'll have a coffee. And I know she was work. I don't accuse you of infidelity every time you have lunch with a woman. But Jonny . . .'

'We need to talk.' His voice was dead. Very final.

She swallowed, and nodded. 'We do.'

They avoided each other's eye while Jonny signalled the waiter for more coffee.

'The boys need you,' she blurted out.

'Yes,' he said. 'But that's not everything, is it? We can't just be about the boys needing us, can we?'

She shook her head, numb.

'I'm sorry, I can't give you that wedding you've always dreamed of . . .'

She put a hand out to stop him going any further.

'No, let me finish,' he said. 'I've been putting this off for so long. You've pretended you haven't minded about getting married, you've always been too cool to let me see into your heart, but I know you've had dreams. I can tell – when we used to go to other people's weddings and you talk about it – the bridesmaids, the food, whether you have a theme or not, whether country or city is better, whether a stately home or a smart hotel, how you could make it different . . .'

'But the one thing we've never talked about is us,' she interrupted.

He nodded. 'Yes. We've never properly talked about us.' He drummed his fingers nervously on the table. 'There's a slot at Brixton Registry office a week on Saturday, and if we go back and

402

have lunch at home afterwards, Heather said she'd do the cooking, and Olivia and Si would bring the champagne, and I know it's not very romantic, but . . .'

Kate stared at him. 'A slot for what?' He didn't seem to be making any sense.

'Us. You and me. To get married. To stop being "um, er" and start being husband and wife.'

Kate froze.

'Kate? Say something. Even if it's no.'

'This seems very . . . sudden.'

Jonny tried to smile. 'You mean after nearly sixteen years together?'

'I wish I could believe,' she said softly, 'that a wedding ceremony could be like a sticking plaster over our problems. But it can't. The main issue is that you are passionately involved with your work, rather than with me. And I'm dying of loneliness out here.'

'Yes, I know.' He laid a hand on hers. 'And I'm sorry. But I've been thinking about that too. You and I are very alike. We really need our work. I didn't understand that until the night that Callum ran away. But you need to be with the boys too, and they need you. I can see how it's tearing you apart, and making you too tired.

'That woman you just saw is Paula Webber of Webber TV, a small indie that wants to get bigger. We were talking about a merger, and one of the things that would make it make sense is that we'd be able to hire. We both agree that we need a development manager, and you always have lots of ideas. You'd be great.'

'Me work for you?' Kate had visions of their domestic arguments writ large in the narrow Soho offices.

'Not for me directly. For the new merged company. Although you'd be able to get input from all or any of us, you'd be doing your own thing, and once a project got the go-ahead, it would be passed to one of the directors, maybe me, maybe not. Kate, believe it or not, I have tried to talk about this before, but every time I mention your career you clam up. So I thought I'd get it all set up, then you could decide whether to do it or not. But it would take work off me, too, which would mean more time for us to spend together as a family. And I think being part of a team, and working fairly regular hours would be good for you too.'

Kate nodded. 'It could work.'

'We'd probably only be able to pay a three-day-a-week role, but I think it would be good for you. And now both boys are going to school on the bus, you wouldn't be so tied to the school day.'

'I'd want to mix working in the office with work from home,' she said. 'I have to keep my own hours. Because of the boys.'

'Keep your own hours. We're only interested in results, not how you get them.'

'And what if I was no good? Suppose my projects don't go ahead?'

He smiled. 'Some of them will, some of them won't. You'll never know until you try, will you? I can promise to fire you if you don't bring home the bacon.'

Kate took a deep breath. 'I won't work with Sasha.'

He shrugged. 'So don't. We're tied to her for the *How To Be Rich And Famous* series, which is a good money-maker, but she's pretty tricksy on set and we won't be looking for another series with her when *HBRF* finally folds.' He looked at her intently. 'I thought that the best way to deal with Sasha was not to talk about her, and not to encourage you to either, but I think that might have been a bit of a mistake. All I want to say about her is that I never fancied her, never wanted her, never encouraged her.'

'Did she try?' asked Kate.

Jonny hesitated. 'It's difficult to say. Yes, probably. Look Kate, forget about Sasha once and for all. You're good at what you do. We could be good together.'

'So this isn't just you trying to make us work?'

'It is absolutely me trying to make us work. But I wouldn't suggest it unless I believed in it, and Paula Webber does too. She loves radio, and knows some of your programmes.'

'Everybody loves radio,' muttered Kate. She took a deep breath. 'Is this proposal linked to the marriage one?'

Jonny looked away. 'I'm offering you this job because I think you'll be good at it. If you don't want to get married, or even if you think we should split up, the job is still open.'

'Then I accept. If you can get the merged company together, I'll start on a six-month trial basis, and even if you don't, I

404

know . . .' She leant forward, suddenly excited. 'Maybe there's a programme in wives and husbands working together, we could take three couples, no, it would need six, and—'

'You haven't answered my other question yet. It kills me that I can't give you that one day you want so much.'

'I don't,' declared Kate. 'You make me sound as if I was some little girl with fantasies about being a Barbie bride, I—'

'No, of course you're not. But it is the most important day of a woman's life, and . . . well, anyway, what I wanted to know . . . or say . . . is . . .' He twisted his hands together.

'Jonny, why has this come up suddenly?'

'Because I love you,' he said. 'And I'm losing you. Ever since we decided to buy the car rather than spend Ella's money on getting married, you've been slipping away from me bit by bit. I thought that was what you wanted, to get the car instead, but Virginia talked to me and I think I've been a bit of a fool.'

Kate stared at him. 'Virginia?'

'Er, she said she'd do the catering, if we did get married. She and Heather talked about it.'

'You've all been talking about it, have you?'

'Kate!' he shouted. 'All I want is to stand up in front of the people I care about most and say, "This is the woman I love more than anybody else in the world." But it wouldn't be the wedding you'd always dreamed of.'

'No,' said Kate. 'It would be much, much better.'

Chapter 65

Kate spent the first three days of the following week looking for something to get married in that wouldn't cost too much and would make her feel fabulous, settling in the end for a three-quarter-length coat in black. 'I was always going to get down to a size ten for the wedding,' she wailed to Jonny, on Wednesday evening. 'Do you mind if I wear black?'

'I'm glad I didn't give you the chance. You'd have kept putting it off. All I ask is that you don't back out because you think you're wearing the wrong colour outfit.'

'But these are the pictures our grandchildren will see. The ones that will describe who we are.'

Jonny looked at the wall. 'If you don't like our wedding pictures, don't frame them. We'll have some taken that you do like.'

The phone rang. It was Molly, frightened and incoherent.

'Molly, try to calm down, I can't hear you.'

Molly's voice always rose very high when she was agitated, and it was almost impossible to make out her words. 'We're all alone here, down in Wiltshire, Daddy's away, and Sasha told me to be in charge, that I was a big girl now . . .'

'You are. You're thirteen and so is Grace. And Tom and Daisy are eleven. I think that's old enough to be left alone for an evening. Just lock all the doors and windows and . . .'

There was an incoherent screech from the other end of the line.

'What? Grace and Tom aren't there? Well . . .'

She couldn't quite make out Molly's reply. 'Overnight? That is a bit . . .'

More hysteria.

'Molly, can I speak to Daisy?'

'No, no, you can't, that's the point.' Molly took a deep breath. 'Sasha's gone forever. She's left Daddy. It took her two hours to pack. She got a small van. And then she and Tom and Grace went to the station in a taxi. And she told me to tell him. To tell Daddy she wasn't coming back. Daisy doesn't know.'

'Molly, you must have misunderstood.'

'No, I promise. I haven't. All her clothes are gone. And so are Tom and Grace. It's just us. And I don't know what to tell Mummy, I don't want to upset her. And I'm frightened here. When will someone come?'

'Someone will come this evening. In a few hours. Don't worry. We'll sort it out.'

'I don't want to have to tell Daddy that Sasha has left him,' said Molly, suddenly sounding very grown up. 'Please help me.'

'Of course I will. Do you know where Sasha's gone?'

'I heard her talking about getting into Paddington at about ten-thirty. She was talking to someone called Chris.'

Kate told Molly that she would sort it out, that she must not worry, and put the phone down.

'What?' asked Jonny.

'Sasha's left Jack. And she's left the house in Wiltshire. Molly and Daisy are on their own, and she's told Molly to tell her father that their marriage is over.'

'Are you sure Molly's got it right?'

Kate held out the phone. 'Call her.'

Jonny shook his head. 'I believe you.'

'I can't go haring down to Wiltshire again, it'll be the Travis episode all over again. But we can't leave Molly and Daisy there.'

'Ring Heather. She can go down and get her daughters. They need to be with her. I'll drive her if necessary.'

'Would you? But Heather can't tell Jack his marriage is finished, can she? That would be terrible.'

'No, somehow we've got to get Sasha to do that herself. Do we know where she's gone?'

'I think she's gone to Chris Koski's. Unless there are any other Chrises you can think of?'

'I've got his address,' said Jonny. 'Ring him.'

'I'm not ringing either of them. I'm fairly sure that Sasha got my calls the night Mumma died, and stopped Jack getting the messages by hiding his phone and switching off hers. If she thinks I'm on to her she'll close down and we'll never get through. I'm going to go there in person.' She looked at Jonny. 'You drive Heather down to get the girls. She needs someone with her. I'm going to see if Si will come with me instead.'

But Si was in Paris.

'This is one of those divorce classics.' Olivia sighed. 'People making their children tell their other half that Mummy or Daddy is leaving. It's right up there with all the other horror stories that all of us lawyers encounter at some point. But I'll come with you. I'll tell her I'm Jack's lawyer. I can frighten the socks off her.'

'But you're two weeks away from having a baby. And her socks don't frighten easily.'

'I'm still capable of a short trip across London in a taxi. Let's aim to get there at eleven-fifteen, to give her time to get there from the station.'

Kate agreed. 'Do you think,' she added to Jonny, as he disappeared out the door, 'that there's a six-part series in how people end their marriages?'

'No,' said Jonny. 'Are you going to turn into one of those TV executives who think there's a six-part series in every trip to the newsagent?'

They kissed, with a smile.

Even with Olivia by her side, Kate knew that Sasha could still make her look a fool, twisting words and reinterpreting actions. Dealing with her was like trying to fight a reflection in the mirror.

Chris Koski lived in a traditional terraced house, with a black-painted door and a brass lion knocker. There were lights on in the basement, the hall and at the top of the house. Kate pressed the buzzer, and rapped the door knocker at the same time. She heard conversation inside.

'I've never talked to Sasha about anything directly before,' she said. 'It was all just froth and compliments. If there was ever anything she wanted, Jack would ask us, not her. Perhaps we should just ring Jack, after all.'

'No,' said Olivia. 'We need to talk to Sasha.'

Kate knocked again, sounding, she hoped, officious.

Chris Koski opened it. He was a big bear of a man, with a pointed beard. 'Can I help you?'

'Is Sasha here?' Kate stepped into the hall, with the bulk of Olivia and her bump behind her.

'Well, yes, but . . .'

Sasha's head appeared from the basement stairs. 'Who is it? Oh, Kate . . . Olivia . . .?'

Kate indicated the room to the right. 'Shall we talk?'

'About?'

Kate folded her arms. 'Or we can talk standing here, if you prefer.'

'No, no, do come in.' Sasha visibly recovered herself. She wouldn't want Chris hearing any of this, Kate was prepared to bet. 'Chris darling would you get us all a little drinkie?'

'What's all this about?'

Sasha almost pushed him down the stairs. Kate thought she heard a whispered 'Poor thing, suffers from depression . . . needs help.'

Sasha switched on the sitting-room lights, and Olivia sat down, looking tired and heavy. It was an ultra-modern white room, probably done up by an interior designer. No sign of a wife. Nothing personal.

Sasha, Kate suspected, had found herself a house.

'I gather you've left Jack?'

Sasha folded her arms. 'It was a mutual decision.'

'One that Jack doesn't know about yet.'

Sasha's eyes flickered from left to right as the colour left her face. 'You really have no right to—'

'*You* really have no right to leave Molly, aged thirteen, alone in a house in the middle of nowhere, with her younger sister, asking her to tell her father that his marriage is over. Heather has gone to fetch the girls, by the way. They're too young to be left alone overnight.'

409

'I did no such thing! That child is a liar, I've had such trouble with her, you wouldn't believe . . .'

'No, I wouldn't believe.' Kate stood her ground. 'What I do believe is that you've had a very bad start in life, and you've been trying to make up for it ever since. We know your father never saw you, we've talked to your half-brother about how they paid you off, we've met Adam and Natalie and know the truth about the court cases and the affair you had, and we have no intention of telling anyone anything about any of it. Provided that you yourself talk to Jack about your relationship, and that if it's over, you tell him now.'

'You'd like that, wouldn't you? You've always hated me.'

'No, I haven't. I liked you when I first met you, and if you hadn't been so greedy I'd have gone on liking you.'

'Greedy?' Sasha let her eyes trail down Kate's figure. 'I think you would know more about that than I would.'

'Are you going to talk to him, Sasha, or am I going to sell the story of the real Sasha Morton to the papers? The way you sold Jack's story?'

Sasha's eyes widened imperceptibly. 'Don't be ridiculous. You know that you must have let something slip to one of your journalist friends. I do sympathise, it's very easy to do, especially if you are a gossip, like you are . . .'

'I am not interested in trading insults. Are you going to phone Jack now?'

'And Sasha?' Olivia spoke for the first time. 'We also know about the money you owe Si which you don't appear to be paying back. As for any more money from the Fox family, you earned more than Jack did in this very short marriage, so anything other than a straightforward agreement to take out of it only what you brought into it would probably mean you paying Jack off.'

'Don't be absurd.' Sasha was white, now. 'I have no intention of paying Jack a single penny.'

'You won't need to, as long as you don't go to court. If you are even remotely tempted to try to get any money out of Jack,' said Olivia, 'I shall act for him, for free, and will wipe the floor with you and your lawyers. Is that clear?'

Sasha raised her head up. 'You are both behaving in the most ridiculous fashion. Of course Jack and I will be having a very straightforward financial arrangement. There is no reason why we should argue over it. It won't be like you and Jonny, Kate,' she flashed. 'Jonny's having an affair, you know. He's about to leave you. You'll lose your house. Just like I did. He kissed me, you know, but we decided not to take it further.'

'He's about to marry me,' said Kate, suppressing a flicker of panic. Just about. 'And he's told me about you. Will you call Jack or shall I?'

'You call him,' said Sasha. 'You're the Queen of Fucking Everything. Telling your brother his marriage is over is right up your street.'

Was that how Jack saw her? Kate reeled in pain. But she was determined to stick to her guns. 'It must come from you, Sasha. Don't be such a coward.'

'Coward?' Sasha laughed, brittle and furious. 'Do you know how I destroy families like yours? It's because you're all too spineless to tell each other what you really think. It's all "how lovely to see you" even if you loathe someone's guts. I could tell you did, quite early on, but you went on inviting me round. Because you were too cowardly to tell Heather that her new friend wasn't welcome.'

Chris Koski came in with a bottle and glasses of wine and mineral water. 'Is everything all right, darling?'

'Absolutely fine, sweetest,' Sasha simpered up to him. 'Kate and Olivia are just leaving.'

'Not until you've spoken to Jack,' said Kate. 'And told him the truth.'

Chris raised an eyebrow and Sasha pushed him out of the room again, muttering: 'Family business.' Then she took out her phone and dialled. 'Jack, darling. Kate's here. She's insisted I tell you our marriage is over . . .' she began to sob, 'she's being horrible to me, she's saying terrible, terrible things, please help . . .'

Kate seized the phone. 'Jack, that's not true, all I asked is for Sasha to tell you where she was and why. She's in London, at Chris Koski's.'

'Kate, what have you done now?' shouted Jack. 'Of course she's at Chris Koski's, she's been staying there since your absurd behaviour over Travis. I can't have this ridiculous bullying and interference from you, Kate, you must get out of my life.'

'She's taken all her things away from Apple Tree Farm, and asked Molly to tell you your marriage is over.' Kate held the phone out to Sasha with a trembling hand. 'Sasha, perhaps you'd like to confirm the order of events? Unless you'd like us to go over everything again with Chris in the room this time?'

'I left a letter saying goodbye,' whispered Sasha into the phone. 'Molly must have hidden it. She's such a troublemaker, and she hates me. If it wasn't for your awful children, I wouldn't have left, I just couldn't cope with their behaviour . . . and I don't want to see you again. Any of you, ever again.' She clicked the phone off and burst into tears, running out of the room.

Chris came back in shortly afterwards, as Kate and Olivia were pulling on their coats. 'I'm sorry, I don't know what you've done to upset Sasha – I assume you've been sent to do your brother's dirty work as he hasn't got the decency to talk to her himself – but I'm going to have to ask you to leave.'

'I need to say goodbye to her personally,' said Kate, standing her ground one last time. 'To make sure she's all right.'

Chris shrugged. 'Darling?'

Sasha came out of the shadows, arms folded, her face white and her arms rimmed with red.

Olivia spoke: 'Sasha, be aware of the laws of slander. And of libel.'

'And that I can keep secrets,' said Kate, 'unless I think it's in my family's interests not to.'

Kate and Olivia left the house, as Sasha hurled herself into Chris's arms, murmuring that her ordeal was over, that if he could be very, very sensitive and never mention any of the Fox family again, they were all a bit mad, he didn't know how she had suffered . . .

Chapter 66

Kate and Jonny married in Brixton Registry Office. Callum was best man, and it gave Kate a shock to see that he had suddenly grown almost as tall as his father. He winked at her as he stood beside Jonny, and hugged her hard after the ceremony. Luke held her hand, something he had almost grown too old for. And Olivia and Si were there, with Virginia, Angus with the boys and Caitlin, and Heather, Molly and Daisy. They walked back – only fifteen minutes – to 19 Lovelace Road, where Virginia and Heather had catered for sixty friends and neighbours, and Si and Olivia had filled the bath with champagne bottles and ice. People jostled to get in, packed out the sitting room, flooded into the back kitchen extension, poured out into the garden, talked, laughed, ate and drank. Jonny smiled his big, lazy grin and held Kate's hand, and occasionally Luke came back and held the other one. Piles of presents mounted in corners everywhere.

'We did it,' said Jonny, kissing her. 'We finally did it.'

Kate kissed him back. 'I wish Jack had come, though. He thinks I wrecked his marriage.'

'I've told him you didn't. So have Olivia and Heather, I think. And Si, although he probably made it worse by shouting at Jack and telling him he was a fool. No, he knows she found Chris Koski all by herself.'

'Do you think they'll stick together?'

Jonny laughed. 'Highly unlikely. That man is a serial shagger. I'd say they deserve each other.'

'Jonny, were you ever tempted?' Kate thought of Sasha saying, 'We kissed but decided not to take it any further.' She knew that Jonny was always honest, and she had never felt strong enough to hear the true answer before.

He stroked her cheek. 'No,' he said.

She believed him. 'I've always wondered if Sasha saw a happy family,' she said, 'and couldn't resist tearing it apart, or whether the cracks had been there all along, just waiting for someone destructive – or damaged – to work her fingernails into them. But when I first saw the three of you – the three Fox men – and her, I had this image of her choosing one of you to run off with. But I told myself it could never happen . . .'

'And then it did,' interrupted Olivia.

'I'm not a Fox man.' Jonny wound an arm round Kate's shoulders.

'Oh yes you are. You're Mr Fox now,' joked Si.

'No, I'm Mrs Rafferty,' said Kate, surprising them all.

'Are there going to be any speeches?' asked Virginia. 'You can't have a wedding without speeches.'

Kate nearly told her you could have a wedding without anything, but remembered how delicious that last crab cake, brought down from Scotland with seventy others in a coolbag, had been. She didn't think Virginia was ever going to be a soulmate, but she was growing surprisingly fond of her.

'I haven't even thought about it,' said Jonny. 'What do you think, Kate?'

'Let's say something together,' she suggested. 'Just thank you for coming, nobody wants any tasteless jokes about your or my past.'

Heather wondered if Jack was staying away because of her.

Or maybe he couldn't face them all. The way Sasha had left him had been humiliating and Jack, in his own way, was as proud as Si. She had tried to call him, to get him to come, but hadn't managed to get through. Then she'd texted. 'Don't blame Kate. Don't blame yourself. Please come to the wedding.' An hour later, when she still hadn't heard from him, she texted again. 'I have something for you. Please come.'

Sometimes she wondered whether her relationship with Jack

would have been strong enough to withstand Sasha if she'd been honest about her past with him. Maybe, she thought. But then again, she worked out, painfully and slowly, you could never know what something would have been, only what it was.

And perhaps she hadn't been supportive enough when he came back, traumatised, from Temanistan. The fear overwhelmed her again, the thought of life sliding out of control, the feeling that everything was all her fault, and she wondered if she could make it to the kitchen and start clearing up, get ahead before . . .

A pair of square shoulders blocked her light. 'Hi, Heather.'

'Jack.' She jumped. 'I'm so glad you came. Kate is really missing you. Have you seen her?'

He nodded. 'All kissed and made up. Insofar as it can be. Where's your drink?'

'Oh, er, I'm not drinking . . . I'm responsible for the catering with Virginia. In fact, I'd better see if things need clearing away . . .'

'They don't.' He poured them two glasses, and raised his. 'You're looking good.'

Heather raised her head up and banished the guilty, anxious thoughts. Maybe she hadn't been supportive enough. But that didn't justify Jack's behaviour either. They were each responsible for their own actions. 'I feel good,' she said. And she meant it.

He touched his glass to hers. 'To you, then. To us.'

Heather raised her glass and touched his. 'Us?'

'Heather, I'm sorry. Sorry for everything . . .'

'I'm fine now,' said Heather, briskly. 'Which is the important thing. I'm sorry it didn't work out between you and Sasha, though.'

He winced. 'It was never a marriage. Just an act of revenge. To show Adam Taylor that she could. And I was the stupid sucker who was so shocked after the Temanistan thing that I couldn't think straight.'

'But you fell in love with her.'

'I was infatuated with her, which isn't the same thing. But from the day we married we never had sex.'

Heather let out a cry. 'I really don't want to know anything like that.'

'Sorry. I just wanted you to know that it wasn't quite the shock you thought it was when she went. I'd started to get the picture.'

'Did you find out about her father,' asked Heather. 'How he never saw her?'

Jack nodded. 'Olivia called me. She wanted me to know why she and Kate went over there. She hoped I'd understand that it wasn't just Kate being interfering, that they were doing it because of Molly. And I suppose I have. Understood, that is. Did you know Si gave her money?'

'Well, I think she felt she was owed. She thought everyone had more than she did. It can't have been easy. Still, that doesn't excuse everything. My mother was an abusive drug-addict and no one has the faintest idea who my father was.'

'I'm glad you feel strong enough to tell me that now.'

'I would have thought Kate might have told you,' said Heather. 'You can have the full story, if you like, but another time.'

He smiled. 'I look forward to that. And no, Kate didn't tell me. She can keep a secret if necessary. I just query whether this should have been a secret at all. Certainly not a secret between two people who've promised to—'

'Jack, I know you feel that I should have talked to you, and you were right,' interrupted Heather. 'And I will take responsibility for that. But you have to take responsibility, too, for what happened.'

His face darkened, and she thought he might walk off, but he managed a smile. 'You've been talking to a therapist, I suspect.'

'Yes,' she said. 'And you should try it. What with your father's death, and what happened in Temanistan, and your addiction to rescuing damsels in distress, which is definitely unhealthy . . .' she smiled to take the sting out of her words. 'You need someone properly qualified, though,' she added hastily.

'Well . . .' He raised his glass to her again. 'Heather, you're amazing. You've turned this whole terrible thing around and made it work for you.' He took her hand. 'I don't suppose there's any chance we could try again? We were so happy – we belong together, you know we do. And I am so, so sorry for everything I did. I've no excuse, except that I was—'

'You don't have to explain.' Heather smiled her dazzling, beautiful smile and withdrew her hand from his. Heather had dreamed

416

of this moment, in the darkest of nights, but now that it had arrived she suddenly realised how far she had come. 'Jack, I do love you. But not in that way. I want us to be friends always, but I'm a different person now. The Heather you knew has gone. She never really existed. I invented her, I tried to create the perfect army wife, because it looked like a world where I could be safe. You found me in the street, Jack, you knew nothing about me, and I got the chance to be a completely different person. I wanted to be her. But I was always so afraid of everyone finding out who I was underneath – and I'm not prepared to go on being that frightened any more. I have to learn how to live alone before I can live with anyone else.'

'Have you met anyone else?' There was a sharpness in his voice, as if he suspected the 'living alone' to be a sham.

Heather put a hand briefly on his arm, to reassure him. 'At the moment, I'm just enjoying being on my own, having a home where I can do what I like, bringing up the girls, getting to know Gerald, the man we lived with in Broadstairs, again and . . . all that. Did you know I've applied for the job of head housekeeper at the girls' school? I think they are better off there, but I do want to be closer to them.'

He nodded, a careful acknowledgement. 'I hope you get it, you'd be brilliant at it. But we could also . . .'

'Jack, the answer is no. Some things break forever.'

'And some don't. What about Si and Olivia?'

She shrugged. 'They're them. It's worked for them. It wouldn't for us.'

'How can you tell until you try?'

'I just know. Now are we going to have a nice time here not talking about anything important, or shall I go off and start clearing up now?'

Jack sighed. 'Let's have a nice time not talking about anything important. Maybe you'll . . .'

Heather laughed. 'No, Jack. I won't. But I've got something for you. Molly found it when she was looking for the note that Sasha said she'd left you. She was very upset that Sasha accused her of lying. So she looked everywhere, and she found this in an old handbag that Sasha left behind.' She handed him Ella's last letter.

417

Jack read it, and handed it to her with tears in his eyes. 'She's asking me to take care of the girls. You can read it. She obviously didn't think we'd get back together either.'

'She was a wise old bird,' said Heather. 'I miss her. I wish I'd been a bit more open with her – I always thought she was a bit of a snob, and would think I wasn't good enough to be an army wife, but . . .'

'She would never have thought that. I've only just begun to miss her, you know. At first I couldn't bear to think about it, and now I think about her every day.'

Heather touched his cheek, seeing herself reflected in his eyes. Strong, happy, confident Heather. The self she had never known before, but who, she now realised, had been waiting for her all along. 'Don't be afraid of pain, Jack. Face it – it's the only way to stop it growing and taking everything over. Now that's more than enough serious stuff for a wedding. Look – Kate and Jonny are doing speeches.'

Kate and Jonny clambered on to their dining table, and everyone began shouting 'Spee-ee-ch' and tapping glasses.

'Unaccustomed as I am . . .' shouted Jonny . . . 'my wife and I . . . would just like to say one big thank-you.'

Everyone roared and clapped.

'To everyone,' added Kate. 'Especially my sisters-in-law, Heather, Olivia and Virginia, without whom today would never have happened.' She raised her glass. 'To sisters-in-law.'

'Sisters-in-law,' everyone echoed, raising their glasses.

'And to Kate and Jonny,' screamed someone else. 'And Luke and Callum.'

Another roar and more glasses were raised.

'And that,' yelled Kate above the hubbub, 'is that.'

'Awfully short speeches,' frowned Virginia, picking up a bottle. 'Oh well.'

Si and Olivia elbowed their way through the crowd to Jonny and Kate. 'You've got one last present.' Olivia put a box in Kate's hand. 'Your mother asked me to keep this for you. Open it.'

Inside there was her mother's favourite diamond brooch, and a pair of her father's cufflinks. And a short note.

'I'm so proud of you,' said the spidery hand. 'You've done the right thing. Give these to Jonny with my love. He can give them to Callum one day.'

'So she left this for me if I got married?' queried Kate, pinning the brooch to her jacket. She had got her last letter from Ella after all.

'No,' said Olivia. 'She asked me to keep it until you made up your mind. She said you would make a decision one day, and whichever way it went, it would be the right one.'

'Why did she give it to you Olivia, not Si?'

Olivia smiled. 'She said she thought Si might pressurise you to do what *he* thought was right for you. And that because I was part of the family, but just that little bit more detached than a proper brother or sister, then I'd see things a little more clearly.'

Acknowledgements

Thank you so much to everyone who has helped with the book: Nicole Hackett of Family Law in Partnership (www.flip.co.uk) on the life of a divorce lawyer and the issues that surround divorce; Bill Rudgard of Rawcut TV, one of Britain's best-known independent crime and reality television companies (www.rawcut.tv), and freelance director and writer Andrew Williams on life in television; Susan Marling of Just Radio, one of Britain's top independent radio companies (www.justradio.ltd.uk) on the world of independent radio; on army life, David Eccles, Katie Forsyth, Richard and Lizzie Iron, the Army Families Federation (www.aff.org.uk), Liz Rhodes, Emma Stein, Caroline Bourne and everyone else at the coffee morning were so helpful; on post-traumatic stress disorder, Simon Wessely is the expert par excellence; and Helen Jones of the Caldecott Foundation, which looks after children who have suffered abuse and neglect (www.caldecottfoundation.co.uk) advised on the kind of childhood Heather might have had. Thanks to friends should include the dog-walkers: Emma Daniell, Rosie Turner, Posy Gentles and Amanda Mannering, and also Hilary Talbot and Jackie Jones-Parry for various introductions.

Thank you, too, to everyone at David Higham Associates, especially Anthony Goff and Georgia Glover, and to the team at Little, Brown: Zoe Gullen, publicist Tamsin Kitson, Charlie King and Emma Williams in marketing, Emma Grey in design and Frances Doyle, Adrian Foxman, Andy Coles, Sara Talbot, Melanee Winder and Robert Manser in Sales, and, most of all, Joanne Dickinson, who is a great editor.

Finally, my own sisters-in-law have been very patient about the difference between fact and fiction – having lived through my writings over the years they know that I never put my own family in books, but the title means they might have to explain this to people a little more often than before, which could get very tedious for them. Although none of them are templates for Olivia, Heather, Kate or Sasha, I have learned from them: without sisters-in-law you would barely even have a family. It's a relationship that is rarely acknowledged in print (mothers-in-law get all the jokes, parents the angst and siblings the best support roles), but in terms of emotional and practical issues sisters-in-law are right there at the heart of it all, keeping everything going, however different they are from each other in temperament or background. So thank you, Anna Ferri, Penny Balding, Lizzie Iron, Anna Campbell and Jane Campbell.